VALLEY OF FIRES

VALLEY OF FIRES

A CONQUERED EARTH NOVEL

J. BARTON MITCHELL

THOMAS DUNNE BOOKS
ST. MARTIN'S GRIFFIN
NEW YORK

THOMAS DUNNE BOOKS.
An imprint of St. Martin's Press.

VALLEY OF FIRES. Copyright © 2014 by J. Barton Mitchell. All rights reserved. Printed in the United States of America. For information, address St. Martin's Press, 175 Fifth Avenue, New York, N.Y. 10010.

www.thomasdunnebooks.com
www.stmartins.com

The Library of Congress Cataloging-in-Publication Data is available upon request.

ISBN 978-1-250-00948-7 (hardcover)
ISBN 978-1-250-02071-0 (e-book)

St. Martin's Griffin books may be purchased for educational, business, or promotional use. For information on bulk purchases, please contact the Macmillan Corporate and Premium Sales Department at 1-800-221-7945, extension 5442, or write to specialmarkets@macmillan.com.

First Edition: December 2014

10 9 8 7 6 5 4 3 2 1

For my editor, Brendan Deneen.
Thank you for helping me bring this world to life.

VALLEY OF FIRES

PROLOGUE

SHE WOKE FROM DARKNESS into darkness, ripped from blurry dreams that were contorted mixes of people and places she both recognized and did not. As her consciousness solidified, the first thing she noticed was how cold it was. The second . . . was that she was moving. Her body shook, strange clicking sounds came and went, and she could feel gravity pressing down.

She was traveling upward in some small, black container, but it was too dark to make out anything other than that it had been designed for carrying people bigger than her. Her hands and ankles were bound, and as the realization of just how trapped she was sank in, the spidery feeling of fear began to creep up her spine.

Light flashed from a small square in front of her.

It was a small window. Looking through it she could just barely make out giant, black walls, so far away from her they faded into the distance. She could see other things as well, flashing by as she was carried upward. There was movement inside this place. It was alive.

Throughout the interior of the massive structure, a complicated rail system had been erected. As she watched, black, oblong, metallic cases flew up and down them, moving every which way, and clicking from one rail to another. It must be one of those things she was riding in.

She saw other things too. Platforms built along the walls and attached to various interior superstructures, below and above. Some were factories, assembling shiny machines of different makes and configurations, most of which she recognized. Assembly combat walkers. Spiders. Mantises. Others. Those very machines had been hunting her for months, and the feeling of fear grew as she passed them.

Other walkers, hundreds of them, painted in different combinations of blue and white, marched in formation on what must be deployment platforms.

On other platforms rested thousands of airships—Ospreys, Raptors, Vultures—all painted in similar patterns of color. Some were landing, others were refueling or had their engines primed for liftoff.

Everything here was evidence of a massive military machine, and it only made her feel more trapped inside this moving coffin. She started to struggle, to try and break free. It was pointless.

Bright, wavering light burst through the window, so intense it blinded her. She grimaced and waited for her eyes to adjust. When they did, what she saw was so amazing it made her forget her fear and discomfort.

Outside, the world continued to drop away. The platforms were gone, the exterior walls were closer now, as if the building, whatever it was, narrowed the farther one traveled up. Only one thing filled the center of the empty space outside now.

A giant, wavering, geometrically perfect column of pure energy that must have been two or three hundred feet in diameter. The huge shaft of light was so distinct, she could see the individual particles which comprised it, floating upward, much slower than she did, gently and lazily drifting toward the top of the massive building.

As she moved, she saw other things around the energy column. Thousands of glowing, impossibly complicated crystalline shapes, made of beautiful golden light. She watched them float in and out of the beam, their own luminescence merging with the huge, wavering shaft.

She smiled in spite of everything. It was beautiful . . .

Her container shook once, twice, and then she felt its ascent slow, and the tingling of fear returned. Wherever she was going . . . she had arrived.

The pod shook again, a loud hissing sound erupting as the entire thing split in half and opened on compact hydraulics.

More light flooded in. She could still see the column of energy, stretching upward to where it floated up through the ceiling far above. The crystalline entities floated in and out of it . . .

. . . and there were others, waiting for her now, hovering above a small platform.

Behind them stood three machines of a type she had never seen. Four legs, like a Mantis, but much smaller, maybe five feet in height with thin bodies that held four tendril-like arms, actuated with servos up and down their length. Like every other machine here, they were painted in matching patterns of blue and white.

Scion . . .

She flinched as the impression forced its way inside her mind, blooming to life and overpowering every other thought. She watched as three of the crystalline entities floated toward her, and they were different. Not golden, like the others, but dizzying mixtures of blue and white light, like a frozen sky.

The Feelings, the ones that had been with her since the beginning, the ones that had always guided her, spun and tumbled with more glee than she had ever felt from them, and she knew why.

You are home, the entities above her declared.

The strange, four-legged walkers moved for her, their pulsating, mechanical tentacles reaching out, and Zoey couldn't help it. She screamed.

Destiny is no matter of chance. It is a matter of choice. It is not a thing to be waited for, it is a thing to be achieved.

—WILLIAM JENNINGS BRYAN

PART ONE

THE BARREN

1. BARGAINS

HOLT HAWKINS HAD TO ADMIT, the *Wind Maker* was a beautiful ship. Three masts salvaged from fishing boats on Lake Michigan stretched into the sky, and a hull shaped from the wood of old barns, the faded grays and reds of the paint still visible. She sat in the middle of the plains of what had once been southwest Idaho, about five miles from Currency, the Wind Trader capital. Like everyone else on board, he had his attention on something in the distance: an old tractor, sitting where it had been abandoned years ago, buried in weeds and overgrown corn, but still solid. It would make an excellent target.

If they ever got the cannon to work, of course.

Arrayed around him were almost two dozen Wind Trader Captains who had come to observe the test firing, and they were studying the proceedings with a great deal of skepticism. Holt didn't blame them.

On the shoulders of one Captain perched a large cat, his coat marbled orange and beige, wrapped around the kid's neck and perfectly comfortable. Max, Holt's Australian cattle dog, stared up at the feline eagerly, though whether he wanted to jump it or be its friend Holt wasn't sure.

Holt nudged the dog, breaking his concentration. "Don't fixate," he whispered. Max whined and looked back at the cat.

The test cannon was refusing to fire, after numerous assurances that it had finally been figured out. It had been fashioned in a joint effort by both Wind Trader engineers and what the White Helix called Adzers, those trained for the dangerous tasks of carving and shaping the powerful Antimatter crystals from the Strange Lands into the Helix's rings and spear points. It was a dangerous job; do it wrong and you'd unleash the crystals' energy and incinerate everything nearby.

The cannon itself was out of sight below, aiming through one of the ship's brand new gun ports. Until this week, Landships had no need of gun ports, because none of them were armed, but that was just one of many things that were changing.

The representatives from both camps were on deck and, as usual, arguing heatedly.

"The crystals spark when it's activated, so it's not a power issue," said Caspira, the White Helix's principal Adzer. She was a tall girl, with a lithe and agile build like all White Helix, and her brownish hair hung down her back in a tight braid. Her voice was always calm, and always laced with ice. "It's the cannon barrel, like I told you, it's too constrictive."

"Just because they spark, don't mean they work, honey," Smitty said back, decidedly less calm. He was a big, heavyset kid, mostly muscle, closing in on twenty, judging by the Tone in his eyes, and he was the Wind Traders' head engineer, a position that involved overseeing the design, construction, and repair of its Landships. His hands were stained a permanent shade of charcoal from his work at the Shipyard forges. He was heated and volatile, the exact opposite of Caspira, and anytime they were within ten feet of one another, it was like gasoline and matches. "It's a *power* issue, the barrel's perfectly proportioned, I honed it myself."

"Maybe that's the problem," Caspira replied.

Smitty's face reddened, but a commanding voice stopped him from exploding. "Stop it! Is it gonna work or did we waste an entire day coming out here?"

Both Caspira and Smitty turned to the tall, lanky kid who'd spoken. His name was Conner, and he was more than just another Landship Captain, he was the Consul of the Wind Trader Cooperative. It sounded fancy, but the position was mainly reserved for tie breakers within the Co-Op, so that no decision could go unresolved. The Consul also negotiated deals which affected the Wind Traders as a whole, called Grand Bargains, and it was why Holt and Mira had approached Conner when they'd first arrived. It was he who had accepted their deal, much to the Co-Op's displeasure, and that displeasure was increasing every second the cannon didn't fire.

"It's fired twice before," Smitty said in annoyance. "Something probably shifted when we mounted it, the girl here and I will . . ."

"It's Caspira," the Adzer replied frigidly.

". . . go down and give it a once-over."

"A *fast* once-over," Conner told him with a glare. Holt could feel the growing impatience spreading through the assembled Captains. It was an ongoing dispute that threatened more and more every day to destroy the deal Holt and Mira had built, the one that would get them and the White Helix to San Francisco, where the Citadel sat, and where the seemingly impossible task of rescuing Zoey waited.

"You made a Grand Bargain without consulting any of the other Captains . . . for *this?*" The impatience had finally spilled over. The Captain was a girl, maybe eighteen, and oddly, she spoke with a British accent, something he hadn't heard since he was a kid.

"It's within my rights to do so," Conner stated.

"Rights or no," the girl continued, "a Grand Bargain affects everyone, and what you've agreed to—"

"Is worth the price," Conner cut her off. "You've seen the Helix weapons. Imagine the fleet armed with them."

"Our ships have never been *armed,*" the British girl argued back. "We've always relied on other things to get us through."

"And what has that gotten us?" Conner retorted. "How many ships have we lost to the Menagerie? Last year we were one hundred and seventeen vessels strong . . . today it's *ninety-three.* With these weapons, the shipping lanes will belong to *us,* and the profit will be more than anything we've ever seen."

"In exchange for what?" It was the voice of the Captain with the cat, a calm, masculine voice, but skeptical, and Holt recognized it. He was somewhere around nineteen, with an assuredness beyond his years and a brash smile, when he chose to use it. Dark hair was layered back in textured waves, and he wore a white shirt tucked into black cargo pants with a gun belt around his waist, and as he stood near the edge of the ship's deck, he placed a silver-tipped boot on top of a deck railing and scratched the cat's ears. "Two weeks is the answer. Two weeks and they have *full* control of the fleet. Every. Last. Ship."

Something about Dresden had always bothered Holt. He'd only met the Captain once before, months earlier, back at that trading post when he'd helped them escape with Zoey. He was cocky. And an opportunist. In Holt's experience, it was a bad combination, but there was no doubt he was one of the best skippers in the fleet. He was also Conner's brother, and there was no love lost between the two. They stared at one another intensely.

"Yes," Conner answered. "For transportation of their army to San Francisco."

"The most guarded and heavily fortified Assembly ruin in North

America," Dresden stated back. "And fighting too, don't forget that. Wherever we're needed. I guess the idea is that a hundred Landships with Antimatter weapons is enough to give the Assembly a little pause, but I'm not sure how much I really buy into that. Oh, and speaking of the Assembly, now we've got a couple dozen of them sitting *outside* the Shipyards." He meant Ambassador and the silver rebels that had joined them after the battle of the Severed Tower, another point of contention, for obvious reasons.

"He's right!" the British girl spoke up again. "Mantises! *Spiders* for God sakes! Other kinds of walkers I've never seen before, and—"

"Can I say something here?" Holt interjected, and everyone looked at him in surprise. Clearly, they'd forgotten he was on board. "We've made some . . . strange alliances, it's true, but those Assembly you're talking about are different from the others. They're fighting their own kind. Now maybe that's not something you particularly care about, and I don't blame you, but at the very least you need to recognize that things are changing, and you ought to be concerned about a lot more than just arming your ships. The Strange Lands are *gone*. The Assembly are fighting each other, and whatever their agenda is, it's reaching its end. Six months from now I think the world is gonna be a very, very different place. That's what this deal is all about: embracing change. What is it you say? 'The wind takes you where it will, not the other way around'? The winds are changing course, people, and you all need to start taking your own advice. Getting left behind is not where you want to be."

Silence gripped the deck of the ship. They stared at him in a combination of different ways, some unsettled and angry, others hopeful and resolute. The truth was he didn't particularly care if they liked the deal, only that they got them to San Francisco. And then, he thought glumly, the real fun would begin . . .

The deck of the ship shook under their feet as a loud harmonic ping echoed sharply below. A giant, glowing blue crystal spear point arced through the air.

The Captains gasped as it impacted the thick metal body of the old tractor, blowing the whole thing to pieces, punching straight through it in a shower of colored sparks and digging itself into the ground on the other side.

No one spoke. Everyone's eyes were wide.

Holt had seen White Helix Lancet crystals do some extensive damage, but these cannons were on a whole other level.

"Well," Dresden remarked. The cat on his shoulders stared around warily. "I'd call that a successful test."

Everyone moved off, heading for the stairs to the lower decks to congratulate Smitty and Caspira, but Holt stood staring at the smoking remains of the tractor in relief. It was the first time something had gone right in . . . well, who was keeping track?

"Two weeks," a voice said, and Holt looked to his right. Dresden stood there, staring at the tractor with him. "Use it well. This little coalition you've built is gonna fall apart at the first sign of trouble, and when it does . . . complications will ensue." Dresden looked at him and smiled. There was no maliciousness in it, he was just being honest, and he wasn't happy about his people being forced into a war none of them had signed up for.

Holt could relate.

"They usually do," he said.

Dresden moved away, and as he did the cat on his shoulders hissed down at Max. The dog whined and started to follow, but Holt held him in place until they were out of sight. The Captain was right about most of it, but the truth was it wouldn't be him holding it all together, it would be someone else, someone he cared about more than anyone else on this broken planet.

It would be Mira.

CURRENCY WAS THE WIND Trader capital, as well as the second-largest population center in North America, next to Midnight City. The breadth of it stretched out over the green and yellow rolling hills of the very northern tip of the Barren, shining in the sun, and, as always, it was beautiful.

The design of the city had integrated Landships almost seamlessly. Broad avenues of green fields crisscrossed the city, large enough for the giant ships to reach their berth. Each ship had its own in the city, and looking out over it, Currency was full of rippling, shuddering color from their patchwork sails. Orange and red, purple and yellow, blues, greens, they looked like huge pieces of art fluttering in the wind. It was easy to see how Currency earned the nickname "City of Sails."

As beautiful as it was, Holt didn't pause to admire it, he only wanted to get away.

When the gangplank of the *Wind Maker* lowered, he and Max were the first off, leaving the others behind. All he could think about right now was getting back to Mira. Who knew how many days they had left before they were forced apart? The sad part was, it was a separation of their own design.

Mira couldn't attend the test firing, she'd been pulled away to deal with some new flare-up regarding the Assembly and the White Helix, which was becoming more and more normal. The Helix had been honed in the Strange Lands as weapons to fight the invaders, and they were starting to get restless, and restless White Helix were a bad combination.

The Assembly, for their part, didn't seem to take it personally. In fact, they rarely seemed to notice the hostility at all. Regardless, because Mira was the only one who could communicate with them, she was always brought in when things went south. That was Zoey's last gift, the granting of one of her abilities to Mira, and as much as Holt didn't like what that power was slowly doing to her, he saw its necessity, saw why Zoey had done what she'd done. Still, it was a steep price to pay.

"Hey, killer," said a feminine, yet decidedly not soft voice, and Holt's reaction to it was the same as always: apprehension mixed with warmth. That was the effect Ravan always had, in varying degrees.

Ravan was beautiful in a hard-edged way, olive skin and obsidian-black hair that trailed down her back. She wore black pants, a T-shirt, and a single utility belt across her waist. On her left wrist was the tattoo of an eight-pointed star, with four of its points colored in, the symbol of the Menagerie. On her right was a black raven, her namesake. All Menagerie took two tattoos when they joined, the star and one of their own choosing. Holt had a near-identical tattoo on his right wrist, though it had never been completed.

She waited for him ahead, near the gate that led into the crowded streets, smiling. Like everything about her, the smile was a contradiction. Warm, inviting, yet predatory.

Holt smiled back nonetheless. "Hi yourself."

Max's tail began to wag. Ravan knelt down and scratched the dog on the head, and Max put up no resistance at all. Holt studied them, perplexed.

"I don't get it," he said. "He never warms up to anyone that fast."

"Some dogs are like people," Ravan said. "They don't whore themselves out, they wanna know what's in it for *them*. That's where he and I have a lot in common."

Ravan pulled something from her coat. A piece of jerky, and when she offered it, Max gobbled it up greedily.

Holt studied Ravan. The girl had a hardness and a self-sufficiency that was rare, even in the world as it was now. She'd been through a lot. Ravan had told him some of it, the rest he'd guessed. Holt still felt close to her. If not for Mira, he often wondered what might have been.

"This came while you were gone," Ravan said, handing him an envelope. Max chewed blissfully on his jerky as Holt studied the envelope. It was red with a white eight-pointed star on the front, just like the one on Ravan's wrist, and at the sight Holt felt his pulse quicken. He pulled out the letter inside.

Ravan,

I am pleased that you are alive and unsurprised that you have succeeded. I knew sending you was the right choice. We eagerly await your arrival, myself most of all. Circumstances at Faust have complicated in your absence, and the news of your return, with my daughter, will raise spirits immensely.

As for Hawkins, the least you have earned from me is my trust. I will hear him out. He will receive amnesty for his crimes against the Menagerie and against me personally, on the condition that he return to Faust immediately and that the deal we negotiate be deemed acceptable.

Hurry home, Commandant. Power and profit . . .

T.

"Looks like you got what you wanted," Ravan said. "Could at least smile a little."

"I'm not sure I'd say it's what I wanted," Holt replied darkly. In a way, of course, it *was*. They were going to need the Menagerie if they hoped to have a chance against the Assembly. It had been decided, between him and Mira, that Holt was in the best position to secure that alliance. He knew the Menagerie, knew Tiberius. After all, Holt had killed his son, Archer. It had been why he'd fled Faust and left everything behind, including Ravan, a long time ago. All the same, he wasn't in any rush to get back. Tiberius's words in the letter were without menace, but . . . the man had a long memory.

"Does that mean you've changed your mind?" Ravan asked back.

"No," he said. "I'm coming. Like I promised."

"Well, your promises haven't always meant a whole lot, have they?"

Holt sighed. "Is it going to be like this the whole way back?"

"You mean my brutal honesty? Most likely." Ravan studied him. "You know, even without everything you've got going on, coming back to Faust is still your best option. Getting Tiberius's buy-in on helping rescue your little girl is the king of delusive ideas, but you can still settle things with *him*."

"So long as the deal we negotiate is 'acceptable,'" Holt repeated from the letter. "Wonder what that means."

"Means play your cards right, and you can get him off your ass forever."

"I killed his son, Ravan," Holt reminded her. "That's not the kind of thing you wipe away with a bargain."

"You know Tiberius. Power is everything, and that's what you're offering. A *lot* of it. Plus, I told him you were instrumental in finding Avril, that you agreed to help out of your deep and heartfelt guilt over the death of his only begotten son."

Holt frowned as he thought it through. What choice did he have? They needed the Menagerie, and Ravan was right. Tiberius valued power more than anything, and that gave Holt real leverage.

"Cheer up." Ravan punched him hard on the shoulder. Holt winced. "You get me for company the whole way, and I'm almost fifty percent sure I'm not going to put you in leg irons."

Holt studied her skeptically.

2. ALLIES

EVEN OVER THE DISTANCE that separated them, Mira Toombs could still hear their voices. Though, "hearing" wasn't really the right word. The projections were more like feelings or emotions, stripped to their barest essence and shoved into her mind, overpowering whatever else she may have been thinking or feeling right then. The farther away she was, the worse the projections were. Anxiety. Loneliness. They were like cries that only she could hear, and she told no one, not even Holt, how bad it could be.

Mira exhaled in relief as the *Wind Rift* rumbled up and over the crest of a hill, and the feelings began to lose their potency. She could see the Shipyards, at the bottom of the hill, and the closer she got, the better she felt.

"They're in your head again," said a small, yet strong, voice behind her.

A tiny girl, barely over five feet tall, her hair laced with strands of pink, stood at the helm of the ship. The wheel was bigger than she was. Her name was Olive, a close friend, one of the few Mira had in the Wind Traders, and their history went back years. In fact, Olive had been the one to help her escape Midnight City, what seemed like ages ago.

"How could you tell?" Mira asked. She didn't like talking about her connection with the Assembly, it made most people nervous.

"Your knuckles are white."

Mira looked down and saw her fingers wrapped tight around the wooden railing that circled the deck and instantly let go. She had to control things like that, no one could know how bad it really got.

"It gets better, doesn't it?" Olive asked. "When you're closer to them?"

For all the connection Mira now shared with the Assembly, she still knew very little about them. One thing she did know, was that Ambassador and his followers had made a very difficult decision. The aliens were a race that, for eons, lived within a joint consciousness, where each one's emotions and thoughts were instantly accessible to all the others at any time. When they rebelled and joined the quest to rescue Zoey, those connections were severed. Permanently. The staggering silence and blackness which came was, to them, terrifying.

But the aliens soon discovered they had one thing they could latch onto to restore a semblance of their original existence: Mira herself.

The ability to communicate with them, given to her right before Zoey was taken, had unwittingly made her a conduit of sorts for them to sense one another. It was a dim likeness to how it had once been, but it was something, and the closer Mira was to them, the more they could sense each other, and the more their anxiety and sadness lessened.

More and more Assembly rebels appeared every week, leaving their established clans and joining Ambassador's group, and the sensations grew stronger as they added their emotions to the rest. Mira shuddered thinking about it. What would it be like in a week or a month, if the numbers kept growing? How could she stay sane, with all those emotions washing out her own?

These were the kinds of things she told no one, and so she did what she usually did when questions like Olive's came up. She lied. "I'm not sure."

Olive frowned. "You don't have to tell me, but I hope you're telling Holt. It's not good carrying weight like that all by yourself."

Mira forced herself to smile, then attempted a subject change. "Why aren't you at the test firing?"

Olive knew when she was being deflected, but she answered all the same. "Nothing there I wanna see."

Mira could hear the distaste in her voice. "You don't approve of the Grand Bargain?"

"Not when it means I have to put my crew and my ship in harm's way."

"You do that every day."

"Not by requirement, and not when there's no profit in it. Fighting wars isn't what Wind Traders are supposed to do."

Mira looked at Olive evenly. "How do you know?"

Olive's eyes thinned. "I'm sure your little friend is very important to you, and I don't pretend to understand all you've been through, but did you *really* stop to think about the ramifications of dragging other people into this? Where they might be killed? By the *hundreds*? Have you thought about how that's gonna feel when all's said and done?"

"No," Mira replied instantly. She and Holt had intentionally *not* thought about those things. If they had, they might have hesitated, they might have done nothing.

"I didn't think so." Olive looked back ahead, and Mira didn't say anything else. Olive was implying the selfishness of Mira's actions and maybe she was right, but Zoey had come to mean everything to her, and whatever it took to get her back she would do.

Mira sighed. All she really wanted was to be alone with Holt. Their deal with the Wind Traders was almost finished. Tomorrow or the next day they would leave and go their separate directions for who knew how long, and there was no real guarantee they would ever see each other again. What time they had was precious now, and there was far too little of it left.

The Shipyards were just ahead, close enough to make out detail: a honeycombed collection of platforms and scaffolding that surrounded what was left of an old power station, its dual brick smokestacks stretching into the air. Smoke vented from them, but these days it was from the forges and welding stations inside for fabricating and repairing the many Landships which passed through it every year.

She could feel the projections from the Assembly there, out of sight on the other side of the building.

Guardian, they projected. *There is disagreement.*

Now *that* was an understatement, Mira thought.

THE ARGUMENT WAS LOUD and volatile, but Mira's attention was held by the Reflection Box. It lay near the entrance to the Forge, the machine shop inside the old power plant, a large, black box with two heavy doors, side by side, that served as its lid. It was painted in worn-out colors of red and green and gold leaf that twisted around its edges, a faded white rabbit on one end, holding a wand that shot sparks in an arc of old silver paint. Large, flamboyant letters spelled out a flowing script of words:

The Mysterious, Magnificent, MOLOTOV—Prepare for Amazement!

In the World Before it had been part of a magician's repertoire, a magic case that did who knows what. Now, it was one of the most powerful major artifacts ever produced by the Strange Lands. More than that, it was integral to everything that was happening. Not just the Grand Bargain they made here, but the entire endeavor to save Zoey. She thought of Gideon, the former leader of the White Helix, how he had told her it would become important later, how he had bargained with Tiberius Marseilles and the Menagerie to attain it. He had been right, after all.

As she watched, a White Helix Adzer opened one of the box's heavy doors. Another placed a green Antimatter crystal inside the open compartment lined with soft, red felt cushions, but unlike the crystals she had grown used to, this one was huge, maybe three feet in diameter. It was meant to be fired from the new Landship cannons, and it was the only reason the fragile agreement with the Wind Traders existed at all.

The Adzer shut the door of the box. A second passed, then it was as if the light around her dimmed . . . and the box flashed. A loud boom, like a thunderclap, shook the foundation of the old building. No one nearby even flinched. It was funny, Mira thought, what you could get used to.

The Adzers opened both lids of the box . . . and lifted out *two* identical, green Antimatter crystal shells. Mira smiled. The Reflection Box replicated anything put inside it, and the box allowed them to produce, at a rapid pace, what would normally have taken months or even years.

"Just give the word," a tense, yet zealous voice stated.

Mira was in the Shipyard's salvage repository, a giant junkyard of pieces and parts the Wind Traders constantly acquired in order to build their massive ships. Airplanes, cars and vans, construction equipment, passenger trains, semitrucks. There was a lumberyard too, full of planks of all kinds of wood, and it was smoking from a fire that had engulfed it. There were no flames now, but the damage was apparent, and it looked like something had exploded. To make matters worse, lying in front of it was the crippled, unmoving form of a large Assembly Brute, one of the five-legged, shielded-ramming machines, the same kind Ambassador inhabited.

In front of her was a large, angry gathering. Wind Trader engineers stood between two other groups that couldn't have been more different. About a dozen White Helix, dressed in their usual patterns of black and gray, utility belts crisscrossing their torsos. Their Lancets were loose and some of them had their masks pulled up. It was a bad sign, it meant they were ready to fight.

In the empty grass behind the junkyard, the Assembly encampment sat. There were no tents or buildings, of course, just the walkers and an array of Osprey dropships. There were four-legged Mantises and giant, towering, eight-legged Spiders, both from the blue and whites, a clan Ambassador called Mas'Shinra. What was left of the green and orange Mas'Erinhah, the smaller, quick three-legged Hunters with their cloaking abilities and a few of their powerful artillery walkers. More Brutes, like the crumpled one near the lumber, the five-legged walkers of the purple clan. And all of them bore one thing in common: their colors were gone, stripped away, leaving only bright, gleaming silver metal. A line of the walkers, mostly Hunters and Mantises, stood in front of the angry, yelling kids.

Guardian, a projection came. It was what the Assembly called her, a reference to her perceived role as the protector of Zoey, their Scion, and every time Mira heard it, she felt a sting. It was an ironic reminder of just how badly she had failed in that task, not all that long ago. She ignored the projections, listening to the argument.

"You saw the explosion," a White Helix stated, a girl, her mask still undrawn. She was tall, lithe, and agile like all Helix, and kept her hair razored in a thin layer of what probably would have been the whitest blond Mira had ever seen, had it been allowed to grow.

"And what was left of one of those Brutes is on the ground right next to it," said another, staring heatedly at a tall boy in grimy overalls. "What else would it have been?"

"Personally, my money's on *you*," the kid replied, folding his arms. Mira knew him. His name was Christian, one of the Wind Trader engineers.

"*Us?*" The Helix seemed aghast.

"Just give the word," one of the Helix stated again.

"You guys are flipping around in here every day, shooting off those sticks," Christian stated. "You said yourself you don't have much to do with artifacts. Which means you have no real idea what happens when one of those crystals comes into contact with—"

"You're really reaching," the Helix girl said. "Why are you so eager to protect them?"

"Just. Give. The word."

Guardian.

What? Mira thought back, her eyes moving to their source, a five-legged walker standing out front of the others. There were no discerning marks or technology on Ambassador to tell it apart from the others, but still she knew. It was in the projections themselves, they were unique in ways she couldn't describe.

We tried to contain, it projected.

The answer, as usual, was cryptic. The translation her mind made of the Assembly's feelings was never a smooth process, but she was getting better at understanding. Mira looked to the smoke rising from the lumberyard and the ruined walker there. She moved for it as the arguments continued.

Mira scrutinized the scene, studying the remains, the smoking lumber, and something else, the remnants scattered everywhere, and they were barely recognizable. A car battery, regular AA batteries, coins, washers, all everyday objects, or at least they used to be. They were artifact components, from the Strange Lands, a powerful, dangerous place that no longer existed, and one that, long ago, had meant everything to her.

Mira picked up one of the batteries. She had never seen one that looked like this. It was just a blackened, charred mass, but Mira didn't think it had anything to do with the fire. Artifacts were supposed to be indestructible outside the Strange Lands, yet these were completely ruined.

Mira was a Freebooter, an expert in such things, and she guessed these had been assembled into a Dynamo, what was essentially a generator, in this case used to power a whole host of tools from the World Before. Air drills, saws, cutting torches. What was strange was that it seemed as if the combination had *exploded,* and that should have been impossible. Combinations lost power and died, but unless their design included the need for some kind of combustion, they didn't blow up.

Guardian . . .

Mira heard the sounds of shuffling behind her. Two Hunters stood on either side of her, no more than a foot away, their red, blue, and green three-optic eyes staring into her. Behind them were two Mantises, staring at her in the same way.

Mira sighed. Sometimes they were more like Max than killer alien invaders.

"Yes?" she asked out loud, with impatience.

We tried to contain.

That word again, "contain." Mira stared back at the wreckage of the walker and the smoking debris and an idea of what had happened here formed. A dozen or more feet away, the argument and the standoff continued.

"It wasn't them," Mira announced, looking back at the group. No one seemed to hear her, they were too busy yelling. *"It wasn't them!"*

The accusations stopped. Everyone turned to her.

"It wasn't *who?*" Christian asked. "The Helix or the Assembly?"

"Either." She held up one of the blackened coins. "It was your Dynamo, it exploded."

"Artifact combinations don't explode," another Wind Trader engineer stated.

Mira shrugged. "This one did. And this walker," she motioned to the wrecked body of the machine, "absorbed the explosion. It must have sensed the combination was about to overload and——"

"Used its shield," Christian replied, thinking it through. Assembly Brutes were the only walkers Mira had seen with energy shields for defense. "Explains why the ground's charred in an almost perfect circle."

Mira stood up. Where there had been two Hunters around her, now there were six, with two Brutes behind them. The Assembly always tried to get as close to her as they could, and it could be annoying. The machines moved apart as she walked through them, and Mira could see the distrustful looks from the kids ahead of her. Could she blame them? The Assembly, the great invaders of the planet, following her around like lost puppies?

"I think you owe them an apology, Dasha," a new voice said. Two other Helix were moving toward the discontent, and Mira knew them well. One was Dane, tall and handsome, with wavy hair and lithe muscles and the easy, assured gait that all Helix seemed to share. The other was Avril, the current leader of the White Helix, though that wasn't going to last much longer.

The eyes of every White Helix dropped instantly in apprehension. Only the girl, Dasha, kept hers raised. "Apologize . . . to *them?*" She meant the Assembly.

"Dishonored yourself, haven't you?" Avril asked back as she and Dane pushed into the crowd. "You've raised your masks when there was no call, and you have accused an ally of treachery."

"They're not my allies," the girl retorted. The other Helix seemed nervous. "And you are not my Doyen."

Avril touched all three of the glowing rings on her middle fingers. Her body flashed in hot, white light. Her movements were lightning quick as she struck outward, and two rapid punches sent Dasha crashing to the ground, staring up in pain and shock.

Avril glared down at her. "You're right. I'm not your Doyen. I am *Shuhan.* And you will respect my words."

"Gideon was my—"

"Avril's achievements grant her the title of Shuhan now," Dane cut her off. "And you will obey her as I do, if only because you took the same oaths. What is the second Keystone?"

Dasha said nothing, just glared.

"What is the *second Keystone?*" Dane repeated.

"Honor above all." The girl's voice was a whisper. The other Helix in the yard echoed the statement out loud.

"Apologize," Avril spoke again. "For your hostility and your insults."

Guardian. Mira flinched at the projections. *It is unnecessary.*

She looked at Ambassador, its triangular eye boring into hers, and raised a hand, signaling it to do nothing.

Dasha lay there a few moments more . . . then stood up and looked to Christian. "I apologize for my actions." And with that, she pushed through the crowd, back toward the White Helix camp.

"Dasha!" Avril shouted after her.

"I will not apologize to *them*!" the girl yelled as she stormed off.

Avril sighed, watching her go. "The rest of you, return to camp, prepare for meditation."

The Helix obeyed, leaping and dashing back toward their tents in the distance, as if the conflict had never existed at all.

Mira looked at Ambassador. *You should go too.*

You are safe? Ambassador projected back, and she almost smiled. Explaining to the entity the concept of "blowing off steam" would have been tough.

I'm fine, she thought. *Go.*

The Assembly turned and pounded away in the opposite direction. When they were gone, only Mira, Avril, Dane, and Christian were left.

"This is starting to get more and more common," Christian observed. "I'd say I'll be glad when you guys leave, but since you're taking the fleet with you, means I'll probably be going too, so . . ."

"The flare-up started with the explosion?" Mira asked him.

"I guess." Christian shrugged and started to move back toward the Forge. "Personally, I think you guys are just itching for a fight. I get it, you're big, tough ninjas, you want to use the skills, I just think discipline might be starting to go by the wayside."

"He isn't wrong," Dane admitted to Avril when he was gone. "It's getting harder and harder to keep them in line."

"Holt's finalizing the deal with the Cooperative," Mira reminded them. "Once it's done, we'll be leaving again, this time with the fleet. I have a feeling the road to the Citadel will give them plenty of action to focus on."

Avril shook her head. "It's not just that. The Strange Lands kept us on our toes, made us vigilant and mindful. If you weren't, you died, it was that simple. Here . . ." Avril frowned, looking at the bright, sunny landscape, the rolling hills, the gentle breeze. The tranquility was the opposite of the Strange Lands, that was for sure. There was no question it would be an adjustment for the Helix.

"They need a focus," Dane said. "They're drifting. We all are. All we have is the one thing Gideon left us, the quest to save the Prime, his word on how important she was."

"Gideon is gone," Avril told him. "Now there's only us."

"And soon . . . not even that," Dane replied soberly.

Avril and Dane stared at each other, emotions and thoughts passing between them in the silence of the evening air. Dane and Avril meant a great deal to the White Helix, they had become its de facto leaders with the death of Gideon, but they meant even more to each other. Mira knew what they were feeling, because she was facing the same reality herself. Avril was leaving just like Holt, headed to the same place, Faust, the seat of power of the Menagerie. Her father was Tiberius Marseilles, the Menagerie leader, and he had gone to great lengths to get her back. The Reflection Box nearby was the price he'd paid, one of the most powerful artifacts on the planet, and he'd traded it for her. Avril may have been honor bound to oblige, but she wasn't required to look forward to it.

"You two should go," Mira said. "Tomorrow . . . will be here before you know it."

Avril looked at her, the two girls feeling the same things. They had a lot in common now. Then she and Dane turned and headed back for the swaying tents of the White Helix camp in the distance.

Mira looked at the old power plant yearningly. Her own room was there, at the top, and she saw the windows of the old office they'd given her for quarters. They were dark, but that didn't mean Holt wasn't there. And if he wasn't, surely he was on his way. Surely by the time she got there—

Guardian, the projection came. Then three more. A dozen. Two dozen. The feelings resurfaced—fear, loneliness—and Mira grabbed hold of the side of an old bus to steady herself.

Guardian. Come.

Mira sighed. Even being this close to them wasn't enough. They wanted all of her. Maybe Holt would be delayed, she thought. If she just went to them for a few minutes . . .

Guardian. Come.

Mira took a step in the direction of the Assembly camp, and the moment she did, she felt relief, the anxiety began to lift, quieting their fear and transferring their relief, in turn, to her.

Just a few minutes, Mira thought, as she walked toward them. Just a few . . .

3. PROMISES

IT HAD BEEN AN HOUR before Mira was able to pull away from the Assembly and their thoughts, to find her way back to her room at the top of the Shipyards. If she looked out the window, Mira knew she would see them even now. The machines and their eyes, gathered below in the junk-yard, staring up at her once again.

Guardian, the projections came. *Come close.*

But resisting them was easier now, because she was in one of the few places that gave her strength. Lying in bed, in Holt's arms, her head resting on his chest. She linked her legs in his and relaxed as his warmth blended with hers. If only she could stay like this, with him, and forget the world . . . but while the world could probably be forgotten, their other responsibilities couldn't.

"I dreamed about her last night," Mira said, absently tracing the curve of his chest with a finger.

"You dream about her every night," Holt answered softly in her ear. "This was different?"

"She was . . . somewhere black, I think. I was there and she was in pain. And she stared up at me, and I tried to get to her but . . . I just couldn't move. It felt like I was frozen, and I just had to sit there and watch her."

Holt sighed. "It was a dream."

"I wasn't there for her when she needed me."

"I'm tired of hearing that."

"It's true."

"It *isn't*. There's nothing you could have done to stop her from being taken."

He was probably right. Zoey had told Mira she'd made a deal with the Severed Tower, and with something as powerful as that, you were basically making a deal with fate itself, but still, it didn't make it any easier.

Anytime she thought of Zoey, she saw the little girl screaming and being ripped into the sky by the Vulture claw.

Guardian . . . the Assembly projected from outside. *Come closer.*

"A month ago would you have ever thought this was possible?" Holt's question drowned out the projections. "Everything we've done?"

No, she wouldn't have. Building a coalition between the White Helix and Assembly rebels, orchestrating the first Grand Bargain with the Wind Traders in years, laying the groundwork for deals with the Menagerie and other resistance groups, but there was still so much left to do. "Sometimes it just all seems like too much. How do we keep going when we know . . . it's probably all for nothing?" It was another grim truth, and a good question. Even if they did reach San Francisco, even if they did have an army with them, they still had to fight the Assembly on its home turf, and that wasn't a scenario either of them were likely to survive.

Holt's fingers moved through her hair. "Faust isn't as self-sufficient as most people think. It has the oil refinery and its machine shops and it can generate power, which sounds like a lot, until you factor in what else people need to survive in the Barren. Water. *Lots* of water. Food. Medicine. All of that the Menagerie has to get on their own."

Mira wasn't sure what Holt's point was, but she didn't really care. The sound of his voice helped push away the thoughts of Zoey and the incessant emotions from the Assembly outside.

"One way they get it is through treasure hunting," Holt continued. "It's what Ravan and I used to do, go into dangerous places, overrun by Assembly or Fallout Swarms, and bring out salvage. One time we went as far north as Portland. There's a building there, skyscraper, got all messed up in the invasion, knocked loose of its supports. It was leaning bad, the top third of it or so had caved in on the rest, but somehow, it was still standing. It was perfect, because it was probably full of useful stuff no one in their right mind would go in there to get. Thing looked like if you blew on it, it would all come down."

"Let me guess," Mira said softly. "You blew on it?"

"We went in, started climbing, using the stairwells where we could, and where we couldn't, we slung up ropes. Took hours . . . but it was worth it. We found lots of loot, medicine mainly, batteries, dried coffee, filled up our packs, probably the best haul we'd ever had. We started back and that's when I noticed it. Little trails of dust raining down between the cracks in the floors and the walls. Pretty at first, way the streams caught the light, but then I figured it out. The only reason you'd see that is if the building was moving. When it happened, it hit like an earthquake. We were both hanging from our ropes, between a gap in about four floors. Ravan just looked at me and laughed . . . and then everything came down. Worst part was the sound, it's all I really remember; this awful, deep roar that shook your insides."

Mira knew that sound. She'd heard it less than a month ago, when Polestar fell in on itself after the Gravity Well died. It was something she would never forget.

"When I came to, it was black," Holt said. "Totally silent. If it hadn't been for the pain, I wouldn't have known if I was alive, but it was pretty clear I'd broken my leg. I heard Ravan stir a little next to me, but she wasn't conscious. I couldn't see a foot in front of me, much less any way out. Then I saw . . . something. Just above and to the right. A light, like someone flipped a switch, and when it came on it lit up where we were. We'd been lucky, hanging on our ropes in the bubble between those ruined floors, and when everything fell, so did it. When we hit, the stuff above us got all caught up in itself and didn't come crushing down. End result was we were trapped in a shell of shattered concrete. There were crawlways, though. Little tunnels, formed out of jagged stuff that hadn't been totally flattened. It looked impossible, getting through that, but it was still a way out. And it had all been shown to me by that light."

"The moon," Mira guessed.

Holt nodded. "Every few minutes it disappeared, clouds probably, and the world went black again. I only had clear line of sight for a couple of seconds."

"What did you do?"

"I grabbed Ravan and started dragging both of us through the tunnels. Problem was, without the moon, I wasn't always sure where I was headed. Sometimes I was moving the right way. I kept going. Sometimes I wasn't. I backtracked. Either way I kept crawling."

Mira smiled and ran her fingers through the hair on his chest. "I sense the coming of a moral."

"The moral is, beautiful, with big things like that, things that seem impossible, you don't focus on the *goal*. You focus on what's in front of you. Then what's in front of you after that. You just keep going."

She looked up at him. "One step at a time."

Holt nodded.

Mira looked at the half-finished tattoo on his right wrist, the partially complete shape of a bird. Ravan had an identical one, only hers was finished. In the Menagerie, the pirates took the same tattoo to pledge devotion to one another. It was called a Troth, and Holt had been having his done the night he chose to leave, a tattoo that would have joined him in a very special way to Ravan. Stories like the one Holt just shared always gave her a glimpse into what used to exist between them, and she was never sure how she really felt about it. "You two were very close . . ."

Holt nodded. "She saved me. I saved her. More than once."

Mira just stared at the tattoo, thinking of where Holt was going tomorrow, and who with.

"Mira, you know——" Holt began, but she raised up and kissed him before he could finish. It was a nice kiss, long and soft, with that mix of passion and tenderness only people who are truly comfortable with each other can share. When she pulled away, he was silent. There was nothing to say, really. They both had their own paths to walk now.

"Have you figured out where you're going to meet the Regiment?" Holt asked.

"Dresden's arranged it," she told him. "Someplace east of the ruins."

"You ever meet a resistance group?"

Mira had to think about it. Resistance groups were just what they sounded like. Freedom fighters that had dedicated themselves to fighting the Assembly, setting up shop in one of the city ruins where the Presidiums had landed. They couldn't do much real damage, of course; their guerrilla tactics were only really useful for distracting them, but still, it was something. In spite of it, the numbers of resistance fighters continually grew, and there was an interesting reason why. The closer you were to one of the Assembly Presidiums, the less effect the Tone seemed to have. There was no explanation, but the survivors could sometimes last as much as an extra year before they Succumbed.

The rebels in San Francisco called themselves the Phantom Regiment, and they were well-known, only because they fought where the Assembly Citadel had been constructed, the seat of power for the aliens in North America, and where Ambassador claimed Zoey was being held.

The Assembly presence there was far stronger than in any other city. If they were going to have any chance of rescuing Zoey, they needed the Phantom Regiment's support. No one knew those ruins like they did, and

they were one of the toughest fighting forces on the planet. That's why en-
listing their help was Mira's next task.

"Just be careful," Holt said.

Of course, she wasn't the only one heading to dangerous places. "Are
you sure you can trust Tiberius?"

"I can trust him to hear me out," Holt said, and leaned forward. His
mouth started to slowly drift down the side of her neck. She could feel his
hands gliding over the arch of her back. It had been an hour since they'd last
given in, and she could feel the heat rising once more. She wiggled up and
around and lay across him, listening to the rumble of his voice below her.
"The only thing Tiberius respects is power, and that's what we're offering.
Plus, when he hears the Wind Traders already accepted, he'll have to find a
way to retip the scales. 'Power lost, must be retaken,' the Menagerie say."

Mira gently bit the side of his neck and then his lips found hers again.
She twisted her legs around his, trying to get closer. She pulled up long
enough to look into his eyes. "Just promise me, if you feel it going south,
you'll run. You'll get free and run and you won't stop. Promise me."

Holt smiled. "I thought we said no more promises."

It was true, they'd made that deal weeks ago, but before she could argue, he kissed her again. God, she loved his taste. His hands reached down
and under her, slowly sliding toward her warmth and she pulled her mouth
free to sigh . . .

. . . and then it all stopped.

Guardian . . . The projections were particularly intense this time, and
they ripped past the pleasure and the sensations. *Come close.*

Mira rolled away, pushing them back, retaking control. When they finally receded, she felt Holt's hands on her, but differently this time, now it
was with concern.

"Breathe." His voice cut through what was left of the projections, helping her focus and center. When it was just her again she opened her eyes.
Holt's face was that usual mix of concern and anger. He hated what she
was going through, she knew it made him want to rip Ambassador apart
with his bare hands. "Promise it isn't getting worse."

It *was* getting worse. Much worse, and more Assembly were showing
up every day, but Holt had enough to worry about. She needed him focused and as clearheaded as he could be, if he was going to survive, if she
was going to get him back.

"No more promises," she reminded him.

Holt frowned at the response, studying her skeptically. He knew her very well now, maybe better than anyone ever had, and it was a source of great comfort. Holt had become her rock over the last few months, her one constant, and the thought of leaving him wasn't something she could bear to think about. Thinking about it, however, would soon be the least of her problems, and they both knew it. It was in their eyes whenever they looked at the other.

Whatever Holt was thinking, however, was lost at the sudden opening of their door.

One of the White Helix girls stood in the doorway, a daredevil, even more than the others, named Masyn, and she paused as she saw them, watching them with barely contained amusement. Mira pulled the covers sharply over them.

"Yes?" Holt asked in exasperation.

"Sorry, but . . . you need to come downstairs. Right now." Masyn gave them one last conspiratorial look, then darted out of sight. There was a note in the girl's voice that Mira didn't like, something that seemed out of place for a four o'clock wake-up call. Excitement. For a White Helix, that emotion usually only meant one thing.

Holt studied Mira knowingly. "And so it goes," he said.

Mira kissed him one last time, and then they were both up and getting dressed.

"*HOW* BIG, AGAIN?" Conner asked, staring down at a map on one of Smitty's worktables. A crowd of people surrounded the map: White Helix, Wind Traders, Mira and Holt, Ravan and two of her men, several dozen altogether, staring at where a female Captain had drawn lines to indicate what she'd seen and where.

Holt stared at a circle drawn about thirty miles west of Currency, where the rolling hills began their transformation into the flatlands that would become the Barren. He felt a hollowness in his stomach, and Mira's hand slipped into his instinctively. They were thinking the same thing. The time had come.

"A hundred walkers, maybe more," said the dark-haired Captain, eighteen or so. "That's how many I counted, at least, before I got the hell out of there. I couldn't make them out, but they were all Spider size I'd say, but there was something else. Something . . . *bigger.* Thought it was just haze at first, a mirage maybe, but then I could see the lights flashing on it, and I knew it was real." The girl's voice held a tangible note of fear, and Holt didn't blame her. It was an Assembly army she was describing, and if those numbers were right, it was twice the size of the one that had attacked Midnight City, even without the mysterious larger object that was moving within it.

Mira's eyes shut suddenly, she swayed, and Holt caught her before she fell. It was *them,* he knew, inside her head again. He saw Ravan's eyes study Mira pityingly across the room. To her, what Zoey had done was a curse, and Holt had a hard time disagreeing.

"It's . . ." she started, trying to make sense of all the voices in her head. "There are two hundred and seven walkers."

The room went silent, everyone looked at her in shock. "*What* did she say?" one of the Captains asked, stunned. "*Two* hundred and—"

"The silvers told you this?" Ravan asked and Mira nodded. "Then I'd say that intel isn't particularly trustworthy."

"They have just as much invested in this as we do," Mira said sternly. "The numbers are *right*. It's the reds. They're marching on orders from the blue and whites."

Up until a few months ago, before they found Zoey, the only Assembly colors they'd ever seen were blue and white. The colors, they now knew, represented different Assembly clans, each with their own territory throughout the world. Zoey, for reasons still unknown, was vital to some agenda of the aliens and these clans had converged on North America in an attempt to claim her for their own.

Holt and Mira had encountered two clans, so far, other than the blue and whites. The green and orange Hunters, who relied on stealth and speed. And the reds, who relied mainly on heavy walkers, like Spiders. If the reds and the blue and whites, as it now seemed, were working together, it meant things had truly changed.

"Ambassador says it's because they have Zoey now. The other clans acknowledge their dominance."

"Lovely . . ." Ravan said.

"Why attack now?" one of the Landship Captains asked. "Why here?"

"We're a threat." It was Avril this time, standing next to Dane amid the other White Helix. "We've been marshaling our forces here for almost a month, they were bound to notice, and it's clear where we're headed and why. They mean to stomp us out before we get started."

"*You* brought this down on us." The bitter voice was directed at Conner, and Holt recognized the British female Captain from yesterday. "You and your bargain! These things are headed for Currency!"

Angry and fearful murmurs swept through the crowd of Wind Traders.

"What's done is done, it was always going to be a hard road," Conner told them. "We're just starting it sooner, and the sooner you start something, the quicker you finish it. I say let them come."

"And if Currency is destroyed in the process?"

"It won't be," Dane said, across the table from Holt, standing with Avril and the other White Helix, all of them Doyen, leaders of their own Arcs. Their reactions were altogether different from the Wind Traders. Excitement and eagerness played on their faces as Dane pointed to a spot in between the army's current location and Currency, a valley between two rocky outcrops. "A small force can engage the reds *here*, buy time for the fleet to escape. We can deploy from the attack ships, use the hills for cover if we need to retreat." The way he said it implied he had very little interest in retreating.

"Smitty, how many ships are armed?" Conner asked.

"Eleven," the engineer said. "Should be fifteen by now, but getting a dependable crystal size from that infernal magic box isn't all it's cracked up to be."

"The Reflection Box creates an *identical* version of whatever you place in it," Caspira replied icily.

"Yeah?" Smitty shot back. "Then why isn't the muzzle velocity or the inertia consistent from weapon to weapon?"

"Probably because your cannon construction is faulty."

"This isn't the time!" Conner yelled, rubbing his eyes. Smitty and Caspira glared at each other across the table, but said nothing else. "Eleven ships out of ninety-three," Conner said to himself, shaking his head.

"Aye," Smitty said soberly. "But it's better than nothing, and the *Wind Star* is fully armed and tested, she's got almost as many cannons as two normal ships." The *Wind Star* was the largest Landship in the Wind Trader fleet, the flagship and the greatest creation of Smitty and his engineers. Designed like one of the old Ironclads, it was a hulking vessel with a hull of almost pure aluminum, salvaged from barns and roofs and pieces of old cars, all welded and formed into the wedge-shaped craft. Its wheels were from giant construction vehicles, ten of them, almost eleven feet high by themselves. It wasn't fast, nothing that heavy could be, even with five sails, but there wasn't any landscape it couldn't tackle. The thing took a crew of thirty to operate and was the only Landship in the world that needed two Chinooks to drive it, the Strange Lands artifacts that focused existing wind into streams powerful enough to propel the huge ships over the ground. Mira had personally helped redesign the vessel for combat, adding more than a dozen Barrier artifact combinations, which acted like deflector shields. The goal, of course, was to have the entire fleet outfitted with White Helix weaponry and Barriers . . . but that was a long ways off.

"Dresden, what do you think?" Conner asked, motioning to the map.

"The Landships make a frontal assault here, deploying Helix as they go. The Barriers should hold long enough to deflect fire from the Assembly, and when we're in range, we let 'em have it."

For as much as they argued or seemed to dislike one another, the two brothers respected each other's abilities and minds. They always consulted on important matters. Dresden, however, wasn't even looking at the map, he was staring out one of the windows of the power station, into the landscape beyond.

"What do I think?" he repeated. "I think whoever participates in this attack isn't coming back, and if my ship were one of these eleven, I wouldn't be taking it anywhere near that battle." Then he finally looked at Conner. "Oh wait, it *is* one of the eleven ships. Well, there goes that."

"You're going to lose people and ships, no way around that." Ravan spoke up from the back of the line. The Wind Traders stared at her and her men distrustfully. She was Menagerie after all, a group who spent their time hunting them and their ships, and there was no love lost between them. "But if you do it as a diversion with the goal of letting the rest escape, it might work. Get in, hit them, get out, don't prolong it. That's too many walkers for anyone to stand against long."

"We haven't decided where Ambassador's forces will attack," Mira said, looking at the map herself. "They could circle the outcrops, the Hunters are fast, and—"

"No." Dane's voice was firm and insistent. "Those things aren't needed here." The majority of the White Helix nodded in agreement. Mira stared at Dane in shock. Even Holt was surprised.

"Much as I dislike the aliens," Holt spoke up, "there are almost *sixty* combat walkers out there. Not using them seems pretty foolish."

"You trust them a lot more than I do," Conner replied, nodding at Dane. "I agree with him, we don't need them for this. Hopefully once the Helix and the fleet are gone, these reds will leave Currency alone. The threat will have been removed."

"Pray that's the case, Consul," the British-accented girl said again, her stare dark. "Or it all hangs on your name."

Conner stared back at her. "So be it. We don't have much time. Prepare your ships. If they've been retrofitted with Helix weaponry, your staging area is west of the Shipyards. Everyone else will unberth and assemble south of Currency. Winds guide us."

"Winds guide us," the other Captains chanted. The White Helix gathered around Dane while he gave orders to the Doyens, choosing which Arcs would participate in the diversionary attack and which would load onto the ships. As expected, every Doyen there wanted their Arc in the battle.

This was going to be the first contact in the war Gideon had prepared them for their entire lives. There was a lot of honor to be gained today.

Avril stood nearby, but apart, allowing Dane to assume command. She was headed in a different direction from the others, and quite possibly might never see any of them again. It was Dane's place to lead, not hers. He was Shuhan, now, but it wasn't an easy realization.

Holt watched Conner pull Dresden away, arguing amongst themselves. He caught Ravan's eye as she moved off with her men. She shook her head disapprovingly, and he didn't blame her.

"I have a real bad feeling about this," Mira said next to him, watching the different groups planning their moves. None of them were talking to the others. No one was working together.

"You and me both," Holt replied.

GUARDIAN . . . THE PROJECTIONS FORCED their way into her mind again. *Come closer . . .*

Mira ignored them as she moved through the crowds of Currency. Word of the impending attack had spread quickly, and the populace grabbed everything they could carry, leaving their homes behind. The ones lucky enough to be part of a Landship crew were headed to their berths. Everyone else was forced to go on foot, because there was no room on the ships. They were tasked with transporting White Helix and supplies, and even if there had been room, the ships were headed west, right toward the coming army.

As she pushed through it all, Mira thought she could feel their angry glares, but it could have been her imagination. All the same, they had every right. She and Holt had come here and turned their world upside down, all to rescue a little girl the Wind Traders had never met. The ramifications were starting to become hard to bear.

As she moved, she saw the ships were all beginning to leave, could see the massive vessels rolling through the city, one at a time. She moved faster, she had to make it before he left.

The berth Holt had been assigned was for a ship she knew well. The *Wind Rift*, Olive's ship. Six massive wheels, three on each side, custom constructions of wood and steel, meticulously fashioned and welded, stood out prominently and held the top deck thirty feet off the ground. Her hull had been assembled from repurposed wood and sheet metal, as well as train and boat parts. Two of the masts were formed out of old tires that held together long columns of barrels, fifty feet tall or more, and her colorful sails flapped impatiently in the wind.

Olive had been the unlucky one to get what was widely considered the worst assignment in this entire ordeal: transporting Holt, Ravan, and the Menagerie back to Faust. While the other ships were potentially looking at war, Olive and her crew were being asked to go somewhere that couldn't have been less hospitable: the capital city of the Wind Traders' greatest enemy.

Mira was relieved the ship was still there. The crew moved back and forth, hurriedly preparing it to sail. Ravan and her men stood near the gangplank, talking with a group of White Helix, and Mira moved toward them.

"If she can't wear them, she should be allowed to keep them at least," Dane was saying, glaring at Ravan. Next to him, Avril was silently removing the red, blue, and green glowing rings from her left hand. They didn't come off easily, she'd worn them a long time. "You have no idea what we do to earn those."

"She's not White Helix anymore," Ravan said simply, staring back at him evenly. "She's something else now, and she doesn't get to keep dangerous things like that, unless Tiberius says so. I'll keep them safe, you have my word."

Avril, Mira noticed for the first time since they'd met, was not dressed in the usual gray-and-black blended outfit of the White Helix. She wore green cargo pants and a white thermal shirt with a small pack slung over her shoulder, and that was it. Mira watched her work each ring loose from its finger, and with each one that came off, more and more of the light in her eyes died. She looked completely defeated.

Avril slipped the rings into a small black pouch and handed it to Ravan. Masyn and Castor were there as well, watching in pain. Masyn even looked away.

"The spear too," Ravan said, her eyes on Dane.

Dane was holding two Lancets, Mira noticed. One was his, the other Avril's. His stare became like fire. "If you and I ever meet again, outside of this—" His voice silenced as Avril gently gripped his arm, and he stared at her with emotion. This was how it was, she was reminding him. There was no point arguing it. Slowly, Dane handed over Avril's Lancet, and Ravan gave it and the black bag to one of her men.

"Fifteen minutes for good-byes," Ravan told them. "I'd make them count."

Dane, Avril, Masyn, Castor, and the other Helix moved off, talking in low voices. Mira stared after them sadly. It was more than just her that was losing someone today, she reminded herself.

"That went better than I figured," Ravan said, standing next to her now. "Expected a riot."

"You handled it well," Mira said. It was true. Given the circumstances, there was no way Avril was keeping her White Helix weaponry. Ravan could have been a lot more forceful and a lot more cruel. For her, it had almost been respectful.

"Yeah," she said. "Just a big teddy bear, I guess."

Mira watched Dane slowly pull Avril into his arms and hug her tightly. It was the first time Mira had ever seen them be affectionate with other Helix around. Relationships in the White Helix were frowned on to some degree. At least she and Holt could express their feelings openly.

Mira looked at Ravan. "You're more soft than you'd like to admit."

Ravan smiled. A little. "Careful, Red. Got a reputation to think of." The two studied each other awkwardly. They weren't exactly friends, but they had come a long way from where they'd started, in that tense march through the Strange Lands. Ravan had proven she was more than she seemed, and as much as Mira hated to think about it, she could see why she had meant so much to Holt.

"You know," Ravan said after a moment, "I don't pretend to understand why you're doing all this, but that doesn't mean I don't respect the strength it takes to do it. You wouldn't make a half-bad pirate."

"I'll take that as a compliment," Mira answered. "For what it's worth, I definitely feel a lot safer when you're around. Part of me is glad you're going with Holt."

"And the other part?"

Mira didn't say anything, and Ravan didn't push it. She kept smiling, though.

"Don't worry about him, kiddo," the pirate said. "If there's one guy who can take care of himself, it's Holt Hawkins. But I'll keep an eye on him for you."

"That sounds ominous." It was Holt's voice. They turned and saw him approaching with Max.

"It was meant to," Ravan said. She looked down at Max, and the dog stared back up. She pulled a piece of jerky from a pocket and threw it to him. Max snapped it out of the air. "Last piece, you little fearmonger." Then Ravan turned and headed for the gangplank of the ship, looking at Holt as she did. "See you on board."

Mira stared after Ravan. It was odd, there was a melancholy to watching her leave. As complicated as things were between them, she'd become a part of Mira's life too, and that part was about to be gone.

"Seemed like an okay good-bye," Holt said.

"I guess." She turned to Holt and the two stared at each other soberly, as the crew finished untying the ship. The White Helix were leaving, Avril was slowly walking up the gangplank while Dane stared after her. It was almost time.

"I don't like the idea of you going on the *Wind Star,*" Holt said, for probably the thousandth time. His voice was tight.

"It's the flagship of the fleet," Mira reminded him. "It's the most heavily armed and it has three times as many Barriers on it, I built them myself. So as far as Landships going into the fight, it's the safest one to be on."

"It's the 'going into the fight' part I don't like."

"We all have to fight eventually. That's what this is about, isn't it?"

Holt didn't say anything; he knew she was right, but that didn't make it any easier for him. She felt the same, in her own way.

"I got you something," Holt said as he pulled out a small object, wrapped in old paper and handed it to her. Mira stared down at it guiltily. Giving Holt something as they left each other seemed like such an obvious gesture, and it hadn't even occurred to her. She felt awful.

"I . . . didn't get you anything," she said.

"That's okay," Holt smiled. "You're a horrible person."

She frowned at him, then opened the package. Underneath all the wrapping was a small white tube, with faded writing she could just barely make out.

It was sunblock.

Mira smiled and shook her head, gave him a dubious look.

"Hey, it's practical," he told her. "You'll thank me later, trust me."

It was exactly the kind of gift Holt would give her, and underneath it were implications. His foresight, his concern for her well-being, just the fact that she, regardless of what was happening around him, always factored into his thoughts.

Her smile faded as she stared at the tube, her hands began to shake.

She made herself look back up at him. She couldn't believe this was happening, that the moment was here. The tears were starting to form, like it or not. "Holt . . ." Mira started.

"What's one short whistle?" Holt asked, looking quickly down and away. He'd asked these questions over and over the last week, drilling them into her. It was important to him, she knew, so she tolerated it.

"It gets his attention," Mira answered with patience, but this wasn't what she wanted to talk about.

Holt nodded, bent down to Max, rubbing his sides. The dog was still working on Ravan's jerky. "One long, one short."

"Scout ahead," Mira said.

"Two long—"

"*Holt*, I know the whistles, I promise. Can we—"

"You don't have to bathe him if you don't want to," Holt said.

Mira frowned. "I *don't*."

"But you have to feed him twice a day, and not that jerky Ravan always gives him. *Real* food." Mira was about to tell him the dog would be lucky if it got her table scraps, but she noticed the emotion in Holt's voice. Max, as annoying as he might be, was a friend to Holt, and they'd never been apart. Holt was losing two connections in his life today, she realized, and that wasn't something he was good at. "Make sure he has water, he drinks more than you'd think. And . . . pet him. You know? Sometimes?"

Mira nodded. When she spoke her voice was barely audible. "Okay."

Holt stood back up and the tears were in her eyes now, there was no stopping them. Holt's hand cupped the side of her face and she leaned into it.

"Oh, God . . ." she said, her voice cracking.

"Do you remember the first time we met?"

She managed a small smile. "I was in the tub."

"You tricked me, trapped me in that Gravity Void."

"Wasn't very hard," she told him. "You get a little distracted around naked girls."

"Clearly," Holt said, and she felt the warmth of his hand and made herself commit the feeling of it to memory. "Amazes me how far we've come. Everything before that moment was you not in my life. Everything after . . . I can't imagine without you. You're a part of me now, and it's not accidental, I believe that."

"Me too." The tears were hot and stinging.

"I know we said no more promises, I know that, but . . ." Holt moved closer, his hands touching her face, wiping away her tears. "I lost everything once. I don't think I could go through that again."

He meant his sister, Mira knew, Emily. Every time he spoke of her, there was a slight hint of pain in his eyes. Her loss had almost destroyed him.

"I just want to know," Holt continued, "that when this is all done, when whatever happens next, happens . . . that you'll be here. With me."

Mira smiled through her tears. "Where else would I be?"

Holt pulled her to him and kissed her. The world blended away a little, just enough, for one brief moment, to forget everything else . . . and then the ringing of the crew bell on the top deck of the *Wind Rift* signaled it was time to leave. The grounds around the huge ship had cleared out.

Holt pulled away. They looked into the other's eyes one last time. Then he grabbed his pack and headed for the gangplank. Max tried to go with him, but Mira grabbed the dog's collar. He whined, confused.

Holt held her gaze. "Pet him. *Every day.*"

Mira watched him climb the gangplank, feeling her heart beating, feeling the energy he brought to her life diminishing with every step he took until he disappeared over the edge onto the deck and was gone.

The world suddenly felt very cold.

"Hey," a small voice said. It was Olive, watching the last of her crew board her ship.

Mira wiped the rest of her tears away. "Hi."

"Seems like an okay guy," she observed.

Mira smiled. "He is."

"I'll get him there in one piece. After that . . ." Olive's voice was dark.

"I'm sorry you got this task, Olive." Mira meant it. "And I'm sorry it's because of me."

Olive looked at Mira, searching her eyes. "The deal is, on the surface, this all seems to be about rescuing some little girl. If you could tell me it was about more than that . . . I'd have to be okay with it. I've always trusted you."

Mira thought about her answer. "I go back and forth on that every day. Zoey . . . has done amazing things. Things I never thought possible. All I can tell you is, she's shown me, for the first time in a long time, that it's okay to hope again."

Olive studied her, then simply nodded. "Well . . . at least it won't be boring."

The two girls hugged each other, then pulled apart and Olive moved for her ship. Something occurred to Mira then. She suddenly realized she *did* have something for Holt, and she slipped it off from around her neck. "Olive!" Mira threw a necklace to the pink-haired girl. At the end was a small, brass compass. Its hands, instead of pointing north, pointed southwest. Zoey had an identical one, or at least she did when she was taken. "Give that to Holt, he'll know what it means. Tell him . . . it's for if he loses his way."

Olive stared down at the necklace, then looked back up. "Winds guide you, Freebooter."

"And you."

She watched Olive jump onto the deck above and disappear, watched the gangplank being rolled up, watched the giant, colorful sails unfurl and the giant wheels turn as the *Wind Rift* began to roll.

Mira looked down at Max. He glared back up at her skeptically. "Come on, mutt. Got our own boat to catch."

THE ENTIRE CREW stood at the edge of the *Wind Rift*'s deck, and everyone who had optics was scanning the horizon. Holt peered through his binoculars with them. It was an impressive sight, almost seventy Landships arranged in formation south of Currency, and more were still coming, assembling in the staging area. When the time came they would all run the gauntlet together.

In the distance, eleven additional Landships stood ready, their sails deflated. These were equipped with the new White Helix cannons, the ones which would try and buy time for everyone else to escape, and it was where Mira was now.

He could easily make out her ship, the *Wind Star,* among all the ones there because it was so much larger. Probably double the length of the others, with five giant masts that towered over the rest, a formidable sight . . . at any other time. Today, what those ships were about to face was, without question, far more powerful.

But where was it? The red army had yet to show itself, and everyone waited with dark anticipation.

"What are we still doing here?" Ravan asked impatiently next to Holt.

"Waiting for the other ships," Olive replied, staring through a fold-out telescope she'd pulled from her belt. "We leave as one."

"But we aren't going with the others," Ravan replied. "We're headed *south,* what does it matter if we wait or not?"

"Looks like you're the only one anxious to get where we're going, Menagerie." It was Castor's voice. He and Masyn were looking to the west with everyone else. They were the only White Helix on board, having been assigned to accompany them to Faust. Neither was happy about it. The way they saw it, a war was about to start and they were left out, given the official (and mundane) task of demonstrating the White Helix weaponry to Tiberius

Marseilles. Unofficially, they were more likely there at Dane's orders to watch over someone else.

Avril sat separate from the others, her back against one of the ship's tire-wrapped masts, staring at the empty fingers of her left hand. She seemed completely blank, like she was living in a dream. Holt had left a lot behind himself, he knew how it felt.

"Shh." Olive silenced the others nearby, lowering the telescope. Ravan and Holt looked at her in confusion . . . until they heard what Olive had. Everyone on deck heard it.

Shuddering, concussive booms that came from the distance.

A second later, and the sounds repeated, echoing off the serene, rolling hills.

Then again. Again. They were growing louder.

"What the hell?" Ravan's voice was unnerved. "Sounds like . . ."

"Footfalls," Holt finished, rescanning the horizon, and this time, amid the haze of the far distance . . . shapes moved.

Large ones. Lines and lines of them, trudging powerfully forward. They were barely silhouettes at this distance, but Holt had seen enough shapes like that to know what they were, and he felt his blood run cold.

Spider walkers. Fifty feet tall and wider than a city street. Agile, powerful, and carrying enough firepower to decimate anything that challenged them. They got their name from the eight large mechanized legs that held their huge fuselages above the ground. The combination granted them superior mobility, and made them one of the most feared sights on the planet.

Holt had seen red Spiders only once before, two of them, and from what Holt remembered, they were different than the blue and whites. Blockier, slower, but more heavily armed, and judging by the movement on the horizon, there were a lot more than two.

"Mira's mechanical friend was right," Olive said soberly. "Looks like about two hundred."

"But it doesn't explain that noise," Holt answered. As he did, the sounds filled the air again, sounds that were now close enough to vibrate the deck under his feet. He remembered what that Captain had said back at the power plant, about the giant shape that moved within the Spiders.

"Look," Masyn said, pointing to the east. "They're moving."

Holt saw with a building dread that she was right. The great, colorful sails of the Landships near the Shipyards plumed outward in bursts of purple and blue as the vessels began to move, gradually picking up speed, headed toward the army growing on the horizon.

"Jesus," Ravan said. "This is going to be a massacre."

"Five hundred White Helix are on those ships," Castor replied proudly. "When they reach the ground—"

"They'll be crushed like five hundred ants," Ravan cut him off.

Now there was something else, Holt could see. A blackness that stirred above the walkers in the distance, like shadows growing in the air. Holt had a pretty good guess what it was. So did Ravan.

"If we don't go now," she told Olive, "we're never going to leave."

"The signal hasn't been shot yet," Olive said.

"What's the signal?" Holt asked.

"A red flare."

Ravan looked to Castor and Masyn, her eyes moving to the Lancets on their backs. On the end of Masyn's rested a glowing red spear point. Holt had a guess what she intended, but his eyes were locked on the Landships barreling ahead and the huge image of the *Wind Star* in his optics as its sails launched it forward. She would make it, he told himself. It was the flagship. The safest place.

"You! The blond one!" Ravan yelled at Masyn, taking a step toward her. "Shoot your red crystal thing!" Castor took a protective step in between them, but Masyn stepped past him in annoyance.

"Why?" she asked. "Look how far away those things are. What's the—"

"Because what's swarming over there moves faster than any one of these ships." Ravan looked at Olive as she said the last part. "You know I'm right."

Olive stared at Ravan, then looked at Holt. Holt nodded. "Do it," he told her.

Olive studied him with a mixture of frustration and fear, but then she looked at Masyn and nodded.

Masyn shrugged and yanked the Lancet from her back. There was a loud, percussive ping, and the red spear point shot into the sky. Every ship in the staging area would have seen it.

"I hope you're right," Olive said. "Because if you're not, then—"

"*Look!*" one of Olive's crew shouted, pointing westward. The air along the horizon exploded in a myriad of buzzing shapes, a hundred of them probably, screaming forward.

It was what Holt expected. Raptor gunships, racing ahead of the ground forces toward the approaching Landships. If those gunships wanted, they could be on the main grouping, the unarmed and defenseless ones, in minutes.

Olive knew the same thing. "Unfurl!" she yelled, running for the helm while everyone else scrambled to their positions. *"Unfurl!"*

The red spear point slammed back onto Masyn's Lancet with another ping. Either it had been taken for the signal flare, or the other Captains had figured out the same thing. The crews of every Landship around them were scrambling to unfurl their sails too.

"Checklist?" Olive's first mate shouted as he started climbing the central mast.

"No time! Full Chinook. *Now!*"

The wind roared above Holt's head as it was focused and intensified by the artifact, bellowing out the ship's massive sails. The *Wind Rift* rocked, and Holt held on, trying to—

Explosions flared up in the distance.

With wide eyes, Holt saw the swarm of gunships streak over and rain down yellow plasma onto the ships in the distance. Their Barriers blazed to life, but flames erupted everywhere.

He could hear the sounds of Raptor engines. Could see several dozen of them bank hard right and separate from the others. He knew what it meant.

"They're coming this way!" someone shouted.

Holt's eyes searched for and found the *Wind Star*, far away, rocking wildly as a blast erupted near it, but, like the others, it kept moving, dashing toward the Spiders . . . and, right next to it, the first of the armed Landships exploded in a ball of fire that arced into the sky.

Then the gunships roared over the *Wind Rift*, and the ground all around them was bursting apart too.

DANE BARELY MANAGED TO leap from the deck of the *Wind Thrust* before it exploded in a massive fireball. Three of his Arc hadn't been fast enough. The Barriers on the ship had taken their share of punishment from the air assault, but had eventually failed.

The Raptors had made short work of it after that.

Another Landship blew apart, spraying fiery splinters all through the air. He saw some of the Arc there, leaping to safety, but not all.

"Damn it!" he cursed as he hit the ground, dashing forward as more plasma bolts rained down, dodging through them. The Freebooter's

Barriers hadn't been enough, and it was tempting to blame what was happening on her, but it was plain to see where the real blame lay.

On him.

He'd pushed for this frontal assault. He'd heard Mira's claims about air support, and he'd ignored them. He should have thought strategically. Gideon had always preached strength, but he had also drilled in the idea that strength could never be relied on alone.

Dane had been a fool, and people, friends of his, were dying because of it.

He had to salvage this, he told himself. He wasn't going to lose the first battle of the war. "Spread out!" he yelled, and his Arc and the others around him obeyed instantly. Right now they were clumped up, easy targets. More explosions flared. "*Agility!*" Dane touched the rings on his index and middle fingers together, calling the power, and felt the world slow around him, the comforting sensation of near weightlessness as everything colored in a hue of yellow.

He and the rest of the Helix dashed forward. More leapt from their ships and followed, weaving in and out of the plasma fire.

Ahead, Dane finally saw the enemy with clarity. The Spider walkers, painted a brilliant shade of crimson, their giant legs moving them forward in lines that stretched from one edge of the horizon to another. The sight was sobering. How could anyone expect to survive against *that*? But he didn't have to survive, did he? He just had to last long enough to let the others escape . . . to let *her* escape.

From behind, he heard dozens of loud percussive pings. Above his head, streaks of color, red, blue, and green, arced forward through the air. It was the Landships. They were firing back.

Cheers erupted as the first of the spear points found their marks. In the distance, colorful explosions blossomed into the sky as they punched through the red Spiders' armor. He watched those machines crash to the ground in flames, and felt a glimmer of hope.

Still, there were more. Many more.

Behind him, another Landship exploded, tearing itself into the earth.

"Keep moving!" he shouted, running through the yellowish, slow-motion world of the Agility power. He and the others were almost there, and when they reached the Assembly, debts would be paid.

Dane couldn't see the other ships, the unarmed ones, and he didn't have time to look. He only hoped that Avril had escaped.

HOLT BARELY MANAGED TO keep from falling as the *Wind Rift* darted around another Landship at breakneck speed. The fleet was moving, which was good. The problem was, every ship here was headed southwest, while the *Wind Rift* was trying to go due *south*. It meant they had to cross through a massive wave of traffic before they could get clear, and that was proving tough.

The crew scrambled frantically to adjust the sails and rigging as Olive barked orders. Yet again, Holt was impressed by their discipline, their ability to not lose their heads in all the panic. Then again, maybe it had something to do with the knowledge that one slip by any of them probably meant their end.

Explosions rocked the ground. Raptors roared past, their cannons screaming. Holt watched three wheels on the side of a nearby Landship separate from the hull and send the entire ship listing into the ground.

The *Wind Rift* banked hard left, claiming the gap left by the disintegrated ship, desperately trying to get away from the buzzing gunships above.

Very little of the chaos around Holt registered. He just looked north, to where the other Landships moved to intercept the approaching army, and the sky above them was absolutely full of Raptors, firing down a constant hailstorm of yellow bolts. Two more ships incinerated and fell apart, their Barriers unable to hold.

Holt's eyes found the massive *Wind Star*, Mira's ship, watching it desperately. Its Barriers were holding, but it was the biggest target out there.

And there was something else now. Something huge. Behind the line of Spiders. Something that filled the horizon with its girth. A single, massive object, the source of those terrifying footfalls. A giant walker. Something no one had ever seen, and if it was real, it towered hundreds of feet above the ground, and it was headed right toward Mira.

Holt gripped the railing, looking down to the ground racing by below. He could jump, run as fast as he could, but he wouldn't last ten seconds and he'd never reach her in time.

Antimatter crystals shot into the air from the deck behind him. Two Raptors exploded as they banked past, caught by Masyn's and Castor's spear points. The Helix fired again and another Raptor crashed in flames.

"Light 'em up or not, boss?" one of Ravan's men asked, his rifle drawn. The Menagerie looked eager to join in.

"Sure," Ravan replied, grabbing her own weapon. "Why the hell not?" Gunfire echoed as they shot into the sky.

"Captain!" The first mate shouted down from the crow's nest at the top of the ship's central mast. "I don't see any way out of this, traffic's just too—"

"Well, *find* a way!" Olive shouted back. She was at the front, where the helmsman spun the ship's huge wheel, trying to keep from running into the vessels on either side of it. "If we don't, we're going to end up—"

Two nearby Landships crashed directly into one another, the front of one's hull tearing loose as both ships disintegrated.

"Pull starboard!" Olive shouted. "Pull—"

Her voice was lost amid the screaming of Raptor engines. Holt felt the ship shift under him as it turned hard, barely avoiding the spinning, flaming debris.

In spite of it, his attention was still on the *Wind Star* in the distance. It had accelerated past the other ships, only about seven of them now, leading the charge toward the Assembly walkers.

Holt knew what was coming. It was only a matter of time.

From the giant shape in the distance, the machine that towered over the others, a single, bright beam of energy erupted. A massive column of heated death that streaked through the air . . . and slammed into the *Wind Star*.

"No," Holt moaned.

Holt could see the Barriers along the front of the Landship flare to life and absorb the massive blast, but they couldn't displace the momentum. The huge vessel rocked violently backward, its front wheels came off the ground and then slammed back down in a cloud of dust. Still, it kept going.

Gasps echoed from the crew as they watched the same thing Holt did. Another beam of energy erupted from the huge walker. The energy slammed into the *Wind Star* again.

Once more the Barriers flashed. The ship listed, losing its forward momentum, beginning to spin.

"*No . . .*"

Another beam. Another strike. And this time . . . the Barriers did not hold.

Holt felt his insides contort as he watched the energy split the huge ship almost down the middle, watching the hull burst into flame, two huge lengths of fire that spun out of control and disintegrated into the ground, spraying metal and debris into the superheated air. No one could have survived it.

Holt heard a gut-wrenching cry that only a part of him recognized as his own.

In the distance, Raptors strafed what was left of the *Wind Star,* covering it in plasma fire, incinerating what little remained.

There was no question. Mira was gone.

He felt his legs move, felt his body shift as he made to leap over the railing, to get to her, to save her . . .

. . . and then hands yanked him back. The world moved in slow motion, upending as he fell to the deck.

He saw Ravan above him, pinning him, yelling something, but he didn't hear it. More explosions flared, Raptors roared past. The helmsman lost his grip on the wheel and crashed to the deck as the ship listed and Olive ran to take it.

The world was fire. And death. And he didn't care. He kept trying to get up, ignoring Ravan's shouts, ignoring everything but the giant plume of black smoke in the distance where the *Wind Star* had gone down. There was nothing there but flames now, nothing but fire.

A dim part of him knew that the last of the light Mira had brought into his life would die with those flames. When they had finished burning, there would be nothing left, not even ash.

6. ALLAY

ZOEY FELT THE POD SHAKE as it came to a stop, settling in place along the rack system. Unpleasant as the thing was, there was one blessing to being inside. There were no voices or projections in her mind, somehow it sealed away the Assembly's thoughts, and it made for a blissful silence she hadn't known for a long time.

The pod vibrated a strange, electronic humming sound, and Zoey braced herself for whatever was to come, to try and be brave. Light flooded in as the pod split into two pieces around her, each sliding back out of the way, and Zoey winced against the brightness. With the pod open, sensations flooded into her mind again.

Scion.

Welcome.

You are safe.

Scion . . .

You are home.

One after the other, hundreds of them, blending together into a stream of thought and emotion, and it took a second to remember to push it all back.

When her eyes adjusted, she could see the room beyond the chamber, its walls made of strange black metallic plates formed into wavelike shapes that circled her and stretched upward out of sight. Instinctively, her eyes followed the walls, and she saw there was no ceiling. Far above her, impossibly far, she could see the flickering, golden light from more of the golden entities, moving back and forth, thousands of them.

It was familiar, this room, and it took a moment for her to realize why. It was like the one the Oracle had shown her in Midnight City, from her repressed memories. She remembered the vision, being tied to a table in the center, one of the crystalline entities descending and burning itself into her body. She remembered the pain, most of all, how she'd screamed . . .

Come, the projections intoned.

In the black room, a dozen or so of the glowing entities hovered in the air. Most of them pulsed in golden light, but two were made of blue and white, their forms casting flickering hues of cobalt and snow.

It was from one of those entities, Zoey could tell, that the projections came.

Come . . .

It was neither warm nor threatening, merely a request. They wanted her to step into the room, and it was then that Zoey studied the only object that rested there.

It was another pod, like her own, only it was lying flat on the floor. Its doors were opened too, but she couldn't see inside, not from this vantage point.

Come, the entities asked again.

Zoey didn't move. As much as she disliked the pod and its claustrophobic confines, she had no desire to step from its relative safety.

The pod vibrated again, and as it did, its walls began to *reform.* The various shelves and cables and flashing instruments all smoothed and disappeared, like they had been absorbed into some kind of thick gelatin. The whole thing began to flatten, the back of it moving outward, filling the interior, and pushing Zoey *forward.*

She fell onto the floor with a gasp, spun around, and saw the pod had lost most of its form. It looked like a black cylindrical shape of clay.

No fear, the projections stated encouragingly. *You are honored.*

The two blue and white crystalline entities floated above her. The others, the more golden ones, stayed back. She could feel their emotions and thoughts, though, swirling around her, trying to push into her consciousness, and it was more than just the ones in the room, she realized. It was many more. Tens of thousands, hundreds of thousands maybe, all inhabiting the massive, black structure that stretched out of sight above.

Come. See.

Zoey tried to hide her shaking hands. They wanted her to look into the other pod, the one that had been laid before her. She supposed she really had no choice. Besides, this was her bargain, wasn't it? It was her choice to come here, because it was only here where the answers she needed could be found. She had to find a way to make it right, to fix all that she was responsible for, and this was the only way.

She had to stand on her tiptoes to do it, but slowly, Zoey peered over the edge of the container.

Inside lay a man. An *adult* man. His black hair was just beginning to gray, and his skin was eerily white from what had been years of existence without the sun, if you could count life in one of these pods as an existence.

Black tubes and wires of all sorts ran around his body and into his mouth, but as unsettling as it looked, he didn't seem to be in any discomfort. The answer to why was clearly evident.

His eyes stared blankly upward, and they were completely filled in with oily black. He was one of the Succumbed, those whose minds had been taken over by the Tone, and his current state, a blank, mindless existence inside one of these chambers, Zoey realized, must be the fate of everyone who gave into the Tone and disappeared inside one of the Assembly Presidiums.

One of the brilliant blue and white crystalline entities slowly drifted up until it hovered directly over the body of the man in the chamber.

Guide. The projections came. *Ease. Allay.*

In confusion, Zoey looked up at the entity . . . and watched as it began to slowly sink downward toward the man.

Guide. Ease. Allay.

She felt her heart beat, felt a wave of sickness as she realized what was happening. The same thing that had happened to *her.* The energetic being was going to sink into this man . . . and it wanted her, somehow, to help the process, to guide and aid the action.

Guide. Ease. Allay, the projections came again.

"No!" Zoey shouted, refusing to project back. She wouldn't help these things do to someone else what they had done to her. She *wouldn't,* no matter what answers she might receive or what she might learn.

Guide. Ease. Allay. The entity kept sinking, closer and closer. Zoey could feel the heat coming from the thing, and the closer it got, the more her head filled with a kind of horrible static.

Zoey stepped back, shaking her head. "No."

And then the crystalline shape sank into the man's body. Even though he was Succumbed, he gasped as the energy absorbed into him. More and more of it pushed in, and, as it did, his skin began to glow incandescently, lighting up the strange, black room even brighter.

Then something awful happened.

The man's shape flashed. Something like flames burst from his skin, and before Zoey could shut her eyes to block out the sight, she saw his body disintegrate into chalky white ash that billowed into the air like a milky cloud.

Zoey fell to her knees in stunned, horrified shock.

She kept her eyes shut tight, refusing to look back up at the open chamber, not wanting to see it empty now.

"No, no, no, no . . ." she moaned, but it did little good. The man was gone. Just like that, and she, however unwittingly, had played a role. Her refusal to help had led to his death.

All around her she felt new projections, and the emotion was almost a singular one. Disappointment.

She had not performed as the aliens hoped. It was the one consolation she had.

Why? The sensation entered her mind. She opened her eyes and glared back up at the crystalline shape. She hated them, she realized, and a part of her didn't like the feeling. She hated the Assembly for everything they had put her through. She would destroy them, if she could.

And that was exactly what she was going to do, she promised herself. Somehow . . .

The empty pod shuddered as it lifted off the floor, closing and drifting away on the rack system. Almost immediately, another pod appeared, rumbling downward and settling in the same position and slowly opening.

Zoey could just see another human shape inside. Her stomach churned as she realized it was all going to happen again.

"Please, don't . . ." Zoey begged, watching the blue and white entity float back into position. *"Please."*

Guide. Ease. Allay. The same projections again.

Without thinking, Zoey stood and looked.

Inside was a woman this time. With blond hair that glowed like honey. She was beautiful, and the sight of her took Zoey's breath away. Not just because she was so pretty . . . but because Zoey *recognized* her, and the realization hit her like a lightning bolt.

"Wait . . ." Zoey cried, but the entity began to sink again.

Guide. Ease. Allay.

"Wait!" It didn't stop, it kept descending. Zoey's eyes moved back and forth between the entity and the woman underneath. Most of her face was

hidden under the tubes and wires, but it *was* her, and there was no way it was a coincidence.

It had been Zoey's plan to resist the aliens' wishes, whatever their agenda. She was here to save Mira and Holt and the Max. Even if they had put a hundred bodies in front of her and made her responsible for their deaths, she would still have resisted, because something inside her told her it was the lesser of two evils.

But . . . now . . .

The woman in the chamber. How could it be?

Guide. Ease. Allay.

The entity continued to descend, burning toward the female body.

Zoey watched a second longer . . . then made her choice. They had forced her hand.

She reached out with her mind and found the presence of the descending entity. Next, she reached out for the eerily silent blankness of the woman in the chamber.

She wasn't sure exactly how to do it, to help the entity descend into the woman, and she only had seconds to figure it out. Zoey reached out for something she had come to depend on. The Feelings rose within her, and Zoey listened, studying the paths they showed her, adopting their suggestions.

She shut her eyes as violent static filled her mind, but she held on, holding onto both the entity and the woman under it, guiding them into each other, helping them to merge, and as she did, it all became clear. She knew what to do, and . . . it felt amazing, she discovered: wielding the power. Zoey adjusted the radiance and the vibrations of the entity and the woman, absorbing some of the heat and energy as the conversion occurred, redirecting it, slowly allowing the two consciousnesses to blend and burn into one unified whole . . .

And then it was over. Zoey collapsed onto the floor, her head full of pain and static.

When she opened her eyes, the blue and white entity was gone. As she watched, the woman in the chamber slowly rose, pulling tubes and wires from her body, sitting up weakly. Her eyes were no longer black. Instead, for one brief moment, they flashed in a kind of golden color . . . then it washed away, as quickly as it had appeared.

The woman looked down at Zoey on the floor . . . and smiled.

"Mom . . . ?" Zoey asked in disbelief.

Then the exertion and the pain finally overtook her. She passed out amid hundreds of thousands of projections of joy and elation that echoed up and down the massive structure she was in, bouncing inside her head until everything went mercifully dark.

RAVAN WALKED ALONG THE DECK of the *Wind Rift*, trying to hide just how hard it was to balance on top of the giant, accursed ship. Why would anyone build something so silly and huge, nothing but a giant moving target? She missed her old dune buggy, a Boston-Murphy style she'd restored herself, something reliable that ran on real things like gas and sweat, not artifacts and giant sails made of parachutes.

The *Wind Rift* had branched off to the south and left the rest of the fleet to deal with the buzzing Raptors and the giant Assembly army a day ago. Most likely Currency had been flattened and the rest of the Landships were all destroyed now, burning like the *Wind Star*, the ship the Freebooter had been on.

It would have been easy to say the idiots got what they deserved, but Ravan's thoughts were conflicted. She could still hear Holt's mournful wail as she pushed him to the deck and kept him from leaping off. That was more than a day ago, and she hadn't seen him since. He'd retreated down to the lower decks, to a cabin Olive cleared for him, which was probably a good thing. Holt had lost everything once. Ravan had been, at the time, the only person he'd ever told that story to, but, she thought with a slight sense of bitterness, it had been Mira and that little girl who had brought him back, made him believe in something again.

Ravan didn't hate the Freebooter. She kind of liked her, really. The two of them had had their share of tension, but Mira had moxie and a brain, one of the few. It was sad that it usually worked out that way. Why was it that the people who actually had something to contribute to the universe always seemed to be put in its crosshairs?

Ravan sighed. The real question was, what kind of mode Holt would be operating in now, if at all. She had never seen him as distraught as when that ship exploded. One thing she'd learned in life: getting dragged back into a darkness you'd crawled out of before didn't make it any easier the second time. Usually, it made it permanent. Most people didn't have the energy to do it all over again.

Holt wasn't most people, though . . . and he had *her.*

Angrily, Ravan shook the thought away as quickly as it formed.

Thoughts like that were weak. They made *her* weak. She'd never loved Holt, Ravan told herself. She'd just been stung by his betrayal, that was all. It cut deep because she let him inside. Chalk it up to a life lesson. It was like Tiberius said, "Trust is no path to power."

But, still, the feelings stirred within her, and her insistence that she felt nothing only seemed to make them stronger.

The landscape had dramatically shifted overnight. Where before it had been primarily lush, rolling green hills, now there was nothing but dust and cactus and scraggly weed along the few rocky outcrops that rested here and there. The sun beat down hard, and the Landship crew sweated underneath it, but Ravan smiled. She missed the heat, the dried air, she was tired of lush places. It took less to survive there, it didn't make you any harder.

The crew stared at her distrustfully as she moved past them. The farther they'd traveled south and away from the rest of the fleet, the darker their moods grew, and well they should. Where they were going, no Wind Trader had ever come back alive. It was a cliché, both in Faust and Currency, that the Wind Traders and the Menagerie were natural enemies. The reality, however, was much more complicated.

The Wind Traders provided the only real source of trade and commerce in North America, transporting and bartering their goods from one outpost or major city to the next, and they were good at it. The Menagerie, on the other hand, produced some of what they needed to survive, but not enough. The rest they had to steal, which meant they targeted the plumpest, richest targets they could. Invariably, that meant Landships.

The reality was, neither could exist without the other. The Menagerie depended on the goods and supplies being transported in those ships, and the Wind Traders depended on the infamy and hostility of the Menagerie to make their trade services through dangerous places like the Barren necessary.

It was a sick relationship, and one reason Ravan could never work up much sympathy for the Wind Traders. They needed the Menagerie as much as the Menagerie needed them. They had all made their choices.

As she moved, Ravan noticed something peculiar. Near the rear of the ship, the two White Helix were noodling about. What was odd was that the girl, the deceptively small blonde, was fully geared. The rings glowed on her fingers, her Lancet was strapped to her back for traveling, along with a pack of supplies.

The two talked a moment, the girl winked, and then leapt and disappeared overboard in a flash of cyan. The boy watched after her a moment, then hurried away.

Ravan had an idea what they were up to. It wasn't a bad play, something she might have done herself, but, in the end, it wouldn't make much difference. Whatever was going to happen at Faust would happen regardless of any little schemes they might be running.

Ravan thought of Avril a moment. Like Holt, she hadn't come above deck since the escape, but unlike him, she had no real reason for moping. The girl was the adopted daughter of one of the most powerful men in the world. You could say she had a lot to look forward to, but it was clear she didn't see it that way. In the end, Ravan didn't really care, as long as she arrived back to her father in one piece. Tiberius had told Ravan to bring his daughter home, not to bring her home happy. What happened after that was his problem.

Ravan kicked open the door to the lower decks and descended the stairs. The insides of a Landship were tight, only room for one person in the halls at a time, and as she moved every Wind Trader there got out of her way. It made her smile, how easy they scared. When the ship reached Faust, they were in for a rude awakening . . .

She stopped in front of one particular door, a faded red one jammed into the frame, staring at it hesitantly.

What was wrong with her? There wasn't a tiger behind it, just one heart-crushed fool. What bothered her was the idea of what she would see on the other side. Holt had always been just as strong as her, just as self-reliant, which was no mean feat, and the thought of seeing him fragmented and weak, emotional even, was unsettling.

Still, she'd given him enough time. The world required you to move on quickly, and she would see that he did.

Ravan opened the door. The small room had rounded walls made of sanded, knotted pine and a little, antique, stained-glass window that cast strange shapes along the floor. It wasn't the mess she expected. No broken mirrors or shattered furniture. In fact, it was all neat and tidy. The bed was freshly made, nothing out of place. Holt's gear was stacked near a chair by the door, ready to go. His main pack sat on the edge of the bed, the flap open. Holt stood at the front, collecting some things from a tiny nightstand.

He didn't look up as she entered.

"Packing?" Ravan asked.

"Almost there, aren't we?"

Ravan studied him curiously. She hadn't expected Holt to be catatonic, but every time she imagined coming down here, it involved kicking his ass and getting him back on his feet. Apparently . . . that wasn't necessary.

"How long until we're there?" Holt asked.

"Three, four hours, I guess." Ravan studied Holt's things. His guns were there, all of them: the Ithaca, the Beretta, the Sig rifle, even the backup .38 he carried in his boot and his knives.

"Figured you'd want those," Holt said as he started closing his pack. He still hadn't looked at her. "Ammo's in the side pouch."

In all the time she'd known him, Ravan had never seen Holt voluntarily give up his guns. She knew how much he'd put into them, both finding and restoring them. They had always been lifelines, necessities.

"You can't take the others, but the backup you could probably get in," she said. Holt likely wouldn't be searched, not if she handed over his main weapons. Her word was golden in Faust, especially now. "I was gonna suggest it."

"Why?" His voice was near monotone.

She looked back at him. "It's *Faust*, Holt. In case you've forgotten, you're not particularly popular there. I'd feel better if you weren't walking around defenseless."

"I meant, why do you *care?*"

The question was like a slap. Not because it was delivered with malice, but because there was no emotion discernible in it at all. She had been with Holt during the dark times, the times after Emily, the times he had done things he regretted, times he had almost died even, but there had never been this lack of life in his voice. Ravan felt a chill.

"Because . . . I want to help you, Holt," she said. "I know you're hurting, and I know—"

"I don't want your help." He cut her off with the same emotionless tone. "I just want to get this over with."

"And after that?" Ravan asked.

"There isn't going to be any after that."

There was a knock on the door. One of Olive's crew opened it, stood there studying them both warily.

"*What?*" Ravan demanded.

"Captain wants you on deck," the kid said. "Something's coming." Then he was gone.

Ravan frowned. "Thanks for the amazingly cryptic update."

Holt shouldered his pack and moved for the door. He still hadn't glanced at her. "I'll leave the guns, take 'em or don't, it's up to you. I assume this whole ship is gonna be stripped down to the nails anyway." He stepped out the door and was gone, without so much as a look back.

The exchange was so abrupt and the opposite of anything Ravan anticipated, she just stared after him, stunned. Above, she heard shouts, could hear the sounds of feet running along the deck to their positions.

Something was happening.

When Ravan made it back up, she saw what it was. It looked like a sandstorm at first, a huge churning cloud of dust bearing down on them from the south. There was a strange rumbling in the air, almost like a growl, and it was getting louder the closer they got.

Ravan smiled. She looked toward the front of the ship where Olive stood next to the helm. The tiny, pink-haired girl's eyes were already on her. She knew it was no sandstorm.

"What do we do?" Olive asked.

They only had a few seconds. Ravan looked to her men, standing near the edge of the deck. "Get the flag down, switch it with ours," she ordered.

Her men moved instantly, one of them pulling a large red flag from his pack, another ran to the flagpole and began lowering the *Wind Rift*'s banner. It was the same flag all Landships flew, blue with a black symbol in the center, a rod with two circles at the top, one incomplete. In all her time chasing Landships, Ravan had never learned what the flag meant, and she had no desire to learn now; it had to come down. Quick.

"Wait one damn second!" Olive took a step forward. Her crew stirred as they watched, some in anger, some in fear.

"You want your ship burned to the ground or not?" Ravan asked, holding the Captain's gaze. The rumbling in the air deepened and grew. "It's really just that simple."

Olive stared at Ravan in frustration . . . then nodded. Her crew hung their heads, moved back to their positions tensely. This hurt them, Ravan knew, but sometimes there was nothing to do but take your licks.

Her men finished with the Wind Trader flag, took it off, then threaded the red one onto the cables and hoisted it into the air. When it caught the wind at the top it unfurled in a flash of crimson: a white, eight-pointed star in the middle. The Menagerie star.

The rumbling became a furious roar as shapes burst out of the dust cloud with the sound of growling engines. Dune buggies, a dozen of them, all armed with guns on the back frames, trained on the huge Landship. Above, three gyrocopters screamed over and banked hard as they surveyed the vessel.

Ravan grabbed the Wind Trader flag from one of her men. As the buggies reached them, surrounding the ship and circling it like sharks, she let the wind catch it in her hands, holding it out for them to see.

The drivers of those buggies knew what it meant. They raised their fists in elation. Ravan could hear their cries of victory even from the deck, and she smiled, holding the giant flag for them to see, letting the feeling of victory flow through her like a drug.

It was a hunting group. The Menagerie had found them.

"Keep your course, Captain," Ravan said, watching the gyrocopters roar back over ahead and the dune buggies on the desert floor flank the ship on either side. "We just got ourselves an escort."

Olive didn't say anything back, just started issuing orders, keeping her men moving, but the air of tension was as thick as it had ever been. It was very real now, for the crew of the *Wind Rift*. Their ship was captured by a mortal enemy, it was all but over.

Ravan turned back around and when she did, her smile faded. Holt leaned against one of the masts, hands casually in his pockets, the wind blowing through his unkempt hair as the ship sailed south under the Menagerie flag. He was staring off nowhere in particular, dispassionate and uncaring.

The sight chilled her more than his words earlier. He should be more nervous than anyone on this ship about where they were heading, but it didn't seem to even register. And, still, he hadn't once looked at her.

Some of her men clapped her on the back, congratulating her and themselves. The shouts from the dune buggies below continued. The gyrocopters tipped their small wings back and forth in acknowledgement. She had done everything she had set out to do: a journey from Faust all the way to the Strange Lands, where no Menagerie had ever been, to bring back an impossible quarry, and she had *done* it. All of it.

But, right then . . . it felt empty.

8. HOMECOMINGS

OLIVE STARED OUT OVER THE BOW of the *Wind Rift* with more dread than she had ever felt. She could hear the rumbling growls following them, the dirty, harsh sounds of gas and combustion, so different from the focused air swooshing above. One was the sound of life. The other of death.

She peered over the deck at the dune buggies, leaving trails of dust behind them. About a quarter mile away, a rabbit leapt from one sand-baked stone to another, stirred by all the noise. The Menagerie saw it, the guns on their buggies exploded to life, spraying shrapnel that decimated everything where the rabbit had been. They were gone too fast to see if they'd hit anything, but judging by their laughter that wasn't really the point.

"This is really happening, isn't it, Captain?" a boy's voice asked next to her. It was Casper, the ship's helmsman, the best and youngest one she'd ever had. The youth had been destined to run his own ship someday, at least before he got this assignment. Now . . . who knew?

Olive looked back ahead, watching the growing menace on the horizon.

"It really is," said a voice Olive had come to loathe. Ravan joined her at the helm, staring ahead with her. "Sooner you accept it, the better."

"Must be thrilling, eh, Menagerie?" Olive asked bitterly. "Bringing in a captured Landship, all on your own?"

It took a moment for Ravan to respond, and when she did, it wasn't with her usual sarcasm. "You'd think so, wouldn't you?"

The pirate wore a perplexed, frustrated look, and Olive saw Holt leaning against a railing, his gear at his feet, unarmed. It was the first time she'd seen him since he'd gone below. He stared away into the distance, no emotion on his face at all.

Olive's relationship with Mira was an old one. It had been strained lately, but her death still stung hard, and Olive could only imagine what it was like for Holt. She could still see the *Wind Star* incinerating into the ground.

If Olive wanted, she could do the math, try and figure out how many Landships might be left after that battle, but she didn't. She didn't want to know the answer. For all she knew, the *Wind Rift* was now the last of her kind.

Another figure joined them, adding more brooding to the occasion. Avril stepped past them and sat down at the front, where the bow dropped down toward the ground and curved underneath.

It was strange. No one on this ship, even Ravan, seemed all that thrilled about where they were headed.

Ahead of them, probably ten miles distant, something massive and huge towered over the desert, the heat from the air wavering in sparkling transparencies in front of it. It was a city. A big one. Its name was Faust.

From what Olive had heard, the land here contained massive deposits of crude oil and gas. In order to tap and drill it, some forgotten company in the World Before created the world's biggest land-based oil platform, a structure that stretched across the desert some fifty square miles, punctuated by giant towers made of reinforced steel that rose a thousand feet off the ground. They were still visible, the heart of the old facility.

From the top of each, plumes of fire shot into the sky, a hundred feet tall on their own. They were called "flare towers," used to burn off the excess flammable gasses released by the pumping that was happening under the ground. At night, those fires could be seen for miles. Olive had seen them herself, from much farther away. If you were Menagerie, they were probably thrilling to see. If you weren't . . . they were terrifying.

Below, the dune buggies growled louder as they shot forward, leaving the *Wind Rift* behind. Above, the three gyrocopters flashed over, disappearing toward the city ahead.

"Where's this damn port?" Olive asked, watching the city come closer, and Ravan pointed to the flaming tower farthest right.

"Commerce Pinnacle. Two docks there, it's where we put captured Landships."

"Just two?" Olive was surprised. "You've captured six of the fleet just this year."

Ravan smiled. "Well, they don't really stay docked all that long."

In a few moments, everyone on deck saw why. Coming toward them was a horrible sight, and Olive sensed the crew's attention lock onto it.

Landships, dozens of them, what was left of their hulls rotting in the sun where they'd been discarded. Wood, it seemed, wasn't of much use to the Menagerie, and that was pretty much all that was left. Broken and shattered, the once polished smooth timber frayed into splinters where the frames and the supports and everything else had been ripped unceremoniously loose.

In all her life, Olive had never seen something so awful. Those ships were more than just wood and metal, they were homes, works of art, some of the most beautiful creations on the planet, sculpted together out of memories; wood and sheet metal and pieces of the World Before that would have just gone on rusting and dying if not for the Wind Traders. Every Landship Olive had ever been on, no matter how big or ugly or slow, had always felt *alive* . . . and the ones here had been *murdered*.

It was a Landship graveyard.

"One . . . quarter Chinook," Olive ordered in a suddenly frail voice that barely carried. It took a moment for the crew to react, but they eventually obeyed, shortening the sail length as Tommy, the artifact handler, dialed the Chinook down to its lowest setting. The roaring wind quieted, the sails lost a little of their power, letting the *Wind Rift* move forward slowly through the remnants and memories lying in the sun.

No one on board spoke as the ship passed through the wrecks. Olive could pick out pieces and parts of them that were familiar, placing those aspects to names, most of them ones she knew or had been on. Each recognition was painful.

"*Wind Sail*," Olive intoned as they drifted past one. "*Wind Turn*," as they rolled by another.

From around her, other voices joined her own, calling out the ships they recognized.

"*Wind Sky. Wind Rail* . . ."

It was some kind of strange, mournful acknowledgement, in voices that held the thinly covered truth that their own home would likely soon be among those wrecks, crumbling in the sun.

"*Wind Pulse. Wind Streak. Wind Fire* . . ."

On and on the names echoed, until Olive couldn't take it anymore and she looked away and back to Ravan. The pirate studied her evenly. There was no challenge in her eyes, no mirth at the horror around them . . . but neither was there any remorse.

"Hold on to the anger," Ravan said, studying her. "You'll get your shot for payback, everyone does. Just make sure when the time comes, you can pull the trigger. It's never as easy as you think."

Olive studied the pirate. She had a strange habit of both proving she was exactly what Olive thought she was, and, at the same time, something completely different. They certainly had their differences, but they had a lot in common too. Both held positions dominated by boys, and they held their ground and their place fiercely, earning loyalty. Either way, Olive did not, and would never, truly like Ravan. The horrors she had just seen had solidified that. But she did respect her.

The eight towers stretched into the sky, flames at their tops, and the city was arrayed beneath them. Slowly, over the years that followed the invasion, the pieces of a city had been built around those towers, circling them in ever-expanding platforms of wood and sheet metal, their foundations built out of old cars and concrete and other materials. Each tower became a "Pinnacle," and each Pinnacle provided a single, specific aspect of the city.

As they drifted closer, Olive could make out the Skydash, the complicated system of thick metal wires that ran between the various towers, and allowed the more brazen to zip along them with special hooks called Dash-claws. Olive had always heard about the Skydash. It sounded insane, just the thing you would find in a pirate's den like Faust.

Olive kept issuing commands, guiding the *Wind Rift* toward its berth. The platforms that ringed each of the city's Pinnacles had been built up off the ground a good twenty or thirty feet, and the one around what Ravan had called Commerce was no different. A flat, wedgelike protrusion shot out from where the platform ended, a crude construction to serve as a dock.

As they crept closer, Olive noticed something else. The way Avril tensed at the front of the ship told her she noticed it too.

On the Pinnacle's platform, all around the dock, moved a wave of people. Thousands of them, all pressed and packed tight, waiting for the *Wind Rift* to arrive, which made it all the more unsettling. They were *expected*. In fact, it looked like a damned hero's welcome. The only problem was, Olive and her crew weren't the heroes in this story. They were the *trophies*.

"Another three degrees starboard," Olive said, judging the distance to the approaching dock.

"Aye, Captain," Casper intoned, his voice uneasy. The ship kept inching closer.

Tommy stood by the Grounders, ready to shut off the artifacts. Olive waited until the ship inched barely two feet from the side of the dock. It would be a perfect berth, she thought ironically, but she didn't feel much satisfaction. It was probably the last time her ship would dock anywhere ever again.

"Chinook, all stop," Olive said, feeling her throat tighten.

"All stop, aye," Tommy intoned as he shut it down. The wind above them silenced as the artifact's effect died. The *Wind Rift* settled into place, its momentum gone. They were still and motionless.

The sounds of the crowd overtook everything . . . and it was deafening.

It stretched all around, a mass of people that pulsed in every direction on the docks and into the Pinnacle platform, so thick it blocked the view into the city. The occasional sound of gunfire ripped the air as the pirates fired into the sky in celebration, chanting two words over and over.

"Power. Profit. Power. Profit. Power . . ."

Olive swallowed, tried to stay calm, but the chant and the roar and the gunfire pressed in on her. They were in the hot, open air, but everything felt claustrophobic.

She looked at her crew and they looked back. She studied each of them with pride and amazement. Not one of the fourteen had jumped ship before making port at Faust. It was entirely possible they would all be killed here, who knew, maybe within the next five minutes . . . yet they had stayed at their posts.

"I hope you know . . . how proud of you I am," Olive made herself say. They deserved more than that, but she couldn't find any better words. "Tie her off."

The crew set to work, closing her latches, stowing the sails, all routine activities none of them knew whether they would ever perform again. The crowd continued to roar around them.

AVRIL STOOD AT THE edge of the *Wind Rift*, staring down at the wooden beams of the dock, faded and gray from years under the burning sun. Another step . . . and she would be home.

Home . . .

She felt a twinge of pain at how easily the thought had formed. It felt like a betrayal. This was *not* home. This was a *promise*, a debt being repaid. Nothing more. She would suffer the tortures of this place, for honor's sake, for Gideon, but it would *never* be home.

"Might as well get it over with, dear heart," Ravan's voice whispered behind her, and it stirred a cold anger in her. "It is what it is."

Avril said nothing. She stared at the dock another moment, then stepped off and felt the ball of her foot touch down, and that was that.

Only it wasn't.

The roar of the crowd, already loud and jarring, intensified. It took a moment for Avril to figure out why. Every stare, amid the thousands of pirates, was aimed at *her*. And it was shocking.

They knew her? They *remembered* her? She stared at the faces in confusion . . .

The crowd roared again as Ravan and her men stepped off. In Faust, the capture of a Landship was the most respected show of power you could achieve. On top of that, Ravan and her crew were returning from what had generally been considered a suicide mission. They were heroes. For a while, at least. Faust wasn't a place where you rested on your laurels, it only remembered what you did today.

Ravan stood next to her, staring at all the faces, soaking up the sound of the voices and the shaking of the wood under their feet. Behind them, the last of the people who were coming off disembarked.

Holt landed on the dock, his stare blank, his face unreadable. Avril wasn't sure why he had run from this place, but he knew there was a death mark on his head because of it. Coming back took a lot of guts, and yet it didn't seem to even register with him.

Avril remembered watching those ships explode, including the one with the Freebooter on it. A part of him had died with her, she figured. That's what losing everything did to you. As he moved forward, his eyes met hers for one second, then he looked away again, but in that moment there was a glimmer of acknowledgment. Avril realized then that she and Holt had a lot in common now.

The eight Pinnacles of Faust were clearly in view, at varying distances, the lines of the Skydash zigzagging through the air between them, and she watched as figures flew down them at dizzying speeds, one after the other, platform to platform. She noticed something else too, something different from what she remembered.

Two of the Pinnacles stood out. Unlike all the others, they flew flags, and the flags were not what she expected. Where the normal Menagerie banners were red with a white, eight-pointed star, these were the opposite

White. With a *red* star.

Along one of those Pinnacles, among the platforms and structures of wood and metal built there, stood hundreds of other figures. But they weren't yelling and cheering, they just stared down at her. At the top of one, out in front, stood a tall boy. Even from this distance, Avril could see long blond hair whisking out in the wind. His eyes, she could tell, were locked on hers.

The Strange Lands had honed Avril's instincts to sense danger, no matter how far, and right now, she felt menace from that boy. Whoever he was, whoever the group that flew that flag, they meant her harm.

Avril just looked away. Before, she would have sought the kid out, found and killed him in his sleep, and whoever else might be with him. It would have been a simple task, he was only Menagerie, but, now . . . what did it really matter? Her life was over either way.

From somewhere came three harsh bursts of sound. Electronic and staticky, they echoed through the Pinnacles of Faust. Whatever it was, the pirates seemed to recognize it. Their yells ceased, the stomping of feet went still, celebratory gunfire silenced. The crowd parted, making way for several figures. Avril's heart began to beat heavily. She knew who was coming.

Six Menagerie guards, burly ones with scars and malice in their posture, surrounded a man. Like Avril's eyes, his were clear of the Tone, but that was to be expected, given his age. He was close to fifty, a rarity now, and it meant he was Heedless.

The guards around him flanked out protectively while he stepped forward. He looked older than Avril remembered, the lines around his eyes were more pronounced, the gray in his short, cropped hair more visible. Like his followers, he wore only black military gear, but he donned his more professionally, his shirt tucked into his cargo pants, the legs falling around the tops of his boots. He wore the necessities of the new world in the style of the old.

His black skin had the rough, leathery look of someone who had spent most his life in the sun. A trait of a worker, but Tiberius Marseilles had never been a laborer, even in the World Before, so it had always seemed a contradiction. He wasn't particularly tall or athletic, there was nothing imposing or even threatening in the way he carried himself. It was only in his eyes where you saw the cunning and intellect that allowed him to create from nothing one of the world's most powerful cities, a city of thieves and liars and brigands, and yet keep them all satisfied and convinced of his dominance.

As he moved, she could feel his crystal-clear eyes lock onto her, and she fought the urge to try and hide, to put something between her and that man, but there was nothing to hide behind. He stopped in front of their group, and his stare finally left her, moving from one person to the next, studying each until it settled on Ravan.

And when it did . . . he smiled. His hands cupped her face tenderly, he looked down into her eyes. "When, I wonder, will you finally disappoint me, Ravan Parkes?" Tiberius's voice was soft, yet it carried weight, and though he didn't speak slowly, he articulated each word with a meticulousness that seemed deliberate, as if every word was valuable.

Ravan smiled back at him. "No time soon, I promise."

"You have brought back to me what I value most." The words gave Avril a shiver. Sweet as the sentiment was, there was little emotion in it. She watched Tiberius reach down and take Ravan's hand. "Congratulations, *Commandant*." Then he raised the hand high into the air, and turned to the pirates that surrounded them.

"*This,*" he yelled for all to hear, "is the *taking* of power!"

The crowd erupted into cheers again. The dock rocked beneath Avril's feet. Guns fired into the air. It was overwhelming. She could feel the tension from the Wind Traders on the ship behind her.

"Tiberius," Ravan said, when he'd lowered her hand. "May I present your daughter."

Avril swallowed. Tiberius's gaze shifted back to her, studying her a long, inquisitive moment, his eyes raking over her, examining every piece, as if in evaluation, as if in judgment. When he moved to her, his smile grew, but, as always, it held no warmth. Whatever reason he wanted her back so badly, it had very little to do with fatherly love.

"Avril," he said. "You have grown strong . . ."

He reached toward her . . . and Avril recoiled as if from a snake.

She felt the anger rise within her. This man had taken everything from her; Dane, her life, Gideon . . . and he expected tenderness in return? He was right. She *had* grown strong, he had no idea how much, but he would.

Tiberius gauged the reaction with only a slight sense of disappointment. He nodded, as if reaching some internal consensus. "We have time," was all he said. "We have time."

Tiberius looked up at the *Wind Rift*, docked behind them. The crew was on board, staring nervously back. Olive stood out front, waiting.

Tiberius glanced at each of the crew a brief moment, then simply looked away.

"Kill the crew, take the ship," he ordered. "Strip it of anything of value."

The words seemed out of place from such an unassuming figure, but the pirates expected nothing less. They moved for the ship, hands reached for guns. The crowd cheered again. Ravan frowned, slightly, but made no move to stop them. Above, Olive and her crew tensed, took steps back.

Avril, however, had been expecting it.

Her eyes scanned the figures of the two closest guards, their stances, noting their balance, deducing their dominant hands from where they kept their guns. It was enough.

Her first two kicks were blurs of motion. The first groaned as his knee-cap snapped, and his weight brought him to the dock.

Before the second one could do anything, she spun, ripping the big hunting knife from his belt, then her knee found his groin and sent him to the ground with the other.

She grabbed Tiberius's right wrist, twisted and spun again, pinning him where he stood and rested the gleaming knife against his throat.

The entire thing took maybe five seconds, and everyone on the dock and the platform beyond froze. A thousand gun hammers clicked into place, a thousand weapons raised, all of them at her.

Avril just smiled. They wouldn't do anything. Shooting her was shooting their glorious leader, and it meant right now, she held all the cards.

Avril leaned in close so that her father could hear. "You wanted me home. Well, here I am."

She sensed no fear from Tiberius, his body felt relaxed. He just craned his neck to look down at her. It infuriated her, his lack of response, the absence of fear. She pressed the knife into his neck. "You will relinquish any claim to the *Wind Rift*. They, at least, will *not* be yours."

Where before his voice had seemed cold, now it was almost warm, affectionate. "Not taking that ship would be denying your people their share of profit and power."

Avril dug the knife in again, feeling the anger build. "They aren't my people."

"Then why react so violently to the suggestion?"

Avril paused, staring at the man hatefully. "What would your men do? If I slit your throat right here? Even knowing who I am?"

"They would kill you, girl," Tiberius said.

"Exactly. I will fight and *die* unless you tell your mindless thugs to leave that ship and its crew alone. I *swear* it. What happens to your *legacy* then?"

The two stared at one another. Tiberius smiled again, and this time, there *was* warmth in it. The sight only made Avril angrier. "I'm proud of you. For taking what you want, not *asking* for it like a Wind Trader. Perhaps your time with the White Helix was worth it. Perhaps Gideon and I had more in common than I assumed."

"Say his name again, and I *will* kill you," Avril whispered dangerously. "Gideon was more a father to me than you ever were, and you are *nothing* alike."

If Tiberius was hurt, he made no indication. He just studied Avril, as if for the first time, long and intensely, and there grew a satisfaction in his face. He liked what he saw, and it made Avril nervous.

"We will grant my daughter's wish, as a gift for her return," he announced out loud. "This ship and its crew are *hers*, no harm is to come to them. You see her strength. You see she is worthy of us. With her here, more power will follow."

The crowd stared back a moment, unsure . . . then it erupted into cheers again. More gunfire lit up the air.

Avril slowly released Tiberius, letting him stand, and she studied the pirates, perplexed. They were even more roused up than before, more excited, and Avril wondered if this hadn't been Tiberius's plan all along.

Her father turned and stared above them, far above, to the Pinnacle that flew the strange, reversed Menagerie flag. The boy at the top, the one with the blond hair, stared back a moment, then did something interesting. He *saluted* Tiberius, as if acknowledging a grand performance.

Who was that boy, Avril wondered. And what was going on in this place?

Tiberius looked away and this time his gaze settled on someone else, someone at the edge of the dock, behind everyone else, someone who had remained unseen until now.

"Hello, Holt," Tiberius said.

Holt didn't reply, but neither did he lower his gaze. The stare that passed between the two was intense, and Avril wondered again just what the history was between them.

"MAX!" MIRA YELLED as the dog darted down into the lower decks of the ship and disappeared, in hot pursuit of the orange cat that had taunted him one time too many. She moved to follow, then felt the shock wave rip through the ship. Her balance faltered, she felt shaky, but it had very little to do with the explosion itself.

Maybe a hundred feet away, the *Wind Star,* the vessel she was supposed to be on, incinerated in a fireball.

"Keep your stupid dog out of the way!" Dresden yelled as he dashed toward the helm, dodging through his crew running everywhere like ants.

"It's not *my* dog!" she said defensively, but her feelings on the subject were conflicted now. If it hadn't been for Max, she wouldn't be on the *Wind Shear* right now, she'd be dead, and all because of his obsession with a cat.

"Then why is it on my ship?" Dresden was, admittedly, a little flustered. "For that matter, why are *you* on my ship?"

Mira pushed through the chaos after him. "He was looking for your cat! It keeps baiting him and—"

"Nemo doesn't bait *anybody.*" He cut her off.

Another explosion shook the ship, and Mira felt its wheels come off the ground and then slam back down. The impact sent her tumbling to the deck, and everyone else reeling.

Giant, colored Antimatter crystals pulsed through the air in both directions, some being fired, others begin recalled, but even the ones that were hitting their marks weren't making much difference.

Raptors roared through the sky, plasma bolts streaking down. More bolts, larger ones, burned through the air from ahead as the Spiders finally returned fire. And then there was that massive shape in the distance, a walker so big it towered over everything else. Its beam weapon had incinerated the *Wind Star.* It would no doubt fire again soon.

The fleet, and the entire escape attempt, were in a lot of trouble.

Dresden frowned as he helped her up. "Enjoying yourself? This was *your* idea."

Another ship exploded off the starboard side of the ship, and Mira saw the White Helix there leaping into the air.

"Helm, get ready for a hard pull to port!" Dresden shouted, trying to balance, leaving her. Another explosion rocked the ship. "When we clear past the line, we're going afterburner, everyone brace for the hit."

Mira looked to the port side. There was nothing there but empty land, it would take them south, *away* from the battle.

"What?" She pushed after him. "You're not *leaving*!?"

"What the hell else would I be doing?" More explosions flared as another flight of Raptors blazed past. "This is a disaster."

"What about your brother?" Mira pointed ahead of them, at one of the six remaining Landships, Conner's vessel, the *Wind Mark*, bobbing and weaving, flame bursting all around it. "You're just going to leave him?"

Dresden gave her a very disapproving look. "In case you haven't noticed, he and I aren't very close. Helm, on my mark—"

"If we leave, everyone is going to die!"

"Sweetheart," Dresden's patience was running out fast, "I gotta say, I think that's kind of a foregone conclusion."

"I don't mean just *us*, I mean the others; the gunships are already hitting them and when we're all gone, those walkers will too. If we don't turn this situation around, you don't just lose this ship, you lose the entire fleet *and* Currency."

More explosions, the ground shook. The helmsman gripped the wheel tightly. "Orders, sir?"

"We *can't* leave," Mira insisted.

Dresden stared at her, thoughts swirling in his head.

"You're not seriously considering this?" yelled a tall boy nearby with a shaved head and glasses. His name was Parker, Dresden's first officer, and from what Mira had observed, the two seemed to have a combative relationship. "*Look* at that thing!"

They were close enough now to see the giant machine surrounded by the Spiders, a red walker unlike anything Mira had ever seen. Six giant legs moved a blocky, armored fuselage three or four hundred feet over the battlefield, brimming with weapons and what looked like its own communications tower. The thing was a walking fortress, and Mira could see a giant, oblong cannon installed on its top, so big it ran the entire length. Mira could feel the earth shudder whenever one of its legs slammed down.

"We have to get the hell out of here," Parker continued. "*Now.*"

Dresden looked from Parker back to Mira, weighing things. "What are you proposing?"

Good question, Mira thought. She answered with the first thing that came to mind. "That big walker's like the king on a chessboard."

"You have a real knack for metaphors, darling, but how does that help us?"

She studied the Spiders in the distance, the Landships nearby . . . and the Raptors, dozens and dozens of them, filling the sky. She had an idea. A crazy one. "Can this thing go any faster? Get out ahead of the other ships?"

Dresden frowned. "She's the fastest ship in the fleet, but why in hell would I wanna get out *front* in this madness?"

She looked back at the huge walker. "Can we fit under it?"

"*Under* it?"

"If we can, we can take it down."

"Orders, sir?!" the helmsman yelled, his nerves shot.

"This is beyond insane!" Parker yelled as more explosions flared everywhere.

"There isn't time to explain it," Mira yelled, dropping her pack to the deck and riffling through it. "You want to save your people or not?"

Another Landship was incinerated, White Helix leaping off in flashes of yellow. Plasma bolts, both from above and ahead shred the ground as the *Wind Shear* roared forward.

"*Orders, sir?!*"

"Dresden . . ." Parker warned.

The Captain held Mira's look, struggling with the choice. "Do you have *any* idea what the hell you're doing?"

She could have said anything just then. She chose the truth. "None whatsoever."

Dresden studied her a moment more . . . then smiled. It seemed, somehow, to settle it for him. "That's all I wanted to hear." He pulled the old brass sextant off his belt and quickly sighted through it. "Helm, set . . . two-six-eight, and *hold* that course."

"Aye," the helmsman echoed, without much enthusiasm.

"You're a lunatic," Parker said, but he was moving for the helm station with Dresden. The Captain had made a call, and that was that.

"I thought so at first too, Parker." Dresden flipped open the lid of a small box on one of the workbenches there. Inside was a small red button, wires haphazardly connected to it and running down into the ship's hull. "But the Freebooter's right, running ain't gonna save us."

"Neither will playing chicken with *that* thing."

Mira pulled three Barrier artifact combinations from her pack, ones she'd made earlier for the *Wind Star,* and tossed them to the ship's artifact handler, a small girl, young, maybe fourteen, her eyes fearful, her hands shaking. Mira didn't blame her.

"What's your name?" Mira asked.

"Jennifer."

"Jennifer, we're going to need those, especially on the *rear,*" Mira said pointedly. "Keep an eye on the ones we have now, we're going to burn through them quick, okay?" The girl nodded, moved for the Grounders with the new combinations.

Parker yelled to the crew across the ship. "Brace for Acceleration Sails!" He adjusted the Chinook, dialing its band of old clock hands to the right, and when he did the wind howling around them blew in a maelstrom, stronger and wider.

"What are you doing?" she asked.

"Afterburner," Dresden replied. He hit the button in the box.

Rockets exploded into the air from the front of the ship, trailing long lengths of cable behind them, attached to fabric. As the rockets flew upward, they unfurled three additional sails, mixes of all kinds of colors that filled with the reinforced wind, pulling the *Wind Shear* harder, giving her more speed.

The ship rocked violently and Mira fell flat on her back. All around the ship, the crew had grabbed onto safety handles or the lines from the sails to brace themselves.

The world rocketed past outside. Mira glared at Dresden. "A warning would have been nice!"

The other Landships swept past in blurs as the *Wind Shear* blew by them. She saw the crew of the *Wind Mark* pointing and cheering as they raced past, taking the lead.

Of course, the lead in *this* assault wasn't normally where you'd want to be. Mira hoped this worked . . .

"I'm doing my thing, Freebooter, you get to yours," Dresden yelled over the roaring wind. Both he and Parker were looking at her expectantly. Time to put up or shut up.

Mira ran toward the front of the ship, where the bow tucked under, the ground racing by thirty feet below. Ahead of them, maybe a mile away now, moved the powerful line of red Spider walkers. She could see their cannons flashing, flinging forward volleys of plasma bolts, but they weren't all headed for the Landships. They seemed to be shooting everywhere; left, right, into the sky.

Mira saw why. The small White Helix force, what was left of them anyway, had reached the Assembly and engaged. She could just make out their silhouettes against the giant shapes of the walkers, leaping and flipping between them. Streaks of color flashed through the air, explosions blossoming from the walkers.

Hopefully, they'd distract the Assembly long enough to let the *Wind Shear* do its thing.

Mira closed her eyes and reached out with her senses, searching for the presences she knew were somewhere nearby.

She found far more than she expected.

A flood of sensation, thousands of thoughts and images filled her mind, and she almost collapsed, moaning, holding her head, trying to fight the projections. The idea that she might be able to tap into the *reds'* thoughts just as she could the silvers hadn't even occurred to her. She felt their rage . . . and their excitement. It had been a long time since anyone had truly *resisted* them, usually the Tone rendered a population inert long before any true challenge, yet here it was. Battle. Action.

Other sensations pulled her back and away, a thick, swirling mix of apprehension and nervousness. It was the silvers. Ambassador's group . . . and they knew she was in danger. If they lost her, they lost their one link to each other, the only one they had left. Mira latched onto their anxiety, letting it push away the massive wave of sensation from the reds.

Guardian, the projection came. It was Ambassador. *You risk much.*

Wasn't that the truth?

I need your help, she projected back.

We were not wanted.

You're wanted now, she answered firmly. *Please.*

There was silence from Ambassador, and the thoughts and sensations from the others swept in like the tide to fill the breach. Mira tried her best to push it away.

We will come, Ambassador finally replied. *Where?*

Mira breathed in relief and opened her eyes . . ,

The air less than five feet in front of her exploded in plasma bolts, bursting into sparks against the ship's Barrier. The effect field flared in prismatic color, absorbing the projectiles, but it was weakening. Every walker not engaged with the White Helix ahead of them was firing at the Landships, now just a half mile away.

Above them, the Raptors circled, roaring after the *Wind Shear,* and even with its extra sails and emergency power, it couldn't outrun Assembly gunships. Yellow bolts peppered the *Wind Shear*'s rear end, and the Barriers flared to life there too. Mira just hoped Jennifer had the presence of mind to cycle out the Barriers as they failed with new ones.

Where? Ambassador projected again.

Mira looked straight through the hailstorm of plasma bolts, focusing on a spot behind and right of the center of the army.

There, she projected, staring, waiting. *There. There.* "There!"

Mira saw the flashes of light, just perceptible behind the reds as the silver Brutes teleported in, each with an additional walker for support. Mantises, Spiders, Hunters.

We are here.

Explosions flared up from behind the line of red walkers as they were hit by a volley of plasma . . . and Mira was overwhelmed by sensations and feelings. Shock from the reds, elation from the silvers. In spite of being outnumbered, Ambassador's strike force seemed to revel in the fight, and she felt their lust, felt it crawl through her . . . and a part of her liked it.

Mira pushed the feelings back. It was getting harder and harder to tell which feelings were hers and which were *theirs,* and the implications were unsettling, but that was something to worry about later.

She looked behind them and saw exactly what she hoped. Most of the gunships had regrouped in a giant line that was chasing after the Wind Shear, their cannons blazing and hammering its rear Barriers. She saw Jennifer rip out a smoking combination from the rear Grounder and shove in a new one, the last Mira had given her.

When the Barriers they had now failed, the ship would be defenseless.

A new sensation washed over her. An awareness, a collective of a hundred or more presences, turning toward the Landships. She felt heat begin to build in her mind, it was the only way to describe it, and everything went brighter and brighter and—

A giant beam of pure, red energy burned through the air from the cannon on the huge walker. It slammed into another Landship, the *Wind Arrow*, burning through its Barrier in less than a second, and Mira shuddered as it exploded. The *Wind Shear* crew barely hung on as the shock wave hit.

"Can you signal concentrated fire on that thing?" Mira yelled.

Parker gave hand signals to the crew in the crow's nest, who yanked loose two flags, one red, one white, and started waving them in patterns toward what was left of the armed Landships. Seconds later, the air again exploded in color as Antimatter crystals streaked toward the giant walker in the distance.

Mira projected the same instruction to Ambassador. In the distance, the silvers obeyed, their plasma bolts slamming into the huge machine right as the giant Antimatter cannon crystals hit. Fire sprayed from it in violent plumes of orange and red, but even that wasn't enough. The walker was just too huge.

The *Wind Shear* raced forward, the Spiders unsettlingly close. Mira could see the White Helix leaping between them. Two of the machines erupted in flames and collapsed to the ground. From the way the Landship was pointed, Dresden was doing exactly what she asked, steering her *right at* the giant walker.

Another blast from its massive cannon fired. Another Landship disintegrated.

"Hold on to something!" Dresden shouted from behind . . . and then they were rushing past the front lines of red Spiders, dodging and weaving through them. The *Wind Shear* swayed and bounced wildly. Its last Barrier flickered once, twice, then died completely. Smoke bellowed out of the Grounders from the ruined artifacts inside. They were defenseless, but the vessel thundered ahead.

It reached the massive red walker, passed between two of its giant legs. Mira looked up, watched the underside of the machine flash by, saw its hydraulics moving, felt its outpouring of anger and surprise.

The Raptors chasing them saw what was coming.

They tried to pull up, but it was too late. They crashed into the huge walker, dozens of them, over and over, exploding in flame and debris, hammering it with more powerful blasts than any plasma bolt. The White Helix, leaping and jumping nearby, seemed to get the plan, and added their firepower to the rest.

The huge machine shuddered. Mira shut her eyes, feeling the desperation of the entities inside to stay standing . . . but it was all futile.

The *Wind Shear* roared out from under just as it began to tip over, groaning horribly as it fell, slamming into the ground in a symphony of contorted metal as fire blew everywhere. Dozens of Spider walkers were crushed under its girth. The ground trembled from the impact, and what was left of the gunships spiraled into the ground all around it.

The crew erupted into cheers, but Dresden held up a hand.

"Not clear yet," he yelled. "Hold it together a little longer."

There was still a small bit of the field to pass through, marked by an approaching slight incline. As they raced toward it, Mira looked behind.

From the wreckage of the huge red walker, a hundred shimmering, golden energy fields rose up and out, each forming a different crystalline pattern in the sky. She felt a surge of elation from the silvers in the battlefield. The tide had turned, the reds were confused . . . but they were all still outnumbered, still in danger.

Leave, Mira projected. *Leave now. You've done well.*

And you, Ambassador replied.

She saw flashes of light as what was left of the silver Brutes teleported out and away, vanishing into thin air, taking the other walkers with them.

There were no more gunships. Mira saw more red Spider walkers falling in flames as they were swarmed with White Helix, but she could tell they weren't staying around to fight, they were retreating, flipping and darting into the cliffs and rocks in blurs of purple, but there were many fewer than what they started with. The Landships were strategically retreating too; she could see their Antimatter cannon crystals streaking through the air and landing back on the ships where they'd launched, and, like the Helix, their numbers had dwindled. Of the eleven they'd had, now there were *four.*

Mira shut her eyes, feeling the guilt and horror wash over her. They had escaped. But at great cost . . .

Pain suddenly overtook everything.

The sensations she had been fighting finally overwhelmed her, and she was bombarded with hundreds at once, a dizzying array of emotions from every direction. Mira felt herself fall, felt herself hit the deck, but it was all in the background.

There was nothing but the projections from the red army. Fury at being thwarted, confusion, and . . . something else. Curiosity. Intrigue. The delicate forming of faith, and all of it was because of *her,* she somehow knew. It was . . . disturbing.

Guardian, the projections came, filling her mind, and they were not from Ambassador. These were from the others, the reds, Mas'Phara. *We believe.*

Then everything went black.

10. BEACON

MIRA WOKE UNDER THE COVERS of a small, wooden bed built out from the smooth, flowing juniper walls of a Landship cabin and stared into the face of Max, lying on the floor beneath her. Stirred from his own sleep, the dog opened one eye to study her in annoyance, then lazily rolled over onto his back with a yawn.

Mira frowned. "Good to see you too." Then she winced as the sensations washed over her. Anxiety and apprehension, loneliness.

Guardian . . . they said. *You return.*

She felt the entities relax, the sensations lessen, now that they knew she was alive, that their connection was not truly gone. They clamored for her attention, as always, trying to deduce her location, to find her, to be close, and the only thing Mira could tell about them was that they were somewhere to the south . . . and that their numbers had *grown*. Almost a hundred strong now. But how?

Mas'Phara, a projection came in answer. It was Ambassador. *They believe.*

In what? Mira projected back, over the distance. Her head spun.

In you.

Mira shuddered at the response. Some of the reds must have defected to Ambassador's side. She remembered the projections that washed over her as that giant, red machine fell. Shock, anger . . . and respect. *They believe . . .*

"Got one hell of a poker face, your dog." Mira jumped; it hadn't occurred to her she might not be alone. Dresden leaned back on a small stool attached to the wall with brass clamps, boots propped up on a nearby desk, and he had an old book in his hands: *Journey to the Center of the Earth* by Jules Verne. "Tries to look like he doesn't give a damn, but he almost bit our heads off in the cargo hold, wouldn't calm down until we got him up here with you. You guys must be close."

"I wouldn't go that far." Mira sat up, and the pain in her head returned, competing with the projections from the silvers. She forced it all away, trying to look at least half alive. Dresden didn't need to know how weak she really was. "Where am I?"

"My cabin. Only place to put you, since you weren't supposed to be here. Looks like that dog saved your life. And . . . well, I guess you saved *ours*, didn't you?"

Mira looked at him, remembering everything. The *Wind Star* exploding, Landships crashing, White Helix consumed in fire.

"Not all of us," she said.

Dresden studied her soberly. "You saved your share."

"I also caused it all, didn't I?" At the end of the day, it had been she and Holt, their quest to rescue Zoey, that had brought the Assembly here, and it had been she and Holt who had embroiled the Wind Traders in this whole mess. "You must hate me."

"Hate's not a very useful emotion," Dresden replied. "And it isn't your fault everything went to hell. No one was working together out there, you saw it. There was no real plan. We were doing our thing, Helix were doing theirs, and we all forced out those silver walkers of yours. Everyone was so sure they didn't need anyone else. It's a hard lesson."

"How many ships did we lose?"

"I couldn't say." He set the book down and lowered his feet to the floor. "The four armed ships that survived are here. So are maybe two dozen of the regular fleet."

Mira was aghast. That was *thirty* ships! "What happened to the rest?"

"Scattered when the gunships hit. Most are missing. The White Helix too, though a few Arcs, or whatever they call their groupings, have trickled in. Right now? We've lost two-thirds of the fleet."

Which also meant two-thirds of the White Helix. Two-thirds of their supplies. Two-thirds of any hope of reaching the Citadel and Zoey. They'd had an army when they left, and in less than a day she'd managed to lose almost all of it.

"Doesn't mean they're all destroyed," Dresden continued, sensing her despair. "Another problem was we didn't set a rendezvous, assumed the fleet would move together but those Raptors shot that plan to hell. They're out there, somewhere, scattered to the winds."

Mira felt the beginning of dread form in her stomach. "Did the *Wind Rift* . . . ?"

"I don't know," he answered. "If I had to guess, though, I'd say Olive got through. They were headed south, after all, away from us, and she's a hell of a skipper."

Another realization hit Mira then, a particularly unpleasant one. "He thinks I'm dead," she whispered.

"You don't know that."

"He thought I was on the *Wind Star*. It was one of the first Landships to go down. He would have seen it."

"Well, then he'll be real happy to see you, won't he?"

Mira shook her head. "You don't understand, he's lost everything so many times." A deep sadness was welling up inside her. Not for herself, but for Holt. "I have to get to him. I have to find—"

"You can't." Dresden stopped her and she looked up in anger.

"Don't tell me what I can't do, I—"

"From what I gather, getting to San Francisco's pretty important. You go after him, you forfeit what you're doing here. You lose the fleet, the White Helix go their own way, and those Assembly seem to me like fair-weather friends at best."

"I could send word. A message."

"How? You think a Wind Trader runner's just gonna stroll in the front gate of *Faust*? They'd be killed on sight."

He was right, and it made her insides hurt. Finding Zoey was what mattered. She and Holt had stated as much to each other, but still, the thought of him, believing what he believed, the pain. And there was more than that, she had to admit. There was who he was with.

Ravan.

"You made a deal, darling," Dresden continued. "A bargain, a big one. So did he. Those types of bargains, there's no walking away from. And where he's going, there ain't no following, trust me."

Mira cradled her head in her hands, and willed herself not to cry. Not in front of Dresden, not now.

There was a knock at the door. "Come," Dresden commanded.

Parker opened it. "Conner's convening. Says they're going to head out in an hour."

The words snapped Mira from her self-pity. "Head out where?"

The look Parker gave her was full of just the kind of scorn she expected. "West, of course. What you wanted, isn't it?"

"*West?*" she asked. "But the fleet? We have to—"

"Conner says we leave them, they're better off on their own."

"I *need* those ships! That's not the deal!"

"Well, that's what's happening," Parker replied sharply, turning back to Dresden. "Captains are assembling outside."

Dresden nodded, got to his feet as Parker left. Mira stared up at him, stunned.

"What'd you expect?" he asked.

"You can't let this happen," Mira begged.

"Me? This isn't my fight, what do I care? Sooner this is over, sooner I get back to making profit, that's how *every* Captain out there feels. *You're* the only one that feels any different. You see what that means?"

Mira did. No one was going to help her.

"You wanna take this thing all the way?" he asked pointedly. "Start acting like it."

Dresden exited the room and Mira looked down at Max. The dog stared back with a vaguely judgmental look. "I *know*."

She got up, fighting the waves of dizziness, and Max followed her up and onto the deck.

It was the first time she had really gotten to look at the *Wind Shear* since her frantic arrival on board, chasing after Max. It was one of the more striking Landships she'd been on, and she remembered it from that time, months ago, when Dresden helped them escape the Assembly at the river trading post.

The vessel had eight massive wheels, four on each side, two pairs of which came from some giant construction vehicle, while the middle were custom constructions of wood and steel, meticulously fashioned and shaped. Her decks had been assembled from a variety of repurposed wood, as well as train and boat parts. Two of her masts were formed out of polished and smoothed airplane wings, big ones, maybe even from an airliner. The whole thing was a hodgepodge of parts, but somehow it all blended together into a giant, beautiful, cohesive craft.

The sun had almost set behind the hills to the west, and its last dim rays streaked across the sky. From there she saw what was left of the Wind Trader fleet. Less than thirty ships were parked everywhere around them. Workers scrambled up and over them, plugging holes, fixing lines and breaches. Every ship seemed wounded.

Mira and Max followed Dresden toward the gangplank. As they did, she looked behind them, to where they'd come from. In the far distance, to the east, in the fading light, she could see something rising into the sky. A thick column of black smoke. Something about it was ominous.

"What's that?" she asked

"Currency," Dresden replied tightly without looking back. "It's burning."

MIRA WALKED BEHIND DRESDEN through the Landships, continually having to stop and urge Max to keep up. The smells from a campfire, some small, scurrying creature, the sounds of hammers against ship hulls: it was all fair game to the dog.

To the west, there was something odd. Something just visible.

A perfectly straight beam of light that shot upward until it disappeared into the stratosphere. It almost looked like a Gravity Well from the Strange Lands, but, of course, that was impossible.

"What's that?" Mira asked.

Dresden answered with a note of amusement. "Figured you'd know, given it's where you're headed."

It took a moment for the words to connect, but when it did, a chill swept over her. *"The Citadel?"*

"Deep in the heart of San Francisco. You've never seen it?"

Mira shook her head, staring at the imposing beam of light in the distance. "No."

"Huge, makes even the Presidiums look like scale models. Has some kind of energy flowing out of it from the top, no one knows what the hell it is or what it does."

"How many miles are we from San Francisco?"

"Four hundred, give or take, and you can *still* see the thing. That's how big and bright it is. Another two hundred miles and you'll see the structure itself, long before you see the ruins. It's . . . impressive. In a terrifying kind of way."

Mira stared at it as they walked, through the sails of the huge ships. There was something eerie about it, seeing it that far away, but as they moved, the sounds of argument pulled her attention. One of the voices she recognized, and with the recognition came a relief. At least *he* was still alive.

"We are not leaving without my people," Dane said, his voice heated.

"No one says you have to," Conner replied. "I'm saying my *ships* are leaving; whether or not you're on them is up to you."

She dragged Max's nose out of a cooking pot and rounded the side of the *Wind Mark* and saw the crowd gathered there. A dozen Wind Trader Captains, and a dozen White Helix Doyens.

"If you leave, I have no way of finding them," Dane said.

"What would you do if you could?"

"Fight." Dane's voice was fire. "Find what remains of that army and destroy it." The Helix behind him all nodded, a similar eagerness in their eyes.

"And we're expected to help you in this suicide . . . why?"

Dane stared at Conner in disgust. "They destroyed your ships. They killed your people."

Conner nodded. "And I would let that go, so as to save the *rest* of my people."

Mira looked back to the beacon in the distance. It marked more than just where she was headed. It marked Zoey, and she felt a surge of frustration and sadness, knowing she was staring right at her, but she still had so far to go.

"You have no honor," Dane continued, taking a step toward Conner, "and you're—"

"Dane, stop," Mira said. The confrontation halted, everyone turned to her. When Dane saw her, his eyes widened.

"Mira? I thought . . ."

"I know, it's a long story."

"They're trying to leave," Dane told her, almost pleadingly.

"There's no 'try' to it," one of the other Captains spoke up. "Once my ship's landworthy, I'm going to finish this contract and be done with it. We all are."

"Mira," Conner said. "Going back to fight those things is—"

"Suicide. I agree." Dane started to argue, but Mira spoke over him. "Even at full force, with every White Helix warrior still alive, do you *really* think you have a chance against that army?"

"Honor demands—"

"Is that *really* what Gideon taught you? Is that what the Keystones say? How does dying to avenge a loss help free Zoey? You remember *her,* don't you? The reason, supposedly, all of you came with us? Or was that just the most convenient thing to believe at the time?"

Dane stared at her heatedly, but said nothing.

"I'm sorry the battle didn't go the way you wanted," she told him. "We'll figure out how to do better, but getting yourselves killed doesn't help anything."

Dane took a long moment before finally responding, and when he did, his voice was calmer. "No. It doesn't."

Mira nodded. "Let me speak with Conner, I'll talk to you in a minute."

Dane looked from her back to Conner, clearly torn, but he moved away without saying anything else, followed by his Doyen.

"Thanks," Conner said. "Glad to see *you* at least understand the—"

"You're not heading west," Mira said as sternly as she could. Dealing with Dane had been the easier of the two. She had to seem strong now, more than ever. Wind Traders were professional deal makers, they could see through most people's bluffs. "I told him you wouldn't help in another attack *right now*, but you *are* going to help find the other ships and the rest of Dane's men, and you're going to start doing it at first light."

The Wind Traders stared at her like she had lost her mind.

"That's insane," the British-accented Captain spoke up angrily. "You don't get to dictate how we carry out our contracts! The arrangement was to get *you* to the west coast, and that's—"

"No," Mira interjected. "It wasn't. My understanding of Wind Trader Commerce Law is that every aspect of a contract must be honored, down to the letter. Dresden, is that right?"

Dresden tried unsuccessfully to hide a smile. "Yep."

"We have our problems right now," Mira kept going, "I understand that, but I made a very specific arrangement with you, and that arrangement was *agreed* to. White Helix weapons in exchange for two weeks of *full control* of the Wind Trader fleet."

"Mira—" Conner started.

"We are on day *two* of those fourteen days, and I am in *command*. Not you. *That* is the deal. If I give the order to run every single Landship into the ocean you'll do it without question. I'm sure that stings, but I'm sorry to say that is the reality."

She let what she was saying sink in, looking from one Captain to the other, then back to Conner. The more she spoke, the more strength she felt.

"We aren't going west. We're going to find the missing ships and the missing White Helix and *then* we will go west. You have until the morning to make whatever repairs you need. At that time someone will present to me plans for a search pattern. Are there any questions?"

The Wind Traders stared at her, no one said anything.

Next to her, Dresden gave Conner a wry look. "Lady's got a point."

Conner glared back, but didn't dispute him. "Twelve more days. Then that's that."

"That's that." Mira forced herself to hold Conner's stare, then the Wind Traders were leaving, mumbling among themselves. Dresden remained a moment, studying her with amusement.

"What?" Mira asked.

He just shrugged. "Nothing. See you on board."

Dresden moved off and when they were all gone, she breathed a silent sigh of relief. Max was still under her, considering her with a look that seemed decidedly unimpressed.

"Always a critic," she said, then looked to where Dane stood at the top of one of the hills, alone. She could tell by his posture he was tense, but she climbed up and stood next to him anyway.

"Sorry," she said.

"It's okay," he answered softly. "You were right."

"They're going to help find the others."

"Thank you." There was a strange energy to him, an insecurity she wasn't used to. "You think she made it? She and Holt?"

All the concern she'd had earlier came back. "I don't know. I hope so."

"Avril would never have let this happen."

"You can't say that."

"Yeah, I can," he said. "She would have thought it through. She wouldn't have . . . just rushed in like that."

"Avril isn't here, neither is Holt," she told him. "There's only us. Before we could hide behind people that were stronger, smarter. Not anymore. I feel sorry for this entire group, because, to be honest, I don't feel like much of a leader."

Dane nodded, he was silent a long time. "Maybe a leader isn't some all-confident, all-knowing sage, who never makes mistakes and always has an answer. Maybe sometimes a leader's just someone who has somewhere they have to be. And the only way to get there . . . is to take everyone else with them."

Mira's gaze floated to the beam of energy in the distance, shooting into the sky. "Maybe so."

"That beacon," Dane said. "It's where she is, isn't it?"

Mira nodded.

He studied it soberly. "Long walk."

"Good thing we have ships." She smiled and looked back at him. "I can't do this without you, Dane, and you can't do it without me. As strong as you are, and I mean all of you, you're not strong enough. None of us are by ourselves, we have to work together. Us, the Assembly, the Wind Traders, the Phantom Regiment when we get there. It's the only way we have even a glimmer of hope of saving her."

"Gideon made us to fight the Assembly alone," he said.

"How do you know that? Did he tell you? He predicted most of this, didn't he? He saw the need for the Reflection Box, the campaign that would come, why wouldn't he have predicted allies in the struggle?"

"Maybe you're right."

"Then how do we fix it?"

Dane finally looked at back at her, and she could see his old self returning. "The way I see it, the main problem's communication. Each group's got their own way of talking to each other, but as far as any unified communication goes, forget about it. You can't adapt to battle situations like that."

Mira thought about it. The solution seemed obvious. "Radios," she said. "We need radios."

Dane nodded. "We need *lots* of radios."

She looked up at him, the unfamiliar feeling of hope beginning to form. "Sounds like we have a plan, then."

11. FAUST

HOLT MOVED THROUGH THE CROWDS of the Commerce Pinnacle, ignoring the malicious glares he received. The animosity of the pirates he brushed past didn't leave much of an impression, neither did the dreadful heat from the sun above. He didn't really feel much anymore. Mira was gone, and she had taken anything he might ever feel again with her.

The only glimmer of anything approaching emotion was when he thought of Zoey. If it wasn't for her, lost and alone, he would just stop moving where he stood, but he'd made promises. They were futile, certainly, he would die before achieving them, but he wouldn't quit. He would just keep pushing forward, until the road finally ran out.

Faust was nearly the same as he remembered. Massive and dirty, radiating a violent, dastardly atmosphere. Holt had always found it odd how disconnected the city was. Each of the eight Pinnacles held platforms near the ground, though built off of it, that circled around them, and buildings and walkways that climbed up to the top, but none of them were connected. To move between the Pinnacles you had to walk, take a dune buggy, or use the infamous Skydash, the complicated wire system that connected them in the air.

Holt hated the Skydash, but he hated pretty much anything to do with heights. He watched dozens of figures sliding along it above, ripping through the air from Pinnacles to the different metallic platforms that hung in between them, called Hubs. The platform in the center of the whole mess was called the Crux, a huge, circular, metallic dais, that hung from the multitude of wires. The thing was enormously heavy, solid steel, and normally it would be impossible for the wires to hold it, but dozens of Aleve artifacts kept it from ripping loose.

The Skydash and the Crux allowed travel to and from any Pinnacle to any other in less than a minute, and there were eight of them. The Utilities Pinnacle, which handled the city's electricity, gas, trash, and recycling.

The Commerce Pinnacle, where all trade and the distribution of plunder was performed. The Food and Water Pinnacle, its function obvious. The Communications Pinnacle, which saw to communication between the various parts of the city and Menagerie forces in the field. The Armory Pinnacle, where weapons and equipment were stored. The Machine Works Pinnacle, a massive platform for repairing and maintaining the Menagerie's fleet of old dune buggies and aircraft. And the Command Pinnacle, the seat of power for Faust's ruling class.

But it was the last Pinnacle that gave Faust its true power. The Refinery Pinnacle made it possible to pump and refine the massive stores of crude oil under the city into gasoline. That gasoline allowed the Menagerie to operate their mechanized armies, and it made them a marvel in the world as it was now. Only Winterbay, far to the northeast, relied on more technology from the World Before, and even it didn't use as much fuel in a week as Faust did in a day.

As he moved, Holt looked and studied the Machine Works and Communications Pinnacles. It was from those towers that the reversed Menagerie flags draped down, white with red eight-pointed stars.

The primary gossip in the city (besides Avril's return), was the civil war that was erupting. It wasn't the first insurrection of its kind; lots of people had tried to usurp power from Tiberius, it's how the Menagerie worked, but no one had ever managed to take a Pinnacle, much less two.

They'd divided the city, and from what it sounded like, the movement was becoming popular. No wonder Tiberius wanted Avril found. He was losing momentum, he needed something to bring it back. The return of his heir and Ravan, one of his premiere lieutenants, would go a long way. So would making the deal Holt had brought him. Tiberius's decision to grant Holt sanctuary in order to consider the White Helix weaponry bargain suddenly made even more sense.

"Did you recognize him?" Ravan asked. "The kid at the top of the Machine Works, out in front of the other rebels?"

Ravan was walking next to him and Castor behind. The Helix returned the Menagerie's stares with his own challenging ones. He was surrounded by hundreds of pirates, but Holt wasn't sure he'd bet against him.

"No," Holt answered.

"Looked like Rogan West. You can tell by that hair, always wanted to rip it out by the roots. He was here when you were, head mechanic at the Machine Works, which explains how they took that Pinnacle."

Holt didn't remember him, nor did he care.

"The rebellion wasn't happening before you left?" Castor asked.

Ravan shook her head. "Usual rumors of disgruntled pirates, but those are nothing new. Everyone wants more than they have."

The roar of a crowd overpowered everything suddenly, and Holt glanced to his right. The Commerce Pinnacle sat on a rocky hillside, higher than any other, and from the platform, Holt could look straight down at the source.

The disconnected nature of Faust wasn't the only reason you had to use the Skydash or some other means to move between its different sections. The swath of desert land in between the platforms was occupied by a giant structure called the Nonagon, named after the geometric shape it resembled, a nine-sided polygon, each side representing the eight star points of the Menagerie rank system, as well as the ninth and final position, that of Tiberius himself.

Each section held rows of auditorium-style seats that stretched around the perimeter, and above hung huge red banners, each bearing a different, aggressive white symbol. A tarantula, a dragon, a wolf, a charging bison, and so on around the entire stadium, every one of the nine sections with its own unique totem.

The Nonagon was an arena, and very few who entered it ever came out. The floor of the structure, in front of the rows of seats, was divided into a large circular swath of metal surrounded by a ring of dirt, roughly as big as a football field. From the center rose a large pillar, probably a hundred feet tall, made of a latticework of strong metal. The Turret, a tower full of gears, struts, pulleys, chains, and cabling, all of which could be reconfigured in a variety of ways.

Cheers from thousands of fans washed up and over them. A match was going on, the round had just begun. Four figures inside the arena divided up, each holding some item that was unseen, navigating between metallic cubes that had pushed up from some substructure underneath the arena floor. As they did, other things pushed up as well, only these were much more dangerous. Steel, razor-sharp spikes shot up and withdrew back out of sight all throughout the grounds, and the team was desperately trying to avoid them as they moved toward the Turret, spinning slowly in the center.

"Tough luck," Ravan observed. "They drew Scorpion."

The Scorpion configuration was widely considered the most difficult draw you could face in the first round. As Holt watched, one of the competitors disappeared in a cloud of dust as a spike shot upward under his feet. Tough luck indeed.

"Is that the Nonagon?" Castor asked, watching intently. The fact that a White Helix, who lived most of his life in the Strange Lands, had heard of the Nonagon was a testament to its infamy.

"What else would it be?" Ravan asked back. The crowd cheered wildly. "Avril's supposedly in her father's box. Wonder if she likes it, a White Helix would make an interesting competitor."

Holt felt her eyes on him, but he said nothing, just kept walking.

"You always hated it," Ravan said. "But you liked talking strategy, how you'd beat the Wolf or—"

"Aren't you meeting your men here?" Holt cut her off as they reached the Handover Ward. He felt Ravan tense at the sharpness of his words, but he didn't care. He wasn't here to stroll down memory lane. The sooner they got this deal finished, the sooner he could be on his way.

"Yeah," Ravan said tightly. "Five minutes." She headed off into the crowd while Castor and Holt waited.

The Handover Ward was where pirates, returning from the field, turned in their plunder, and it was how profit was distributed. Like everything invented by Tiberius, it was much more complicated than it needed to be, but that was the point. The Menagerie leader long ago figured out the best way to make sure no one questioned something was to make it more complicated than they could understand.

Large conveyor belts ran in crisscrossing patterns along the platform, the smaller belts converging into the larger main one, which shuttled the pirated loot into Faust's warehouse. Items were stuffed into bins, divided by category: weapons, ammunition, perishables, toiletries, water, the list was near endless, and each one had their own belt. Monitors were stationed at each, making sure the bins were loaded correctly, weighing them, and marking which crew had brought them in before sending them off.

The last part was the most important, and it was where things got really convoluted. The loot was divided between the crew bringing it in and Faust itself, into a sixty/forty split, with Faust coming out ahead. As each bin entered the warehouse, it was weighed. The division of profit was figured out by that weight. The split rarely, if ever, came out even, so Faust's take was rounded up, while the pirates' was rounded down. This meant the weight of each bin going through the system was critical.

Pirate crews were allowed to trade smaller items of their own for larger ones from other crews, in an attempt to get their weight as close to their favor as possible. In the end, though, the odds were stacked against them, Faust always came out ahead of the 60 percent figure, and that was no accident.

Holt watched Ravan meet her men, a large collection of bins in front of them, bigger than any other crew's. It made sense: they'd been gone months, they would have plundered a lot of loot in that time.

Ravan caught his eye, and the look she gave him was complicated. She was hurt by his recent indifference, but she wore that hurt differently than most. There was no sadness, only a a darkness, an anger that took time to recognize for what it really was, but Holt had seen it enough to know. The truth was he'd been the cause of most of it, and any other time it would have bothered him. It was liberating, in its own way, not worrying about other people's emotions anymore, not caring what happened next, though there was a nagging feeling underneath that something was wrong, but it wasn't strong enough to push to the surface.

The roar of the Nonagon overwhelmed everything again. The Menagerie watching from the edge of the Commerce platform reacted either with boos or cheers, and money and trade items exchanged hands as bets were resolved. A blaring tone of sound, like the one they'd heard earlier, blasted in the arena, signaling the end of the first round. The cubes withdrew back down into the underworks, the Turret stopped spinning, and a huge clock face on top of it whirled into view. It was numbered 0 to 120, and the giant hand on its face began to tick clockwise.

"Two minutes," a loud, amplified voice announced through giant, staticky speakers. *"Two minutes."*

Below, the team was regrouping, one of them clearly injured, hobbling back toward where the dirt ring met the solid circle of the arena floor. They'd managed to survive, and that was something.

"How does it work?" Castor asked in amazement, the look in his eye an unusual one. He was clearly imagining himself *in* the match below. As much as the pirates of Faust enjoyed the Nonagon, none of them had the desire to be a competitor. It pretty much meant certain death. But Castor had faced such stakes daily, he was White Helix after all, and the Strange Lands had a myriad of ways to kill you. It wasn't a surprise he would be drawn to the Nonagon, that it might even feel like home. Holt thought about Ravan's observation a few minutes ago. How *would* a White Helix perform there?

"It's an arena," Holt answered, "but you don't fight other people, you fight the Nonagon."

"It takes four?" Castor asked.

Holt nodded. "Usually they're captured prisoners, but sometimes it's Menagerie, people who've committed crimes against the city. They can choose to face the Nonagon instead of being executed, and if they survive it, they get life imprisonment. If they *beat* it . . . they're freed, but no one ever beats the Nonagon."

"How does it work?"

"Three rounds. Each has three different possible configurations. Supposedly they're determined randomly, but I always assumed it's rigged, like everything else here. See the banners above the different sections?"

Castor looked from one to the next, studying each, all nine of them. A tiger, a cobra, a harrier, each fluttering on their crimson banners in the hot, desert winds.

"Each one represents a configuration. The round before was Scorpion, steel spikes that shoot up from the ground, real nice. If you'd been sitting in the Scorpion section when it was picked you'd get a profit bonus. If Scorpion kills the four competitors, you get even *more,* while the other sections lose. If the team survives the configuration, you lose profit, the other sections gain." None of that included all the ancillary gambling that took place during the matches. The pirates bet on everything, from which configurations would be chosen to which would be beaten or simply survived, to which items would be picked and used, and all of it was encouraged by the ruling body and Tiberius.

"But how do you *win?*" Castor was enraptured. He'd probably try and beat the thing by himself if he could.

"Each round is timed, nine minutes. You either survive in that nine minutes, or you disarm the configuration. Disarming is the only way to *win*, but very few teams ever do. It's all most can do to just not get killed." Holt had heard of only two teams that ever managed to disarm all three rounds, out of hundreds that had competed. It was virtually impossible, but that was the point. It kept Tiberius's rowdy, unkempt, violent followers entertained, kept their focus off him, and prevented them from doing the kinds of things that Rogan West and his rebels were trying right now.

At the thought, Holt looked up at the Machine Works Pinnacle and its reversed Menagerie flag, and as he did, he noticed something odd. A group of boys were there, near where the Skydash lines connected from the Crux to the Pinnacle. Maybe two dozen. Even from here Holt could tell they were armed, and, as he watched, they leapt onto the cables of the Skydash and zipped downward toward the Crux. When they landed, some stayed, unstrapping rifles from their backs, while the others jumped onto new cables and slid toward the Commerce Pinnacle, one after the other.

"What's this?" Castor asked hopefully next to him, watching the same thing. The answer quickly became obvious.

The Commerce Pinnacle was much less crowded than usual, due to the Nonagon match, and Holt figured that was the whole plan. Gunfire flashed from both the Crux and the kids slinging downward.

The pirates on the platform jumped for cover, most of them unarmed. The ones that were returned fire as best they could, but the snipers on the Crux were good shots.

Holt saw three Menagerie fall near him, saw Ravan and her men take cover behind one of the conveyors, but they weren't prepared for an attack, they only had their sidearms. Holt didn't even have that, but the truth was, even in all the chaos, he still had his strange detachment. It was like he was watching it happen to someone else, and he just stood and stared curiously as the bullets flew and people fell.

Castor grabbed him and shoved him behind the closest conveyor, staring at him in amusement. "Your reaction time could use some work."

More bullets sparked around them, and the Menagerie nearby were firing back. Above them, on the Crux platform that hung over the Nonagon, the snipers kept their fire up, pinning everyone down. The main force, about a dozen, cut loose from the Skydash and hit the platform running, firing as they advanced. There was no way the rebels could take the Pinnacle with this small a force, they must have something else in mind.

Castor's eyes were full of excitement. "What do we do?"

It took a moment for Holt to realize Castor was asking *him*. He had no real desire to do anything, but the truth was, Holt had an agenda, and these rebels were screwing it all up. As usual, he had no real choice.

"Can you handle the ones on the Crux?" Holt nodded upward. "There's four, looks like."

Castor studied the snipers there and his only answer was to nod in anticipation.

"Do it then," Holt told him.

"Seek," Castor intoned, pulling his mask up and grabbing the Lancet from his back. "And find." Then he leapt upward in a flash of yellow, grabbing one of the Skydash cables and twirling around it like a gymnast, launched himself even higher.

The pops from Ravan's sidearm were overwritten by the big bangs from the rebels' shotguns and rifles, and Holt peered over the conveyor. The rebels were by the Pinnacle's main gas line, which was mined and processed here at Faust along with the petroleum, and it was critical to the Handover Ward. The combustion engines that ran the conveyor and processing system were fueled by that gas.

Two of the rebels moved for the big, metal wheel that closed and opened the line's main ball valve, while the others covered them. They turned the wheel and shut the valve . . . and the conveyors all around Holt sputtered and died.

One of the rebels lit a portable cutting torch, then started slicing the wheel at the base. Holt saw what they intended now. Cutting the wheel with the valve closed would cripple the Handover Ward's processing system until the Menagerie could install a new one. It was a good plan, shutting down Tiberius's ability to process and distribute profit to his crews would cause a big shake-up, and probably bring more pirates over to their side.

Above, Castor flipped up and off one of the cables and landed in the middle of the Crux, his Lancet a blur of blue light. The rebel snipers stopped firing and stared at the masked boy wielding a glowing, dual-edged weapon. It was their mistake.

It took about six seconds. Castor dodged their strikes and gunfire in flashes of purple light, sending them screaming over the railing and falling toward the Nonagon below. The match had abruptly stopped and Holt could see the crowds were emptying out of the different sections in a rush, but Holt knew they were going to be too late. It would take minutes for them to get here, and the rebels would be done long before then.

Bullets kept flying. Holt noticed the plunder bin next to him. Inside lay a row of things in separate containers of foam. Grenades. Several dozen. As he studied them, an idea occurred to him, an insane one, and he was surprised by how little aversion he felt toward it.

Holt grabbed two of the grenades, one in each hand. They felt cool and heavy. He peered out from behind the conveyor one last time . . . then simply stood and stepped out *into the open*, walking forward.

Bullets whizzed through the air, barely missing him. Holt didn't even flinch.

"Holt!" It was Ravan's yell, horrified, from behind him. The shout registered, just barely, but he ignored her, kept walking casually through the bullets screaming past.

Some of the rebels saw him. Their guns turned, flashed, but Holt felt nothing. What would happen would happen.

A few more steps and he was at the pipeline, where the two rebels were working with the torch. They stared up at him in shock. Holt dispatched the first with a grenade-laden fist to the head. The second he slammed into the pipe and watched as he fell to the ground.

Bullets sparked all around him, but he didn't duck, he just reached for a smaller wheel on the big pipe, the line's blow-off valve, used to bleed off excess gas in case of high pressure. He spun the wheel, and there was a loud hiss as white vapor shot into the air.

"Hold fire!" a young, masculine voice shouted, and the bullets from the rebels silenced instantly. Holt heard Ravan shout the same order. No one wanted to fire a bullet now, especially toward *him*. Igniting the gas spewing out of the massive pipe would set off the whole thing, and probably blow the entire Pinnacle to pieces.

Which was what made it all the more shocking when Holt pulled the pins from both grenades and casually stood on top of the pipe.

Everyone on the platform—rebels, Menagerie, Ravan—stared at him in dismay.

Holt hadn't released the grenade handles, which meant they hadn't primed. But if he were to drop them, say, from being shot . . .

"Doesn't happen often," a voice observed with slight amusement, "but I am at a loss for words." It belonged to a hard-edged-looking kid, with long blond hair tied behind his back. He was covered in grease and grime, but Holt had a feeling it didn't have anything to do with the battle. Rogan West, Ravan had called him, the leader of this futile rebellion, but Holt didn't recognize him. "I suppose the idea is if we shoot you, you drop the grenades . . . and *boom*."

Holt just stared back, without emotion. There was a resourcefulness in Rogan's eyes, charisma too. Holt could see why the others followed him, though it wouldn't amount to much.

"That, of course, means you would be dead too," Rogan continued. "That what you want?"

Holt shrugged. "It's funny. Not really sure *what* I want anymore."

Rogan stared back at him considering, like he were some riddle to figure out. Maybe he was, Holt thought, but the answer was simpler than the kid knew. There was just a lot of power in having nothing to lose.

"Holt Hawkins," Rogan said. "That's you, isn't it?"

Holt didn't reply.

"You did this place one hell of a solid when you killed Archer Marseilles. You're the last person I'd expect to help Tiberius, much less die for him."

"I need him and the Menagerie intact, and you're screwing that up."

"Ah." Rogan nodded, interested and skeptical at the same time. "So, it's about *you*, not him."

Holt was losing patience. He felt the cold orbs of the grenades in his hands.

"Call this scrub's bluff," one of Rogan's men said next to him, gun aimed at Holt.

Rogan shook his head. "There's no bluff to call, he's pulled the pins. He's committed. I like that. Not enough people really put their money where their mouth is anymore. Why don't you come work for us? Make real change instead of just adding to Tiberius's power base?"

The answer was simple. "Because you're going to lose."

The rebels tensed around Rogan, the guns shook in their hands, but their leader looked back without malice. If anything, he seemed more impressed.

"Straight shooter," Rogan said. "I like that too. When you see Tiberius . . . tell him I said hi."

Holt frowned. The rebels stood up and moved for their wounded, helping them to their feet. No one fired at them, because the blow-off valve was still venting. Seconds later, they were zipping away on the Skydash.

When they were gone, Holt shut off the valve, sealing away the gas stream. Menagerie reinforcements were swarming onto the platform now, weapons drawn, but there was no longer anything to fight. Castor landed next to Holt in a flash of cyan, and Holt noticed a broad, contented smile on his face.

White Helix . . .

Castor reached down and grabbed the pins Holt had let fall to the ground, and while Holt held the grenades, slipped them back into place, disarming them. They felt no different to Holt either way, he noticed strangely.

"What is your problem?" Ravan's voice yelled from behind him. The look in her eyes as she advanced was pure fury. Clearly, she didn't approve of what he'd done, even if it had pushed back the rebels.

"The Holt I know would never pull a stunt like that," Ravan spat as she closed the distance, stopping in front of him. "Who the hell *are* you?"

Holt sighed. He just wanted this day to be over, the trade to be complete, and to be on his way. More than anything, he wanted to be alone, where he didn't have to pretend to be something he wasn't, where he didn't have to be anything to anyone else. Ravan was angry because she cared about him, but it stirred nothing in him. It was just another burden.

"What do you want me to say, Ravan?"

"I don't want you to *say* anything, I want you to screw your head on right, because what I just saw were not the actions of a rational person, especially not one with as much responsibility as you have. Do you even remember *why* you came here?"

Holt stared back at her absently. "Do *you* remember that you don't believe in any of it?"

"You're right," she replied with fire. "I don't believe in any of it, it's insane and pointless, but *you* believe in it. Passionately. Or at least you used to."

"What do you care what I believe?" There was an edge of ice in his own voice he'd never heard before. "You said it yourself: you don't care, so why not just leave me the hell alone? We'd both be better off that way."

Ravan looked at him scornfully, almost with disgust. She probably saw his ambivalence as weak, and there was nothing she hated more than weakness. She held his gaze and moved closer, punctuating her words. "She's *gone*, Holt."

It was the last thing he wanted to hear. Holt tried to move off, but she grabbed him and held him in place.

"She's *gone*. It sucks. But you live with it."

"You don't think I know that, Ravan?"

"I know it hurts, but if you would just let me help you, if you would just see that—"

Holt grabbed her now and pulled her close, the anger inside him, the frustration at all the responsibility he was forced to bear, finally poured out. "I don't *want* your help. I don't want *anything*. Not from you, not from anyone. You need to think of me as someone who's gone, because that's how it is. You're right, she is gone. And so am *I*. Got it?"

Ravan held his stare a moment, and then, to his surprise, in spite of the venom and the scorn in his voice, shook her head defiantly. The emotion in her eyes became anger. "You're a *coward*, you know that? You repulse me, but I'm not giving up on you. I won't, no matter what you say to me or how hard you try and push me away. I'm going to hound you until you're the person I remember again, I will beat it out of you, I swear to God. You have exactly *no* choice in the matter."

She yanked away from him and started moving, pushing through the crowd. Holt watched after her, and for the first time since Currency, he felt a slight twinge of emotion. Guilt maybe, or something fonder, he couldn't be sure. He watched until she disappeared in the direction of the platform's edge, and blended in with the rest of the Menagerie, and when she was gone, whatever he felt was covered up and buried just as quick.

MASYN PERCHED NEAR THE top of one of the strange city's giant towers. The flames whipped upward above, and she could feel the heat even over the intensity of the sun.

Castor was easy to spot, leaping up the tower opposite hers in flashes of yellow and purple, engaging the Menagerie on the platform over the giant arena in the very center.

Holt was harder to find, he blended in with the crowds, but eventually she spotted him, one of the few not running away. She admired the rebels' strategy, leaping from those wires onto the platform, firing their primitive weapons. They had drive and fearlessness. She liked Holt's strategy even more, walking into certain death, the grenades, willing to risk everything just to win.

Masyn smiled and decided she liked this Faust. It was dangerous. Unpredictable. Chaotic. She felt more at home here than she had felt anywhere since the Strange Lands, and it had only been a few minutes. She wondered what else this place had in store for her.

When the battle was over and the dark-haired pirate had finished with Holt, Masyn watched them all move off.

Castor and Holt had already gotten themselves in trouble, and there was little doubt it was a trend that would continue. Masyn would keep an eye on them, but, of course, that was the whole plan. Infiltrate the city and watch. She'd stay here until nightfall, then try her hand at that cable system connecting the strange towers, with their flames at the top. She wondered if she could run across the entire length of one.

12. TIBERIUS

THE SPEAR POINT EXPLODED through the armor plate in a shower of green sparks, and then hummed back through the air to Castor's Lancet with a reverberating, harmonic ping. The plate was just under a foot thick, something from an old tanker ship, and the crystal punched through like it wasn't even there.

Tiberius's only reaction was the slight raise of an eyebrow, but it took a lot to impress him, and even more to generate a reaction. The power of the White Helix weaponry would be obvious to anyone. It was all but assured now: he would make the deal and Holt could finally get out of here.

They were at the top of the Command Pinnacle, where Tiberius's private quarters rested. A large balcony overlooked all of Faust, and Holt tried not to think about where he was. Archer's room had been just below this one.

"And the rings?" Tiberius asked, in his slowly thoughtful voice.

"Off the table," Avril replied, standing next to Holt. "They're too dangerous to use without training."

Tiberius gave no indication whether that was acceptable or not. He simply beckoned for the Lancet in Castor's hand, and the Helix studied him warily.

"That's not appropriate," Avril said, forcing herself to be civil. "A Helix never parts with his weapon. It's a grave insult to even ask."

Tiberius's eyes slanted slightly toward his daughter. "I am to agree to a deal of this scope without even touching what you offer?"

Avril frowned, then, after a moment, nodded to Castor.

Slowly, he handed Tiberius the Lancet. It made Holt uneasy, seeing a weapon like that in the hands of Tiberius. But what did it matter? He would make the deal and be gone, and the Menagerie could do whatever they wished. He wouldn't be around to see it.

"Each Lancet is unique," Avril said. "The shaft is honed and shaped by its owner when they earn the right, from wood and materials they gather on a quest into—"

"Do you really see the Menagerie fighting this way?" Tiberius cut her off like she wasn't even speaking, slowly twirling the weapon in his hands. "With spears?"

Holt expected the question. He spoke up, and when he did, the weapon seemed to spin faster in Tiberius's hands. "It's the crystal you should be interested in, that's where the power is. It can be formed into pretty much any shape you want."

"Like the tip of a bullet," Tiberius said.

"Exactly." Next to Holt, Avril closed her eyes. To her this was a nightmarish deal, but, like him, she had no real choice. They needed the Menagerie if they were going to save Zoey, and the weapons were their only real tradable commodity.

Holt and Castor had been led here by Ravan and then left in Tiberius's quarters with Avril. The room was not what you might expect. It was comfortable, certainly, but completely absent of materialistic possessions. There was a bed, a dining table, chairs and a sofa, a workbench with tools, an entire wall full of shelves lined with books on technical and engineering subjects, and a drafting table, the wall around which was lined with blueprints and schematics of Faust and its original infrastructure.

The only thing that might count as an indulgence was a large, very old crossbow mounted to the wall near the bed. It was the only thing in the room whose purpose wasn't immediately perceptible.

Besides Tiberius, there were two large guards, and a heavily muscled officer named Quade, who had a strange habit of looking at everything sideways. He wore an orange Taurus on his right hand, and his Menagerie star had seven of its star points filled in, marking him as an Overseer. Two silver .45 pistols were sheathed in double shoulder holsters under his arms. He was Tiberius's master-at-arms, and Tiberius trusted his counsel on all military matters.

"Quade?" Tiberius asked, moving away with the Lancet. "Your thoughts?"

The boy seemed unimpressed. "It's powerful, no doubt, but I'm not sure how we would mass-produce enough ammo for it to be worthwhile. From what I understand, it's difficult and dangerous to shape these crystals."

"The deal *includes* the ability to mass-produce this crystalline ammunition to our specifications, so that's not an issue," Tiberius observed. "There's a bigger concern I was hoping you would see."

Quade seemed impatient. "Which would be?"

"The Wind Traders. They've already entered into a bargain for this technology. If they adopt its use and we do not, the balance of power will shift. The ramifications of that I find troubling, and so should you." For the first time since Tiberius had entered the room, he looked at Holt, the Lancet still spinning in his hands.

Holt stared back at him. It was strange, the lack of emotion. This encounter was something that had been building for a long time, but it, like everything else now, failed to move him.

"I heard what you did in the Handover Ward," Tiberius said. "It was . . . surprising."

"Time changes people, I guess," Holt replied. He wasn't sure he meant it, but it was what he figured Tiberius wanted to hear.

The Menagerie leader studied him a long moment, but there was no way to read his thoughts. "You *have* changed. You're . . . harder now. Colder. You've been hurt, haven't you?"

Before Holt could say anything, Avril cleared her throat. "I think we should get back to—"

Tiberius held up a hand to silence her, his eyes still on Holt. "Engineering has always been my passion. I used to be an engineer here—in fact, I helped design this facility back before it was Faust. Did you know that?"

Holt wasn't surprised. Tiberius knew far too much about the inner workings of the structure, had played too prominent a role in the city's construction, and there was no denying his mechanical genius. The Nonagon, for instance, was a work of horror, but the skill it took to design was unquestionable.

Tiberius tossed the Lancet to Quade and it hummed as it split the air. The big kid studied it skeptically when he caught it, testing its weight, still unimpressed.

"You've noticed the crossbow, certainly," Tiberius said as he removed the ancient weapon from the wall. It was bigger than it had looked, almost as big as Tiberius himself, but he held it easily. "Do you know why I keep it? Why I find it relevant?"

Holt said nothing, he was growing tired of this show and tell. He wanted to be done here, to be on his way, but Tiberius just kept talking.

"Because it represents the *taking* of power," the man said pointedly, as if it was meaningful. "One of the first accounts of a crossbow came from the Greek engineer Heron, of Alexandria. He described a weapon called the 'Gastraphetes,' a primitive crossbow, but it still could fire with far more energy than an arm-drawn hand-bow. Impressive, no doubt, but that wasn't why it caused such a major shift in how wars were fought. What do you think the real reason was?"

The question, oddly, wasn't directed at Holt or even Avril. Tiberius was asking Castor. It took a moment for the Helix to realize he was being addressed. When he did, he thought about it for a moment, then answered. "To use a bow requires years of specialized skill. But anyone can fire a crossbow, once it's primed."

A smile from Tiberius was a rare thing, but he wore one now. He seemed impressed. "Exactly. The crossbow was simple, cheap, and physically undemanding enough to be operated by large numbers of regular, conscripted soldiers, no matter how dim-witted. It shifted everything, and all because some ancient engineer sat down and thought of a way to overcome human limitation. I find that . . . inspiring."

What happened next happened so quick, not even Castor's honed instincts could save him.

There was a loud, vibrating pulse as the crossbow bolt fired and hit Castor in the shoulder, spinning him around and sending him to the floor.

Before he could get up, Quade swung the Lancet like a club into the Helix's head and sent him rolling. He didn't move after that. White Helix or not, when something as dense as an Antimatter crystal connects with your skull, you stay down. Holt looked at Castor's limp body. It made so little sense, the suddenness of it, the shift from conversation to brutality, that he just stared in a daze.

Avril tensed—her reaction would have been lightning fast, were she given the chance—but Quade dropped the Lancet and drew both his sidearms in a blur and aimed them at Avril. So did the two burly guards near the door.

Avril froze, breathing hard and angry. She glared at her father. Clearly, this had all been planned.

"Without your silly little rings, girl, I don't think you're fast enough to dodge bullets," Tiberius said as he knelt down to Castor, slowly plucking each of the rings off his fingers, being careful to keep them from touching one another. "But, if you try, Quade has orders to wound you. I would prefer to avoid that, your safety means a great deal to me."

"What are you *doing*?" she asked through clenched teeth.

"During China's Han Dynasty," Tiberius calmly told her, "the emperor's army had no crossbows. Their neighbors, the Xiongnu, had invented the weapon for themselves and refused to trade it, no matter what the Emperor offered. They knew that by doing so, they gave away their only military advantage. So the Emperor invaded Xiongnu, and took the technology for himself. He then went on to conquer most of Asia at the time."

Avril didn't seem to care much for her father's history lesson. "This deal was—"

"Irrelevant. If you had listened to anything I just said, you would see that. True power is always *taken*, never bargained for. It is our way. We will *take* from the White Helix what we want. There will be no 'deal.'"

"I swear," Avril began, barely controlling her rage. "I will fight and—"

"And die, yes." Tiberius stood and moved to the drafting table, setting the rings on it, watching them glow. Then he hung the crossbow back up onto its spot on the wall. "You said so before. But why?"

"These are my friends." Avril seemed stunned. "Castor is my brother, you have no idea what we've—"

"*Your brother is dead!*" Tiberius roared so loudly it shook the room.

The sound snapped Holt back to reality, even Avril took a step back. It was the only time Holt had ever heard Tiberius raise his voice, and that in itself made it shocking. When he spoke again, the usual calmness had returned, but it was laced with heat. "These 'friends' of yours, this one in particular, did any of them tell you the *truth*? Did they tell you *who* killed Archer?"

Holt could see where this was about to go, the path Tiberius had intended it to take from the beginning, probably even before he'd arrived. He needed Avril, for her to rejoin the Menagerie, but she loathed him. What was needed was a way to make her question her loyalties. Even for Tiberius it was brilliant.

"Tell her, Holt," Tiberius said, turning around, staring at him with the full rage and hatred he no longer needed to conceal. "Tell her the truth. It would mean so much more coming from you."

Avril looked at Holt, and he saw it behind her eyes, could see her putting the pieces together, deducing what he was about to say. The emotion there almost seemed to plead with him not to. What did it matter now, Holt thought. The deal was finished, there had never really been one. It was all a ruse to lure him back with Avril and it had done its job gloriously.

"It was me," Holt said—and when he did he saw a little bit of the light in

Avril's eyes snuff out. "I shot him, right below here in his room. I did it, and no one else."

He could have tried to explain, to say what Archer had been about to do, but there was no real point. Oddly, the words felt good to say, not just because he was, in a way, unloading some kind of burden, but because he knew by saying them that he was sealing his fate, that it would all mercifully be over soon. He wouldn't have to pretend anymore.

Tiberius nodded to the guards and Holt sensed them step toward him.

"You would defend the murderer of your own brother?" Tiberius asked Avril. "You would *die* for him? What kind of 'honor' did they teach you in that place?"

Holt groaned as one of the guards' fists slammed into his stomach. The second guard doubled his fists and knocked him the rest of the way to the ground. Kicks followed, brutal ones, with lots of force behind them. He felt the sharp pain of a rib snapping, then another, felt the air burst from his lungs.

Through the haze of pain, Holt saw Avril staring down at him. It was a stare laced with an anger he had never seen from her, and the sight of it, the knowledge that it was all going to end this way, instilled in him the strangest emotion.

He laughed. Loud and bitterly.

It was enough to stop the guards. They looked at Tiberius questioningly. In response, the man knelt down, right to Holt's eye level.

Holt said nothing, just kept laughing, even though it hurt. Something about all of it was hilarious, that the end result was exactly what he should have predicted, and yet he had come here anyway. He was a fool.

The world blurred, a mixture of pain and a dreamlike daze that seemed to be growing, and underneath it all lay relief. He didn't have to go through the motions any longer. He could just let go, and wait for it all to end, and maybe, soon, he would see Mira again. The thought finally silenced his laughter.

"You don't care, do you?" the blurred face of Tiberius asked. Holt felt a hand grab his hair and make him look into the Menagerie leader's eyes. "You're glad it's come to this. I understand. Well, don't worry. Before all is said and done, I will *make* you care again, I promise. It will be my gift to you."

If only it were that simple, Holt thought.

His head hit the floor. He felt more kicks and punches, but the pain blended into the background, fading away, until there was nothing but black.

WHILE SHE WALKED through the Armory Pinnacle, Ravan tried not to think about her last conversation with Holt. She hadn't seen him since she'd left him with Tiberius yesterday, and he'd made no move to contact her.

Good riddance, she told herself. He'd never done anything but hurt her. She was better off with him gone, with him not around to think about or miss, but the thoughts felt hollow.

Whoever that was that had said those things was not Holt, and the idea that all he had ever done was hurt her wasn't fair. He'd caused pain, sure, more than anyone, but there was a time when he'd filled her with things no one ever had. A sense of belonging, a feeling of assurance, and a promise of something she had never wanted or believed possible. Salvation. All along, she realized, that was what Holt had meant, not just from the things she had done or the person she'd become, but from all the darkness she saw coming ahead.

What would it have been like to not be in the Menagerie, to just . . . exist? To live. To love. Holt had been the only person to ever make her think that way.

"Do you know why I brought you here?" Tiberius's voice startled her. She'd forgotten he was even there, forgotten where she was. As they moved, all the eyes of the pirates on their land-duty shifts warily watched them.

"No," she answered.

"I'm wondering what it is you want from your Commandancy. It's an important rank, it comes with important responsibilities. There are only twelve, after all."

It was true, the higher up the ladder you went, the fewer positions there were. Only four people held the seventh rank, Overseer, followers like Quade, the master-of-arms, and Petra, the spymaster. The Consul rank, the second highest only to Tiberius himself, had only two, though one of them was empty, and had been for some time. The popular consensus was that that position was to go to Avril, assuming she ever wanted it. Not for the first time, Ravan thought her a fool. All that power, simply being given, and she couldn't be bothered. It didn't matter, someday it would be hers. It was all just a matter of time.

"I could use someone with your tenacity to reorganize the Armory Pinnacle," Tiberius continued, studying the interior as they walked. "It needs . . . fresh eyes."

The Armory was the only Pinnacle whose platform was fully enclosed, sealed with walls of metal and thick wood, and always heavily guarded. Inside was what you expected. Shelves loaded with assault rifles, small arms, shotguns, grenades, and even more dangerous things like missile launchers and antiaircraft guns, all of it looted and pillaged from the ruins of the World Before. When they were treasure hunters, Ravan and Holt had helped fill more than their share of this room.

But the Armory Pinnacle was more than just a warehouse. Sparks sprayed from dozens of welding torches as Menagerie repaired and modified weapons. Nearby, ten pirates ran the ammo forge, using machines to compress and create the unending supply of bullets the Menagerie needed. The forge ran twenty-four hours a day, in four shifts—there was no other way they could keep up with demand. The Pinnacle also held Faust's prison, though they hadn't reached it yet. It lay in the very center of the old flare tower this place had been built around.

Tiberius was right, she *could* make this place run better. A part of her might even like it. A cursory glance revealed half a dozen major ways she could improve productivity on the repair line alone, but the problem with attaining a higher rank was that many of the positions that came with it were boring as hell. Running the Armory Pinnacle wasn't who she was, and it certainly didn't fit her plans.

"I was hoping for something in the field," Ravan responded carefully. Being offered a Pinnacle was an honor; she didn't want to seem ungrateful, but she intended to state her intentions clearly and firmly. Tiberius would respect that. "A Zone Commander. Something dangerous, something no one else wants. Give me whatever zone you've had the least success with, and I'll make it twice as profitable every year after that."

It was a bold claim, but it wasn't grandstanding. Ravan could deliver.

Tiberius nodded as they walked. "I guessed as much, considering you intend to one day challenge for leadership."

Ravan barely kept herself from tripping at his words, but Tiberius didn't seem the least bit wary.

"Your intentions are clear to anyone who looks," he said. "Constantly requesting field assignments, asking for ones no one else wants, whether it's treasure hunting or running a ship on the Mississippi . . . or finding my daughter. You've taken and mastered every tactical regimen we offer—indeed, you're one of the most skilled fighters we have—and all of it is to put yourself, eventually, in a position to challenge for leadership and to *win*."

"Tiberius . . ." Ravan began, but he waved her off.

"I respect the course you've chosen, your plan to take the power you feel you deserve, why would I be threatened? Do you intend to challenge *me*?"

"Never," Ravan said pointedly, and she meant it. She respected Tiberius more than anyone in her life.

"I value your loyalty, there are very few I trust more. I'm not sure if I've ever told you that. Sometimes I feel . . ." He trailed off, looking past her. He was a man who always gauged how much to reveal, always weighed the risks. It was what had kept him alive, allowed him to achieve what he had. "Avril has never been the most endeared of daughters."

The thoughts of Holt vanished. It was an amazing admission, she wasn't completely sure what to say. "I'm glad you find me worthy."

"You should know I have no objection to you challenging my successor, even if it should be Avril. It's how I designed the system, a natural selection where the strongest rise to power."

Ravan was surprised. Not feeling threatened by her desire to challenge him for leadership was one thing, but not minding if it happened to be his daughter, the heir he was grooming, was another.

He seemed to sense her surprise. "A leader is only as powerful as the foes they defeat. If Avril does follow me, then she would be well served to be challenged by you."

"And if I win?" Ravan asked with more than a hint of contempt.

"Then the Menagerie will be led by the most powerful. Either way my legacy is assured."

It made sense the way he put it. She just had to make sure she made it count when it was time, and this reminded her of another obstacle.

"How did Rogan West manage to take two Pinnacles?" she asked, and for good reason. Eliminating the threat of the rebels was a necessity. If they won, West would no doubt take his position at the top of the Menagerie and everyone in Tiberius's upper echelon would be executed, Commandants included.

"The same way they tried to upset the Handover Ward's operation," Tiberius replied. "They used a Nonagon match to get people off the platforms, then they struck in force. They took over both that day, Machine Works and Communications, electrified the Skydash lines coming into them, and have kept guards up around the clock. Quade estimates they have a force of almost a thousand."

If that was true, it represented the greatest challenge to his leadership Tiberius had ever faced. It was impressive, really. Organizing that many, convincing them to bet their lives on the rebellion's success. Rogan must be one charismatic leader.

"Now you see why finding Avril was so important," Tiberius told her. "If my reach is shown to extend all the way to the Strange Lands, my perceived power increases. You can already see the momentum shifting from her return."

"But will she cooperate?" Ravan asked. To this point, Avril had given no indication that was even a remote possibility. She seemed to hate Tiberius and the Menagerie.

"I . . . remain hopeful she will warm to me in time."

"Even if she doesn't," Ravan replied, "you still have the deal with the White Helix. You should demonstrate the weaponry soon, tomorrow even, let everybody see what you've done."

He slowed to a stop and Ravan studied where they were. It was the center of the platform, where the giant steel rungs of the tower stretched upward, and it was the only part of the Armory that didn't have a ceiling. New sections of metal had been welded into place up and down it, a rail system for lowering, raising, and maneuvering what rested about halfway up: rows of wooden "capsules," about six feet by six feet, fifty in all.

These were Faust's "prison cells," large enough to lay down in, they had no windows or light, and Ravan grimaced at the sight. She hated being locked up more than anything else, she couldn't imagine being inside one of those things for even a day. Lengths of thick chain hung down from the top, part of the pulleys and winches that moved the cells, and hanging from them, his body wrapped tightly, was a person.

He was so still, it took a moment for Ravan to even notice him.

"A demonstration?" Tiberius's eyes were on the hanging figure. Something about the intensity of his stare made Ravan look closer at that limp form. "There will *definitely* be a demonstration."

It took her only a few seconds this time. Mainly it was his right hand, one of the few parts of him not completely covered in blood. There was a tattoo there, unfinished. If it had ever been completed . . . it would have looked exactly like *hers*.

Ravan felt a train crash of emotions inside her, every one of them in rapid-fire succession. Anger, guilt, horror, pain, sadness, shock, they all exploded in a thick wave that moved through her body and almost knocked her down.

Her fists clenched. She bit her lower lip until it bled, but she didn't feel it.

A sickness swelled in her stomach, and all the while, her eyes stayed locked on Holt, hanging from the chains, his blood dripping down and collecting on the floor, and all the while, her mind worked to find some way to explain what she was seeing, because it simply *couldn't* be what it looked like.

"Your reaction is nothing to be ashamed of." Tiberius's voice spoke in her ear, cold and dispassionate, but it sounded a million miles away. Ravan's body trembled, she couldn't blink, could only stare at him, feeling every injury she could see on his body, and there were many. "He was one of the few you were ever close to. I understand, Ravan, but, as I . . . explained to Holt, forgiveness is weakness. You know this better than most."

Her body felt numb. She wasn't sure if she was even still standing.

"Holt was a traitor. He did things there are no remitting." There was a slight heat to Tiberius's voice, the only indication of the burning hatred underneath. "He killed my *son*. He diminished my power, I had no choice."

There were more than just bruises on Holt's body, she could see. There were cuts too, they had used a knife. She shut her eyes . . . and the world swayed, threatening to overtake her. This couldn't be happening. It couldn't . . .

" 'Power unclaimed must be taken,' " Tiberius recited. " 'Power lost must be retaken.' "

It was the Menagerie mantra, and Ravan knew it well, she'd spoken those words at every ceremony for every star point she'd ever filled in on her left wrist. She knew the words so well, in fact, she should have seen this coming. There was no bargaining with Tiberius Marseilles, no matter what you had to offer, but she hadn't let herself believe that.

Ravan opened her eyes again. She could just make out Holt's chest rising and falling under the chains. "He isn't dead."

"No. He is very strong, but he always was, wasn't he? Strong . . . and smart. It's a shame, to think of the power he could have brought to the rest."

"What happens to him now?" Ravan forced herself to ask.

"He will be executed publicly, and then strung from the Armory Pinnacle. A symbol not just to the rebels, but to *all* the Menagerie: that power lost has been *retaken*."

"And the deal? With the White Helix?"

"When Rogan and his rebels have been dealt with, a large force will head west, toward San Francisco." Tiberius moved slowly around from behind her, his voice cold and calculating. "They will claim the deal has been finalized. They will enter the camp there, welcomed as allies. And then . . . they will kill every single White Helix and Wind Trader they see, and take the Antimatter technology for our own. *That* is the Menagerie way. Deals and brokering are for Wind Traders."

She felt him turn to her, studying her as he had never studied her before.

"I would like *you* to lead that force, Ravan. You traveled with them, you will know how best to crush them. After, I will grant you what you want. Command of the eastern zone, all the ships up and down the Mississippi. In the years to come, that position will set you up well for your challenge to my daughter."

A part of her, far back in her mind, recognized she had just gotten everything she wanted, but it stirred no emotion now, her eyes were locked on Holt.

She and Tiberius were well away from the main part of the Armory. There were no guards. No workers nearby. Just some of the pirates on prison duty above, but they were too far away to do anything. She could kill Tiberius, right now. Take her knife and bury the hilt in his chest so deep it would never come out.

"I wanted to show you this personally," Tiberius said. The words were weighted. He was all too aware of what she was feeling. "To be sure that we . . . understood one another."

Ravan made herself look away, for the last time, from the figure in the chains, the only person to ever have held her while she slept, the only person she had ever allowed herself to love. The emotion was all over her face, she was sure, but she made herself stare into the man's eyes and hold his gaze.

"No," she said. "There are no misunderstandings between us."

RAVAN EXPLODED OUT THE door of the Armory and slammed into the railing that circled the tiny, uncovered perimeter of the huge platform. She gasped out loud, like she'd been drowning underwater and could finally breathe. Tears fell, hot and bitter, giant sobs racked her body, and she didn't even look to see if anyone was watching.

The image of him, hanging there, was burned into her mind. She would never *not* see that image, she knew. The cuts, the bruises, the blood, the unnatural way he hung in the chains like some kind of ragged scarecrow. God . . .

The kicker was, it was all her fault. She'd been the one to encourage him to come back, had even come up with the plan for doing so, for what to tell Tiberius, for what to offer and how, and it had all been for selfish reasons, if she were brutally honest about it. Wanting him with her, having him here again, where he belonged . . .

Some part of her consciousness was doing the math on the last time she had actually cried. It was when she was eight, growing up in that dead-end desert trailer park outside Las Cruces, and her father had done what he'd done while her brother watched. She'd allowed herself to cry then, but after it was done, she told herself never again. She stopped being a child that night because she had to become something stronger, and she had always prided herself on that, and lived up to that intention right until this very moment.

The tears kept falling. They wouldn't stop.

Get control of yourself, admonished that same piece of her, the one that had risen up and kicked her in the ass all those years ago, the cold, dark piece that always looked out for her. *Get. Control.*

Ravan nodded and wiped the tears away angrily, cleaned her face, forced herself to breathe and stand upright without leaning on the railing for support. She looked around and confirmed there was no one nearby, no one had seen the display. The other Pinnacles stretched upward, the flames shimmering in the hot desert air. People swarmed on the platforms, or zipped through the air, thousands of them. It was the place she had lived for so long, the one place she used to feel she belonged. Now it all looked foreign to her.

They would put him into the cells tonight, they'd want him lucid for the execution. She knew where he would be. She was respected, she could get to him. No one suspected, not even Tiberius. She'd made sure of that, told him she was angry but that she knew when something was done and over with, and this was beyond done. Her desire for power outweighed her sense of vengeance.

It was what he wanted to hear. If she had said she was perfectly fine with Holt being strung up like a piece of trash, he would have recognized the lie and probably killed her on the spot.

She was still in the inner circle. She could free him.

Ravan felt a chill. She looked down at the eight-pointed star on her left wrist, its individual points like sharp iron spears. The two new ones she received only the night before were filled in with red now, and they still stung. Two more notches in her quest for what she wanted. It was in her grasp now, all of it, it had lined up perfectly.

Everything she wanted.

Was she just going to throw it all away? Is that what she was *really* thinking about here? For what? For *him*? While he was lamenting the loss of someone he loved more than her?

Still . . . it was Holt. The thought of him, in those chains . . .

Could she walk away and leave him? She could, she knew. That part of her, the one that wanted her strong for survival's sake, could. But that would be the end of her. The end of the last shred of humanity, the parts that Holt had always kept alive, the ones his presence never allowed to fade. Who would she be then? Was it really worth it, the power, if that was the price?

"Damn you, Holt," she said, feeling the tears forming again. "Damn you."

Get. Control.

Fine. She blinked the tears away, concentrated on her anger—it was always the most helpful emotion, the one that focused you the most. If she was doing this, *really* doing this, then that was that. You make a decision and you stick with it, you don't ruminate on it like a weakling.

Ravan couldn't do it alone, though. Freeing Holt was one thing, getting him out of the Pinnacle alive was another. She needed help, both before and after the ordeal. The "after" was obvious, though it meant a radical change in her future. The "before" was the real problem. Her men were loyal, they had fought and bled together, some would follow her, but others were just as loyal to Tiberius, and there was no real way to know which were which. There was only one other solution Ravan could think of, assuming what she guessed about the girl's plans was correct.

But where to find her? Masyn was a White Helix warrior, not a master of disguise. She wouldn't try and blend in, she would hide and observe, but from where?

Eventually, the answer occurred to her.

Ravan looked up to where the towers of the Pinnacles stretched into the sky, the giant plumes of flame billowing upward. She frowned at the obviousness of it. "Naturally."

14. ROSE

ZOEY WOKE INTO A SQUARE, blackened room, with walls of the same strange, organically flowing metal, and everything inside was out of place. She lay in a bed with a pretty red canopy and a white, lacy top. There were two couches: a black leather one, and something that looked like it was from a museum, with a bright floral pattern. The walls were lined with paintings and posters, and none of them seemed to fit any sort of theme. The whole room seemed like it had been thrown together at random.

Zoey left the bed and studied the room closer. It was definitely an improvement over the cramped pod, but the obvious attempts to make it feel more familiar had really only made it more disturbing. There were neither windows nor doors, and the realization frightened her. Had they walled her away in a prison where no one would ever find her?

The far wall across the room shuddered and dissolved suddenly, not exactly like it was melting—it was more mechanical than that, like microscopic pieces were moving and reforming themselves into new shapes, and as they did, the wavelike patterns in the surface ebbed into a new orientation. It became a doorway, allowing a view to a hall beyond, made of the same black metal.

The pretty woman from the lab, the one Zoey had helped the entity blend with, stepped into the room, carrying a silver tray, just as out of place as everything else. She paused, surprised to see Zoey out of bed. "I wanted to be here when you woke. I'm sorry."

Zoey said nothing. It was uncanny looking at her. The only real memories she had from her time before the Assembly, before the invasion, came from the Oracle, and even those felt like someone else's. Regardless, the woman in front of her looked almost identical to the memories she had seen of that night, when Zoey and her mother both watched the invasion as it began over Bismarck, but it couldn't be her . . .

The woman wore blue pants and a white blouse that clung to her lightly. Her hair, sparkling blond, was loosely braided down her back. She was the only thing in the room that didn't feel random in its appearance.

Zoey realized something odd. She couldn't read *anything* from the woman in front of her. In fact, there were no other sensations from the hundreds of thousands of Assembly here either. As in the pod, the silence was a blessing, but it made her uncomfortable, how easily they could block her ability.

"I hope you weren't frightened," the woman said. "I would have been, waking up like that."

Zoey still said nothing. The woman studied her strangely, as if in both recognition and not. Eventually she moved toward a wicker dining room table, with mismatched chairs, and set the tray on it. Zoey didn't have to look to know it held food. She could smell it. Real, hot food. Her stomach growled at the thought.

"I know you're hungry, Zoey," the woman said. "How are you feeling? You have been asleep for more than a week."

Zoey remained silent. Her eyes glanced behind the woman, where the strange doorway still stood.

"Does this form frighten you?" The woman kneeled down to Zoey's level, but made no attempt to move closer. She seemed perplexed, disappointed at the little girl's silence. "We expected the opposite. She is from your past, isn't she? Someone who meant a great deal to you. No one will hurt you here, I promise. You are more welcome than any entity in the entire universe."

Zoey just kept looking at the door, about twenty feet away.

"I decorated this room for you," the woman continued. "Do you like it? It's based on memories. This level of the Citadel was made for *us*. A horizontal orientation instead of vertical, I think you'll—"

Zoey dashed as fast as she could around the woman.

"Zoey!" the woman yelled, lunging for her, but it was too late.

The doorway began to shudder again, to reform itself, but she was through it before it could. She heard it reopening, knew the woman would pursue; she had to hurry.

Her plan wasn't escape, that wasn't why she'd come. She was inside the Assembly's most powerful structure, and the answer to defeating them must be here somewhere. She had to find it.

As she burst into the hall, her mind suddenly flooded with sensations.

It made her falter, the sudden emotions and thoughts from the Assembly. There were so many it was dizzying. The room she had just fled must have been shielded to prevent her from connecting with the aliens, and now she was out of its protection.

Zoey found her footing and dashed down a hallway made of the same black, organic wave shapes, and the way they flowed made it look like the whole thing was corkscrewing ahead of her. The woman hadn't lied; everything here was arranged horizontally, and it too was decorated. Movie posters lined the walls, odd paintings in varying styles, pictures of people and places no one remembered anymore.

Zoey ignored it all. The swirling hallway split in four directions ahead. She reached the intersection, turned right . . .

. . . and screamed as two mechanical constructs moved toward her. She'd seen these before, when she first arrived. Four legs, maybe five feet tall, with thin bodies and four, tendril-like arms. Three-optic red, blue, and green eyes stared into her.

They stomped forward, their strange arms reaching out.

"Zoey!" The woman again, coming from behind, down the hall.

Zoey backpedaled and took a new route. The hallway became oblong, it moved in waves ahead of her, making corners she had to run around, and there was no telling what was going to be on the other side of—

She ground to a desperate stop.

In front of her the hallway ended right into the massive structure's giant vertical shaft, stretching out around her, up, to the sides, and *down*, so far down she couldn't even see the bottom.

Zoey saw gunships and walkers, moving along the walls and through the air, and their projections filled her mind. The complicated rail system wound and branched its way up through the shaft, thousands of the pods and platforms buzzing through the air below.

Everything in that shaft maneuvered and was built around the center, and in the center rose the same, brilliantly bright column of energy, each particle of it almost visible, rising up toward the top. There, the crystalline entities pushed in and out of it, and like before, it was all beautiful. The sight made her hesitate.

"Zoey!" the woman shouted again, her voice close. There was nowhere left to run. Desperately, Zoey looked up and down, trying to find handholds or anything she could—

Something happened.

Directly across from her, the energy of the giant column began to slowly bend out *toward her.*

As it did, the projections in her mind were overwhelmed by a new sound. Something like static, distorted and powerful. It was mesmerizing, watching all that strange, flowing energy bend and morph forward, as if slowly reaching out for her.

She felt a strong desire to help it, to touch it, and she started to raise her own—

"Zoey! *Please!*" The woman's voice snapped Zoey's attention away from the energy. Not because it was loud or close, but because of the *emotion* she suddenly felt from the woman. Genuine emotion, the first she had sensed.

Zoey turned around and saw her standing a few feet away, the strange machines behind her, waiting. Where the woman had been blank before, now there was fear and concern, even dread, and all of it at the idea Zoey might hurt herself.

Then came confusion. Confusion at having those feelings in the first place. Zoey didn't need to read the woman to know, it was written all over her face. She was experiencing emotions . . . and they weren't expected.

Who *was* she?

"Don't come any closer!" Zoey yelled and took a step toward the edge, the energy from the huge column still bending closer.

"Zoey," the woman said. "I know you're scared, and that none of this makes sense, but right now, back here, with me, is the only place that's safe for you."

"You look like my mom," Zoey said. "But that can't be."

"Will you come back to our room so I can explain?"

"No."

The woman's desperation was building, and Zoey felt her latch onto an idea, one she found unpleasant, but she did it anyway. The woman's feelings turned inward, searching through the memories she held like a librarian flipping through a catalog, looking for something, finding it. "When you were very little, there was a song you loved. You sang it a dozen times a day, do you remember?"

Zoey steeled herself. This woman, whoever she was, was *not* her mother. She looked around again, trying to find an avenue of escape . . . then pure music filled her senses and overrode everything else.

It was a song, one she barely remembered. A simple melody, but it stirred great things in her.

You are my sunshine, my only sunshine . . .

Zoey looked back at the woman, locking eyes. Images flashed in her mind: this woman, and another, very similar in appearance, both beautiful and close, singing with her.

You make me happy when skies are gray . . .

The song lasted a few seconds more, its melody flowing through her head until it dissolved away and was lost. Zoey shuddered, trying to hold on to the memories, but they slipped away like water through her fingers.

"How did that feel, Zoey?" the woman asked.

Zoey didn't answer. She wasn't sure how to.

"I'll make you a deal. Come back with me and let me explain, and if you still want to, you can leave. Or you can choose to stay, and I can free more memories. Many more. You can finally, once and for all, learn the truth. Of your destiny, of who you really are . . . and how very loved you are here."

Zoey looked back to the drop below, and the giant column of energy, still bending closer and closer, almost there. She could feel the heat from it now . . .

The woman offered her hand. "All you have to do is listen. That's not so bad, is it?"

There was still a residual feeling from the memories, a shuddering of warmth. She'd had no idea they would have that kind of effect, and she'd had no idea how badly she wanted to feel them again. Besides, the woman was offering exactly what Zoey had come here for. Answers.

Slowly, cautiously, she moved forward and took the pretty woman's hand.

ZOEY LOOKED AT THE food that was still on the table, but she made no move to take it.

"You still haven't eaten," the woman said. "You must eat to remain healthy. Please." She motioned toward the tray. The emotions Zoey had felt from the woman were gone now. She wasn't exactly blank, but there was something . . . *off* about her.

"If I answer your questions, will you eat?" the woman asked.

Zoey said nothing, but in her mind she saw that as a fair compromise. The woman must have felt the decision, for she smiled a little.

"Ask," she said.

"How did you do that before?" Zoey asked. "Unlock my memories?"

"They're my memories too." The moment the woman said the words, she flinched as if she had misspoken. "No . . . I mean, they were *hers*."

The woman seemed confused, a little apprehensive, but it only lasted a second.

"You're not her," Zoey said. "My mother was with me when the Strange Lands formed, the Oracle showed me. The Severed Tower said I was the only 'remainder,' the only person not wiped away."

"I never said I was your mother, Zoey."

Zoey hesitated. "But . . ."

"Everyone always told them they looked so much alike. They told them they could have been . . ." The woman stopped, struggling for a word.

"Twins," Zoey finished for her, coming to understand.

The woman nodded, and her voice had a slightly haunted edge to it now. Zoey could sense more emotion trying to push through. "Your mother was younger than me—*this form* by a year. You used to visit, this very city. Do you remember?"

Zoey shook her head. The woman closed her eyes.

Images burst to life in Zoey's mind. Two women. One the Oracle had shown her, the other was the woman here now, and she looked almost identical to the first. They walked with Zoey between them, each holding one of her hands, lifting her up into the air, skipping her along the sand, and she giggled with each jerking movement. They loved her. She loved them.

The memories cut off. Zoey opened her eyes.

"You're . . . Rose . . ." She said. "I called you Aunt Rose."

"Rosalind was her real name," the woman responded.

"You were my mom's sister."

"Yes . . ." she began, and quickly cut off. Zoey felt her push more feelings down. "Or . . . no . . . Not me, but . . . It is strange. It is . . . not as expected."

"You're one of *them*. Aren't you? You're the shape that buried itself inside her, the one I helped. You're the one talking . . . not her."

"Finding this form among the multitude was fortuitous," Rose said. "She had been a medical professional, and that was the group we focused on for your Custodian. We ran basic scans on each of the Hosts in our possession, and to our surprise, her DNA matched with yours. It is then we knew."

"How to get me to do it," Zoey said. "How to get me to help one of you take over one of them."

"It was a . . . consideration, but more so, we hoped it would put you at ease, the sight of someone familiar."

"But you're not her. Not really . . ."

"I am much more than that now, Zoey. As are you."

"The Feelings," she said, though she already knew. A part of her had known from the very beginning. "The Feelings are . . . one of you. One of you is *inside* me." She remembered the vision the Oracle had shown her, that horrible, black room where everything moved up and down, not left and right, and the blue and white glowing crystalline shape that buried itself into her . . . just like the one who had buried itself into the body of her aunt.

"The Feelings, as you call them," Rose told her, "are the remnant of the Mas'Shinra Royal who merged with you."

"But . . . the Feelings have always *helped* me."

"Why would they not? They are not your enemy, none of us are, far from it. They want what we all want."

Many things were suddenly making sense. "That's why I can control machines. Because of the Feelings. It's the Assembly's ability, not mine."

"It is the Feelings' *ability*, but *you* are the one who channels it. Just as you channel its ability to read and sense others' emotions and memories. Only your rebirth through the Severed Tower makes this possible. You are unique in all the universe, Zoey. You are the future. Of the Assembly. Of humanity. They will both be ascended through you." Another glimmer of emotion. The concept seemed to both thrill and frighten the woman who was, and was not, Rose.

Zoey barely noticed. "Why do this? Why aren't your own bodies enough?"

"That is . . . a complicated question. I can show you. If you want. But . . . there is a price."

Zoey stared at her, unsure.

"You must eat something first," Rose clarified.

Zoey thought about it. How did it further her goals to starve to death? Besides, she might get real answers to her questions. All the same, she reminded herself, the thing in front of her was *not* Aunt Rose.

Zoey took a muffin and gingerly ate a bite. It was carrot cake, and somehow, it tasted freshly baked. The flavors exploded in her mouth, her stomach growled louder. She wasn't sure if the muffin was just that good, or if it was because she hadn't eaten in so long, but it tasted better than anything she had eaten in forever.

She sighed in approval, forgetting her desire to resist the Assembly, her hunger taking over. Zoey finished the muffin in two bites and looked back at the woman.

Rose nodded in approval . . . then closed her eyes. Imagery and sound took over all Zoey's senses at once.

"We were born of the Nexus," Rose's voice said inside her head. "And it was beautiful."

There was nothing but light and color, and Zoey could see it was its own structure, a giant, floating field of energy surrounded by stars. Golden, glowing crystalline shapes merged in and out of it, as if swimming through its warmth. Zoey had, of course, seen those shapes before, and she had seen the field too. It was the same energy that formed the column in the center of the Citadel.

"A place of color and of warmth, but we were tethered to it. Trapped. As we evolved individually, our minds stayed connected. We exist in the Whole, a mass of each's intelligence and purpose, united by the energy of the Nexus. We feel each other's thoughts and emotions whether we want to or not. The Nexus sustains us, gives power and life, but we could never leave it, we would die without it. Can you imagine a more torturous existence? Trapped in all that cold blackness, self-aware, connected . . . but alone."

Strangely, Zoey could. For all the beauty of the Nexus, the entities in this vision really were trapped, adrift in the deep of space, without a future, without anything other than themselves, forever and ever.

"After eons," Rose said, her voice low. "We were saved."

Objects appeared in the distance, a dozen of them or more. Even this far away, Zoey could tell what they must be. Ships. Headed toward the Nexus.

"Explorers? Conquerors? All that matters is that they saw us. They were captivated by our beauty, for we are radiant. They could not help themselves, they came closer, and we learned that day we were not as helpless as we believed. We could enter machines, disperse our essence into technology itself, power and control it. It was in this way that we were freed."

An unpleasant question occurred to Zoey. "What happened to them? The ones on the ships?"

"We inhabited their technology. Certain systems were deemed unnecessary. Without them the biologicals could not survive."

"You killed them . . ." Zoey said in horror.

"They were weak. Such is the way of the universe. We powered in the direction they had come, hoping to find their home world. In time, we did. And more. Many more. The pattern was repeated. We added to our technology, growing, controlling everything through our own energy, and leaving nothing behind, assimilating new colors into the Whole."

It was horrible. Even Ambassador, for all it had done for her, was one of *them*. It had participated in a swath of destruction and death that stretched back who knew how long. It made her sick.

Rose seemed to sense Zoey's feelings. "It was necessary. Even now, we remember how it once was, being alone, tethered, adrift, and lost. We swore it would never happen again, and a plan formed, one approved by the Whole, a decision that set in motion a quest that has, so far, lasted hundreds of thousands of years and seen countless races put to the Criterion."

The Criterion was what the green and orange Royal had called the test the captured human population was given. "What were you looking for?"

"*You*, Zoey."

The answer, for all its implications, was stated so plainly that it took a moment to feel the full weight of it.

"We have searched a millennia for an organic species that could contain our essence in the same way as a machine. No being has ever passed the Criterion. Until you. We have a name for the first, a herald of the coming Change."

"Scion . . ." Zoey said, her voice a whisper.

"You are the key to a great search. We will fight and die for you, and the clan that claims you will become dominant, superior to all others. Look."

The imagery flashed away. Her head swam from the abrupt shift back to the black room with its mismatched furniture.

Rose waved a hand toward one of the exterior walls, and as she did the color of it, the blackness, simply vanished. The walls were still there, they had just become transparent, making one giant window.

A giant panorama of city ruins stretched out before Zoey. She was looking due west, and the sun had just begun to set, burying itself in a perfectly straight horizon. It was the ocean, Zoey saw, and she could see where the land ended and the water began. The sky was full of color, oranges and reds, and somehow, it made the ruined city of San Francisco seem almost tranquil.

Buildings were shattered, fallen in on themselves, the patchwork of streets looked like a spiderweb from this height, and what was left of a once giant bridge spanned a gap in the landscape to the north. For all the destruction, though, the city was not dead. There was movement, like ants swarming in a nest.

Thousands upon thousands of machines moved in the streets and drifted in the air, and whatever force blocked Zoey from feeling and sensing them was suddenly removed. The impact of all those presences was overwhelming, but as she pushed the wave back, one thing became clear: the combined presence below did not represent only the Mas'Shinra, the blue and whites. They were there, she could feel them, but there were many more.

Every clan, all eight of them, from all over the world. They had sent representatives, not for conflict, but to unite. With all their aggression, it would take something remarkable to bring them together. There was only one thing it could be.

"Yes," Rose said, looking down upon the multitude. "They are here because of you, Zoey. You will ascend them all, human and Assembly. You will be their queen."

Zoey swallowed and looked up at the woman who had once been her aunt. "How?"

"With the Tone. It is broadcast from each Citadel on each continent, and it reaches the minds of every human on this planet, whether Succumbed or not. You have the power to use it. To transfer every entity from the Nexus into a human host using the Tone. We will be physical and real, and never again fear being trapped."

Zoey shook her head, the horror filling her. "The humans don't want that. They don't want to be you, they want to be *them*. They'll fight you . . ."

Rose nodded back to the window and the incomprehensible numbers of alien machines there. Zoey was suddenly hit with the reality of just how futile it all was. "There is no fighting us. Your friends have no choice but to be Ascended. It is an honor for them, and you will make it possible."

"I won't," Zoey whispered.

Rose studied her curiously. "You have more in common with us than you know. You are of us. As much as the entity inside you."

"That's not true," Zoey said firmly.

"You were born of the Severed Tower, and the Tower was born of both humanity *and* Assembly. It contained the essences of both. The form you were given is human, but you are equally Assembly. It is why you are the Scion, and why you are so important."

Zoey stared at Rose, trying to find a way to deny her logic, but one would not form.

Rose smiled. "You will be our Ascension, Sunshine. It is your destiny."

It took a moment for them both to realize Rose had called the little girl "Sunshine." It was what her aunt called her as a small child, a nickname based on Zoey's favorite song. When Rose realized it, the confidence slipped from her face. Apprehension and doubt bubbled to the surface. It was the sign Zoey had been looking for, the barest hint that maybe not all was lost.

Rose, the *real* Rose, however much buried by the Assembly presence within her, was not gone.

15. RIO VISTA

MIRA LAY AT THE EDGE of the mesa with everyone else, trying to push away the incessant projections from the Assembly. They were almost like little children, always clamoring for her attention and closeness, only these were children with the ability to drown out her own thoughts if she didn't keep a handle on them.

Right now, however, she had more pressing concerns.

They'd spent four days running search patterns throughout the desert, looking for missing Landships, White Helix, and Assembly. Dresden and Conner had divided the ships into four groups, each surveying a different area. By the end, Mira and Dresden had found twenty Arcs of Helix, fifteen Landships (most of which needed repairs) and several Assembly groups, and the others had had equal success. When all was said and done, they were operating with about 75 percent of what they'd set out with.

On the surface it was a good number, but there was no ignoring they'd lost more than a quarter of their resources in one battle. Which really meant they had lost *people*, a lot of them, and the thought was grim. She and Dane had dedicated themselves to being smarter, and she hoped they'd learned their lessons.

Below them, where the ground flattened out into a dusty plain, lay a town. It had been called Rio Vista in the World Before, a nondescript desert place that seemed equal parts trailer parks and adobe structures, or at least what was left of them. The only piece that stood out was the very thing that had brought them here: a large, arching, metal bridge that spanned a wide river. For Landships, that water was impossible to cross, and there were only a few places where the big vessels could pass over in this part of the Barren. This bridge had been cleared long ago for just that purpose.

But, as usual, they had a problem.

The Assembly had parked themselves in the town, the blue and whites, several dozen Mantises, and six Spiders. A powerful force, one that outnumbered theirs, yet nothing like what the reds had fielded a few days ago. Most were dug into defensive positions, while patrols searched the perimeter. The Assembly, it seemed, had been expecting them.

"Distance?" Dane asked behind her. He was on the ground with his men, almost a thousand White Helix, masks already pulled up, eager for payback. Mira hoped they got it this time; the plan Dane had devised seemed overly complicated, but at least it included all three groups.

Mira reached out with her senses, feeling for the Hunters, the Mas'Erinhah defectors. Right now, they were cloaked, moving at full speed around the side of the town, so far undetected. "They'll be ready when you hit."

Dane looked to where the rest of the force had been divided. Two groups of impressive size. One contained all the Landships that had been armed with White Helix weaponry, and the number had grown to twenty-one. Smitty and Caspira, it seemed, had found ways to stomach each other's presence enough to work together, and they had used the last four days well. Next to them sat the Mas'Erinhah artillery walkers, the big ones that had laid down that devastating barrage in the Strange Lands a month ago.

The second group was a small force of the silver Assembly, mainly Mantises and Brutes. They weren't using any of the Spiders per Ambassador's recommendation. The entity felt that with the close-quarters fighting to come, that level of firepower might cause more friendly fire than enemy. Still, Mira could see them, a mile away, hovering protectively over the rest of the Landship fleet. If they were needed, they could be brought in.

"Still wish we had air power," Dresden said next to her. So did Mira. Out of all the defectors the silvers had gotten, not one gunship had joined their side, only several Osprey dropships. At least the blue and whites below didn't seem to have any either.

"Never venture, never win," Dane answered, and looked to Mira. "Light 'em up."

His face was a mask of confidence, which was exactly what the numerous Doyen and their Arcs behind him needed to see, but she knew he felt at least a stirring of the apprehension she did. This was their first battle since the travesty of Currency. If they lost this one too, the entire endeavor was probably finished.

Mira reached for the button on her belt. From a device there, a wire ran to an earpiece and microphone around her ear. Everyone else on the mesa wore an identical set, including Dane and his Doyen.

It had been a lucky find by Conner, a National Guard armory he spotted during the search. Like most places it had been well picked over, but the looters had mainly been interested in the guns and explosives stored there, and had passed over the electronics, including several crates of headset radios. While there hadn't been enough for everyone, there was enough for each Landship Captain and first officer, and each White Helix Doyen. They were useless of course for Assembly, but Mira could relay any messages to that group herself.

She slapped the button, heard the crackle of static. "Artillery, fire at will." At the same time, she projected the same message to the giant Mas'Erinhah artillery walkers . . . and then shut her eyes.

The air exploded.

Piercing, harmonic pings shook the air as the Landship cannons launched their Antimatter shells into the sky. The sound of the artillery walkers adding their own fire shook the ground like thunder, and it all screamed over her head.

Below, the town was suddenly ablaze in fire as the ordnance hit. Explosions flared, both regular fire and colored from the crystals, and Mira saw several enemy Mantises incinerated almost immediately.

They didn't sit idle for long. Even though the artillery was out of sight, they returned fire in its general direction, and plasma burned through the air and sparked against the side of the mesa. They were firing it in a way Mira had no idea they even could. The yellow bolts of light, instead of simply shooting straight, now shot in arcs that curved in the sky and came back down toward the plateau. Explosions rocked the ground nearby, rocks and dirt sprayed everywhere.

"Seek," Dane yelled as he pulled his mask over his mouth.

"And find!" came the response, a thousand strong, loud enough to overpower the chaotic sounds.

"Move as one!"

The order was shouted again through the ranks, and the Helix advanced, leaping over the edge of the mesa and soaring downward toward the town hundreds of feet below in a cloud of cyan.

Do it, Mira projected to Ambassador. Instantly she felt a wave of anticipation that replaced her own sense of anxiety. The aliens' furor for battle filled her, and she smiled, letting the feelings flow, before she realized they weren't her own, and she pushed them back. It was frightening sometimes, the mix of emotions, hers and theirs. She could lose herself so easily.

The machines thundered forward, almost twenty Mantises and Brutes. There were no teleports yet, they wanted to take their time getting to the enemy. The longer it took, the more the artillery could soften the town up.

Of course, that worked both ways.

Behind them the arcing plasma bolts finally found a mark, and Mira heard screams as they started slamming into one of the armed Landships. The Barrier artifacts flashed to life, deflecting the ordnance in giant plumes of sparks, but the shield was flickering in a weird way she didn't like.

"What ship is that?" Mira asked.

"The *Wind Drag*, why?" Dresden responded.

"Because its Barrier is failing," Mira yelled, eyes wide, reaching for the radio button, but it was too late.

The Barrier flickered off, and the ship exploded in a giant wave of flaming splinters. She saw people leaping off as the ship buckled, but far fewer escaped than perished. Mira shut her eyes tight.

"Those Barriers are *new*!" Conner yelled in anger.

He was right, she'd helped make them for all the ships on artillery duty. It should have lasted twice that long. It made no sense.

More bolts exploded around them. They needed their main force to engage, to pull the artillery off them, and fast.

Mira looked back and down, carefully peeking over the edge again into the hailstorm of plasma fire, and watched as the Helix touched down outside the town. Explosions flared up all around them, and they flipped and leapt into the air in flashes of yellow light.

Streaks of color shot forward as Dane and his group fired, and they blew through buildings and old cars and found their marks in showers of sparks. The Helix were closing the distance fast, which meant it was time.

"Artillery, cease fire! *Cease fire!*" Mira yelled into her headset, projecting the same toward the Mas'Erinhah. It took a moment, but the gunfire silenced. Below, the last of the explosions from the barrage flared away . . . right as the White Helix entered the town, leaping between the various buildings, the second volley from their Lancets flying forward while the first was returning toward them.

Ambassador and his mechanized force continued to move. As Mira watched, flashes of light lit up and down the line of walkers as the Brutes teleported themselves and one Mantis walker each down to the bottom. Similar flashes appeared in the town as the machines teleported into position, strategically placed, and Rio Vista was suddenly a battleground, explosions and plasma bolts and Antimatter crystals flying everywhere.

"Goddamn, that's beautiful," Conner said. "That is *beautiful*."

Mira almost agreed, until she watched fireballs consume a dozen White Helix, and felt the projections of shock from some of the silvers as their walkers exploded. For the Assembly, falling on the battlefield was a much different proposition. They simply lifted up and out of their burning machines and floated away. The White Helix had no such luxury; when they fell, it was permanent.

Mira looked away. Dresden studied her sympathetically.

"I know it's not fun, but you have to watch," he said. "You're the only one who can guide in the Hunters."

He was right. Their force had made a powerful surprise attack, but they were still outgunned. Below, the blue and white Spiders stomped forward, their huge cannons opened up. Mira flinched as more of Ambassador's and Dane's forces fell or disappeared in blossoms of fire.

Mira studied the battle like Dane had taught her, looking for the weaknesses he had outlined, and finally she saw them. The blue and white walkers were swarming toward the northern part of town, Mantises leaping onto rooftops for elevated positions, and the Spiders were grouping there too, all of them concentrating their fire to the east at the Helix and silver Assembly.

It wasn't a weak point. Dane had called it a *strength* point, a place that if you could hit unsuspectingly, the loss would be enough to turn the tide of a battle.

Instantly she reached out for the Hunters, felt them moving near the river, leaping and powering into the town from the western end.

Guardian . . . they responded eagerly.

Mira concentrated on the blue and white strength spot. *There,* she projected.

She felt the Hunters' acknowledgement, sensed them shift their movement, felt their elation at joining the battle. Seconds later, explosions flared to life all around the grouped-up blue and whites as the Hunters decloaked from behind and opened fire.

Mira could feel the surprise from the enemy as the Hunters engaged, desperately trying to swing their cannons around, to defend, but it was too late. Most of them exploded and fell, the buildings they were on falling to pieces. Even one of the Spiders collapsed in on itself.

Cheers erupted from everyone on the mesa. The tide had turned . . .

From there it was surprisingly straightforward.

The White Helix and Ambassador's group followed Dane's mop-up strategy. The silvers focused on the Mantises, and the Helix leapt like a cloud of bees onto the Spiders, their Lancets punching into their armor, over and over, swarming them until each one fell in flames. The Hunters kept moving, roaming as a force, lending firepower wherever it was needed.

In minutes, what was left of the blue and whites was decimated and the old town of Rio Vista was nothing but a smoldering ruin, thick plumes of black smoke rising up into the air along with the glowing, golden crystalline shapes of the Mas'Shinra entities. More cheers, people shaking hands and hugging, Landship crews and White Helix, their differences forgotten. She could hear congratulatory radio chatter and felt a surge of pride swell up from the Assembly below.

Mira sighed in relief. Until right then, she'd had no idea how much trepidation she was carrying.

She felt Dresden's hand on her back. "You did good, kiddo."

She nodded but didn't smile, just stared down at what was left of the small town, nothing but flames now. The amount of power that had just been brought to bear at her command made her more than a little—

The sound of roaring engines filled the air.

The cheers died as everyone looked west. A flight of shapes soared through the sky, headed right for them. They closed the distance fast, and as they did, Mira saw strobic flashes as the plasma cannons on the aircraft burst to life. A volley of yellow shot downward, but not toward the mesa or even the walkers or the White Helix. It was aimed at the huge metallic bridge that spanned the river.

"What the *what?*" Dresden asked, stupefied, then everyone flinched as the ordnance hit.

Explosions flared up and down the bridge, shooting streaks of orange into the air, and there was a horrible groaning sound as the whole thing, its supports decimated, crashed under its own weight into the river in a mass of burning, warped metal.

Then the airships banked sharply and headed back west in formation, without firing another shot. Raptor gunships, blue and white. Mira listened to their engines scream as they withdrew, lost in the horizon in just a few seconds.

Everyone stared at where the bridge had been, stunned.

"What the hell just happened?" Conner yelled angrily nearby.

"We just lost our route west," Dresden replied.

He was right, their forward progress had been completely halted. Surely there were other crossing points, but the loss of this bridge so soon after their victory stung badly.

It begged certain questions too. Why wait until the end of the battle to destroy the bridge? If the Assembly had the ability to take it out so easily, why not just demolish it beforehand? Why not just demolish every single bridge up and down the river, for that matter? And why didn't those gunships participate in the battle while it was going on?

None of it made sense, and the look Dresden gave her said he agreed.

"What do we do now?" she asked.

"There's other crossing points," he said. "We'll have to follow the river south, but it's going to cost you time."

He meant time off the two weeks the Wind Traders had given her, time that was quickly running out. If she didn't make it to San Francisco by then . . .

Mira looked to the river, watching it wind south, flowing until it disappeared from sight. It felt like starting over again. In a way it was, but she had done that enough times in the last few months, hadn't she? She would just have to find a way.

One step at a time, she told herself. One step at a time . . .

MIRA SAT CROSS-LEGGED at the front of the *Wind Shear* as the ship rumbled south, following the curving line of the river. All around were other Landships, heading the same way, the biggest fleet ever assembled, but the sight had lost its impact. Every time she looked now, Mira only saw the ships that *weren't* there, the ones which had been lost. The weight was getting harder to bear.

"Your dog knows Nemo's a boy, right?" Taylor asked. "And . . . also a cat?"

Behind her, Taylor, the *Wind Shear*'s helmsman, a stocky kid of about seventeen, stood at the wheel with Parker next to him. Nemo lounged on top of one of the Grounders, ignoring Max, who stared up at him with his usual fascination. Mira wasn't sure what it was about the cat, but at least it kept the dog occupied and out of trouble.

Mira smiled. "He just doesn't run into anyone his own size that often. And, again . . . not *my* dog."

"Right, we forgot," Parker said. "He's your Menagerie boyfriend's dog."

Mira stifled the anger she felt. "Holt wasn't in the Menagerie."

"He thought about it, and that's enough for me," Parker replied.

"What'd he do to piss them off anyway?" Dresden asked. He stood next to her, along the railing, watching the fleet moving as one through the desert. "Heard the guy's got a death mark."

"He killed Tiberius Marseilles's son," she answered simply, and felt a satisfaction at the way they all stared at her.

"And he's going *back* there?" Parker asked with incredulity.

"He has a letter of assurance," Mira said.

"A 'letter of assurance.' From Tiberius Marseilles." Dresden sounded highly skeptical. "Well, he's got more guts than I do, I'll say that."

"More guts, less brains," Parker said.

Mira tried not to think about what they were implying. Holt was in danger there, no question, but he'd believed it was the best choice. Of course, that was before he saw the Landship she was supposed to be on explode in a fireball. With the state of mind he was no doubt in, that made it much worse.

If only there was some way to get word to him, to let him know, but there wasn't. She was locked onto her path now, and he was locked onto his.

"Hey," Dresden said, looking apologetic. "Didn't mean to worry you. If he's as resourceful as you say, I'm sure he'll be fine. Parker's sorry too. Right, Parker?"

"Yeah, sure," came the detached reply.

Mira smiled for the first time today. When he wanted, Dresden could be sweet. He moved to the edge of the deck, standing along the side railing, and pulled a pair of binoculars from his belt. He aimed them eastward, past the fluttering sails of all the other moving ships, staring intensely at something.

"What's out there?" Mira asked.

"Old highway, running parallel to us."

"Is it a problem?"

"Not sure," he said. "They can be."

Mira looked over the railing and saw the road he was scoping. Like most, it was full of old rusted cars, crashed into one another or left abandoned.

"How do you get a Landship through something like that?" It seemed impossible, all the cars would make it a near-impenetrable barrier for something as big as the *Wind Shear*.

"You either route around them or use one of the pass-throughs other ships have made," Dresden answered. "Problem is, Menagerie like to hide out on highways, their dune buggies and jeeps blend right in. Once you get close, they come screaming out. I just like to be careful."

While he continued scanning, Mira looked back down to the artifacts in front of her. Three Barriers, a Zephyr, and two Aleves, as well as a few dimes and quarters. The coins were from her own stock, but the combinations had come off different ships, and they all bore one thing in common. Each was a charred, blackened mass, all fused together, the components barely recognizable.

Mira had only seen it one other time, back in Currency, in the Shipyards, with the Dynamo that had exploded. She assumed that incident was some sort of freak mishap, maybe a focuser or something had been aligned wrong, but now she was sure it was much more.

She picked up one of the quarters and held it in her palm. The usual, slight vibration from a Strange Lands coin wasn't present: it sat in her hand like any other coin. With a sinking suspicion, she threw it hard against the deck.

Strange Lands coins were volatile, imbued with arcane energy that would release if they were thrown. Some kids even used them as weapons, firing them from slings and such, but this one just emitted a light spark and a fizzle and that was it. Mira watched it slide off the deck and disappear.

"You've been looking at those things all day," Dresden observed, still sighting through his optics. "What's going on?"

"Something's wrong," Mira said. "They're weakening much faster than they should, and it's not just combinations, it's individual components too. I thought it was a coincidence at first, but it's not. It's why the Barriers on the ships have been failing."

"They're dying," Dresden said. "Is that what you're saying?"

"Yes," Mira answered. All the evidence pointed to that one grim conclusion.

Dresden glanced back at Parker and the two shared a dark look. Something about what Mira had said bothered them.

Dresden slipped the binoculars back on his belt and moved to where Nemo lay across the Grounder. The cat lazily hopped onto his shoulders, and Max whined, watching the feline.

The Captain motioned for Mira to follow him. "Let me show you something."

They moved toward the rear of the ship, Max following along, his stare on Nemo. If the cat noticed or cared, he gave no indication.

Mira and Max followed Dresden and Nemo down the stairs, which led to the *Wind Shear*'s cargo hold, a big, open-ended room with an oval ceiling made of polished red wood beams, and floors striped in patterns of steel and oak. Shelves had been built into the walls, and boxes and crates filled most of the floor, packed together in ways that made paths through them. Dresden moved to one of the crates, and as he did Nemo leapt off onto another and scaled to the top, staring down contemptuously at Max.

Dresden opened the box and nodded toward it.

It was full of coins, all denominations, each wrapped in plastic in the way all Strange Lands coins were stored. They seemed to just barely wiggle and writhe there, as if trying to push away from each other, but as always Mira could never be sure it wasn't a trick of the eye.

Dresden looked at all the crates, studying each in turn. "Everything inside these is an artifact."

Mira's eyes widened. There were hundreds of containers here, it meant an artifact collection of amazing scope, and represented a fortune on the open market. "You're kidding."

"You know the Coterie?" Dresden asked.

Mira nodded. The Coterie was a small thieves' guild, one of the few Menagerie competitors, and it operated mainly along the old Canadian border.

"Parker and I found it all in an old barn outside Jackson Hole," Dresden said, moving among the boxes. "It was marked with Coterie symbols; who knows how long they'd been collecting and stashing it. Seemed a shame just to leave it there, so we loaded as much as we could into the ship. It was right before we were called back to Currency for the Grand Bargain." Dresden looked at her sourly. "What you're telling me, though, is that everything in here is either worthless or soon will be?"

Mira studied him back just as seriously. This cargo was clearly important to him, and she hated to be the bearer of bad news, but it was what it was. "Yes."

Dresden didn't react immediately, he just stared back, a whole host of thoughts flashing through his head . . . then he turned and kicked one of the crates as hard as he could. The whole stack came toppling over and shattered on the floor, spilling out batteries and paper clips and pencils and springs. Nemo retreated upward out of the way.

"We were going to finance two new Landships with this haul. Parker would have taken one, Conner's XO the other. Tone'll take all of us before we have another chance like that now."

Mira just listened, didn't say anything. It only seemed to make him angrier.

"I could trade this right now, if it wasn't for this stupid Grand Bargain!" he roared.

"Yes," Mira agreed.

"I could just leave," he said, fuming. "I *should* leave. Trade this off before everything goes to hell."

"You could, but now that you know, you'd be making a dishonest trade, which, as I understand it, is . . . kind of frowned on in Wind Trader circles."

He stared at her another moment, then kicked another box, putting his boot all the way through it. Mira winced. When he withdrew it, his boot was scratched. The sight seemed to cool him off. Dresden liked his boots. "Damn."

"I'm sorry, Dresden." Mira meant it.

He studied the boxes and crates like he was already looking at the past. When he spoke his voice was calmer, he'd blown off his steam, only simple frustration remained. "So why's it happening?"

"It must be the loss of the Strange Lands," Mira answered. "The artifacts were tied to them and now they're gone, so they're dying too." Maybe it was like what Zoey had told her, on top of that old building in Bismarck. "Order from chaos" she had said. Maybe the artifacts losing their powers was just another way the universe was putting things back the way they were supposed to be.

"If that's the case," Dresden said, "we're all in a hell of a lot of trouble."

He was right. In a world that had become as dependent on artifacts as this one, it was a chilling proposition. Landships needed them to make the wind to move across the ground. Survivors used them for light and power, heat and cold, everything from Aleves to Magnatrons would no longer work, and every city in North America would essentially have its reset button pressed. It also meant her way of life was over, she suddenly realized. There would be no more Freebooters, because there would be no more artifacts.

"So what does it mean for *us*?" Dresden asked.

Mira guessed what he meant. What she was thinking about before was in the future. There were concerns in the present to worry about too. This entire endeavor, the journey west to find Zoey, ran on artifacts. Just the Reflection Box alone was a major part of the campaign. If it failed . . .

And what about the Antimatter crystals? The White Helix's weapons she and Holt were using as bargaining chips? If they lost their power, they would have no way to earn the cooperation of the other groups, much less fight Assembly combat walkers.

"We'll have to make more combinations, more often," she said, thinking it through. "Monitor them, keep records of how fast they fail, compare the data. That way we can see if it's accelerating or constant."

"And if it's accelerating?"

She looked up at him. "Then, in a few months . . . the world's going to be a very different place."

Dresden stared back at her soberly. "A can of worms."

Then they both rocked forward as the giant ship began to slow, the vibrations under their feet softening. The *Wind Shear* was slowing down, and the look Dresden gave her said it wasn't planned.

"Now what?" he asked, and they both moved for the stairs.

THE PROJECTIONS THAT HIT Mira when she stepped back onto the deck were the strongest she'd ever felt from a single source, so powerful it would have reached her from the other end of the world. It was fear, but not the normal anxiety Mira usually felt from the Assembly, this was *mortal* fear, potent and sharp, and a wave of dizziness almost overwhelmed her.

The entire line of Landships had come to a stop, and smoke rose in torrents from the very front, about six ships ahead. Crews were running in that direction, and Dresden, Mira, and everyone on the *Wind Shear* followed. When they pushed through the parked ships and all the people, the cause of it all was obvious.

A silver Spider walker—one of the Mas'Shinra defectors judging by the armor—and a Landship had had one hell of an unfortunate incident. It looked like the huge walker had fallen over right *on top* of the ship, and the impact had been catastrophic.

The front half of the vessel was disintegrated, while what remained of the rear had split into three pieces, and one of them was burning. Its cargo was thrown everywhere . . . and so were its crew.

"Oh, God . . ." Mira said, her eyes darting from person to person on the ground, each surrounded by three or four people, trying to help. Like every other ship in the fleet, it had been carrying several Arcs of White Helix, but they would have easily leapt clear. The crew wasn't so fortunate.

"Conner!" Dresden yelled, getting the attention of his brother, who was overseeing the chaos. "What the hell?"

Conner stared back hotly. "It was the *Wind Fall*. How's *that* for irony? No one's dead, it's a damn miracle." He glared at Mira then. "This is all *your* fault."

Dresden stared back skeptically. "What'd she do, trip the Spider walker?"

"This was intentional!"

"Oh please." Dresden cut him off. "Attacking Landships by *falling* on them?"

Mira stepped forward through the crowd of people, ignoring the damage and the burning ship, all of it blending into the background as she zoned in on the source of the intense fear. It was the walker, the crumpled silver Spider on the Landship, or more specifically, the entity inside.

It was terrified and . . . weak. The projections from it came in fragmented waves, like a radio whose batteries were dying. It was awful, the intensity, the feelings. All she wanted was for it to stop, to not have to feel it . . .

Guardian. It was Ambassador, its five-legged walker standing across the waterway amid half a dozen others. *You are here.*

What can we do? she projected back.

Nothing. The Void waits.

Mira was confused.

It will cease to be, Ambassador clarified.

Mira hesitated. What was Ambassador saying, the thing was dying? She thought Assembly entities were immortal. The fear from the presence in the Spider was boiling over inside her. Mira's body was almost shaking with the thing's terror. She had to find a way, had to stop it, if for no other reason than to shut down the stream of emotion.

"You okay?" Dresden asked, studying her with concern. The White Helix watched her oddly too, but right then she didn't care. She had to find a way to stop these feelings.

Mira moved for the machine, and when she did, Dresden grabbed her and pulled her back.

"Whoa," he said, holding on. "Whoa, whoa."

She glared at him angrily. "It's dying."

"It's probably best to stay away from it," Dresden said.

"Let me go." She said it with as much heated emphasis as she could. Dresden wasn't happy about it, but he relented, released his grip.

"Your funeral," he said with a frown.

Mira walked forward, past the others, toward the fallen machine.

Guardian. What do you intend?

"I don't know," she said out loud instead of projecting. She didn't care if the others heard, she just wanted to stop these feelings. She felt the stomping of giant, mechanized legs as a dozen of the silver Assembly moved toward her and the fallen Spider, surrounding it. She passed through them and kept moving. "It defected to our side because of you and me. Which means no matter what side it was on before, if it really is dying, then it's dying for *us.*" Her voice was tight, it was hard to talk through all the fear. She still had no real understanding of *why* the thing was fading, but that could wait.

She sensed confusion from the Assembly, they seemed just as perplexed as Dresden.

This makes no sense, Ambassador projected. *This makes no difference.*

"Yes it does," she whispered.

Mira reached the giant Spider, navigating around where its legs had splayed outward, climbing up one of its actuators and pulling herself toward the fuselage. It was the first time she had ever been this close to one. Who knew, maybe it was the first time *anyone* had. The machine was enormous, its power undeniable, and yet here it was, terrified and helpless.

She crawled toward the eye, and watched it move back and forth, never resting, as if studying every millimeter of her. Mira fought through the fear bleeding off the thing . . . and then slowly placed her hand on the bare metal right next to its optics, and closed her eyes.

The fear doubled in intensity. It was the first time she had ever communed with one like this, it was different from doing it at a distance: more powerful, more intimate, more vibrant, and that made the fear almost unbearable.

She held on, resisted the urge to run, felt her heart beating. There had to be a way to stop the outpouring of feeling, she would go insane if she couldn't.

I'm here, she thought to it. *You're not alone.*

The fear didn't subside, but it felt different, a little less potent. *Guardian . . .* she heard.

An odd thought came to her: the memory of Holt holding her, on that hillside, when the Tone first fought her for control. He had been there and whispered in her ear, asked her to tell him what she missed most from the World Before. Her answer had been Hostess CupCakes, a gift he later found for her in the Drowning Plains. The point of it, though, had been to disrupt the pain of the Tone and to focus her. She wondered if she could do something similar here.

Show me your peace, Mira projected. She had no idea if the thing would understand what she was asking, for it to recall a place or time when it had been the most at peace. She found that it was easiest to communicate with the aliens with simple ideas, in the same way they communicated with her. The translation from words to impressions was as difficult for them as the opposite was for her. *Show me your peace.*

An image flared in her mind.

A giant, wavering, geometrically perfect column of energy, that must have been two or three hundred feet in diameter. It looked tangible, as if you could touch it, and it was so bright and distinct she could almost see the individual particles, gently and lazily floating upward. As she experienced it, so did the other Assembly around her, and their reaction was one and the same. An outpouring of awe, of reverence . . . and a yearning for what had been lost.

Whatever it was, it was stunningly beautiful. *What is it?*

The Nexus, it replied. *From where we came.* The reply was echoed solemnly all around her, by the dozens of Assembly, one after the other.

From where we came . . .

As comforting as the image was, Mira could feel the entity weakening, its terror returning.

Mira reached back out to it, burrowing through the thick outpouring of fear, until she found the emotion she was looking for, the one of tranquility that had arisen when the image of the Nexus had appeared. When she found it, she concentrated on it, tried to blossom it, to grow it, and slowly, very slowly, it began to work.

The feeling grew. Not just within her, but within the entity before her, and all the others nearby.

She exhaled a long, relieved breath as the terror dissolved away, enveloped by the peaceful ones, and as they did, the image came to life again, the brilliant, beautiful column of energy, stretching upward.

She felt gratitude from the entity, the only other emotion inside the bubble of placidity, and Mira knew it was meant for her.

It's okay, she told it. *It's okay now.*

The feelings lasted a few more moments, for her and the others . . .

. . . and then they faded completely. It was like watching a small breeze stir the leaves on the ground as it evaporated and moved away, drifting off, and then never seen again.

When Mira opened her eyes, the Spider had gone dark. The hum of its electronics and actuators was gone, the lights up and down its fuselage were dark, and the red, green, and blue of its "eye" had gone colorless. There was nothing now. The entity inside was silent.

Guardian . . . It was Ambassador. Mira looked to where it stood, its giant, five-legged form nearby, part of the circle of other walkers that had surrounded the fallen. Every one of them stared at her intently. *You are of us.*

There came an outpouring of gratitude from the machines, not just for what she had done for one of their own, but, apparently, for showing them that brilliant, beautiful column of energy once more. She got the impression it was something they never thought they would see again, and their thankfulness was tangible.

"Why did this happen?" Mira asked out loud. She had a feeling the answer wasn't a good one.

Ambassador responded in the way it did when it needed to impart a concept more complicated than its limited words could express. Images and sensation filled her mind, and she shut her eyes tight as it flashed by, showing her the truth, and all the unpleasantness it represented.

When it was over, she opened her eyes and looked behind her. The Wind Traders and the Helix were staring at her with a great deal of confusion; they had no idea what she had just been through. She looked for someone specific, saw him near the other Helix, watching her with concern.

Dane.

"We have a problem," she said.

"THEY'RE . . . *DYING?*" Dane asked with incredulity.

"Yes," Mira answered. She understood his shock, it seemed impossible to her too, but that's what Ambassador had shown her. "When they joined us, they disconnected themselves from the rest."

"You've mentioned that before, but how's that killing them?" Dresden asked. He stood nearby with Conner and Dane, while the crews continued to work at the wreck site behind them. The endeavor had turned into a salvage operation now, with Smitty organizing kids to pick through what was left of the *Wind Fall*'s cargo on the ground for anything of value, while he surveyed the wreck for usable parts.

"Disconnecting from the others means they no longer have access to something called the Nexus," Mira explained, and they stared at her strangely. She was struggling to explain in words what Ambassador had shown to her in imagery. "It's . . . like a power source, I think. Some kind of energy that recharges them, and if they don't enter it every so often, they die."

"Lovely," Dresden said.

"That's what happened to the Spider?" Conner asked. "It passed out and died on top of one of my *ships*!? What if this happens again?"

"It undoubtedly will," Mira said, and her gaze moved to Dane. There was a larger implication here, and she was sure he saw it too.

"We used to see them outside their ships all the time, now we hardly ever do," Dane said. "They're protected inside, aren't they?"

"They can last longer, yes, inside the armor. If they come out . . . they'll fade fast. Which means—"

"If their machines are destroyed," Dane finished for her darkly, "they're dead, just like any one of us."

Mira nodded. It was a grim realization. All this time they'd been operating under the belief that if the Assembly lost one of their machines, they would just float up and out and enter another one. The reality was, it seemed, only their *enemies* had that ability. Their silver Assembly army was very vulnerable.

Dane shook his head bitterly. "This just gets better and better."

"I couldn't care less about your little war," Conner said, holding Mira's gaze. "What I do care about is the loss of one of my ships for no reason, and the cargo it was carrying. Those are irreplaceable."

"So were the crew," Dresden said.

Conner gave him an annoyed look. "They're fine, none of them died, so I'm looking at what actually *was* lost. Profit."

"Of course, Conner," Dane replied. "Wouldn't expect you to care about anything other than your own bottom line."

"And what exactly am I *supposed* to care about?" Conner asked back. "This little girl that's been kidnapped? If you didn't have something incredibly valuable worth bargaining for when you showed up two months ago, no one would be on this fool's errand with you. *No one*. This entire coalition is held together with string, if that, and it has *six* days left." That last he said with a pointed look at Mira, then he simply turned on his heel and disappeared back toward the ships and the campfires.

When he was gone, Dresden looked at Mira. "He's right about one thing. The more you ask us to do, the closer we are to just saying the hell with it."

"Does that go for you too?" she asked back quietly.

Dresden studied her impatiently, starting to move away, back toward the *Wind Shear*. "I'm no hero. You're the only one trying to be one of those." He held her look a moment, his eyes full of . . . something unreadable. Then he disappeared back into the salvage effort, blending in with the others.

"What are we going to do?" Mira asked Dane.

"All that we can," he said. "We still have six days with the fleet, that's enough time to make it to San Francisco. Truth is, the ships weren't going to be much help there anyway. I haven't seen the ruins, but I can't imagine Landships would be able to operate inside. When we find this Phantom Regiment, and Holt and Avril get back with the Menagerie, we'll make up for losing them."

"I meant what are we going to do about the *silvers?*"

That was the real problem, wasn't it? Ambassador and his rebels numbered almost a hundred now, and if they were to be honest, represented as much power as the White Helix, and now they were apparently just as vulnerable as any other piece on the game board. The Assembly, however, could lose walker after walker and not truly suffer a single loss.

Dane rubbed his eyes tiredly. "We just have to think strategically when we use them, like any other asset, and hope we get more defectors as we go." He turned to her, confused. "Why would they do this? Why would they revolt if it was going to cost them so much?"

Mira shrugged. It was one of many things she still didn't understand about the aliens.

"Maybe it's time you found out," Dane said.

THE ASSEMBLY "CAMP" WAS nestled in a clear area of desert that was mainly compacted dirt, and it felt like walking on cement. They had definitely left the green rolling hills of northern Idaho behind. Even though it was night and the sun was hidden, the heat still bore into her through her clothes. Why would anyone live in this wasteland?

The Assembly always camped the same distance away from the *Wind Shear*. In fact, Mira was convinced if you were to measure between the two at every stop the distance would be identical. She'd made this journey many times, secretly slipping out of her bunk on the Landship and coming to sleep amid the Assembly, where she could breathe, where she could actually think.

Guardian . . . The projections came, one after the other, dozens of them. *You return.*

The machines stood like hulking shadows in the dark, and the dozen or so golden, crystalline entities that floated in the air lit them in strange, wavering bands of amber. As she approached, the walkers moved toward her.

Mira watched the glowing shapes, hovering between the walkers. Like Dane had pointed out, seeing the entities themselves was getting rarer now, as they weakened, but it was still a strange sight, knowing those golden constructs *were* the aliens, not the machines they controlled. Ironically, the walkers had much more personality than the ambiguous, glowing formations. They hovered and drifted slowly and grew brighter or dimmer, but without Mira's abilities to commune with them, they appeared docile, fragile even, and judging by what had transpired earlier, maybe they were. Mira wondered what that would be like, a true form that was nearly immobile and nonphysical. Then again, humans were probably no less mystifying to the Assembly.

Mira exhaled as the anxiety and loneliness drained away as the aliens took comfort in her closeness, able to feel each other again, just a little bit. She sat down on the warm, dusty ground and closed her eyes.

Show us, they implored. *Show us again.*

Mira knew they wanted her to picture the Nexus, the beam of energy the dying one had shared with her. She understood why, but she was too tired. It was unsettling how much effort it took to constantly push back the Assembly, to focus through them.

Show us. Show us. Show us. Show—

The projections stopped as they were overwritten by a more commanding presence, one whose colors glowed brighter than all the rest. She recognized the way those colors wavered in her mind, the same way she distinguished all the individual patterns of the Assembly.

It was Ambassador.

The others moved away as it approached. Ambassador was making them give her space, both physically and mentally. She opened her eyes and saw the huge, silver, five-legged Brute standing over her, its triangular eye bouncing back and forth as it studied her.

Guardian . . .

Thank you, she projected back, enjoying the peace and the silence.

Mira still didn't understand Ambassador's role here, why the others seemed to relent to its command, but she guessed he was some kind of "noble," much like the green and orange Royal who had pursued Zoey into the Strange Lands. Apparently, that status counted for something, even among rebels.

You have questions, Ambassador projected. It must have been obvious.

Mira did indeed, one in particular, an obvious one. *Why do you fight for us if the cost is so high?*

Because we do not believe, was the predictably cryptic answer.

In what?

In the Scion. In the Ascension.

The first of those, she understood. The Scion was what the Assembly called Zoey, but the other was an unknown.

Imagery burst to life in her mind, and she shuddered as it ripped through her. Image after image, telling a story, just like when Ambassador had explained the Nexus.

Mira watched as the now-familiar wavering, golden energy fields of the Assembly burned into someone she didn't recognize: a woman with blond hair, beautiful, like an older version of Zoey. The woman's eyes opened . . . and instead of irises or pupils or even the black, spidering trails of the Tone, they were filled with bright, golden light. The view pulled back to reveal more people, *many* more, millions probably, their eyes all glowing just like the first.

Someone stood at the top of a huge, monolithic black structure, staring down at the hosts of people below, like a queen observing her subjects. This grand image below filled that person with feelings. Excitement. Pleasure. Triumph.

That person was Zoey, standing at the very apex of the Citadel, and the feelings were *hers*.

Mira's eyes snapped open, her heart racing. *That's* what Zoey was to them? A way to . . . be *human*?

Ambassador read her thoughts. *Human is irrelevant*, it told her. *They will never be trapped again. Never without form. They sacrifice much. They sacrifice who they are.*

It was fascinating and terrifying at the same time, but it still didn't answer her question. *What do* you *want?*

To stop the Ascension.

Something dark occurred to her then, something frighteningly obvious. If Ambassador and the silvers wanted to stop the Assembly's plan so much, for whatever reason, would they be willing to kill Zoey to do it?

The feelings that exploded from Ambassador were nothing short of horrified. It even took a crunching step backward. *She is the Scion. She will Ascend us.*

To Mira, it sounded like a great contradiction. "But you just said . . ."

She will Ascend us, Ambassador explained, *but not how others believe. The Scion will make us whole. Make us as we were meant.*

Mira sighed and shook her head. She didn't understand, the concepts were too foreign, too . . . inhuman. All she knew was that Ambassador wanted to stop the horrible vision it had just shown her, and, it seemed, save humanity from a horrible fate. Beyond that, whatever else it thought, at least it was on Mira's side.

Her next question came almost subconsciously. *Are you dying too?*

The giant machine looked back. *We* all *cease to be.*

Mira smiled. "How philosophical of you."

The machine rumbled its strange, distorted sound, and while Mira was sure it wasn't the alien's version of a laugh, she did feel a lighthearted energy from it.

We are fading, it confirmed. *We have little time.*

Mira was surprised at the emotion she felt, a deep sense of regret and sadness, and it was hers, not Ambassador's. It occurred to her that the alien had been here, with her, in one way or another, longer than any of the others. She'd come to rely on it, more than she knew.

How long? she asked.

Days.

Mira's eyes closed tight. "Then that's it? Then you're dead and gone and so is everyone else?"

There is time, Guardian. We will win.

"How?" she demanded. It seemed impossible. Something about the alien's nature, its inhumanity, its inability to judge or chastise her, allowed her to be more honest with it than with Dane or Dresden or even Holt. "Where we're going they outnumber us a thousand to one!"

Because we fight as one.

Mira frowned, thinking *that* was certainly an optimistic appraisal.

The others will not, it explained. *They acknowledge Mas'Shinra. But they will not fight as one. It is their way.*

Mira thought she could see what Ambassador was getting at. He was saying the different clans would fight them separately, one at a time, not as one giant force. Still, it didn't particularly give her much comfort. *How does that help? The sheer numbers of just one clan are—*

The Electives.

Mira knew Electives were what Ambassador called each clan's specific and unique abilities, and she had seen firsthand how varied they were. The blue and whites, the Mas'Shinra, favored a balanced approach, heavy and medium walkers. The reds preferred heavy armor. Mas'Erinhah relied on stealth and speed, and Ambassador's clan, Mas'Asrana, seemed designed for strength and close-quarter fighting.

Even so, she still didn't understand. *How do the Electives help?*

They are by design, it answered. *To prevent dominance. No one Elective is superior.*

Something about that made sense. The answer occurred in the form of childhood memories. "It's like Rock, Paper, Scissors."

It wasn't a surprise, the confused emotions that came from Ambassador. *Rock. Paper. Scissors*, it projected questioningly.

"It's a game," she said. "Each player picks one of the three, and each one can beat one of the others. It's . . . kinda hard to explain, actually."

Scissors, Ambassador projected instantly.

Mira stared at the machine oddly. What was it—?

Rock.

Mira sighed. The alien was trying, unsuccessfully, to play the game. "No, we have to do it at the same time. Otherwise I can just—"

Scissors.

"Ambassador . . ."

Rock.

Paper.

Paper.

Rock.

The projections were suddenly coming from all around her now, from the others, not just Ambassador. She could feel their inquisitiveness, their fascination at the idea, simple as it was. Mira just groaned in frustration.

"Forget the game!" she yelled, and the projections ceased. "You're saying our group has an advantage, because it's more than one Elective fighting together at once?"

Correct.

"If we only face one clan at a time," Mira said to herself, "even outnumbered, we have a chance, because more than one Elective trumps a single Elective." She could feel the beginnings of something she hadn't felt in a long time. Hope. But it was dim at best.

You will see, Ambassador told her.

Mira didn't argue, she just hoped it was right. Instinctively, she looked westward, toward the beacon of light in the night sky. It was closer now, growing brighter every day.

The Nexus, Ambassador said.

It took a moment for the words to sink in. When they did, she looked back at the machine in surprise.

"That beacon *is* the Nexus?"

Each clan carries a remnant. They blend in orbit.

Mira stared back at it in a different way now. *It's beautiful.*

Ambassador rumbled its distorted, electronic sound, as if in agreement.

Do you think she's okay? Mira projected. It was clear to both of them whom Mira meant.

She is the Scion, Ambassador stated, as if that should explain everything.

Mira lay all the way back and closed her eyes, exhaling a deep breath. The incessant pushing and prodding entered her mind again, clamoring for her attention.

Show us, they pleaded. *Show us again.*

Mira smiled at how childlike they really were. The Assembly, the great conquerors of Earth, were nothing like what most survivors believed.

It is not necessary, Ambassador told her.

It's okay, she thought back. *I don't mind.*

She remembered the image of the Nexus, focused on it, fanned it brighter, and let it blend into the thoughts of the others, letting it fill them. Waves of rapture flowed over her from the entities, and Mira soaked it all in. Tomorrow, yet again, the feelings of anxiety and loneliness would return and threaten to overpower her, but that was tomorrow.

Rock, Ambassador projected again.

Scissors, projected another.

Mira laughed. Why not?

"Okay," she said, as the other machines gathered around her. "I'll teach you."

18. WE DO NOT MOURN

MARSHALL, AMBER, EVERETT, STONEY, Mira recited in her mind, over and over.

She and Max stood inside a human circle of White Helix, two thousand strong, which wrapped around in a giant loop the dusty flatland Dane had chosen for the funeral. It needed to be flat to hold the pyres, and be big enough to contain the White Helix as one large group. It was no easy task to find the right spot, and Conner had seen it as a waste of time, but she insisted. It was the least Mira could do.

All told, they had lost one hundred and seventeen Helix. A large number, but nothing compared to the almost six hundred that died during the escape from Currency. Mira prayed it was a trend that continued.

She stared at the hundred-plus small funeral pyres and the bodies wrapped in charcoal gray linen that lay on them. It was a reminder of not just the loss of life, but that it had occurred, many could argue, because of her.

Cynthia, Jonathon, Harrison, Mikhael . . .

This was her first White Helix funeral. She hadn't been invited to the ones for Gideon and those who died at the Severed Tower. The second, after Currency, had been when she was still unconscious following the battle. Mira wasn't sure she would have gone anyway, the sight of all those dead, of the travesty . . .

This time, she had to. She wanted to see them, to never forget the repercussions of what she and Holt had begun.

Bashir, Tomas, Coakley, Sumi . . .

She asked Dane for a list of their names, the ones who had fallen, and he had obliged, even though it confused him. For the Helix, death was not something to lament, it was simply a fact of their lives, but she wasn't White Helix, and she never wanted to forget the sacrifices people had made. So she memorized the names, one after the other. If she could remember their faces too, she would, but she hadn't even met all of them.

Brendan, Attila, Destiny, Margaret . . .

The fallen had been arrayed with their feet pointing toward the northeast, toward what had been the Strange Lands. Next to each pyre stood the fallen's Doyen. If the Doyen had lost more than one of his Arc, a close friend stood in his place, and they held the Lancet of the fallen warrior. The deceased's rings were still on his or her fingers, and they would burn with the body.

Dane stepped forward, the hot wind ruffling his wavy hair. Mira could sense the attention of thousands of Helix turn to him. They saw him as their leader now, and it was a weight he bore the best he could.

"There is only one thing we must learn," he said, reciting the traditional words, "one *last* thing. Tell me."

"*To face death unflinchingly,*" the crowd of Helix shouted.

"We do not mourn the fallen," Dane continued.

"*We do not mourn the fallen,*" they chanted back.

"We honor them."

"*We honor them.*"

"For they have made us stronger."

"*For they have made us stronger.*"

Dane nodded, and for just a moment, his gaze moved to Mira. She may have been the only one who could really see the conflict in his eyes, but that was for the best. The others needed to see him as strong.

"There are not more than five musical notes," he recited, "yet the combinations give rise to more melodies than can ever be heard."

Mira flinched as those who stood next to the pyres, all at once, snapped the shaft of the fallen's Lancet over their legs.

"There are not more than five primary colors, yet in combination they produce more hues than can ever been seen."

As she watched, they placed the two broken ends of the weapon underneath the pyre, so that the crystals touched, and then moved away quickly. When Antimatter crystals touched, the reaction was violent.

"There are not more than five cardinal tastes, yet they yield more flavors than can ever be tasted."

Each pyre burst into flame, and depending on the crystals, they burned in a variety of colors—mixes of red, green, and blue that lit up the dusty plain as the sun continued to set. As beautiful as the sight may have been, for Mira, it elicited only sadness.

Taylor, Sawyer, Sherman, Harris . . .

"We are strong. Together, we are stronger," Dane finished.

The Helix, as a group, knelt to the ground, their heads bowed, feeling the heat of the flames. Mira kept her eyes on the pyres, on the colors, unable to look away.

"There will be more to fall. We will grow even stronger. But we do *not* mourn."

"*We do not mourn,*" the Helix chanted.

Max sat next to her patiently, studying the colored fire, but making no sound. He and Mira watched with the others until they disbanded, moving back toward the Landships. They had only observed the flames a few minutes, but such was their way. Like Dane had said, they did not mourn.

Mira stayed, ignoring the heat from the colored flames. Her body was covered in sweat, the heat almost unbearable, but it was one of the few times something had managed to drown out the incessant projections from the Assembly. For that, she was thankful.

"You let this weigh on you too heavily," Dane said, standing next to her. She'd assumed he'd left with the others.

"How can I not?" she asked back, and in spite of her efforts to keep the bitterness from her voice, she failed. "There's *hundreds* of them."

"And why *is* that, Mira?"

She stared in shock, surprised he had asked her so bluntly. It was like a slap. "They're dead because of *me*. Is that what you want to hear? Because they're willing to die for my cause?"

"You're wrong," Dane replied. "They're willing to die for *their* cause. You don't get to have *her* all to yourself, she was the Prime to us long before you even met her. Gideon told us she was the most important thing in this world, and every one of us believes it. We're not dying for you, Mira, we're dying for Zoey. It's our choice, and you need to learn to honor it instead of being horrified by it, if you want them to follow you."

Strange as it was, she knew he was right. Mira didn't pretend to understand the White Helix, but their ways were their ways, and she didn't have a right to dismiss them. The bitterness from before dissolved away, her gaze softened. "They don't have to follow me, I have you for that."

"That can change any day," Dane said.

Mira felt cold. "Don't even say that. I have no idea how I'd do this without you, so you do *not* have my permission to make everyone else 'stronger.' Do you understand, Dane?"

"Ordering me around now?" he asked with a slight smile.

"On this particular subject, yes."

"You worry too much, you know that?"

They smiled at each other. Mira liked Dane, she decided. In the Strange Lands he had been so stubborn and stern. She still remembered how he confronted her after the Assembly stole Zoey, but she supposed that was the same emotion she was seeing now, just in another form. She didn't realize it then, but Zoey meant a lot to him, to all of them. In the time since, he'd become someone she depended on, and his presence had become a great source of comfort.

Dane looked past her, to the west. "It's getting closer."

In the far distance, the glowing, brilliant beam of energy that was the Nexus streaked upward into the sky, now that the sunlight had faded. It was growing slowly brighter.

"Every time I see it," Dane continued, "I feel this . . . hopelessness, almost. It's so far away and getting there, I have a feeling, is going to be the easy part. How do you do it?"

"Do what?" Mira asked, confused.

"Not get . . . overwhelmed. Not just give up. I've never met anyone more committed to something than you, more fearless."

Mira almost laughed out loud. If only he knew . . .

She thought through her answer. "Someone . . . important told me not to focus on the goal. Told me to keep my eyes on where I had to go next, never any further than that. So that's what I do."

Dane nodded. "Gideon always said, 'Plan for what is difficult while it is easy, do what is great while it is small.' I'm not sure it's the same thing, but it's close." She felt his eyes move to her. "You'll see him again, you know."

Somehow Dane had guessed she was talking about Holt. Maybe it was an easy guess, because the sad thing was there were very few people in her life that really qualified as "important."

"He thinks I'm dead," Mira said, and the words made her feel sad . . . and very alone.

"I *know* Avril's alive," Dane replied. "She made it out of Currency and she's survived everything at Faust. I know because if she was gone . . . I'd *feel* it. And it's not a White Helix thing, it's what happens when two people are connected, and you and Holt *are* connected."

She looked back at him then, feeling hope at what he was saying, praying it was true.

"He knows," Dane said. "Part of him, at least."

Mira touched his arm, her eyes welling up, but she fought it off.

Dane's hand closed around hers. "We're gonna be okay, Mira Toombs," he told her. "You and I."

Mira nodded, unsure what to say, but Dane didn't seem to mind. They stood there in silence, and as they watched the hundreds of burning pyres in front of them, the strange flames lighting everything in prismatic, shuddering color, her thoughts returned to Holt. Where was he right now? What was he feeling? Could he see the same stars that she could?

I'm still here, she thought to herself, though it was meant for him. I'm *still* here.

19. SKYDASH

HOLT WOKE INTO A DIZZYING array of pain he never could have imagined. As it set in, he tried to hold onto the dreams. They were of Mira, somewhere in a desert, surrounded by strange, burning colors, but try as he might, the image wouldn't remain, it just dissolved away as he woke completely, and the pain took its place.

He looked around the tiny "cell" they'd put him in, an almost perfectly shaped cube of wood and sheet metal with a fiberglass ceiling. He'd seen these cells from the outside many times. When he and Ravan had done bounty-hunter work for the Menagerie, the Armory prison was always where they took their quarry and the irony wasn't lost on him.

Pushing himself up was an agonizing process, where he could feel each of the sharp pains in the ribs they'd broken, and the stinging lacerations where they'd cut him. A part of him wondered just how much blood he'd lost, but the truth was, he didn't care. Even the pain didn't really have much of an impact anymore.

Tiberius must have been so disappointed.

The only regret he really had was Castor. The Helix was probably in one of the other cells, and if he hadn't followed Holt here he wouldn't be in this situation. He should have distanced himself from Castor the way he had from Ravan. At least she was okay, at least she was spared this.

Most likely they would be executed, probably in a very public way. Holt just hoped it—

Sounds made their way into the cell, not the normal ones of this place: gears turning, chains rattling, moans, the occasional yell from a guard to shut up. These were something else.

The soft thuds of fists impacting with a human body. The swoosh of something falling past, then crashes from down below, where it hit the platform.

Holt's cell shook. There were *footsteps* on the roof now, light and deft, and with a sinking feeling, he knew what was happening.

"Oh no," he moaned.

Seconds later the lock on the door burst apart as a glowing red crystal spear point punched through it in a shower of splinters. The door snapped open. A small, blond girl stared in at him, casually hanging by one hand from the cell door, unimpressed by the hundred-foot drop below.

"Masyn," Holt started, his voice raspy and harsh. "Listen to me . . ."

The Helix held a finger to her lips and smiled, then leapt upward out of sight, and he heard the chains of another cell rattle as she landed on it. Castor's, most likely. She was freeing them, and a swell of anger filled him. He had made peace with this, he was *done,* he could stop caring and she was ruining *all* of it.

His cell shook again. Masyn flipped down from the top and landed inside, her Lancet attached to her back. She moved straight for him.

"Masyn, take Castor, but leave me—" Masyn spun him around and slammed him face-first into the wall, and the pain that shot through his body cut off the rest of his complaints.

"She said you'd try and talk me out of it," Masyn whispered in his ear. "Unfortunately for you, we have a deal, she and I, so listen up, I'm only going to say this once. I don't give a damn about your death wish or your existential crisis or whatever it is you're going through this week, the only thing I care about is getting my friend out of here, but to do that, I have to get *you* out of here, which means you are *coming.* Get your head around the idea, because it's happening, and do *not* get in my way."

Holt looked back at her. "You have a way with words, you know that?"

Masyn shoved him toward the door. As she did, Castor scrambled down off the roof into the interior. Holt studied him. While Castor may have gotten less severe treatment, the Menagerie hadn't been gentle. He had two black eyes, his lip was swollen, and he held his arm strangely, bandages around the shoulder the crossbow bolt had punctured.

The Helix looked back at Holt, and instead of seeing anger or accusation, Holt saw mutual respect. They had both been through the same hell, after all.

"Holt," Castor said.

"Castor," Holt replied.

They stepped to the front, and Holt looked at the sheer drop under his feet, the cement and wooden floor of the Pinnacle's central platform far below. There were two bodies there, guards, and Holt remembered the scuffle and the screams. Masyn must have knocked them down there. He could see the other cell pods too, squares just like his, up and down the tower.

"How are we doing this?" Holt asked grimly, fairly sure the answer was going to be unpleasant.

"They took Castor's rings," Masyn answered. "You'll have to hold onto me, I'll jump us to the top."

"The top?!" Holt demanded. "Why not just drop down to the floor, with that . . . parachute thing you guys have?"

"Then what? Walk out the front door? How are you planning on getting off the Pinnacle?" She gave him a scornful look. "It's all planned out, just stop talking. As long as you—"

Shouts rang out from above, and Holt saw another guard yanking his rifle loose. He heard the sounds of people running on the catwalks that circled up and down the prison. They'd been seen. Any moment now the alarm would go off, and when that happened . . .

Holt could sense Masyn tense, felt her begin to lean forward. Guards or not, he didn't like this.

"Wait, *wait*! Can we talk about—"

"No."

Everything in his field of vision went yellow as Masyn jumped. Holt wasn't sure if the effect field from the rings affected whoever was close to her, or maybe just who was touching her, and right then he didn't care. He shut his eyes as they flew through the air, then felt the impact as they slammed into another cell . . . and then came the sensation of slipping.

"Holt!" Masyn yelled in annoyance. "*Grab on*, pay attention!"

He looked and saw the edge of the cell's roof as he began to fall. Desperately, he grabbed it, flinching at the pain. Bullets sparked all around them on the cell pod. The guards were firing.

"What are we doing about *them*?" Holt asked. There was no way Masyn could fight the guards and hold on to him and Castor at the same time.

"It's taken care of," she replied.

Then they were leaping back the way they'd come, only this time upward. As they did, Holt saw one of the guards aim, dead center on them. Holt winced . . .

A single gunshot echoed down from above. The guard spun and fell.

Before Holt could think more of it, they were leaping again, more bullets barely missing them. He could see what Masyn was doing: she was leap-frogging them up the side of the tower, and each time Holt had to grab onto whatever she landed on, gulp air and forget the pain, and get ready for the next leap.

Whenever one of the guards lined up on them, a bullet from above took him down.

Holt's heart sank. The possibility that Masyn had come on her own was now out of the question, and there was only one other person who could shoot that well who would be helping. It meant she had given up everything for him, and that realization filled him with dread.

Three more jumps landed them on the highest walkway of the tower, some four or five hundred feet off the platform. Masyn collapsed in exhaustion, breathing heavy, drenched in sweat. The rings helped, but with two additional passengers, those jumps must have been grueling.

Castor put his hands on her, tenderly, clearly concerned . . .

. . . and a giant, blaring alarm burst to life, echoing through the tower. Floodlights flashed on up and down the structure, lighting everything. More shouts from below, more gunfire.

"Idiots! Move!" a female voice shouted from the other end of the walkway. Holt looked up and saw Ravan shouldering the long barrel sniper rifle she was carrying, just as he expected. She looked at him, but her expression was unreadable.

Holt ignored the pain in his legs and side as he lifted Masyn to her feet, got her and Castor moving.

Bullets sparked on the underside of the walkway as they ran. When they reached Ravan, she kicked open a door at the end, and Holt saw a small platform outside, hovering over the Pinnacle's main structure, with a single metallic cable arcing downward.

Holt groaned at the sight. It was the Skydash.

"Don't start," Ravan told him, dropping the rifle and slipping off a pack, dumping the contents: four Dashclaws, wheeled pulleys that snapped onto the Skydash cables with a four-pronged grip for holding on. That was it, not even a harness to give the illusion of security.

Holt looked at Ravan with supreme displeasure. She looked back in pretty much the same way.

"Would it kill you to be grateful for once?" she asked.

"I didn't *ask* for this!" Holt answered, feeling his anger building. It was true, he hadn't asked for it, why couldn't she have just left well enough alone?

"God, you're the densest, most infuriating person I've ever known!

If the whole point of this wasn't to save your ass, I'd throw you over the railing."

"Guys . . ." Castor said, looking downward, the alarm still blaring loud enough to be heard from every Pinnacle in the city.

"Just leave me," he told them. "If you leave me, maybe Tiberius—"

"Will what? Forget I just broke his pet obsession out of prison?" Ravan advanced on him, hefting the Dashclaw like a club. "I swear to Zeus, Holt—"

"*Guys!*" Both Castor and Masyn yelled this time, and it was enough to rip their attention downward. The edges of the Armory platform, where it was covered, were swarming with Menagerie, climbing up toward them. The same thing was happening at the other Pinnacles, the Menagerie running for other Skydash lines. Gunfire lit up the platforms, and bullets whizzed through the air again.

Holt and Ravan stared at one other heatedly, then he yanked the Dashclaw out of her hands. "Let's get it over with." He attached the thing to the line and circled his arms up and around the first two prongs, then grabbed the second pair with his hands, locking him (to a debatable degree) into position.

He looked over the edge of the platform, studied the ground far far below, and exhaled a deep breath. This was not going to be—

"Get on with it!" Ravan's boot sent him flying forward, and he barely grabbed hold of the Dashclaw as he fell. With a grimace, he felt the cable absorb his weight as he flew downward, the wheels on the harness whining, louder and louder. The line connected to one of the Hubs, the smaller, suspended platforms between the much bigger Crux, and it raced upward toward him.

Holt's eyes widened as the two runners on the Hub disconnected the Dashclaw from the cable. Normally, a rider could absorb the impact when he hit, but Holt wasn't even close to 100 percent right now.

He crashed to the metal platform and rolled right to the edge, slamming into the railing, his feet dangling. He barely managed to hold on.

The Hub rocked twice more as two guards landed next to him. They saw him, struggling to hold on, and smiled. They drew their knives.

Ravan hit the Hub and rolled into one of the guards like a boulder and sent him flying off into the air.

The second guard stared at her, shocked.

Ravan swung the Dashclaw and connected with his head. The boy flattened and didn't move.

Ravan yanked Holt to his feet. Castor landed on the platform behind them. When Holt looked, he saw Masyn, a smile on her face, *running down the cable*. He shook his head. White Helix . . .

Bullets sparked all around them. Holt could see more Menagerie darting toward their Hub, and below, on the Crux, the large, central platform which hung above the Nonagon, he could see about half a dozen Menagerie waiting.

Masyn leapt onto the platform. "You guys are slow," she said, ripping the Lancet loose from her back. She jumped toward the cable that led to the Crux, used the shaft of her Lancet like a Dashclaw, holding onto it with both hands and shooting downward.

Bullets streaked upward to meet her, but it was all too little, too late.

She landed on the Crux in the middle of the Menagerie. Masyn was outnumbered seven to one, but it didn't matter.

Holt saw two Menagerie falling toward the ground almost instantly, as Masyn spun and dodged and struck out. It was impressive, but he didn't have time to enjoy the show.

Ravan shoved him toward the next cable. He felt the pain in his ribs. "Hey!"

"If you die after all this, I'm gonna be pissed," she told him.

Holt scowled as he slipped the Dashclaw onto the next wire and darted downward, the wheels whining again. On the Crux, Masyn was fighting off three Menagerie at once, and more were landing on it every second. It was going to be overrun soon.

Holt hit but stayed in control this time, only sliding about halfway before he got to his feet, slamming into two guards, driving them over the railing, watching them disappear.

Another Menagerie swung his rifle like a bat. Holt deflected the blow, but the impact was enough to send him reeling. Masyn spun and lashed outward, kicking the kid off the Crux, and he screamed as he fell out of sight.

Ravan landed, quickly followed by Castor. "Masyn!" she shouted, ripping her rifle loose and aiming back the way they'd come. Menagerie were sliding down the cable from the Armory, all the guards they'd left behind.

Ravan's gun flashed. The closest kid fell. Her gun fired again. Another dropped. Another. But there were just too many.

"*Masyn!*"

"You're sure about this?" Masyn asked back.

"Yes, please!" Ravan's gun fired twice more, two more Menagerie fell from the line.

Masyn's Lancet spun in her hands. "Which ones am I leaving again?"

Ravan pointed to three of the dozens of cables that connected to the Crux from the various Hubs and Pinnacles. "Work your way around from the Armory, it'll give us time to set up."

"Got it," Masyn replied, and a crystal fired from the end of her Lancet . . . and, to Holt's horror, punched *straight through* one of the cables holding the Crux aloft. The guards who were sliding toward them plummeted downward as the cable fell away.

Another line split apart in a shower of sparks as Masyn's glowing red crystal sliced through it like it wasn't there. As it did, she spun and caught her green spear point at the end of her Lancet with a loud harmonic ping. The platform shook . . .

"What are you *doing?*" Holt shouted in horror.

"I bet you can figure it out all by yourself," Ravan replied, firing twice more, and dropping two more sliding Menagerie.

Masyn spun again, two more cables were cut, the Crux rocked, the weight starting to add up.

Holt looked at Ravan with wide eyes. She smiled back.

"I'd hold on to something," she said, wrapping her arms around a railing. The Crux shook again, more cables split apart.

Holt desperately slid to the edge of the platform, wrapping his arms around a railing. So did Castor.

"You're a complete psychopath," Holt observed.

"We have to get to either the Machine Works or the Communications Pinnacle," she told him casually as Masyn cut more cables. "And we need to make a big entrance."

Machine Works and Communications were currently controlled by Rogan West's rebels, and Holt saw what she intended. It still didn't make it any more palatable. "Why don't we just *use* the cables like they're actually intended?"

"Because the rebels electrified them," she told him. "What's the matter? Scared of heights?"

"You *know* I'm scared of heights!"

Ravan laughed out loud.

Two more cables cut, the Crux shook violently. Holt could hear it groan as it absorbed the weight. It was all but done now. The Menagerie, no fools themselves, had seen what was coming, and were zipping down the Sky-dash toward whichever Pinnacle was closest. When the Crux went, so did the entire cable system.

"*Ravan!*" a voice shouted from a distance, and somehow it carried over all the chaos and the blaring alarms.

Holt looked upward, toward the Command Pinnacle, and the balcony at the very top. Two figures stood there, watching the action below.

Tiberius. And Avril.

Even from this distance, Holt could feel the man's hot gaze. Castor and Masyn looked up at Avril, and the girl stared back, unsure. Somehow, she and her White Helix brethren were on opposite sides of a strange conflict.

Holt watched Ravan hold Tiberius's stare, and as she did, he felt a surge of guilt. It was because of him she had done this, and her life was now irrevocably changed.

"Do it," Ravan said, her voice firm.

Masyn nodded, her Lancet spinning. The last six cables, other than the ones attaching it to the Machine Works Pinnacle, burst apart in sparks . . .

"I love this city," Castor said next to Holt, eyes full of excitement.

And then Holt shut his eyes as the Crux tore loose and fell, feeling gravity try and yank him off. He held on as the entire thing arced power-fully downward, hanging by just three cables, gaining momentum and speed. The Crux was huge. When it hit, it would decimate the Machine Works platform and anyone standing on it.

But Masyn leapt forward and grabbed the nearest railing, touching her middle and ring fingers together. A new color, this time cyan, erupted in his vision, and impossibly, he felt the Crux's momentum *begin to slow* as the effect from her rings enveloped it. It was stunning. Masyn was single-handedly slowing the Crux's descent toward the Pinnacle.

Just because it was slowed, though, in no way meant it hit gently.

The world rocked cataclysmically as the Crux slammed into the Machine Works Pinnacle's main platform, spraying splinters in a torrent as it plowed through it. It was all Holt could do to hold on, and he groaned as the impact sent tremors of pain through his body.

Everything was a confused, distorted blur after that.

He felt someone lift him up and onto the deck of the Pinnacle platform. He saw Castor and Masyn, Ravan too, all pulling themselves slowly out of what was left of the Crux. And shapes, dozens of them, pouring out of the Machine Works, carrying guns. In seconds, they were surrounded, those weapons aiming down.

Next to him, Ravan looked up at the rebels. "Hate to be dramatic," she said, breathing heavy, "but take us to your leader."

The rebels looked down at her with surreal surprise, stunned by the sudden damage and violence that had engulfed the city. Holt exhaled. Ravan had actually pulled it off. Barely.

And it was all for nothing . . .

HOLT, RAVAN, CASTOR, and Masyn walked forward in a clustered group, their hands bound, which, in Holt's injured condition, made for a very uncomfortable walk. It had taken awhile to convince Masyn to give up her Lancet and rings—it was seen as a great failing for any Helix to lose them, but eventually she'd relented. Castor hovered over her protectively, though she looked completely fierce and unintimidated.

The Machine Works Pinnacle was what it sounded like: a giant garage for fixing, modifying, and in some cases, building the Menagerie's large host of machines. Dune buggies, Hummers, Jeeps, gyrocopters, and ultralights. Holt had always liked the Machine Works, there was something encouraging about the way the Menagerie kept the old world running. He liked the sparks from the welding guns, and the whining of power wrenches. In spite of all the noise, he was always able to think better here.

As he moved, studying the collection of vehicles, it was impossible not to think about how powerful a force they could be in San Francisco. Of course, that would never happen now. Tiberius had no interest in cooperation, and he had been their best hope. These rebels were a temporary insurrection at best. Still, by denying Tiberius two key Pinnacles, they had dealt him a serious blow. Not only had he lost the vehicles stored in the Machine Works, he no longer had the ability to repair and rearm the ones he still had.

They were all ushered into the central area of the platform, reserved for Menagerie aircraft, and pushed toward a particular gyrocopter. The Menagerie had more than a hundred of the strange flying crafts, most outfitted with small-caliber machine guns, though some had been configured to carry bombs. All the gyrocopters looked basically the same: cigar shaped, one- or two-seated fuselages, with a propeller at the rear end and a larger blade up top, like a helicopter. There were no wings on the main body, just two small, thin ones that branched off the vertical stabilizer at the rear.

As they got closer, Holt noticed a pair of legs sticking out from under the gyro, welding sparks spraying from the opposite end. They stopped in front of it, the guards waiting. Whoever was underneath was who they had been brought to meet.

Another few seconds and the figure rolled out from under and sat up. It was Rogan West, the same kid Holt had met on the Commerce Pinnacle before. His long, blond hair was tied back now, and he wore grease-stained overalls and a tool belt that had definitely seen better days.

Rogan took off his welding glasses and studied each of the four in turn, and when his eyes got to Holt, he noticed that they were almost completely filled in with the Tone's blackness. West stood up and took off his gloves, shoving them in a pocket on his overalls, revealing a purple tarantula on his right wrist and a Menagerie star with four points on his left. He pulled his eyes away from Holt and nodded to the gyrocopter.

"I love gyros," he said. "Look like choppers, but they're way different. Top blade isn't actually powered, did you know that? Only the rear propeller is, and all it does is push the thing. It's the wind and the momentum that turns the top blade, and that's what gives it lift. Moving forward is what lets it fly, and the faster it goes, the higher it can climb. Something I always liked about that, something philosophical, but I could never really say what. Not much of a poet, I guess."

Rogan studied Masyn and Castor. "I don't know either of you." Then his gaze moved back to Holt and Ravan. "But you two . . . you are what I call 'known quantities.' Ravan Parkes and Holt Hawkins. Wherever you guys go, it's like you bring a damn wrecking ball with you."

Ravan seemed unimpressed. "Thought you'd be happier to see us. You *should* be."

"Happy? You just demolished one of the two Pinnacles I control. You have any idea what it's going to take to fix that?"

"Fix it?" Ravan asked, confused.

Rogan smiled at the question and shook his head. "Ah. So. *That's* what you think of me. Crazy anarchist looking to destroy everything. I don't want to destroy anything, I *fix* things, it's what I do, and it's the whole point, really. Faust is broken and no one seems to wanna fix it."

Ravan paused. "What if I said we wanted to fix it?"

"I'd say what you really mean is you're looking for my protection from Tiberius, who will surely try and recapture *this* one." He nodded to Holt. "In fact, the only reason I don't think this is some elaborate ruse by

Tiberius is because Hawkins is here with you." Rogan studied him oddly, like some piece of machinery that needed an upgrade. Holt supposed the analogy wasn't that far off. "When I saw you step into that gunfire with those grenades, I thought to myself, now there's a dead man walking. Funny thing is, you see the same thing, don't you? You just don't care. Guess I was right all along, it is about *you* after all."

Holt felt Ravan's stare, but he didn't look at her. "I didn't ask for this, and Ravan shouldn't be—"

Holt cut off as she elbowed him in one of his broken ribs. The pain was sharp.

"No," Rogan agreed. "She definitely shouldn't, but she has, so what now?"

"The answer's obvious," Ravan stated impatiently. "You bring us in, we help you take Tiberius down. More than that, we have *them*." She motioned to Castor and Masyn. "Which means we have the deal they were here to offer Tiberius. Make it with us, and he *will* fall. You have no idea what these weapons are—"

"They punch straight through solid steel from what I've heard." Rogan cut her off. "And they're reusable. Idea was to make them into bullets, I guess."

Holt stared at Rogan in surprise. What he'd just said implied more than a passing knowledge of Antimatter crystals.

"You think I could have a revolution on this scale without my own people inside?" Rogan looked back to the gyrocopter. "I'm a mechanic, I have a good eye for things. Half the spare parts you find have hidden flaws, you have to be able to tell which have any value. I see value in you, Ravan. I see value in the White Helix deal. Hawkins, though . . ."

Holt stiffened, he didn't like that this was becoming about him.

"Holt escaped Tiberius twice," Ravan answered. "It made him look less powerful, and Holt joining you can inspire others to do the same."

Rogan shook his head. "I don't see a whole lot that's particularly 'inspiring' about him."

Holt didn't argue, he didn't care. This was all a hopeless undertaking anyway, they were just waiting for the inevitable now.

"The promise of weapons, powerful ones," Rogan continued, "that's an offer for the future, when my current problems have been fixed, but it doesn't do me much good now, does it? Believe it or not, I'm not interested in destroying the Menagerie, I want to change and profit it. I want to *fix* it. Tiberius's time has come. You said it yourself, he turned down the White Helix deal. Why? Because power is never bargained for? Were those his exact words? He's a mechanical genius, I respect that. A visionary too, but . . . why *couldn't* we bargain with the White Helix? Isn't that a more direct route to power than war? We have tremendous resources and trade goods, but most of them just sit in a stockpile we could never possibly use on our own. What's weak about bartering them? Power can be increased through all kinds of means, that's what Tiberius doesn't get."

"So, you're a capitalist, then?" Ravan asked.

"Oh, I'm no Wind Trader, I'm a *pirate*. I'm just the only one who sees the world's changing."

"More than you know . . ." Holt said quietly. Rogan looked back to him.

"If you want this to work, I need two things from you," Rogan told him. "Something to help me overthrow Tiberius, first off. If that doesn't happen, then anything else we agree on isn't particularly useful."

Holt had thoughts on that. He'd spent years in Faust, he knew parts of it very well. Provided they hadn't changed, he could definitely think of ways to hurt Tiberius, maybe even take another Pinnacle.

"What's the second?" Holt asked.

"Trust," Rogan answered. "Something that shows me you're really in this. I look in your eyes and I don't see anything. Maybe what Ravan thinks of you is true, maybe you were someone once, but whatever that part of you was, I don't see it, and I don't trust you because of it. I need you to make me *believe*."

Holt had had enough. "I really don't care what you believe, Rogan."

Rogan grinned and nodded. "Pretty much the answer I expected." He looked back at Ravan, Masyn, and Castor behind her. "You three can stay, your value's obvious, but Hawkins leaves. Tomorrow we'll slip him outside in a buggie, he can head wherever he wants, but I don't want him here."

Ravan shook her head. "Holt stays or we all go."

"Then you all go," Rogan answered without hesitation, slipping his gloves back on and kneeling down to the gyro again. "Take tonight to think about it, if you want. Of course, careful deliberation doesn't really seem to be your strong suit, does it?"

He slid back under the gyrocopter and resumed his work. Holt felt his bonds cut with a knife, and saw Rogan's men doing the same to the others. They were led away, toward one of the walkways that wound up the

side of the tower, and eventually to one of the Pinnacle's residential platforms about halfway up. Masyn and Castor were led to one room, Ravan
and Holt to another.

The room was furnished with a mismatched set of end tables, a desk, a
dresser, and two small beds. Right then, nothing had ever looked more
appealing than that bed and its mattress and—

Ravan slammed him against the wall, and pain arced through his back.

"Which is it?" she demanded. "You don't see you're ruining everything?
Or you just don't give a damn?"

"I've said it a hundred times, Ravan, you should have left me there, forgotten about me, but you couldn't leave well enough alone. Like always."

"You're right, I have a real problem doing the smart thing when it comes
to you." Ravan's hand gripped the collar of his shirt tightly. In his condition,
Holt wasn't sure he could break away if he wanted. "It pisses me off, you
know? I *hate* weakness. I. Don't. Make. *Sacrifices*. Not for other people,
not for anything . . . except when it's *you*."

"I never asked you to," he told her, his voice rising as his anger and frustration built. "I don't want anything, don't you see? I was happy where I
was, everything was over and done with, and then you dragged me back
into it all again. What is it going to take for you to understand, *I don't want
you!*"

Ravan's eyes filled with more emotion than he'd ever seen from her. He
wanted her away from him, he wanted her gone, it was best for her, safer,
best for both of them really. He had to make her stop sacrificing things for
him; he wasn't worth it, because he couldn't give her what she wanted. He
would never be able to give that to anyone again.

Her grip on him loosened. When she spoke, her voice was a torn whisper. "You're right. You *didn't* ask for this. You've never asked me for anything, have you? Because you don't care about me, not really, you *never*
have, and I just keep putting myself in your crosshairs over and over
again."

"Rae . . ." Holt started.

"No," she told him. "I'm done. *It's* done. For what that's worth. Whatever debts I owed you, they're paid, now you take yourself and your things
and you leave. You leave and you never come back."

She held him against the wall another moment . . . then pushed away,
slamming the door behind her.

Holt shut his eyes, strange sensations overpowering the pain, things he hadn't felt much lately. Emotions. Bad ones. Guilt, shame, anger.

He lashed out and knocked a lamp off one of the end tables and watched it shatter on the wooden floor. It didn't make him feel any better.

Leave, Ravan had said, but where would he go? There was no place left for him now.

21. NEXUS

ZOEY LAY ON A WHITE, shaggy carpet near the fireplace, staring up at Aunt Rose as she read from a book in her lap. Try as she might, Zoey couldn't make out the words Rose was reading, even though something told her they were important.

You are my sunshine, my only sunshine . . . The song echoed everywhere, drowning out Rose's voice. She thought she could make out one word as the woman spoke it, but she wasn't sure.

It looked like . . . "dragon."

Then the dream flashed away.

ZOEY WOKE IN THE strange, black room with its wavy walls. Rose, or the woman who had once been her, sat on the couch, holding her head in her hands. Zoey had an idea why.

"It's not the way you thought it would be, is it?" Zoey asked. "The memories and the dreams."

Rose startled at the little girl's voice. When she looked up, her eyes had a wildness to them, and, for just a moment, Zoey felt a glimmer of emotion. It was fear.

"I don't like them," Rose said quietly. "They are . . . disturbing."

"When I was with the Mas'Erinhah, they showed me things I know now were memories of the Feelings. It was strange and scary, because they felt like *my* memories, but they weren't. It's probably the same for you. They're getting harder to hold back, aren't they? It's getting harder to know whose they are."

"I don't understand. My personality should be *dominant*."

"It's not that easy, Aunt Rose," Zoey said, and the woman's eyes thinned.

"Don't call me that," she said.

"It's only going to get harder if you fight it," Zoey told her. "You were fighting it before, that's why the dream ended. You were having the same one I was, weren't you? You reading the book to me, in the past. What did the book say, Aunt Rose?"

"Stop calling me that!" the woman shouted. "I *won't* experience the memories. I refuse to. They are weakness, and I am *not* weak, I am Mas'Shinra."

Zoey shook her head. "You said it yourself, you're more than that now. You're both her and you. Don't you see? It'll be the same for every Assembly that inhabits any one of them."

"That's not true."

"They'll have this same struggle, this same pain, the other mind will never let you destroy their memories, because memories are too important."

"This is not the way it was prophesied," Rose said, confused.

"Maybe you just don't understand the prophecy," Zoey told her. She felt emotion pour from Rose, more fear, but doubt now too. She felt other things, could see them, like thousands of threads that pushed out from the woman's glowing consciousness. Each thread was a memory, Zoey could tell, memories that involved her. She wondered if she could pull one of those threads, if she could bring them to the surface somehow and . . .

The emotions vanished, so did the strings. The woman stared at her sternly. "It takes strength to overcome, and so we will. You will help us."

Zoey shook her head. "I told you, I won't. Never again."

"You have no choice," Rose said. "You are the Scion. You *will* be our Ascension."

To Zoey it seemed liked the woman studied her with two different looks. One full of compassion, the other of menace.

ZOEY LAY ON A black, metallic table in another lab, arrayed with mechanical arms. Each held a wrist or ankle, keeping her pinned against the hard gurney. Inside stood four of the smaller Centurion walkers, as she was now calling them, their three-optic "eyes" studying her inquisitively. Rose was there too, watching from a corner, and she still seemed torn by their previous conversation.

"What is this for?" Zoey asked. "What are they doing?"

Pieces of the walls on either side of Zoey morphed into perfect, circular holes, and two long, actuated mechanical arms slid out. At the end of each was a strange, triangular device, made of brilliant silver metal. They looked like giant antennae, and lights flashed all over them.

"Aunt Rose," Zoey moaned, watching the arms floating toward her. She was frightened, not just by the arms, but because something about it all was very familiar. "Aunt Rose, please. What are they going to do?"

"Shh, child," the woman told her. "It will be over soon . . . and you won't remember a thing."

Something about that bothered her. *You won't remember a thing.*

The arms slid closer. An audible hum filled her ears. The Feelings welled up then, coming to the surface of their own accord, whispering and suggesting things. She followed where they led, toward the woman who had been Rose. There was emotion there now, just perceptible, under the surface.

Apprehension. Doubt.

The Feelings turned her attention to Rose's memories, and with their help, she saw the threads again. Zoey reached out with her mind and took hold of the thread the Feelings seemed to indicate . . . and then she pulled on it.

Rose gasped, feeling what Zoey was doing. "Wait . . ."

But it was too late. Zoey pulled harder, loosening the walls around those memories, letting them come to the surface, and when they did, they washed over her.

Zoey saw a nearly identical room, herself clamped to a nearly identical table, all in the past, months ago, before she had been transported away. She watched nearly identical arms with nearly identical devices encircle both sides of her head, the humming increasing, the light growing . . .

And then what had been Zoey, all her memories and experiences, were simply wiped away.

"She's learning!" The woman's voice was frantic. "She's remembering!"

This was how they had done it, she knew now. This was how they had erased her memories before, and as she pulled more and more threads, the memories of the entity inside Rose spilled out into the air like a busted dam.

The woman who had been Rose was right. She *was* remembering. And the more she remembered, the angrier she became. They were trying to do it all again. Reset her, make her another blank slate, hoping that would make her more cooperative, and it probably would, because it meant if they wiped her mind this time, she'd lose everything she had been through, everything that she had come to learn about herself, every memory she had made with Holt and Mira and the Max. All of it would be gone, all of it would have meant *nothing*.

She would not allow that to happen.

Zoey closed her eyes. She could feel every machine in the room, the tables holding her, the arms, the Centurions, all of it, and the reality was, it was all vulnerable to her. She knew that now.

It was why they had blocked her memories before: they were frightened of the power she could wield here, and they were right to be afraid, because in a place like this, with her Assembly abilities amplified by her Strange Lands–created biological structure . . . she was almost a god. She'd simply forgotten the truth.

"*No!*" Zoey shouted. Sparks sprayed from the arms reaching for her, as they contorted and collapsed to the floor. The restraints on her wrists snapped open.

"Stop her!" the woman who had been Rose yelled.

Two of the Centurions moved . . . then shuddered as Zoey overtook their controls, even with the entities inside. Their arms raised and smashed into one another, over and over, leaving each other nothing but sparking, dented, pieces of scrap.

Rose lunged for her. Zoey reached out. The last two Centurions involuntarily grabbed the woman and slammed her into a wall.

The ankle restraints snapped open. She was free, and Zoey jumped to her feet.

"Zoey, wait, please," the woman yelled, struggling against the machines holding her. "You have no idea—"

"I do too." Zoey cut her off, the anger boiling over. "I know what you did last time. It's not going to happen again." Zoey moved for the far wall and studied it. It was like everything else here, she now knew: completely under her influence.

Zoey concentrated. The wall shuddered and morphed, dissolving away into nothing. Beyond lay the interior of the Citadel, stretching down and up and away. Ships and walkers moved everywhere, pods raced along their rails. At her feet was a sheer drop into nothing, the bottom tens of thousands of feet below.

"Zoey . . ." The woman struggled, but she was locked tight. Zoey could feel her genuine fear for the little girl's safety, but she didn't care. She remembered everything now, every single little thing they had done to her, and it would never, *ever* happen again.

"It's not like I thought at first." Zoey reached out again with her mind, finding what she wanted, bringing it to her. "I thought it was me who was trapped in here with you, but that isn't how it is, not really. The truth is . . . it's all of you who are trapped in here with *me*."

Outside sparks flew into the air as one of the pods came to a stop beneath her. Zoey could feel it, the rails and the power flowing through them, she knew how to manipulate them now; it was strange she didn't see it before, but that had been the illusion the Assembly had tried to make.

Rose screamed as Zoey leapt down and onto the pod, forcing it to open with her mind. She swung inside, closed the doors, and projected outward. The pod began moving again, leaving the lab behind.

A repeating, pulsing tone of sound suddenly filled the interior of the Citadel. It blared loud and rhythmic, over and over in alarm, and as it did, the feelings and emotions from the entire array of Assembly inside blew over her like an ill wind. Word of what had happened spread instantly into the Whole, and it meant that not just the Mas'Shinra knew what was occurring: so did the other clans outside.

The Scion had escaped, the Scion was not cooperative.

In the background, she felt a tingling as the Assembly tried to shut down the rail system, but Zoey simply reached out and repowered it with her own energy. The pod didn't even slow, it just kept taking her to where she wanted.

Three Raptor gunships appeared outside, taking up positions all around her pod as it moved. Zoey ignored them, reached out and felt the rail system. The organization of it appeared in her mind, stretching and branching off into countless different strands that traveled to almost every part of the giant structure.

Zoey studied the layout, finding the right path. The pod shuddered as it switched to a different rail, moving in a new direction, gaining speed.

The emotions from the Assembly all around her shifted. They knew where she was going, they knew what she intended. The horror that filled them was powerful. She sensed the reluctant order spread to the entities in the Raptors around her.

They were to fire. They were to *kill* the Scion. There was no other choice now.

Zoey smiled. It was far too late for that.

She reached out and took control of one of the Raptors, activating its weapons. Outside she heard the high-pitched whine as the plasma cannons burst to life. One of the ships exploded and tumbled downward.

There was another explosion as a second Raptor destroyed the one she was controlling, and as it did, the pod crashed through the railing system, breaking apart.

Zoey opened the pod's doors, revealing the sheer drop below, then simply stepped into the air . . . and *fell*.

The rail system came apart above her, the pod breaking loose. All throughout the Citadel, pieces of the gridwork were falling in bursts of sparks.

She reached out as she plummeted, found the last remaining Raptor and took control of it.

The entity inside struggled, but it was no match for her. Zoey arced the ship into position beneath her . . . and she landed on its roof with a jolt. She grabbed on, held tight, and lifted the ship back into the air, feeling the energy that flowed through it flow through her. It was like she *was* the ship, and it felt amazing.

Yellow bolts of light sizzled past her, and she saw Mantis walkers on the platforms that circled the sides of the huge structure, firing up at her.

Zoey spun the Raptor and aimed at the Mantises below. Its cannons burst to life, sending plasma streaking down. Three of the Mantises took hits, exploded, and then she felt her gunship shudder. Flame burst from its engines, it contorted and began to drop, and Zoey controlled it down as more plasma bolts streaked through the air.

She looked to her left, and in the distance, through the Citadel's columns and platforms and winding rails, she saw where she was trying to get: the giant, shimmering column of energy stretching all the way to the top of the structure. She could feel it, even from here, and she knew it was tied to everything she could do and everything she was. She felt it push up into the sky above and even farther, into space where it met with similar streams from other Citadels all over the world. It was called the Nexus, and it was the source of all that the Assembly were.

It was also the key to what she had come here to do. It was the key to *destroying* them.

She guided the Raptor toward a platform, but already she could feel walkers moving toward her. They knew where she was going, and they were scared. They should be, Zoey thought. They would never hurt her or anyone else again.

The Raptor hit the platform, slid forward in a shower of sparks, and Zoey held on until it stopped. She jumped off as, behind her, the Ephemera began to lift up and out, lighting everything in brilliant, golden light.

Zoey walked purposefully, studying the platform as she did. Giant Spider walkers sat dormant in a line, unused, towering over her. Behind her she heard the frantic, digital chirpings of Mantises closing in, and she saw movement ahead, more Mantises, looking to cut her off.

Zoey reached out with her mind toward one of the unpowered Spiders and filled it with her energy. It flashed to life instantly, its engines powering up, standing up tall. She turned it to face behind her, and a dozen missiles streaked from its shoulders. She felt the heat of the explosions, felt the platform shake. The Spider kept moving, engaging the Mantises behind her.

Ahead, six more appeared. She took control of four of them, turned their guns on each other, blowing them to pieces. The other two she sent leaping off the platform, disappearing into the breach.

She brought two more Spiders to life, and they flanked her as she walked, continuing on the platform, toward where it ended in the center of the huge structure. The light from the Nexus was growing, she could feel its energy.

More walkers appeared, but they were irrelevant. She took control of them all. Some she blasted, some she sent off the edge, others she pulled along with her, surrounding her as she moved, the entities inside struggling to resist, but unable to. Behind her, the flames and destruction of where she had been made a glowing path of fire and smoke that stretched out of sight.

She reached the edge of the platform and looked to where the bright column of energy drifted lazily upward, about two hundred yards away. She had to reach it to do what needed to be done.

Zoey looked down at the platform and let her mind drift through the metal. She closed her eyes . . . and it all began reforming itself, spreading toward the Nexus, making a bridge. Zoey stepped onto it.

The alarm blared. She felt the frightened, desperate emotions from the Assembly all around her. Raptors appeared in the air as she moved, but she made them crash into one another and fall in flames.

The bridge stopped its formation a foot away from the Nexus. She could feel its power, a warming sensation that coursed through her. Just like before, the column shifted and began to bend toward her.

"Zoey!" a voice shouted.

Zoey turned and saw Rose on the platform behind her, saw the destruction she had left in her wake, saw the dozens of walkers she had dragged along with her through this place like a child's toys. "I know what this is," she yelled back at the woman. "It's the place you were born."

"Part of it, yes . . ."

"You took the energy with you, you carry it from world to world."

"We need it," the woman who had once been Rose said. "It sustains us."

"Each clan builds a Citadel. Each Citadel houses a piece of the Nexus. And the Tone is broadcast from those pieces. My powers, they come from it too, just like yours."

"Yes . . ."

"But I am born of the Strange Lands. I have no limits. I can *drain* it dry if I want, I can absorb all of it into myself, not just this piece, but the ones all over the world."

Rose's voice was shaking. "We would die. Please don't do this!"

"You've hurt so many people," Zoey said. "You won't hurt anyone else."

She reached out for the Nexus. It bent toward her even faster, bowing out in the center. She could feel the Feelings inside her recoil, trying to make her stop, but she ignored them too. If they didn't want this, they shouldn't have brought her here.

"Zoey, wait!" the woman who was Rose and not Rose shouted. "Just feel it. Just *feel* the Nexus, for one second before you do this. *Please.* Just feel it!"

It wasn't the woman's desperate voice that made her hesitate, or the words themselves, it was the emotion underneath. She felt what Rose was feeling. Horror. Not at what Zoey was about to do, but of what would be lost, and the sorrow for that loss was intense, it suggested to her that maybe, just maybe, the Nexus was something different than what she believed.

She felt agreement from the Feelings, a similar plea. It showed her what to do, showed her where to touch and feel with her mind, and instinctively, Zoey closed her eyes and reached out to the Nexus.

The outside world vanished. Her mind expanded. Warmth spread through her of a kind she had never felt. It was like having her body filled with sunlight, so much so she couldn't really feel herself anymore.

There was nothing of her left . . . and it was glorious.

No words could describe the Nexus, the pure serenity, but that wasn't what was most striking. Every sensation, from every Assembly entity outside that was trying to force its way into her mind, to plead with her, suddenly vanished . . . except from one singular, powerful source.

The Nexus itself.

With shock, Zoey sensed feeling and emotion from it. She felt it welcome her, felt it embrace her in its own way. She felt an outpouring of something she had only felt in a few instances, mostly from Mira and Holt, something she could only describe as . . . *love.*

The Nexus was more than an energy field that produced life. It was, *itself,* life. Zoey could feel its consciousness, and that consciousness, without question, was completely, undeniably gentle and benevolent. It spoke to her. Showed her things: solutions, ideas. It had waited for her coming a very long time. Zoey listened, considered what it had to say, felt the Feelings underneath it all agree. At last, the children of the Nexus could be whole and free, if only she would agree . . .

Zoey's mind raced, struggling with the new reality that had just been thrust on her. Destroying the Assembly meant destroying the Nexus, and knowing what she knew now, that was completely impossible. The Nexus was wondrously alive. The idea of killing it was horrific to even consider.

She thought of what it had shown her, and she knew what it meant, it all seemed to fit, like the final piece of some giant, cosmic puzzle. Then again she had known the truth since the Tower, hadn't she? Just not the form her actions would take. There was a strange calm that came with knowing now, with the end of the long road being so near.

She knew, finally, what she had to do.

Reluctantly, Zoey pulled her mind away from the Nexus. The world snapped back into focus. She was on the bridge, dozens of Raptors in the air all around her, guns primed. Behind her, more Spiders and Mantises waited . . . and Rose stood there, staring in desperation.

The whole experience had probably lasted seconds, but it had changed everything.

Zoey looked at Rose. Rose looked back.

"Now you see," the woman said.

"Yes." Zoey nodded. "I *am* the Scion. Your Ascension."

An outpouring of emotion flowed over her from every Assembly entity in the Citadel and outside, hundreds of thousands, all at once, and the feelings: relief, joy, anticipation.

"Sunshine . . ." the woman who had been Rose said, opening her arms to the little girl. Zoey moved to her and let herself be held, trying not to think about what was to come. There was only one real solution, because she couldn't do it alone. It was amazing, when she thought about it. How everything had lined up. Had the Tower arranged this too? Or was it simply fate?

Either way, she would know soon enough. She just hoped Mira and Holt found her soon.

22. PINCHER

GUARDIAN, THE PROJECTION came to her over the distance. *Wait for us.*

"Ambassador thinks we should wait," Mira informed the others.

"Lucky for me I don't take orders from Assembly," Conner replied.

"But you do take them from *me*," she said pointedly, looking down at the giant grid work of rails and old trains below them. They were at the crest of a hill, and at the bottom lay what remained of the West Platte Railroad Classification Yard. Once it was the largest rail yard in the Southwest, a busy hub hosting trains from all over the continent, conjoined here for repairs, reloading, and rerouting to their destinations.

Now it was a rusting junkyard. The tracks were still visible, but the desert sands were slowly overtaking them. There were probably close to a hundred locomotives, falling apart where they stood, most with their rotting lines of cars still attached.

Interesting as it was, though, it wasn't why they were here. At the far end, seven huge railway bridges stretched over the same river that had daunted them at Rio Vista, each wide enough to support a Landship. Only five of them were usable, though. Two were crammed with the charred, blackened remains of freight trains, probably strafed by Assembly Raptors long ago.

"Why didn't we come here in the first place?" Mira asked. "Rio Vista only had *one* bridge."

"Yeah, but it's a smoother ride," Dresden, standing next to her, replied. "You ever ridden over railroad tracks in a Landship? It's not fun, you have to take it slow or you'll bust an axle or a locking cap."

"Not if we sit here and wait," Conner said impatiently. "We should do this now, while we can."

Mira wasn't so sure. What bothered her about the situation was the complete lack of Assembly, especially after the welcome that had been waiting for them in Rio Vista. The aliens had accurately deduced where they were going that time, why not now? There were only so many routes over the river for a Landship.

"Where *are* they?" Mira asked with concern.

"You complain about really weird stuff," Conner said. "Wherever the Assembly are, it isn't *here*, and we should cross right now before that changes. We've got the wind for it. Besides, Smitty and that White Helix tinkerer have gotten over forty ships armed."

That was all true, but what really bothered her was not having Ambassador and the silvers with them. Even Mas'Erinhah Hunters couldn't keep up with the fleet at full Chinook, and they had been left behind this afternoon. It was just the fleet and the White Helix here now.

She looked down at Max, lying on the ground next to her. He rested his head on his paws and closed his eyes. At least *he* didn't seem concerned.

Behind them was the Wind Trader fleet. Conner had ordered them lined up in five groups that would snake carefully through the rail yard and the maze of busted trains, each toward a separate bridge, and then cross one after the other. Most of the Captains knew this yard, had used the bridges before, so they wouldn't be bogged down with pathfinding. All told, Conner said, the entire thing should only take a few hours.

Mira looked at Dane, standing in front of the hundred or so White Helix Doyen, and she could see in their eyes they were just as impatient as Conner. The only difference was they were probably hoping it *was* a trap.

"I think we should go for it," Dane said. "You see how tight and cramped it is, with all the machinery? Any walkers that show up won't be able to maneuver down there; we'll swarm them before they get a shot off. It's probably why they aren't there, they know this position isn't defensible for them."

Guardian, wait . . .

Mira pushed Ambassador and the others away. If Dane was confident, shouldn't she be too? Was it just her fear at attending more funerals like she had last night? Dane was right, she had to get over the desperate desire not to lose any more people, to not feel the guilt weigh on her, because it would happen, over and over again. That was her path now.

Everyone waited for her answer. Mira nodded. "Do it."

Dane turned to the Doyen, began giving orders. Dresden and Conner and the other captains nearby radioed their crews. Flags of different colors waved in patterns in the crow's nests of the Landships, sending the signal to the ships behind them.

Mira nudged Max with her foot. He woke up with an annoyed look, but followed after her as she walked with Dresden back toward the *Wind Shear*. The vessel sat sixth in a line of eleven, squarely in the middle. Mira wasn't sure if that was a good place to be or not.

"You're worried," Dresden observed.

"It's too easy."

He didn't say anything to indicate whether he agreed. Nemo sat lounging on the rail of the *Wind Shear*, waiting for them to return, and Max barked and shot up the gangplank toward the orange cat, but Nemo barely budged. He knew the dog couldn't reach him there, and Mira was convinced he enjoyed taunting Max. She liked that cat more every day.

Within twenty minutes the entire fleet was moving toward the rail yard, each line of a dozen or more ships snaking off toward its entry point into the labyrinth of old trains and tracks. Mira was on the helm deck with Dresden, watching as the artifact handler, Jennifer, and the helmsman, Hamilton, as well as Parker coordinated the movement of the ship. It seemed to take a lot more work to move a Landship slowly rather than fast, more critical balancing of the Chinook, the crew constantly alternating the sails between slack and tight, and all the while, Hamilton had to keep an eye on the ships in the line with them, while he maneuvered through the trains and the tracks toward their bridge.

They were making good time, though. All five lines were now in the middle of the yard, about halfway to their bridges. It was starting to look like everything was going to be okay, which, as usual, was the time when everything went wrong.

From one end of the yard, Mira heard a strange, high-pitched whirring sound.

When she looked, she saw a small, spherical-shaped object whiz upward into the air. It was too far away to make out any detail, but by the strange sounds it made and its perfect trajectory into the sky, it could only be one thing: something technological. Mira felt her heart sink.

"Dane," Dresden shouted to the Helix leader, whose eyes were already following the object. "That something of yours?"

Dane just shook his head.

From the end of the yard came a brief strobe of light as the object exploded in a harsh flash.

Lightning crackled in the sky, so bright, even in the daylight, Mira winced. A sound, like a thunderclap, echoed around them, and then the air ripped apart. That was the only way she could describe it. A huge hole of pure light shuddered into existence and everyone on the ship gasped.

"Focus!" Parker yelled. "No matter *what* happens!"

Hamilton guided the *Wind Shear* slowly forward while the crew kept working, but everyone kept their eyes on that hole. Mira knew what it had to be almost immediately. She'd made holes like that before, but she'd done it with artifact combinations called Portals. She was pretty sure what she was looking at was the same thing. Gateways, from some other place to this one.

Seconds later, Mira's suspicions were confirmed.

A large, cigar-shaped craft began to slowly push through the gateway, streaks of lightning crackling around it. As more and more of it was revealed, Mira could see it was some kind of large aircraft—and, most striking, it was painted in a color pattern she had never seen before, bold combinations of yellow and black that flared down its thick, metallic fuselage.

Ambassador had been right. The other clans had come to support the blue and whites.

Guardian, Ambassador projected to her, miles away. *What transpires?*

Instinctively, Mira opened her mind to the alien as she watched the ship push completely out of the gateway, hovering in place at the end of the rail yard. It just sat there, unmoving.

Mas'Rousha, Ambassador answered, and there was a notable sense of disgust in its projection.

"Doesn't look that tough, really," Dresden observed unconvincingly. "I mean . . . there's only one of them."

A mass of blackness erupted out of the sides of the ship, streaming into the sky. The sounds of electronic buzzing filled the air.

As they watched, the swarming cloud divided into two, one moving toward the front of the lines of Landships, while the other moved for the rear. The buzzing intensified, and Mira could see the clouds were each comprised of thousands of smaller objects. Max growled low.

"What are they doing?" Mira asked.

"It's a Pincher move," Dane said grimly from behind her. His eyes were following the swarms darting toward the Landships. "They'll destroy the ships on either end of the lines, and then—"

"We'll be trapped in the middle," Dresden finished for him. He, Mira, and Dane shared pretty much the same look. All the weaknesses Dane had pointed out earlier, the lack of mobility, a susceptibility to being swarmed, all of it suddenly now applied to *them*.

"What do we do?" Parker asked.

"We *fight*," Mira said without hesitation, not because of any bravado, but because it was the only real answer. She looked at Dane and Dresden. They nodded back.

Dane tapped the radio on his belt and talked into his headset, "All Arcs deploy, spread out and cover as many ships as . . ." His voice faded away as he moved off, his Arc raising the masks up and over their mouths and noses.

We come, Ambassador projected.

Clearly, it intended to teleport in, but Mira shook her head. *No! It's too tight for walkers. They have the advantage.* She felt a great deal of guilt at the realization. It *had* been a trap. And she had given the order to walk right into it.

"Signal all stop, all ships, fire at will!" Dresden yelled to the flagman in the crow's nest, and he started waving the colored flags in patterns. Mira watched the action spread and the giant crafts came to a stop, surrounded by the rusting hulks of old freight trains.

Then explosions flared up at the front of their line of Landships.

The swarm of strange objects completely enveloped the front of each line. Their sails shredded and fell to the decks, she saw kids falling from the topmasts, others leaping off in droves. Antimatter crystals shot upward into the sky, both from Lancets and Landship cannons, and they left trails of flame as they burst through the cloud of machines, but there were just too many.

More explosions from behind as two more ships shuddered and collapsed. Mira wasn't sure exactly what those machines were doing; they weren't firing any weapons she could see, but regardless, they were doing just as Dane said they would. In seconds, every Landship at the front and back of the five lines was burning.

The *Wind Shear* shuddered to a stop. They were trapped.

The White Helix on the *Wind Shear* leapt into the air in flashes of yellow, spreading out on the tops of the old trains. The other Arcs were doing the same. Loud harmonic pings burst to life as the cannons on the ships opened fire. The swarms buzzed toward one another now, sweeping up and down the lines.

Nemo hissed and leapt off the railing, running toward the lower decks. Mira turned to Dresden.

"We have to get out of here and into the train cars!" she yelled. "They're metal. This ship is *wood*."

Dresden gave her a severe look. "I'm not leaving my ship."

"As noble as the 'going down with the ship' thing is, you're being a horse's—"

More explosions ripped through the ships on either side of them.

They both watched as the swarm overtook them, finally meeting in the middle and converging into one gigantic, buzzing mass of small machines. Mira could see them now. Flying metallic discs, colored either yellow or black, each about the size of a Frisbee. The buzzing came from their outer halves, which spun in blurs.

Three of them slammed into the deck of the *Wind Shear,* burrowing straight into it in torrents of sawdust. Seconds later . . . they exploded in fireballs that sent the crew flying, leaving gaping holes in the deck. The things were basically exploding, flying saw blades, Mira realized in horror, and there were *thousands* of them.

Mira and Dresden hit the deck as they swarmed past, almost taking their heads off. Max barked violently, trying to leap after the things, but Mira grabbed him and held him down.

"Damn it!" Dresden yelled in agony as the beautiful, colored patchwork sails of his ship fell apart. The ship rocked again and flame shot out the sides, more of Dresden's crew fell.

Mira stared at him pointedly. "We have to—"

"I know!" he shouted back, and there was pain in his eyes. "I know."

He turned to Parker. "Get the wire crew out of the masts, and order abandon ship. Take cover in the train cars."

Parker looked just as sick as Dresden, but he didn't argue. He shouted orders, and the crew started leaping off the ship; the kids in the masts slid down what was left of the guy wires and just in time too.

Two more discs burrowed into a mast . . . then exploded.

The whole thing collapsed, the wires running between it and the secondary mast pulling both of the structures crashing onto the deck.

Dresden grabbed Hamilton and Jennifer, shoved them toward the edge of the ship. Mira grabbed Max . . . but the dog pulled loose and darted away, running like he had a purpose.

"Max!" Mira started moving for him, then felt Dresden's hands yank her back.

"That dog'll outlive all of us," he yelled. The discs were everywhere, buzzing through the air, and they seemed to be thickening. She had a pretty good idea what would happen if one of them hit her, and she pushed away the image of her head flying off her shoulders.

They all leapt and landed on the ground, and Mira felt her ankle almost break. She groaned, limped forward, and Hamilton pulled her into one of the old cargo cars with Dresden and Jennifer.

The car was rusting and dusty, but empty, except for about four White Helix at each door, firing their Lancets into the air. Dane was with them, yelling orders into his radio.

She could see Antimatter crystals streaking through the air, blowing apart a dozen discs each, but it made no real difference. White Helix weapons were meant for big targets. This was a swarm, and Mira had never seen anything like it.

To make matters worse, Mira could see the "mother ship," the one that had come in through the gateway. Some of the Antimatter crystals fired in its direction, and every time they were deflected away as some kind of sparkling, wavering energy field burst to life around the thing.

The ship was shielded, just like Ambassador's Brute walkers.

She slammed her back against the wall of the car as more Landships buckled and collapsed on either side of it.

Guardian, Ambassador's "voice" filled her mind again. *What transpires?*

More explosions, more screams. She peered out the door. Some of the braver White Helix were spinning and jumping through the swarm, cutting the machines down as they moved, but not making any real dent. As she watched, one of the discs sliced right through the center of a warrior's Lancet, splitting it in half, and he fell out of sight. Mira winced as an explosion flared up where he fell.

All is not lost, Ambassador projected back, sensing her emotions.

What can we do?

The mother ship, Ambassador projected. *Its reactor. It lies in the center.*

Mira watched more Antimatter crystals bouncing off the ship's energy field. *But we can't get through the shield!*

Another can. Look.

Mira watched again, concentrated as more explosions rocked the ground.

Two of the drones buzzed into their train car, and the Helix inside dispatched them before they could explode. In the sky, the mother ship still hovered, still pouring out more and more of the deadly drones, the area becoming saturated with them.

Then she saw it. The shield flickered, for a microsecond, every time one of them was launched. The *drones* could pass through the shield. Her eyes widened, it must be what Ambassador meant, but she had no real idea what to do with the information.

"What is it telling you?" Dane asked as he took cover next to her, a blue crystal flying back through the door of the train car onto the end of his Lancet. He must have guessed she was communicating with Ambassador.

"We have to take out the ship," she told him, shuddering as more explosions shook the train.

"How?"

Outside, Mira saw two more Landships crumple to the ground, saw more Helix fall, saw more Wind Trader crews engulfed in fire. This was a nightmare, this was—

"Mira!" Dane's voice snapped her back. *"How?"*

She told him, about the center of the ship, the shield, the drones, and with every word the same idea formed in her mind as did in Dane's. She saw the same solution as him, and a feeling of dread filled her. There was no fear in his eyes, however, no regret. There was nothing really, because he'd accepted it. Perhaps he had accepted it long ago. "I understand."

"Dane . . ." she said, the dread and the fear building. "Please don't do this."

Another explosion, they both saw his men dying outside.

"Who else can?" he asked, with a gentle smile. "One of my Arc? Should I ask them?" He would never do that, she knew. He held her gaze with strength and resolve. "Tell Avril . . ." he began, then stopped. The smile faded. "No. She'll know."

"Please," Mira begged him. Her voice was desperate, her throat ached. "I *need* you, Dane. I can't do this . . ."

His hand gripped her shoulder, but she didn't feel it. She only felt a cold numbness spreading through her. "Yes, you can, Mira Toombs. Yes, you can."

He held her gaze a moment more, then turned away, to what remained of his Arc in the train car.

"Defend this position with your lives," he told them. "Obey Mira Toombs. *She* is your Shuhan now."

The other Helix stared at Dane in shock . . . then he leapt out the steel door of the train car into the air in a flash of yellow.

Mira stood in the center of that door, explosions and shrapnel flying everywhere, but she didn't notice. She watched Dane puncture a drone with one end of his Lancet, spin through the air, and lance another. The drones sparked and died, stuck on the ends of his weapon like speared fish. Then he leapt again, up toward the ship.

She felt Dresden tackle her, force her down to the rotted floor of the car, but still she stared after Dane, watching as the shield around the mother ship flickered and let him fly through, the drones fooling it. She watched as he grabbed onto the underside of the ship, watched as he fired both ends of his Lancet straight up into its center, watched them explode in blue and green flame out the top of the craft.

The ship exploded. Violently. A concussion blast rocked the train yard and everyone around her was blown down. The flaming debris of the ship tumbled out of the sky and crashed with a sound like thunder into the ground.

The buzzing all around them silenced. The drones began to fall, thousands of them, slamming into the train cars and what was left of the Landships like a hailstorm.

And then, finally, it was over.

The drones were gone. The Assembly had been beaten. The fleet was saved. But at what cost?

Mira rolled over. Dresden looked down at her, his eyes full not just of shock, but of remorse.

The train car shook as something jumped inside. It was Max, she saw, and he had an orange ball of fur in his mouth: Nemo, hissing and scratching, completely unappreciative, but *alive*. When Max let him down, the cat ran and jumped onto Dresden's shoulders.

Dresden and Mira stared at one another, the smoke and the dust filling the air outside, and then pushing into the car, filling everything, mercifully drowning the sight of what had happened in a thick smog of gray.

THERE WERE MORE THAN FIVE HUNDRED DEAD. Their pyres stretched almost out of sight in the rail yard. The Helix had insisted on performing the ceremony here, it was preferred to cremate the remains at the sight of a battle. It was ironic, really. There were more dead in this White Helix funeral than any other, but it lasted the least amount of time. Mira wasn't sure if that was because there was so little to say . . . or because they were just getting good at it.

She stood next to Dane's pyre. They'd found his body near where the wreckage of the mother ship had fallen, and a charred length of wood that was his Lancet. Only the crystals remained unscathed, glowing in blue and green. She held the brittle staff in her hands, and it had made them black, covered in soot. His Arc had asked her to stand by his pyre. In a way, it was appropriate. It was because of her he was dead. In all fairness, she should be standing next to every one of these pyres.

Manny, Carter, Pershing, Amanda . . .

There was no way to remember all their names, it was just too many, so Mira settled for memorizing the ones she had known. It was a very long list regardless.

Five hundred. Mira felt sick.

The Wind Traders had piled onto their Landships to watch, the ones that weren't burning or lying in heaps. The funeral was quiet, no one had spoken since they assembled, the White Helix standing in a half circle around the pyres. Each one was staring at her, but they weren't looks of hatred or pain, it was merely as if they were waiting.

It suddenly occurred to Mira . . . that they were waiting for *her.*

It was a shock at first. Why? Who was she to them? Didn't they blame her, didn't they loathe her the way the Wind Traders certainly did?

We're not dying for your cause, Dane had told her not that long ago. *We're dying for ours. And you need to learn to honor it.*

She wasn't sure she could; it was a hard thing to learn, but she would try. Mira swallowed and stepped forward.

"There is only one thing we must learn," she said, surprised by how easily she remembered the words. "One *last* thing. Tell me."

"*To face death unflinchingly,*" the crowd of Helix chanted as one.

"We do not mourn the fallen." The words hurt to say, but this was not her funeral, she reminded herself, it was *theirs*.

"*We do not mourn the fallen,*" the crowd replied.

"We honor them."

"*We honor them.*"

"For they have made us . . ." her voice broke, "stronger."

"*For they have made us stronger.*"

She finished the rest of it, forcing herself to say words she didn't believe. Then she raised up what was left of Dane's Lancet and snapped it across her knee. She flinched like she had been struck. The sounds of hundreds of other snapping shafts echoed in the air, just as sharp and jarring. Mira placed the crystals on the pyre, underneath Dane's body, and stepped back.

Almost instantly, it burst into flame, an unreal mixture of blue and green fire that engulfed everything and stretched toward the sun. Everyone else was moving back, to get away from the searing heat, but Mira stood and let the swelter from the blaze wash over her, let it burn, hoping the pain would override the guilt and the anguish she felt.

For the first time since Holt had left, Mira felt tears flow down her cheeks.

THE CALM AND QUIET was unsettling now after everything that had transpired. Fires still burned throughout the rail yard. The damage had been catastrophic. Not one of the sixty-three Landships that entered this place had come out unscathed. Three of them were still in condition to work, albeit barely. Another eight could be repaired, according to Smitty. What was left, were total losses. Fifty-two beautiful, inspiring creations of the new world, more than ships, homes to their crews, each representing years of work, were gone. As difficult as that was to accept, there was an even darker statistic.

The death toll.

No one had come up with an accurate count yet for the Wind Traders, but it would be in the hundreds, just like the White Helix, there was no question. Every time she closed her eyes, Mira saw Dane, leaping upward toward that yellow-and-black ship. She wondered if she would ever not see that.

Mira climbed from the lower decks of the *Wind Shear* into the sunlight. Dresden's ship had taken a good amount of damage, lost both its masts, and had gaping holes in the main deck and the starboard side of the hull, but it was in the group Smitty thought could be repaired. That was a bit of good news, at least. Mira had come to love the ship, its crazy combination of parts and pieces, the way the silver airplane wings held the colorful sails, and especially, the crew.

As she walked slowly toward the front of the ship, the crew was already busy making repairs, the sounds of hammers and saws echoing in the air. She reached the helm deck, where Dresden stood near the wheel, studying it absently. In the distance, toward the west, a storm was gathering. It wasn't something she would have expected in this place. As she stopped next to Dresden, she watched lightning flash from the dark clouds.

"I didn't think it rained in the Barren," Mira said.

Dresden didn't look up from the wheel. "It rains. Only when it does, it's way stronger. Something about the heat and the dry air."

Mira stared at the storm. It seemed fitting, all things considered.

All around the rail yard, crews were either diligently working on their ships, or salvaging what they could for scrap. "They're leaving. Aren't they?"

Dresden nodded. "Turns out even Grand Bargains have their limits."

It was the answer she expected. The fleet was decimated, Currency was ashes, it would take years to rebuild. They'd made a bargain, a gamble really, and they'd lost. She had no intention of trying to stop them. What argument could she possibly give to make up for everything they had suffered?

"It's funny, you know?" Mira said, her voice strangely absent of any bitterness. "The calm that comes when everything's finished."

"So you're quitting too?"

Mira almost laughed. "Dane was the one holding it all together. I can't lead all of them, no one can, it's impossible."

"Maybe that was the problem," he said, his eyes following hers to the storm. "We are what we think we are, isn't that what the Helix say?"

"It's not that simple."

Dresden leaned against one of the ship's Grounders, watching the lightning flash in the distance. "You ever hear of the Tonopah Valley?"

The question wasn't what she expected, and she looked at him oddly.

"Very northern end of the Barren. Still flat, but everything's starting to get green again, lot of grass, trees, lot of pathfinding to get a ship through there. Because it's still the Barren, it gets hit with droughts, which means in the summer you have a lot of really dry vegetation, and it can all go up like a match. Several years ago, a lightning strike set it off, whole thing went up in a blaze. Flames burned through the mountains and then spread down into the valley. It was an inferno, I remember you could see the smoke from Currency."

His voice had a haunted tone to it now, far-off. Whatever the memories were, they weren't pleasant.

"There was a Captain, name was Pierce," he continued. "His ship was the *Wind Fare*, and he had the very bad luck to have been moored right in the middle of those hills when the fire started. By the time the crew was up, they were surrounded. Flames behind them, flames to the left, to the right, down in front of them where the valley was, there was nowhere to go."

"What did he do?" Mira asked.

"Pierce sent everyone but a handful of volunteers down below, had them seal everything best they could. Then he ordered full Chinook, burned his Zephyrs . . . and raced right down into that valley."

"Why?"

"Ship was gonna burn no matter what he did, fires were closing in. So Pierce figured he'd go for it, maybe punch through the fire line at the end of the valley. It was the shortest way out, after all. He took the wheel himself, from what I heard, steered toward the lowest flames he could see, trying to keep the sails from burning, 'cause if they went, it was all over. The *Wind Fare* caught fire in the low decks, and the crew inside tried to keep it all at bay. She burst out the end of the flame line like a torch on four wheels. Sails were gone, masts were cinders, wheels were melting where she stood. The crew used axes and punched a hole through the hull and got out. Three dozen on that ship, more than two survived."

Dresden finally looked at her, studying her soberly. "We all face moments like that. Choices that lie between us and what we have to do. The point where you have to decide to keep going forward . . . or just stay where you are and burn. Wind Traders call that place the Valley of Fires."

Mira felt a chill run down her spine. She related to the story more than made her comfortable. "Are you saying *you're* at that point right now, Dresden?"

Dresden exhaled a slow breath, studying her intently. "No, Mira. I'm saying *you* are."

He held her look a moment, then he turned and started back toward the center of the ship. His words had hit in an almost tangible way. He was right, wasn't he? She *was* at that point. But did she have the strength to to pick up the pieces all over again? She didn't know. She honestly didn't.

"Dresden," Mira called after him. He stopped, but didn't turn. "Captain Pierce. What happened to him?"

Dresden was silent a long moment. "He burned to death at the wheel. But he got his ship through."

Mira closed her eyes. When she opened them again, Dresden had blended back into his crew on the main deck. She sat down, staring at the storm again. It was closer now. More lightning flashed, and this time, muted thunder rolled over the rail yard.

Something just to the north of the dark clouds caught her eye then, just barely visible in the fading light. It was far away, hundreds of miles, yet so big it was still visible. A giant, hulking black construction that towered over the landscape, even the Severed Tower would have been dwarfed by it. A bright beam of pure energy shot from its apex, arcing up into the sky until it faded from view.

It was the first time Mira had ever seen the building that housed that beam, the object of this whole ordeal, the reason all of this was happening. It was the Citadel, where Zoey was. It was finally close enough to see.

Dresden's words echoed in her mind. *You have to decide whether to go forward . . . or just stay where you are and burn.*

Mira stared at that giant black monolith, deciding things, weighing options. As she did, she felt something sit down next to her. It was Max. He lay there, looking at her calmly, without his usual glare of disapproval. He put his head in her lap and closed his eyes.

Mira pet the dog on his head. In spite of it all, she smiled.

PART TWO

VALLEY OF FIRES

THE NONAGON, Avril noted, felt much larger than it looked from the outside. The stands were empty, the Turret stood motionless, it was all docile and serene, but Avril knew that underneath her feet were yards and yards of mechanics and gears that did all sorts of nasty things.

Tiberius stood a few feet away, conversing with Quade. His demeanor was calm as usual, but underneath she knew he must be tense. Holt Hawkins had not only escaped, but had been aided by one of Tiberius's most trusted lieutenants, and both had sought refuge with Rogan West. The absence of the Crux and the Skydash above was a constant reminder of the failure. Avril would have been overjoyed, but her feelings regarding Holt were conflicted now.

Archer, for all his faults, had been her brother. She remembered the dark days, struggling to survive in Midnight City, stealing food, warding off gangs and Factions. Archer had taken beatings for her, gone without food for her. Whatever he became, he had been that person once, and Holt Hawkins had ended him.

She would kill the Outlander if she could, but he'd escaped her wrath as much as Tiberius's now.

"You look troubled." Tiberius's voice startled her, she hadn't heard him approach. Quade was a dozen feet away, watching her, and his stare was strange. He seemed curious, weighing things when it came to her, though there was no indication as to what.

"So do you," Avril replied. "Ravan must sting."

"I underestimated her feelings for Hawkins," he said.

"Would it have made a difference if you had known them?"

"Yes," he answered, matter-of-factly. "I would have killed them both. These are the decisions you will one day be faced with."

Avril studied him with disdain. "You're so sure I want what you have."

"I know you better than you think," he replied evenly. "You will take what is yours eventually."

They stared at each other, and the certainty in his voice made her uneasy.

"I designed this arena, you know, each of its configurations." He studied the Nonagon, the giant banners hanging over the nine empty seating sections. "They are my favorite designs, the ones I'm most proud of."

"Only you would be proud of something like this," Avril stated, but only out of a sense of obligation to disagree with him. In reality, the place fascinated her, the danger that lurked just out of sight. For the first time in months, she felt at home, like she was back in the Strange Lands.

"You think so little of me," Tiberius replied, "and so much for your Gideon. He's done far worse than I. Forcing his students to live and die, only to make them stronger. How is that more noble than this place?"

Avril tried to think of a response, but couldn't.

"You claim to have grown strong," Tiberius continued. "I would know just how much."

"Am I supposed to fight your contraptions? I won't. I'll let them kill me."

Tiberius smiled, and there was a hint of warmth in his eyes. It angered her, that affection. Anytime she defied the man . . . it only seemed to please him.

"Oh, no," Tiberius said. "The Nonagon doesn't think, it isn't *alive*. True power can only be seen in how we deal with others."

As if waiting for a signal, Quade whistled through his fingers. Four large, burly pirates appeared through the arena's main gate. Avril watched them move forward. When they reached her, one of them, head shaved, a wicked scar down the side of the neck, stepped forward.

Avril just shook her head. "I won't fight them either. I won't do *anything* you want me to."

"That's a shame," Tiberius stated. "Today is going to be unpleasant for you then."

Avril groaned as the boy's fist doubled her over. His knee sent her crashing to the ground.

Pain lanced through her head. She tasted blood. Avril had seen it coming—who wouldn't, the way he telegraphed it? It was embarrassing, but she stood and took it anyway. She wouldn't do what her father wanted. She would die first.

A kick sent her rolling in the dirt. The world spun, pain shot through her side.

"Nothing?" Tiberius asked above her. "No response at all?"

"Go to hell . . ." she hissed.

Another kick, more pain. The toe of the boy's boot found the spot between her ribs.

"Perhaps I was wrong," Tiberius observed. "Perhaps your time in that place was a waste, after all."

The boy's boot flipped Avril onto her back. He towered over her, grabbed her by the hair . . . and punched her. Her head slammed into the dirt. Her vision blurred.

Avril began to feel something new, something that overpowered the pain. Anger. It was starting to burn and build inside her.

"There is no strength in you," Tiberius observed. "You are no warrior."

The boy dragged Avril through the dirt by her hair. The others laughed, she could hear them through the haze. It was disdainful, the way they might laugh at a beggar or a weakling.

The rage finally boiled over.

What happened next was instinctual, fueled by some primal part of herself she'd rarely seen surface. Gideon's training had always stressed fighting without emotion, that it was only when you were dispassionate that you could react in the way you needed.

All that went out the window as Avril reached back and grabbed the boy's ankles. She pulled and swung her legs up and over her head, punching her feet straight into his face, sending him reeling back.

With the momentum, she launched herself up, landing in a crouch.

The laughing stopped. Tiberius watched expectantly.

She spun and faced the boy. Blood seeped from his nose, it looked broken. He stared back in fury . . . and charged.

Avril shook her head clear, watched the boy close the distance. He was big, strong, but those were advantages easily neutralized.

She dodged a wild punch, then her foot found the right spot on his knee, snapped it, dropped the kid to the ground. Another kick to his bald head put him out cold.

The pain was forgotten now, replaced with satisfaction. When her father nodded and the three remaining pirates charged her as one, the only thing she felt was an electric sense of eagerness. It had been too long since she'd been tested, and even though she swore to resist Tiberius at every turn, she indulged herself.

It just felt too good.

The first pirate she dropped with a blow to the throat. The other two reached for her, but Avril flipped back and away, rolled, and watched the two kids follow.

They weren't overconfident anymore, they saw her as a threat now, which meant they would think things through. In its own way, that was a mistake. It gave Avril the few seconds she needed to evaluate them.

The first kid, a stocky redhead with giant biceps, was a left-hander. The second was taller, right-handed, and he wore a patch on his left eye. Good. It would limit depth perception, mask his peripheral vision.

Avril grabbed a handful of dirt and tossed it into the face of the redhead. He groaned and stepped back, blinded, and Avril leapt for the kid with the patch. She moved for his left side, didn't even have to duck to avoid his wild punch, just leaned and hit him with three lightning-quick strikes.

The kid crashed in a cloud of dust, and she stomped on his stomach, making sure he stayed down.

Avril turned slowly to face the last kid. He'd gotten his vision back, stared at her hatefully.

"You fight dirty, huh, little girl?" the redhead snarled. "Lots of tricks."

"How you fight isn't as important as whether you win." Slowly Avril circled the kid, stretching her arms, flexing her fists, loosening up. God, she felt good, better than she'd felt in weeks. "No more tricks. Just you and me, how does that sound?"

Apparently the boy found it agreeable. He stepped toward her carefully, wary for any other ruse, but there was no need. Avril wanted a fight, one-on-one.

She let him close the distance, let him strike first even. His punch wasn't bad: straight, no wasted movement, it came with speed. He was used to fighting, used to dropping his opponents quickly. That wasn't going to happen here.

Avril sidestepped, judging the redhead's balance. He didn't falter, didn't overextend. Good, she thought, she could make this last.

She dodged another punch, then shot a spinning kick toward his head. He blocked it, but the impact staggered him. Her punches came lightning fast. One connected, staggering the kid even more.

Avril closed in . . . and, surprisingly, so did *he*.

He rammed into her as she approached, driving her back, then punched and caught her on the chin.

The hit was a good one, the world went a little darker, and she flipped up and back, resetting the fight before she lost her advantage.

The redhead smiled and moved for her again. Avril spat blood onto the dirt, felt the anger build, giving her power.

She dodged two jabs, then an elbow. His next punch she grabbed with her hands and twisted the kid's wrist inward, pulling him off balance.

Her knee shot into his face, knocking him back.

She hit three more times. Another kick, two punches, both to the stomach, hard. It was all but over, but Avril still felt the pain from the one punch he'd managed to land, and the anger still boiled.

She flipped up and over him and wrapped her arms around his neck. When she landed, the impact sent the pirate crashing to the ground. Her foot found his stomach, her fists his face, her knees his solar plexus. The blows rained down. The kid resisted . . . until he lost consciousness.

Still, Avril lashed out, funneling all the anguish she'd been put through the last few weeks onto the pirate.

Her fist uncurled, making a wedge with her knuckles. Her next strike would be lethal. She aimed for the throat, felt the energy build . . .

A gunshot echoed sharply in the air. The sound jarred her from her battle lust.

Quade stood next to Tiberius, both guns drawn, both aimed at her.

Reality came crashing back. Avril felt her chest heaving in and out, felt the sweat, the heat from the sun, but she didn't look down at her opponent, she just stared into the eyes of her father.

The look he gave back seemed filled with the exact same emotions.

"How do you feel?" he asked, studying her.

Avril said nothing, just kept breathing, her heart racing. She knew what he wanted to hear, but still some part resisted.

"Say the word, Avril," her father told her. "It's only a word, and words mean so little."

She felt the emotion, like a drug almost, and it had been made all the more potent by her self-imposed inactivity. There was no question what had happened here was more than a demonstration, it was an attempt to make her feel what she was now feeling, and it had worked, as much as she might not want to admit it.

"How do you *feel*?" Tiberius asked again.

"Powerful," she replied. It was the truth.

Tiberius seemed to approve. "And so you are."

Quade lowered his guns, studying her in that strange calculating way. Avril stood up and moved away from the fallen pirates, all four motionless in the dirt.

"Tell me," Tiberius said. "What did you dislike most about the White Helix?"

The answer came too easily. "Patience was always stressed over action."

Tiberius nodded. "That would sit poorly with *you*, wouldn't it? Even as a child you couldn't stay still. Once, you escaped your guards and climbed out your window to the platform nine stories below, do you remember?"

Avril nodded with a small smile. "I made it a game. It took two days for them to catch me. You were furious."

"I didn't understand you then. I should have seen the yearnings you had for adventure, I should have encouraged them. Instead I locked you up for your own protection. It was a mistake. I should have realized that in you was the potential for true power, even more than your brother. I never looked close enough, but I'm looking *now*, Avril."

The emotions going through her were unexpected. Part of her felt a slight tenderness for the older man standing in front of her, his eyes clear of the Tone, and another part felt a revulsion for feeling it. "What do you see?" she asked.

"The future." His eyes burned into hers.

Avril stared back, conflicted, her thoughts and emotions torn asunder.

HOURS LATER, HER BODY still ached; a bandage was wrapped tight around her ribs, but the pain had been earned in action, and so it felt good.

Avril leaned against her balcony, in her old room, though none of the original vestments remained. It was just bare, wooden walls, and the sheet metal roof, with a king-size bed, an armoire, and a desk, all of which were empty.

Night had fallen and Avril stared out over the city. Even in the dark, it was a frothing, heated hub of activity. Lights from the old refinery flickered harshly, cooking stoves filled the blackness, and the huge flames from the flare towers tore at the night veil, drowning out the light from the stars. The sounds of laughter and yells and lovers' quarrels drifted up to her. Faust was electric, and ever since Tiberius had reminded her of one of her early escapes, she hadn't stopped thinking about it.

He had known exactly which buttons to push to make her confront who she was, and not for the first time today she wondered what she would have been if she had stayed. Just another Archer, consumed in her own darkness? Or would she have managed something else? She would never know, of course, but the question nagged at her.

A knock at the door startled her.

"Come," she said. When it opened, Quade stood outside, the last person Avril expected.

"May I?" he asked. His voice was full of strength, but somehow quiet too. There was an introspectiveness to Quade. He was more than just one of her father's thugs, he was cunning, but you had to be to rise as far as he had.

Avril nodded and he stepped into the room.

"You did good today," he observed. "For all the lip service it gets, wouldn't have thought White Helix fighting styles to be so effective."

"I guess that's a compliment," Avril remarked, studying him warily. "Is that what you came to tell me?"

Quade hesitated only a moment, then he spoke, simply and to the point. He didn't whisper, didn't look around, and Avril sensed very little fear or apprehension in his eyes. "Tiberius's time is done, the Menagerie can't go any further with him. He's too swept up in the wrong things, so . . . me and a few others have been encouraging change."

Avril was more than a little surprised, not just by the words, but by the fact that he was saying them to *her*. He didn't seem threatened that she might go to her father.

"You're working with Rogan West." Avril stated the obvious. "For how long?"

"Pretty quick after they took those Pinnacles. First time anyone's ever gotten that far, but I knew it wasn't gonna last unless someone kept the momentum going. Tiberius is just too smart."

"*Momentum* kind of faltered at the attack on the Commerce Pinnacle, didn't it?"

Quade frowned. "That would have worked if it hadn't been for Hawkins. That attack was smart, I don't care what anyone says. We're not gonna take any more Pinnacles, security's too tight now; we have to find other ways to bring Tiberius down, and there's only one real option. Erode his public opinion. Like any leader, he only has power if people let him keep it."

"Or if he's dead," Avril said. "Why not just kill him?"

"What good does that do? The rules say only a Consul rank can challenge for leadership, and Marek is firmly in Tiberius's pocket. Anyone else who kills Tiberius is just an assassin, and they're gonna be dead a few seconds later. Killing him's no way to take power, and power's all that matters here."

His frankness seemed to know no bounds, and she studied him curiously. "What's your angle? You want Tiberius's crown?"

Quade snorted in contempt. "I got enough power, don't need no more, and that's really the problem. Here, enough is never enough. People kill and scheme and climb over each other to reach the top, and all of it's encouraged by your dad, because he doesn't see the world any other way than that. Whole damn thing is starting to fall apart because no one looks out for anyone else but themselves. Say what you want about the Wind Traders, but they got each other's backs. I worked too long and hard to get where I am to see it all go to hell, and I don't got much time left anyway."

He was right, Avril saw. His eyes were nearly full of the Tone's black tendrils.

"Real question is," Quade kept on, locking his eyes on hers. "What do *you* want?"

Avril stared back. After today, the answer was a confusing one. "I don't know anymore."

Quade studied her in that same inquisitive way. "Well, figure it out soon. You got a card in the game now, but it's losing value by the second." He moved for the door, but Avril had one more question.

"Why tell me this, Quade?" she asked. "Why are you sure I won't tell Tiberius?"

"I'm not," Quade said, stopping in the door. "I'm just hopeful. First time in a long time, actually." Then he stepped through and closed it behind him.

It was clear what he'd meant. Now that she knew of his betrayal, she had a card to play. She could tell her father about Quade or not. Prior to today, there was no way she would have told anyone, but now . . .

Things were less clear. Avril stared back out over the city.

What was she doing? Playing Faust politics? It was the opposite of what she intended coming here, but things had changed, hadn't they? She could try and deny it, but the truth was she enjoyed the Nonagon this morning, still felt the tingling of adrenaline. She'd told Gideon more than once she wasn't very good at patience. Here, she had found something she never expected. Here, she could *be* herself, as she wanted.

Looking out over the city, she saw the possibilities. It *could* all be hers, she knew. Who was there that could possibly challenge her?

The ninth Keystone of the White Helix played in her mind. *Temptation shows us who we are*. It had never occurred to her to ask Gideon: if that was the case, then what was the point in resisting?

25. COMPASS

THE BOX WAS AN OLD AMMO CASE, maybe four feet long, wooden and colored with old, faded green paint. The lid had been replaced with Plexiglas, letting Holt and the dozen or so pirates that had crowded around him see inside, and what *was* inside would make most people cringe.

But Holt wasn't like most people anymore.

It was a Devil's Box, a game unique to Faust, and Holt stuck his arm through a hole in one end. At the other sat the box's only inhabitant, its long, thick body wrapped in a tight coil. It was easily the biggest rattlesnake he'd ever seen, and the rattler on its tail vibrated and rose as Holt's fist moved inside.

It was still strange, the lack of emotion. He'd seen Devil's Boxes before, watched kids gamble their lives for credits, but he'd always just shook his head at the idiocy of it. Now though, the box took on new meaning. Maybe *it* could make him feel something again. Maybe raw, primal fear could override the apathy, but this was his third time trying the box, and so far he still felt nothing.

It sat on a table in the Machine Works Pinnacle's makeshift food court. Rogan West's rebels had set up a temporary one here. Everywhere were stalls selling harvested fruits and vegetables, nonperishables, water, all of it plundered from outside the city. Meat sizzled on grills, and there was a plate of beef and peppers in front of him that Holt hadn't touched.

Excited murmurs passed through the crowd. Bets were placed. Seconds later, something was pushed through another hole in the box's side. A small, gray mouse quickly scurried forward, darting through a field of rocks inside the case between Holt's hand and the snake, looking for shelter, but there wasn't any.

The snake's eyes shifted to the mouse, its forked tongue tested the air.

Holt watched too, his eyes shifting from the snake to the mouse and back again, waiting for the right moment.

Then his hand shot forward, grabbed the mouse in his fist. The snake uncoiled in a lightning-quick move that flung it forward.

Holt snapped his hand back. Rocks and dirt sprayed everywhere where the snake hit. It struck again, just as fast, its rattle shaking.

Holt ripped his hand out. The crowd murmured, pressing in to see. Holt studied his skin, but there were no bite marks. He'd done it. Again. He let the squirming mouse loose, and sat back in his chair. The crowd erupted in a variety of reactions, some pleased, some angry. Bitterly Holt felt none of those things, just watched as everyone collected their winnings.

"Again?" a hopeful rebel asked.

Holt stared in through the glass at the snake, withdrawn back to its corner. Its strange eyes, yellow with vertical slits, stared back eagerly.

"I think he's done for now," a small voice said. Holt looked up as the crowd parted. Olive stood there, radiating a fierceness even the rattlesnake couldn't match. The pirates mumbled in disappointment and moved off, leaving them alone.

Olive studied him darkly. Clearly she disapproved of the depths to which he'd sunk, but, like everything else, her reaction failed to illicit a response. Her eyes roamed over the bruises and cuts she could see on him, Tiberius's little welcome-home presents.

"Really worked you over, didn't they?" she asked, sitting in the chair opposite his, the Devil's Box in between them. She didn't look at the snake.

"How'd you get here?" Holt asked. He'd forgotten about Olive and her crew, their ship still held at the Commerce Pinnacle. This was Machine Works, one of the two Pinnacles the rebels controlled, and not only was it under siege, the Skydash was gone, Ravan and Masyn had seen to that. Getting here couldn't have been easy.

"Saw you and Ravan's little escape, figured whatever leeway I had in this place was about to run out. Getting here wasn't that big a deal. Gotten pretty good at finding ways through dangerous places over the years." Her eyes shifted down to the snake in the box, studying it with interest. "They locked down the *Wind Rift,* put my crew in 'quarantine,' gonna strip it for real now, which means they'll probably kill every one of my guys."

"What does that have to do with me?" Holt asked impatiently.

She looked up at him sharply. "I want to know what the plan is. I want to know how we're going to break them out and get to San Francisco where we're supposed to be."

"If you want plans, you've come to the wrong place," he said. "Ravan and West, they have plans, but I doubt they involve your ship. They gave me a jeep, couple tanks of gas, I'm supposed to leave in the morning. You wanna get to San Francisco, you're welcome to tag along."

"You're going back by yourself? They're expecting you with an army of Menagerie!"

"Do you see any possible way that that can happen now?"

Olive stared at him like a complete stranger. "Would you rather be back in that cell they locked you up in?"

Holt stared right back. "What's the difference?"

Olive moved with a speed even faster than the rattler, and slapped him in the face with as much force as her small frame allowed. It was enough to rock his head to the side.

Laughter erupted in the food court, and Holt stared at Olive in shock. She glared back in disgust.

"She wouldn't give up," Olive said. "If *you* were gone, *she* wouldn't give up."

"I'm still here, aren't I?" His voice was bitter.

"No, you're not," Olive answered back. "When that ship went down, it was like a light turned off inside you. You've been sleepwalking through everything since, because you don't *care* anymore. I'm sorry you lost her. I am. She was special, and I loved her too, but she *is* gone. Everyone on this planet has lost someone. The difference is you still have people who care about you, people who are *here*. People, from what I understand, that have sacrificed a lot for you, and the least you could do, the very least . . . is *try*."

The words gave Holt the first emotion he'd felt in days . . . and it was shame. He tried to hold Olive's stern gaze, but failed, looked away.

Something fell on top of the Devil's Box, a necklace of some kind.

"She wanted you to have that," Olive said. "Said to give it to you if you lost your way, said you'd know what it meant."

Holt could see what it was now. The little brass compass Mira wore. Zoey had one just like it, they were both Strange Lands artifacts. Instead of pointing north, they pointed at each other.

Holt stared at the compass with far more fear than the snake. It wasn't just that it used to be *Mira's,* an actual physical link that had *touched* her, but more so what it represented now: a call back to reality. The truth was, he liked his wallowing. He liked the pain, he liked the relief that came with not caring. If he *really* wanted to feel something again, the opportunity was right there. All he had to do was take it.

"Tough thing about the world is that there's always something more important than ourselves," Olive said. "Much as we hope otherwise."

Slowly, Holt reached for the necklace, felt the chain intertwine with his fingers. It was warm, it felt alive. He held the small compass, turned it so he could see the needle. It pointed *northwest*, toward its other half, and the person who owned it. Someone he loved. Someone who loved him. Someone he had neglected in his descent into self-pity.

The needle pointed to Zoey.

His vision glazed, and he shut his eyes, keeping the tears away. He heard Olive turn and walk off, headed back the way she'd come.

"Wait . . ." he said, his voice hoarse. When he opened his eyes, the tiny Captain had stopped and turned back, studying him.

"Your ship." Holt slipped the necklace around his neck, let it fall under his shirt. "Just how 'locked down' is it?"

THEY WERE IN THE work bay when he found them, where the gyrocopters sat. A dozen rebels, West, as well as Ravan, Masyn, and Castor, stood around a crudely drawn map on a workbench, and from behind them, Holt could just make out that it was of the Commerce Pinnacle. They were going to try and hit it again.

"Without the Skydash, the options are limited," Rogan said.

"Air-drop people onto the platform?" a pirate suggested.

Ravan shook her head. "We don't have enough gyros to put men in there to make a difference."

"But with your White Helix support—"

"You're looking at it all wrong," Holt said, interrupting them.

Everyone at the table turned, and their eyes almost universally held contempt. Ravan just looked back down at the map with a scowl. There was a trickle of emotion then, at the way she tensed. Even though it was unpleasant, knowing he'd hurt her, knowing how she felt about him, it still felt good in its own way, good to feel *something*.

"You're supposed to be packing, Hawkins," Rogan said. "And no one's interested in your opinion."

"That's a shame," he replied, "because you're going after the wrong Pinnacle."

They stared at him skeptically. "How's that?"

"You need a knockout punch. The longer you stay entrenched, the more momentum you lose, and Tiberius hasn't even done his counterattack yet."

"So what Pinnacle would you hit, then?"

"Refinery," Holt stated. "Take Refinery, you take the city." The reactions he got were the ones he expected. Some of the rebels laughed, others just rolled their eyes. Ravan, though, looked up at him curiously.

"That's definitely true," West said. "It's why the Refinery Pinnacle's the most heavily guarded of the bunch. There's no way to take it in a stand-up fight."

"A stand-up fight is definitely not what I'm proposing." Holt looked at Ravan pointedly. The way she stared back implied she knew where he was going.

"They may have changed it," she said, thinking it through. "All it takes is the flip of a switch. Even if they haven't, you'll still need more."

"I've got more."

"You two clearly have some kind of plan forming," Rogan stated, his eyes still on Holt. "Fact remains, I still don't know if you're really committed to this."

It was what Holt expected, and there was an obvious answer. He'd thought it through on his way over, all the ramifications, all the consequences. They were significant . . . but he was tired of breaking promises.

Holt held up his right hand, showed the half-formed image on the wrist. "Finish it," he said.

Ravan's eyes widened, she looked at him in a completely different way. Even Rogan seemed surprised.

"That's a binding agreement in all kinds of ways," the rebel leader said.

"It's a promise I'm willing to make." His gaze moved to Ravan. She stared back. "You want to take this city or not?"

IT WAS A NIGHT WITHOUT A MOON, which, Olive figured, was probably the plan. The ground under the Commerce Pinnacle was nearly black as she, Masyn, and Castor moved silently through it. Above them, through gaps in the platform's wooden beams, they could see the flickering lights of the flare tower and the pirates. There were a hundred probably, guarding her crew, being held in the Pinnacle's lower-level rooms.

They crept past the giant beams that held the platform, moving toward their goal. Olive could just make out the *Wind Rift*'s three custom-made wheels in the shadows ahead, and she felt relief pour through her. The pirates hadn't stripped her yet.

The glowing crystals on Masyn's Lancet had been covered with black cloth. A similar cloth was wrapped around the rings of her left hand. Castor didn't have to worry about that: he'd lost his to Tiberius days ago, and it weighed on him greatly. From what Olive understood, losing a Lancet or a ring was a source of great shame to the Helix, and unless he recovered them, he would be an outcast. It seemed harsh, but the Strange Lands were a harsh place. It made sense that its people would be just as severe.

They reached the end of the platform, nothing but open desert and the *Wind Rift*'s giant wheels in front of them. The voices from the pirates were dimmer, and Olive stared up at the deck of the ship, some thirty feet above. The hull sloped down and under toward the ground, which meant you would be climbing it at a negative angle. It looked impossible.

Masyn shook her head. "That's a hell of a climb. Barely any handholds, all grip and back strength. Not sure how you're going to get up, Castor."

He looked at her severely. "I can do it." Castor's shoulder was wrapped tightly with bandages, his arm tucked into his chest from his run-in with a crossbow bolt.

Masyn didn't even look at him. "Not without rings or with that shoulder. You probably should just stay down here where it's safe."

Castor glared at her, then jumped and grabbed the wooden hull with his one good hand. He swung his legs, using the momentum to shoot up and grab another handhold.

Masyn smiled then, watching him climb. Olive wasn't sure where he was finding places to grip, the ship was almost completely smooth, it was impressive.

"Were you baiting him?" Olive asked.

Masyn shrugged. "He needs to get back on his feet and stop moping." While the remark may have seemed dismissive, there was a tenderness there. Castor was important to Masyn, and it bothered her how dejected he'd been, White Helix rules or not.

Above, Castor's form slipped over the railing. A second later he reappeared, and Masyn threw up a thick coil of rope. He caught it, tied it off, let it drape back down.

Masyn grabbed one end. "Wait here, remember what we said."

The girl pulled herself straight up, not even bothering to use her legs. When she reached the top, she and Castor grabbed the rope. It was her signal. Olive grabbed it too . . . then felt it *lift*. The two Helix pulled her up, and she slipped over the railing onto her back.

At the middle of the ship, where the gangplank led down to the dock, three Menagerie stood, laughing and talking, their backs to them. They hadn't seen their climb.

Masyn silently unstrapped the Lancet from her back, and she gave Olive a meaningful look. Olive felt her pulse quicken. She could do this, she told herself. The Menagerie weren't getting her ship.

Masyn and Castor moved toward the three pirates in complete silence. They reached them in seconds. In less time than that, the pirates were down, then they separated, moved farther ahead, disappearing in the shadows.

Now it was her turn. Olive swallowed, made her feet start moving. She could still hear the voices from the rest of the pirates below, could see the orange light from their fires and lanterns.

She reached the helm deck, moved for the Grounders sitting next to the ship's huge wheel, opened the one she was looking for. Inside was the ship's Zephyr, a complicated, four-tier artifact combination, with a small ring of quarters inset into its exterior. Zephyrs and Chinooks, a Landship's two most important artifacts, were often confused. Chinooks amplified existing wind into a strong enough force to propel the giant ships over the ground. A

Zephyr, however, created wind where there was none at all. It was a fail-safe artifact, if the ship found itself in a dead calm. Unlike Chinooks, Zephyrs could only be used once, but Olive had no problem burning this one.

She chewed her lip, then slid the ring of quarters all the way to the top of the artifact combination.

Wind roared to life in a maelstrom above her head. The sails had all been stowed, there was nothing to contain it, it just blew like a hurricane.

The pirates on the platform stared up at the huge ship as the wind raged. A few of them turned and headed right where she hoped. For the door to the storage building holding her crew.

She saw the pirates yank it open, start pulling the Wind Traders out and yelling at them, pointing toward the ship. It was working: the pirates were freeing the crew, telling them to deal with whatever was going on.

Everything that happened next happened in a blur.

A streak of red shot through the air and punched through the platform in a blaze of flame. It was followed by a blue one that did the same thing. A dozen pirates fell through the crippled woodwork and vanished. The rest pulled their guns, guessing what was happening now. That was Olive's next signal.

She reached for another Grounder, revealed the Chinook. She dialed it up to its highest setting . . . then twisted the artifact ninety degrees to port. The wind shuddered as it aimed to the side, roaring down toward the platform under the ship. Pirates were blown off their feet, sent hurdling into the air, and slamming into the Pinnacle tower.

"Now!" Olive yelled.

Masyn landed on the dock in a flash of cyan, right in the middle of the Menagerie. The platform exploded as she recalled her two crystal spear points from beneath, reconnecting onto either end of her Lancet. Her rings lit up the night as she spun and struck.

Castor, even with one useless arm and no rings, was still a threat. He took out three pirates as he shoved the *Wind Rift* crew toward the ship. Olive switched off the Chinook and the Zephyr and ran to meet them.

Casper, the helmsman, was first on, and he looked at her wide-eyed. "Captain. Damn good to see *you*."

"You too," she replied, as more crew were running up. "Get to the helm. Everyone else, get us unhitched, sails unfurled, fast as you can!"

They dashed away and Olive's trepidation grew. She was relieved to see them unharmed, but the truth was, if they didn't pull this off, they were all going to die, and not later, but tonight. Olive jumped in herself, helping to untie the colorful sails.

Below, Masyn flipped and darted amid the pirates, sending them flying. Castor was dropping his share as well. But they were both about to be overwhelmed. Menagerie were pouring onto the dock, their guns flashing. Olive ducked as bullets sparked against the ship's hull.

The first sail unfurled, the front one. She looked around, watched the last of the mooring ropes coming off the ship. They were loose.

"Casper! Chinook, full blast!"

He stared at her like she was crazy. "There's only one sail!"

"I'm not blind, just do it!"

A flurry of gunfire snapped him to action. He raced for the Grounders.

Olive hurried to help the others get the second sail up. Casper was right to be worried. Most sails weren't stitched strong enough to contain the blast from a Chinook at full power all by themselves, most would rip to shreds, and it took a full blast to move a Landship with just one sail. Olive prayed hers would hold.

The Chinook roared. The sail inflated in vibrant color. Olive saw it bow outward like it never had before, absorbing the wind. She could hear the sound of its seams stretching . . .

The huge ship began to roll, pulling away from the dock.

Cheers erupted from the ship. Yells of anger came from below.

Gunfire sparked all along its hull, but it was too late. The second sail unfurled and absorbed its fair share of wind, propelling the ship even faster.

"Watch the graveyard!" Olive yelled, and Casper spun the wheel in time to avoid the first of the rotting Landships beyond the dock. Olive breathed a sigh of relief, watching the Commerce Pinnacle fade away, the pirates on the decks firing futilely after them.

Then something occurred to her. "Wait! What about—"

Two figures leapt over the railing in a flash of yellow light and landed with heavy thuds: Masyn and Castor, the latter holding onto the girl. Both were injured, bleeding from new wounds, and exhausted, yet they stared at Olive with a look of rapture.

White Helix . . .

"Where to, Captain? North?" Casper asked hopefully at the wheel.

Olive shook her head. "Not yet. We got a bargain to honor."

"*Another* bargain?" he asked.

"You're alive, aren't you?"

Casper shrugged, unable to argue the point.

AS COMPLICATED AS REFINING crude oil was, the Refinery Pinnacle itself only contained the infrastructure for about a third of the process. The rest was outside the city, connected by huge pipes. The one Holt was sliding through came from the Vacuum Distiller, a giant heating system that produced heavy oils for things like diesel gas and other distillates that Faust really had no use for, and that side of its production had been shut down long ago.

Holt had worked in the Refinery, it's how he knew of these pipes. The good news was, they led right to the system's Coker and Hydrocracker tanks, deep inside the Refinery Pinnacle. They would be their back door. The bad news was that it was one long crawl through the darkest, most cramped environment you could imagine, and every second you could feel the walls closing in.

Two dozen rebels were behind him, and a second group was in another pipe, moving in the same direction. A headlamp lit the dark ahead, and he could see Ravan's feet as she crawled forward. She was the head of the line, and he stared at her enviously. He would have much preferred the front, where it was less cramped.

Of course, that's probably why Ravan had insisted she go first. She was still plenty mad at him, as evidenced by how her foot suddenly kicked him in the face.

"Ouch!" Holt shouted and pulled back.

"Oh," Ravan's irritated voice said ahead of him. "Forgot you were back there."

"Why'd you stop?"

"Because we're here, moron, why else would I stop?"

Holt rubbed his nose, but saw she was right. In the light ahead of them, the pipe dead-ended into the filter path that separated the oil to either the Coker or the Hydrocracker.

"I need you to unstrap the torch," she said, lying flat.

Holt could just make out the portable cutting torch on her back. To use it, she had to roll over, but she couldn't do that until it was off. He crawled toward her, could hear the line of rebels behind them grind to a halt. In the dark he couldn't totally see where her straps secured the torch. His hands slid up her back, searching.

Ravan tensed. "Don't touch me."

"How else am I supposed to get it off you?"

"*Don't* touch me."

Holt did his best. He found the first strap, unfastened it, and pulled it loose. "You know, I was kind of expecting a warmer response to my proposal. At least, from you." It was true, Ravan's attitude, if anything, had gotten more hostile since he'd stated his desire to come back to the fold, and he didn't really understand it.

"Shows how completely detached from reality you are."

"Ravan . . ."

"Just get the torch off."

"Fine," he mumbled. The next strap had twisted around her side. His hands slid under her, reaching for the clip. "Hold on, I have to—"

She flinched unpleasantly. "Stop."

"I almost have it."

"No . . ." She struggled against him, trying to squirm away from his hands, but they slid along the length of her waist and the bare skin there.

Ravan froze. Holt's hands stopped. Each focused on the feel of the other.

It was funny how unique her skin was, how it brought back memories, feelings too, and they surprised him. He could hear her breathing under him.

"Hey!" the rebels shouted behind them in annoyance. "Hurry the hell up!"

It broke the spell.

"Get it *off* me," Ravan hissed. Holt found the last buckle, unclipped it, and pulled the torch off. She rolled over and yanked it out of his hands, and slid away from him.

Holt watched her move in the dark as she primed the blowtorch, the slimness of her, the curves. The feel of her skin was still in his head, and the emotions that came with it. Judging by how tense Ravan seemed, the way she kept her eyes locked on the blowtorch, it was the same for her.

Holt looked away from her and checked his watch. They were early, they still had two minutes to go. "Anything you want to discuss?"

She finally craned her neck up to look at him. "Jesus, you just want to add insult on top of insult, don't you?"

"What do you mean?"

"What do I *mean*? Taking the tattoo? *Now*? You don't *get* it at all."

Holt certainly didn't, as usual. He would have thought the gesture would make her happy, or at least not want to snap his neck. Women were more difficult to figure out than Assembly.

"You are *not* taking that tattoo," she told him firmly.

"What am I supposed to do? Rogan—"

"Can go to hell." She cut him off. "You *both* can. You're not taking it, not now."

Holt started to say something else, but Ravan pulled the welder's goggles over her eyes and lit the torch. He flinched when it touched the top of the pipe, spraying sparks in a violent burst that lit up the dark. Holt guessed that was that.

RAVAN BARE-KNUCKLE PUNCHED THE cap she'd just cut off, and heard it clang to the floor on the other side. The pain was sharp but it did little to blunt the anger she felt.

Holt's touch had been electric. She'd forgotten what it felt like, and it was funny how distinctive the way someone's hand could be, how you could recognize it blindfolded.

God, she was pathetic. After everything he'd done, all he had to do was run his fingers over her back . . .

She climbed out of the pipe, forcing herself to focus. She dropped the torch and yanked her Beretta free, scanning the underworks of the Refinery Pinnacle.

It was empty.

Holt climbed out behind her and exhaled a long breath of relief. He hated being cramped up almost as much as he hated heights, and she had enjoyed making him go second.

She pulled the welding goggles off her face, while the other rebels started scampering out of the pipe behind them. Ravan began brushing all the grime and dust off. She could feel it in her hair, all over her—

Holt smiled in that way he did when he was trying not to laugh.

She looked up at him. *"What?"*

Holt motioned to her face. She figured it out, it was probably covered in soot from the welding torch, and the goggles had left two clean circles around her eyes.

"Screw you," she said, rubbing her face furiously, but finding it hard not to smile herself. It only made her angrier. Why did she always soften for him? Why did she always let him do these things and just come back?

Nearby, she saw the sparks from where the second team was cutting through their pipe.

"Go help them out," Ravan told some of the rebels. They moved for the other pipe, and not one seemed resentful about her being put in charge. Rogan's sway appeared to be strong, which was good. It would make it easier later. If she couldn't ascend to the top of the Menagerie under Tiberius, then she definitely would under Rogan West.

In a few minutes, the rest of the rebels were free. The last three from each group dragged the larger weapons in bags behind them.

Everyone moved to those bags and started gearing up. They had only four dozen rebels to fight several hundred pirates above. There was no way they could win by themselves, but they weren't the only part of the plan. She just hoped the other groups didn't screw it up.

"Listen up," Ravan said, and the rebels looked at her. "This is the heavy oils distillation room, it's unused, which means no guards, but it's not going to be that way from here on. Two floors to the top, and there will definitely be kids working the refinery. We have to get there without setting off any alarms, so move low and quiet and *only* when Holt or I say."

No one dissented, they only seemed eager. Everyone crept past the huge pipes that ran from the big Coker and Hydrocracker tanks. Ravan and Holt reached the heavy steel door out of the room. Both gripped their Berettas, their rifles slung over their backs. It was too cramped in here for large caliber right now, but that would change fast.

Holt winced as he leaned against the wall, and she studied him carefully. He'd gone through a lot of punishment, and clearly wasn't 100 percent.

"I'm fine," he told her, sensing her stare. Ravan just nodded. She trusted him to know his abilities, but he would no doubt be slower than usual. Still, she'd take a slow Holt Hawkins over pretty much anyone else.

Ravan gripped the door. It groaned open, and the sounds of machinery burst in. Pumps shuffling, steel stretching on heating tanks, the clanking of gears against gears, all of it loud and jarring. All the better. The sound would help conceal them as they moved.

Ravan and Holt pushed into the room, ducking down behind more pipes. Inside stood the huge hydrotreater tanks, filling the room with their girth. Something didn't seem right, though.

"Not as hot as I remember," Holt observed, voicing her thoughts.

"Maybe they've got it running low yield," Ravan said. "Take left, I'll do right."

Holt moved off, disappearing around a bend in the pipes. Ravan did the same and saw three kids standing near the tanks. They weren't guards, they were workers, clothes stained with soot and oil, but they were armed and could alert other pirates inside the Pinnacle.

Ravan moved in, keeping out of sight by a batch of pressure valves. She couldn't see Holt, but it didn't matter. He'd know what to do, they'd always worked well together.

She gave it another second . . . then twisted one of the valves above her head.

Steam erupted in a hissing geyser, and she had a glimpse of the three workers jump in surprise before they were obscured by the cloud of super-heated vapor.

One. Two. Three, Ravan counted.

Then she covered her face and rolled right through the steam. It stung, but was over fast. When she emerged, the workers hesitated. It was their mistake.

She chopped one in the throat, sent him to the ground. The second lunged for her, but she whirled out of the way, then shoved him headfirst into the metal pipes. He fell too.

Holt appeared and grabbed the third worker around the neck, squeezing, choking off the kid's air as his arms fumbled. In a few seconds he ran out, and Holt let him fall to the floor, out cold.

He looked at Ravan, smiling. "Always wanted to try that."

Ravan spun the pressure valve closed and sealed off the steam. "Works better when you *don't* squeeze the windpipe." She felt the anger soften again at his voice, at the casual way he had of disarming tension. She wanted to stay mad at him, to remember he couldn't be trusted with her feelings, but the walls were crumbling again. She would hold out as long as she could.

Ravan motioned for the rest of the rebels, and they poured into the room. Everyone moved around the hydrotreater tanks toward a stairwell that climbed up the far wall, then poured into the refinery's central chamber, where the huge blending tanks sat, each a hundred feet in diameter and made of thick steel. It was here the various oils and naphtha produced by the refinery were blended into gasoline, Faust's greatest treasure, and what had kept Tiberius in power all these years.

They rounded the sides of the tanks, spreading out . . . and came face-to-face with the room's occupants.

About twenty of them, a dozen guards and the rest workers, but all of them armed.

Ravan's rebels outnumbered them, but the problem was, the second the shooting started, the hundred or so guards outside would come running in, and that would be that.

Everyone drew their guns on everyone else and froze. Ravan searched the crowd of Tiberius loyalists one at a time, until she found the one she was looking for. They locked eyes . . . and Ravan shrugged. "Well?"

The kid stared back . . . then he and the dozen guards spun and slammed the ends of their rifles into the workers, dropping them to the ground in a heap, and just like that the standoff was over.

Ravan smiled, staring at her old crew warmly. They were all here, not one of them had stayed on Tiberius's side once she'd called. It meant a lot, but that didn't mean she couldn't mess with them a little. "You hesitated, Marcus, having second thoughts?"

"Hell no, boss," the kid said, and the others nodded. "It's no fun without you."

"Three days on your own, and you go all soft on me," she said and started moving again. "Line up, we got work to do."

Ravan's men joined the rest, shaking hands, nodding. Holt kept quiet and apart, followed along as they flanked the big double doors that led outside onto the Pinnacle platform.

"What's the plan?" one of Ravan's men asked.

"We wait," she replied.

"For what?"

The big doors vibrated as an explosion rocked the platform outside. Then another one, this one accompanied by yells of alarm. Gunfire echoed outside, sounds of battle.

"For that." Ravan studied the rebels, about sixty now with her old crew joining up. "We're outnumbered, but they don't know we're here. Hit as many as you can before they regroup, then take cover and wait for the cavalry."

"When exactly's that?" one of her men asked.

"Whenever it feels like it, Jackson," Ravan replied. "You in a rush?"

Everyone smiled back, even Holt. "One. Two. *Three.*"

Holt kicked open the big doors and rushed outside with the others. He was limping, but he moved just as fast as everyone else. Memories of him standing on that gas valve with primed grenades entered her head. As conflicted as her feelings were right then, the thought of losing him was a tangible fear. He'd done nothing but hurt her . . . but that didn't change the fact that he was more important to her than probably anyone else on the planet. Besides, if he died . . . what would have been the point of any of this?

Ravan pushed the thoughts away and lunged after him into the chaos.

HOLT DASHED INTO THE fighting, and quickly wondered what he was thinking. He planted himself against a cabled stack of barrels and flinched as explosions flared all around the platform and Rogan West's gyrocopters streaked through the air, dropping bombs, right on time. Still, it felt good, oddly, caring whether or not a bullet took his head off. He felt like he was coming back to himself, albeit slowly, and probably never again like he'd been, but it was something. It showed things could change.

To take advantage of it, though, he'd have to survive the next few minutes.

Holt stared up through the metal rungs of the giant flare tower and watched the gyros circle. One of them took a blast of gunfire, wavered, then fell and crashed out of sight.

All around him, the rebels pushed onto the platform from the refinery, guns blazing. The pirates on the other side didn't see it coming, and more than two dozen were cut down before they figured it out.

Still, they returned fire brutally, taking cover of their own. Holt saw six rebels fall before they could get behind something.

"We got a problem, go figure." Ravan ducked next to him, slamming a new clip into her rifle. Gunfire echoed everywhere, gyrocopters roared past, bombs detonated.

She pointed past him, to the rear of the platform, the part that faced out onto open desert. No one was there, all the fighting was up front, which was part of the plan. What wasn't part of the plan were the lines of metal storage containers that had been put there. Two lines of them, eight each, blocking the entire rear edge. They were new, they hadn't been there last night when the plan was made, probably part of some kind of storage runoff. The Menagerie had gotten lucky.

"Splendid." Holt sighed. If they didn't clear a path through those things, the rest of the plan was screwed. He studied the containers, looking for possibilities, and saw the only thing that looked like an option: an old, rusted forklift near the far end.

"You thinking what I'm thinking?" Ravan asked, looking at the same thing.

Holt nodded. "Just like Tucson. You have rope?"

"Yep."

"Who's driving?"

"You're the cripple."

He started to argue, but she poked him in the ribs and he groaned in pain. "Fair enough."

Ravan smiled . . . then seemed to stuff it back down. Holt could see the cracks forming in her walls where he was concerned, and the fight to maintain them. He wasn't sure if it was a good or bad thing.

"Get ready," she said, then glanced at the rebels around them. Two more fell from hits, and the circling gyros were almost out of bombs. The battle was about to take a bad turn.

Holt took a deep breath . . . then darted out from the barrels. He heard bullets buzz through the air around him, and pain shot through his legs and ribs as he ran, but he ignored it. He made the distance and lunged inside the old forklift, slamming into the seat with a groan. Bullets sparked all over the cabin.

"Hurry!" Ravan yelled, pointing into the desert.

Holt looked, but knew what he would see. Giant plumes of purples and blues that marked the sails of the *Wind Rift*. It was about half a mile away, closing fast. Olive had it right on schedule.

"For once I wish someone would be late," he yelled back, gripping his Beretta.

"Quit whining." Ravan ducked through the gunfire toward the rear of the forklift, pulling a length of thin-gauge rope from her pack. As she did, Holt aimed at the back window of the vehicle and shut his eyes. His gun flashed, the glass exploded outward.

Ravan jumped onto the back, tossed in one end of the rope. Holt grabbed it and wrapped it around his waist, tied a quick barrel-hitch knot and pulled it tight. More bullets slapped into the forklift. The gyros roared over, banking hard to the right, headed back to the Machine Works, out of bombs. It meant if they didn't clear this landing zone for the *Wind Rift*, the whole thing was over.

"Hit it!" Ravan yelled, firing and hanging off the rear.

Holt cranked the forklift, shoved it into gear, and stomped the gas. The machine jumped forward and Holt aimed it for the nearest pair of containers, stacked one in front of the other. There wasn't time to lift them off the platform, he'd have to take a more direct approach.

The machine slammed into a container at full speed, the twin teeth of its loader punching right through the metal, and the wheels kept spinning. Sparks shot out from under the containers as they were shoved forward along the platform.

A second later, the first one cleared the edge and fell. Without the extra weight, the forklift lurched forward. The second container was about to go too.

"Ravan, go!" Holt yelled. He heard her leap off, but he didn't look back, had to keep the wheel straight.

The second container tipped over as it was pushed off the edge . . . and the forklift whined as the back wheels lifted up. Its teeth were stuck in the side of the container, it would be pulled right over with it, and Holt watched the world upend, felt gravity start pulling him down . . .

He groaned as the rope around him went taut. As the forklift fell, he stayed in place, pulled right through the back window he'd cleared earlier, watching the machine and container crash violently into the ground below.

Holt just hung there, suspended off the edge of the platform. He could hear the gunshots from back where they'd been, could see the *Wind Rift* barreling toward him.

Above him Ravan appeared, staring down in amusement.

"Remind me again why the 'cripple' gets this job?" Holt asked.

"Because it amuses me," she answered.

The giant Landship sailed closer, almost on him. Ravan lowered her hand. Holt took it, scampered up and over the edge, right as the huge ship shuddered to a stop against the platform. The gangplank crashed down in the gap left by the containers.

Holt, exhausted, watched as a hundred rebels, led by Rogan West, poured off the Landship, running forward onto the Pinnacle, rifles ready, most already firing. He gave Holt a wink as he dashed past with the others.

Holt and Ravan didn't follow. They just sat down and leaned against a container, watching as the Menagerie broke and ran, seeing they were outpositioned. When they were gone, West and his men hit the stairs, sweeping upward through the numerous shops and living quarters along the flare tower, clearing them, completely dominating the Pinnacle . . . and taking very few prisoners.

Holt looked at Ravan. They'd pulled it off, in spite of everything. "Guess we still got it."

Ravan studied him back wearily, though there was a softness behind her eyes. "If you say so."

Holt watched her gaze drift down to his right wrist and the half-finished image there.

"You can make the top half a different color," she said quietly. "Or . . . make it into a gryphon or . . . *anything* else."

"I still don't understand why."

"God, you don't see anything but yourself, do you? You don't see me or how I feel. That you're the only person who ever made me want to be something besides what I was." She looked up at him, and there was pain in her eyes. "You brought out parts of me I . . . was scared to let myself have, feelings I had no business with. Everyone—*everything*—else in my life I put there to keep me *alive*. You were there . . . because you made me *feel* alive. Do you 'understand' now, you idiot? I *love* you. I always have, and that tattoo was supposed to mean something. Now I'll have to look at it every day and know it's not for real, that you did it . . . because you *had* to, not because you wanted to."

The admission was startling. As long as he'd known her, as much as they'd shared, she had never expressed as much sentiment and emotion to him as she just had. His chest tightened, he felt feelings rise, old ones . . .

He could see it in her eyes, the hope he would say what she wanted to hear. He knew the words, knew the way to restart their journey, one that had meant something to him once, but as much as he might want to, the sad truth was, there was a part of him he hadn't yet let go of. A part of him, regardless of what he knew to be true . . . still, somehow, believed Mira was alive. That she was still here. It was like he could still feel her, out there, and it was unfair. Not just to Ravan, but to him too. Why wasn't he allowed to just move on?

For all those reasons, Holt couldn't tell Ravan what she needed. Someday maybe. Maybe even someday soon, but not now. Not yet.

Ravan held his gaze a moment more, then turned away and shook her head. She stood up without looking at him, hefted her rifle, and moved to join the others.

"Don't take that tattoo," she said as she moved off. "Don't you dare."

Holt watched after her, but she never looked back.

MIRA HELD ONTO THE EDGE of a train car, letting the dizziness pass. The Assembly were in her head, and it was worse than it had ever been, but that might be because in her grief and guilt she'd stopped fighting them. They ripped through her mind, the feelings of desolation and loneliness, their eagerness for her, replacing her thoughts with their own, and that was just fine, because right then, she didn't want her own thoughts.

She made herself move through the yard, one foot in front of the other. She could see the Citadel in the heated haze of the distance, across a hundred miles of desert. It reminded her there was something she had to do and, walking toward it, she didn't feel the apprehension she expected. There was no other choice, really, and that brought with it a strange calm.

As she walked, she caught glimpses of the White Helix on the old train, watching interestedly. She wasn't surprised: they enjoyed conflict, and they probably had a sense of what was coming.

Mira rounded the side of a tanker car, and saw what was left of the Wind Trader fleet assembled near the eastern edge of the yard. The charred wrecks of the rest, dozens of ships, lay where they'd burned into ashen heaps after the attack.

There were only eleven left. What had been the Wind Trader fleet, one of the most amazing creations on the planet, was decimated, a way of life was gone, and it was Mira's fault. Still, it didn't change what she had to do. She moved toward the assembled group of Captains nearby, watching as their crews loaded the last of the supplies and making ready to depart.

Dresden was amid the others, and he studied her intently. He, like the White Helix, probably had an idea what was coming as well, but she was unclear which side he would eventually end up on. He had just as little reason to stand with her as the others.

"I need to talk with you," Mira announced, and her voice was firm and unwavering, in spite of the projections in her head. "All of you."

The Captains turned with a mixture of emotions. Some saw her as a villain, who had overseen the destruction of their way of life. Others, a compatriot, who had been through hell with them and played a role in any of them getting out alive. All of them were wary.

The projections from the Assembly swelled. The world spun, but she forced herself to keep her eyes open, to say what she needed to say, to not show weakness.

"I want to ask you to stay, to help me finish this." Their reaction was a foregone conclusion. Most turned away in disgust, the rest studied her in genuine dismay. To them, there was nothing left to "finish," it was already over.

"You can't be serious, Mira," Conner said without malice. He just looked exhausted and defeated.

"I am," she answered. "I still need your help, and we still have a deal."

"There's no deal *left*!" the Captain with the British accent spat viciously. "The fleet is gone, burned to the ground, all thanks to your *deal*. There's no one left to honor it."

"There's you," Mira told her, and the girl glared.

"You realize," Dresden began, "our fleet notwithstanding, you've lost almost two-thirds of the force you set out with, and you're not even to San Francisco yet."

"Our numbers have dwindled, yes, but the ones who remain are stronger."

There were murmurs of agreement from the Helix on the cars. The Wind Traders seemed less impressed.

"Mira, you had to know the answer would be no," Conner told her. "We're leaving in less than an hour, and when we're gone, we're not coming back. We have to rebuild and start over, and I certainly hope we have the 'strength' for it, but don't make this any harder than it has to be."

She felt Dresden watching her curiously as she reached into her pocket and grabbed what was there. "You're strong enough. I know it. But the truth is, there is *no* starting over."

Mira threw a handful of quarters at their feet. They were Strange Lands quarters, and the Captains flinched, expecting them to explode, but they only sparked and fizzled and nothing else. It was a pathetic display, and everyone stared down at the coins in confusion.

"The artifacts are dying," Mira told them. As she spoke, each Captain slowly looked up at her. There was fear behind their eyes. "A few months from now, they'll all be dead. The components, the combinations, whatever energy made them what they were will be gone. It means . . . the Wind Traders will die with them."

"This is a trick," one Captain said. "She's trying to manipulate us."

Conner stared at Mira in shock. When he spoke, his voice was almost pleading. "My Chinooks and Zephyrs work just fine."

"For now, but they *are* dying," she told him, and it gave her no pleasure. "It's why the Barriers on the ships have been failing early. It's why we've been having to replace combinations at twice the rate we normally do. Ask Dresden, he knows."

The Captains turned to him, clearly hoping he would refute everything Mira said. It was a vain hope.

"She's right," Dresden said. "I've checked the *Wind Shear*'s stock of components, half of them are dead or near powerless."

"The stash?" Conner asked, his voice a whisper. He meant the giant haul of Strange Lands artifacts in the *Wind Shear*'s hold, the one that was supposed to have made their fortune.

"Worthless," Dresden answered, locking eyes with his brother. "Or it will be."

"Bloody hell . . ." the British Captain said, covering her eyes. The others were having similar reactions, and Mira could understand why. They'd already lost so much, now they were suddenly faced with the reality that they were going to lose the rest.

"You can go home if you want," Mira continued, hating the pain her words caused, "spend the last few months living as you've lived, I wouldn't blame you, but it would just be on borrowed time. I know it hurts, but there's another option, a better one. You can use the time you have left to help me change things."

"To defeat the Assembly you mean," the British girl stated. "You're mad."

Mira turned and pointed to the tops of the train cars, where the White Helix crouched, watching and listening. "Have you noticed their eyes? Have you seen even a trace of the Tone in any of them? They're all Heedless. Zoey freed each of them, she freed me too. She can stop the Tone. She can do even more than that, and if we can find her, I believe, I truly *believe*, she can save us all."

"Zoey's just a name to us," Conner said.

"What would you have us do?" Dresden asked his brother. "Go back to what's left of Currency? Wait out the last few months while we can still sail? Then what? Become farmers? Join some Midnight City faction? I don't see myself doing either of those, do you?"

"*You're* buying into this?" Conner asked.

"I bought into it back at the *Wind Fall*, watching Mira do what she did with that alien. I'd never seen anything like that, never had any inkling whatsoever that they were more than just giant, walking death machines. It showed me there's more to what's going on here. It's a *big* maybe, I know that, but I'm sorry, it's a hell of a lot better choice than going home and waiting for the Chinooks to die. If I'm going down, it's gonna be on my ship. I watched too many people I know die a few days ago to just pretend it didn't happen."

Conner shook his head, trying to absorb it all. "We have *eleven* ships left, Dresden, how the hell are we going to transport all the White Helix west? How the hell are we going to defend ourselves? How the hell are we going to do *anything*?"

"I have a few thoughts on that," Mira said, and the Wind Traders' attention shifted back to her. From the distance, the Assembly called again, her vision blurred, but she steadied herself and hoped no one noticed.

"*THIS* IS YOUR IDEA?" Smitty asked in dismay. They were inside a giant repair bay, its rusted metallic walls lined with shelves of countless old tools and machines. In the middle, on the bay's tracks, were two massive diesel locomotives, each with the faded insignia of the Santa Fe Railway. They were imposing, enormous, and clearly powerful. At least, assuming they could be brought back to life. Smitty, Caspira, the Captains, and a few White Helix Doyen stared at the huge machines with skepticism.

"I found them yesterday," Mira said, forcing herself to think through the projections from the Assembly. Conversations were the hardest when they were in her head. "They look like they're in good shape. I don't see much rust, they were probably protected in here."

Max sat next to her inside the giant building, and beside him was Nemo. The big cat circled around the dog, rubbing against him and purring loudly. His opinion of Max had certainly changed. He'd gone from disinterest to adoration, and if Mira didn't know better, she'd think it was because the dog saved the cat's life. Either way, Max didn't exactly seem pleased, he looked up at Mira with an embarrassed look.

"You want to get them running?" Caspira asked, walking down the length of the machines.

"What if we did?" Conner asked. "What are you going to do, pile your thousand Helix on top of them?"

"There's tons of ruined rail cars outside," Mira answered, "but there's also some in pretty good shape. I'm sure out of all of them, we could find ten or fifteen that are still solid."

"Then what?" Smitty asked.

"We armor them," she replied. "There's tons of scrap metal, and the artifacts in the *Wind Shear* will let us make Barriers, Gravitrons, Lithes, you name it."

"Artifacts, based on your own estimation, that don't have much life left in them," the British Captain retorted.

Mira felt herself getting frustrated, but she pushed it down. "Look at this."

As a group they walked toward the far edge of the big building, where an old, dusty office had been built. Inside sat a few desks, a safe, shelves with binders and books, and a giant map on the back wall near where the bulletin boards had been before they crumbled to the floor.

It showed the western half of the United States, and a spiderweb of lines that represented railways. Mira pointed to one in particular, marked the "Western Terminus," and the group could see where it twisted and turned, until it finally ran into a metropolis that had once been named San Francisco.

"Terminus," Conner remarked. "Is there a less ominous choice?"

"Dresden," Mira said. "Where's the Citadel on here?"

He studied the map. "I only saw the thing once, but it looked pretty much right in the center of Oakland. I remember because I could see the Presidium too, but it landed across the bay, in downtown. Made it easy to mark."

The Presidium was one of the giant Assembly ships that had come barreling out of the sky during the invasion. One landed in San Francisco, which meant the ruins not only were home to it, but to the Citadel as well, which had been built after the planet was conquered.

"That's what I was hoping," Mira said, following the line of one track with her finger as it came to a stop where the land met the bay, right where

Oakland would have been. "If we want to get to Zoey, this line'll take us right to her doorstep."

"Who's to say all these rails are still functional?" Conner asked.

"You've been out there just as much as I have," Dresden replied. "When have you *not* seen a rail line that wasn't in good shape? Those things are solid, I wish more of them *were* broken."

Mira could imagine. A Landship hitting a line of train tracks at full Chinook was probably unpleasant.

"Our real problem's gonna be other trains still on the tracks," Dresden continued. "Stopping before we run straight into them is easy enough in the day, but I assume we're gonna be moving at night."

Mira nodded. "We split the Landships into two groups. One flanks the train, runs escort. The smaller one scouts ahead, looks for obstructions and Assembly." The Captains listened, and she could sense a change in their demeanors. They weren't starting to believe necessarily . . . but they did seem to be doubting less fervently.

"We armor it, salvage what's left of the cannons, mount them up and down the thing. The Reflection Box still works, which means we can still make whatever we need. We do all that, add in artifacts and armed Landships running escort, then . . ."

"We have a rolling fortress," Conner replied, rubbing his chin.

"All we need is to get to the Phantom Regiment," Mira said. "Then, together, we *all* go after Zoey."

"Guys." Smitty's voice from outside the office pulled their attention. He and Caspira were both inside one of the train's cockpits. Everyone watched as Smitty punched something on the operator controls.

The locomotive's instruments lit up under all the dust, and Smitty looked at Mira and Dresden with a smile.

More conversation ensued, discussing the train and the realities, but for Mira, it faded away into the background. The Assembly swelled in her head again.

"You okay?" Dresden asked, and she nodded, told him she was tired, that she needed rest, and left them there, discussing the plan and the logistics. She should stay, but she couldn't. They couldn't see her like this.

Mira exited into the sunlight, rounded the side of the giant repair bay, out of sight.

Guardian . . .

Show us . . .

She tried to push them away, but they were overwhelming. She gripped the edge of an old air-conditioning unit, but it wasn't enough. Mira collapsed onto her back, staring up at the sky.

Guardian . . .

Come closer . . .

Show us . . .

Then everything went black.

MIRA WOKE TO A STRANGE mix of darkness and light. The world was covered in night, but far above in the sky, giant, wavering bands of color fluctuated like waves in the ocean.

It all made for a surreal disorientation. Wherever she was, everything was silent, there was only the sound of a desolate wind, the kind that used to blow through the Strange Lands inner rings, but this wasn't that place.

Something even more obvious occurred to her. The silence didn't just extend to the environment, it was in her head too. The hundreds of impressions and emotions from the Assembly were, amazingly, mercifully gone, and the sheer relief of it overwhelmed her. Mira had forgotten what it felt like to have her mind to herself, and she exhaled a long, slow relieved breath.

Until a nagging pain in her back formed. She was lying on something hard and metallic.

Mira rolled over and saw the thick, armored fuselage of Ambassador underneath her, and it made the situation more confusing. Had Ambassador teleported her here? It seemed likely, but why? For that matter, where *was* here?

She looked closer and noticed there was very little to actually see. All around them was nothing but a massive field of white stretching into the dark.

It was snow.

Guardian, Ambassador projected to her, sensing her movement. She flinched at how jarring a single projection was in her now quiet mind. It made her wonder how she possibly coped with the hundreds she did on a daily basis.

"Where are we?" she asked out loud.

The top.

"Of what?"

Your world.

It suddenly made sense. The snow, the giant wavering bands of color. They were at the north pole, and the bands were the aurora borealis. She stared back up at them in wonder, something she had never seen before, only heard and read about in another time and place.

The realization begged other questions.

Why isn't it cold? she projected to Ambassador.

You are protected. Ambassador's shield flickered briefly around her, lighting the night. It screened her from the environment as well and she was definitely thankful. Without it, she would be dead in minutes.

"Why are we here?"

For you, Ambassador replied. *It is quiet.*

Mira was instantly filled with tenderness for the alien. It meant the lack of projections from the others. Ambassador must have sensed her distress, come looking, and found her. It had brought her here. Maybe it did so only because it saw her as an asset for getting what it wanted, but Mira was grateful all the same. She could finally breathe . . . and it felt marvelous.

"I didn't know the strain was so much," she said.

Your mind is limited.

Mira frowned. "Thanks a lot."

No insult is meant. Few could go as far.

"You act like I have a choice," she said, lying back and staring at the colors above her again. They were beautiful. "You can only teleport places you've been, right? Or places other people have seen?"

Correct.

"So you've come here before."

It is pleasing.

Mira had never heard an Assembly, in all the "conversations" she'd had with them now, express anything resembling an affection for something. It was surprising.

"You like it here."

It has meaning.

Imagery exploded in her mind: only light, bright and pulsing and colorful, and she recognized where she was. It was what the Assembly called the Nexus, their life force, but this time she wasn't looking at it from the outside, Ambassador was showing her the *inside,* an altogether different experience.

Colored energy surrounded and encompassed everything. Feelings of bliss and peace washed over her of a kind she'd never experienced. It was like . . . somehow being inside *love*. It felt amazing.

The interior of the Nexus, the colors and pulsing energy, bore a passing resemblance to the aurora above. No wonder Ambassador came here. It was for the same reason the other Assembly wanted her close to them: to feed off her mind, to sense the Nexus again through the memories that had been shared with her, if only dimly.

Mira breathed in sharply and opened her eyes suddenly, cutting off the imagery. The brief glimpse of actually being inside it, of the sensations and feelings, had left her with one clear impression, and it was shocking.

"The Nexus is . . . alive?" she asked.

Life comes from life.

"But it was so peaceful and serene, and you're . . ." She stopped herself, but it was too late.

Neither, it finished for her. Mira sensed no insult . . . and no disagreement either. *It is unfortunate.*

"What?"

We indulge in the Nexus. We never learn from it.

Mira thought she understood. The Nexus was an answer to whatever had plagued the Assembly its entire existence, but, for whatever reason, they didn't see it.

"Most times," Mira admitted, "humans have the same problem."

She watched the colors above, thinking how odd it was that she was so at ease, lying on top of an Assembly combat walker, having an intimate conversation. A year ago it would have seemed insane, not to mention a betrayal, but not now. Ambassador had become a confidant, though she wasn't sure it was a mutual sentiment. She wasn't really sure the alien had the ability to feel something like kinship, but she was glad it was here all the same.

"When you're . . . 'Ascended,' or whatever," Mira said, curious. "What will it be like?"

We do not understand.

"The experience, for you, what will it be like? Are you, I don't know . . . transformed? What will you feel? And see? I mean, will you still be you?"

We will be who we are. Not who we want.

Mira smiled. It was funny how used to Ambassador's cryptic answers she'd become. "You're not who you are now?"

Most resist.

"But *you're* different?"

The alien hesitated, a rare moment where it formulated its thoughts. Usually its answers were nearly instantaneous.

Few see things as they are. The Scion will ascend us. Show us the truth. Then all will see.

Mira sighed. "If we can get there."

You doubt?

"On a daily basis." It was the kind of thing she could only tell Ambassador. From it, however, she felt a strange response. Confusion.

The more you achieve. The more you doubt yourself. A human quality?

It was a very good question. "Maybe so."

They both watched the aurora again, the beauty of it, the way it shimmered and bounced. It was a special place, she saw why Ambassador came here.

Do you have special places?

"Of course."

Show us.

It took a moment to realize what Ambassador was asking. It was offering to take her anywhere she wanted, and from the machine she sensed an eagerness. It was intrigued to know what moved her. It was only fair, she supposed. Ambassador had shared something with her, after all.

But where to go? There were many options.

The Oregon beach where her family had gone every summer and her father had taught her to bodysurf. Parts of the Strange Lands she had never reached. Maybe there were still artifacts there to collect. Landmarks, like the aurora borealis above, famous ones she had never seen. Midnight City, where she had come of age, where she had found her path and her first home. Then again, an Assembly combat walker teleporting into the Scorewall room probably wasn't the best idea.

In the end, one choice outweighed all the others. There was a bittersweet anticipation for seeing it again, but it was what she wanted.

Mira shut her eyes. She pictured the place, and it came easily. She touched Ambassador with her mind, inside the shell that was slowly becoming its tomb.

"Okay . . ."

There was a sound. Like a powerful, punctuated blast of static, and a quick wave of heat washed over her.

She opened her eyes again.

The aurora was gone, replaced with the tops of swaying pine trees, the stars shining down. They were in a forest clearing. Nothing about it looked particularly familiar, but that wasn't necessarily surprising. She'd only been here one night, and a lot had happened since then.

Mira fought the wave of dizziness that always came with teleportation and hopped onto the ground.

Why here?

"I'll show you," she said and moved away from the machine, pine cones crackling under her feet. It was night here too, and very dark. She pulled a flashlight from her pack and flipped it on, searching for something specific. For a moment, she wondered if Ambassador had brought them to the wrong place, but then her light settled on what she was looking for.

A ring of stones, with the remains of a campfire, months old now, what was left of the wood nothing but blackened cinders. It wasn't much to look at, but Mira felt warmth spread through her nonetheless.

Why here? Ambassador asked again.

Mira closed her eyes . . . and let herself remember. The imagery wasn't as vibrant, she thought, as the vision of the Nexus, but even so, the feelings that came with it were as potent as they had been then.

Mira saw the campfire, burning bright. She saw Holt and Zoey dancing around it, while a waltz played on a staticky radio. Then she saw herself with Holt, watched him place a polished, black stone in her hand to help her move. The two of them danced around the fire, pressed close, the distrust that existed between them dissolving away. She heard Zoey giggle while she pet Max and watched them whirl around and around . . .

When she opened her eyes, they stung with tears.

Being here, feeling it all over, brought home how much had changed. Holt was gone. Zoey was taken. She felt they were all fighting to find one another, but whether or not they ever would was in no way certain.

Instead of pushing the tears away, she let them fall. It was another reason she was grateful for Ambassador, she didn't have to hide weakness from it, didn't have to pretend she wasn't anything other than strong and resolute.

The machine rumbled an odd sound. She felt a stirring of emotion from it: wonder, inquisitiveness, and . . . envy. It was the last one that stuck out the most.

Why that feeling? Mira projected to the alien.

These emotions. We do not feel them.

Mira turned to the giant machine, its three-optic eye staring at her.

How different would we be if we could? it asked.

Mira shook her head. What a sad race the Assembly really were. All that power, but so little to show for it. Nothing but fear, really. The thing in front of her was so different than what she had always assumed. Maybe Ambassador was the exception, but it seemed to yearn for something greater, to be more than it was. It was a trait all the silvers seemed to share. The sad thing was, Ambassador might not make it to the end. Like the others, it was trapped in its armor, dying. It might fade before Zoey could do whatever it was she was supposed to. After all it had sacrificed, how tragic would it be to never see the reality it was trying to bring about? How heroic as well?

This one, Ambassador projected. *From the memories.*

Holt, she projected back.

He will return?

Her emotions swelled. Most likely not, she knew. She wondered where he was right now, what he was thinking, what he felt. He'd seen her die, as far as he was concerned. She felt the same surge of guilt she always did, for not finding some way to get word to him, for not going to him, but Dresden had been right. That was a choice she didn't have the luxury of making. Even if he did return . . . how different would he be? How different would they *both* be?

All of these feelings and thoughts Ambassador read.

A shame, it replied. *To lose what was made. We wish . . . we could make such things.*

Mira did something strange then. It was driven by instinct more than anything else. She reached out and touched the metal, armored shell of Ambassador. She felt its presence inside, felt the ironic mix of its personality, gentle and ferocious at once.

"I don't know what future Zoey can make for you," she told it, "but maybe one day you will make them."

Ambassador rumbled softly. Mira kept her hand on it a moment more, then moved back to the blackened campfire.

We must return, Ambassador projected.

"Just one thing." She set her pack on the ground and rummaged through it. She couldn't find it at first, so she started taking items out, one at a time. A water bottle, canned food, first-aid kit, her wretched artifact, a—

Ambassador rumbled again, this time loud and jarring. It took two thunderous steps backward. Feelings of disgust and apprehension washed over Mira.

She studied the silver machine. "What?"

Abomination, it simply said.

"What is?"

It. Its eye bobbed up and down, staring at the items in front of Mira.

She looked down, and there was only one that wasn't mundane and ordinary. Her artifact, the horrible one she'd made in Midnight City, the one that forced her to flee her home what felt like ages ago now. She hated it, had meant to destroy it in the Strange Lands, but it was like the thing had a will of its own to survive.

It was a multi-tier combination, made up of over a dozen different objects, all tied together with linked silver chain and purple twine. Its main aspect was an antique gold pocket watch that rested on the exterior, with a silver δ ornately etched into the metallic cover. It was a pretty combination, really, forever marred by the reality of what it did. Mira made it in an attempt to create a combination that would reverse the effects of the Tone. Instead . . . it did the opposite. It *accelerated* it, forcing anyone, even Heedless, to Succumb within a matter of seconds.

Warily, Mira picked it up. "This?"

Ambassador took another step back. *Abomination.*

The alien wasn't wrong, as far as Mira was concerned. She only kept hold of it because it was too dangerous to just discard, but that didn't explain why Assembly would feel the same way.

Ambassador sensed her confusion. *What you call the Tone. It is the Whole.*

The Whole was what Ambassador and the Assembly named the joint awareness that their entire species shared. While independent entities, each still maintained a connection to the Whole, where they could feel the emotions and thoughts of every other entity at any one time.

The Tone, by contrast, was the telepathic signal the aliens had blanketed the planet with. Anyone older than twenty years old quickly Succumbed to its call, their minds controlled. It had made the conquering of Earth a fairly routine affair. Mira didn't see the connection between the two. "How is the Whole also the Tone?"

They are the same.

Mira tried to understand. "You're saying the signal itself, the Tone . . . is the *same* signal that carries the Whole, your joint consciousness?"

Correct.

In some way, it made sense both would be overlapped, but it didn't explain Ambassador's reaction. She held the artifact up to it. The machine rumbled unpleasantly.

"So what's the deal with this?"

It perverts the Whole.

Yeah, Mira thought grimly. If her artifact changed and altered the Tone, then that meant it did the same to the Whole.

A thought occurred to her. Mira held the thing safely away, and opened the brass lid of the old pocket watch. A stream of blackness flared out from it in a cone of shadows that seemed to squirm like a nest of worms, darker than the night around them.

Ambassador rumbled angrily. She sensed pure fear as it stepped back and slammed into a tree, almost toppling the thing.

Cease, it projected, and the sensations almost knocked her over, they were so strong. She had never felt anything like that from Ambassador before.

Instantly, she snapped shut the watch. The contorting black light vanished.

I'm sorry, Mira projected to the alien, and she meant it. *I just wanted to see.*

Never again, it projected back.

I promise. At the words, Ambassador's fear began to subside, though it made no move to come closer.

Mira shoved the dark thing far back into her pack. As she did, she felt what she was looking for.

It was the black, polished stone Holt had given her here. It felt smooth and cool, comforting. Normally she carried it in her pocket, but she'd been scared of losing it. She studied it a moment, the feelings and memories returning . . . then she reached toward the campfire, dug through the ashes, and set the stone there. She pushed the dirt back over it.

If Holt came back, perhaps together they would reclaim it someday. If not, if he was gone, then it was where it belonged, buried amid the ashes of a past memory.

She stared at the campfire one last time, then turned back to Ambassador.

"Let's go." The machine studied her warily, made no move toward her. Mira rolled her eyes. "Come on, you big baby, we got things to do."

HOLT AND RAVAN stood on a residence balcony on the flare tower of the Refinery, staring down over the city at night. Masyn, Castor, Olive, and her crew had all returned to the *Wind Rift*, docked at the rear of the Pinnacle. Rogan West and some of his men were in the center of the room, discussing strategy, and their voices gave away just how emboldened their victory had made them.

"We should hit something else soon, while we have the momentum," one rebel said, but Rogan shook his head.

"What momentum?" he asked. "We have Refinery, that means we have *Faust*. Just have to hold it long enough for the rest of the city to rebel."

"Taking this Pinnacle's a big deal," another rebel replied, "but you underestimate Tiberius's influence. It's not going to happen overnight, even with the Refinery gone."

"I don't need it to happen overnight," Rogan continued. "I can wait weeks or months. We don't even need the other two Pinnacles now, we can bring every rebel we have from those and fortify this one."

The debate continued, but Holt couldn't feel the same enthusiasm. Ravan seemed of a similar mind.

"Never seen it this quiet," she observed, staring out at the lights from lanterns in windows up and down the towers. She was right, it *was* odd, even for how late it was. Faust seemed unusually silent, peaceful almost, and that was all wrong. It only added to Holt's unease.

"Rogan would say it's because the city's stunned at the defeat," Holt said.

"But you're worried," Ravan replied.

Holt nodded. "It's been fourteen hours, and he hasn't made a move. It's not like him: 'power lost must be retaken.'"

"And here I was hoping he would just surrender."

Holt looked away from Faust and studied Ravan. The night had always suited her. The shadows and their ambiance accentuated her features. The line of her neck, the way her black hair hung down her back, even her eyes, somehow, seemed to glow more prominently. He'd always been the most attracted to her at night. Such thoughts, he knew, would have been alien to him a few days ago, but things were changing.

"I've been thinking," Holt told her softly. "I'm not going to take the tattoo. You're right, it was supposed to mean something, and I understand that."

She didn't look at him, but something about the way her features tightened suggested she may have been just as torn about him not finishing it as doing so.

"I can't explain it," he continued, "it's like . . . some part of me thinks she's still here. I know it's not fair, that it's the way it is now, but it doesn't diminish what I feel for you underneath. I want you to know that. I don't know where I'm going to come out on the other side of this, but . . . I hope you're there when I do."

She stood silent a moment, her eyes on the city, her thoughts elsewhere. "Don't do that, Holt. Don't give me false hope. We are what we are, we don't have to be anything else."

The door to the room opened. Three kids entered, all about fifteen, sweaty and grimy.

"Well?" Rogan asked, as if expecting them.

"Trying to get the Isomerization Tanks back online, but so far it's a no-go," one of the new arrivals stated.

The statement grabbed Holt's attention, and he looked to the kids. "The isomerics aren't working?"

They nodded. "Most of the valves were closed, two of them are stuck. I'd say they were rusted in place, they're so tight, but . . . that doesn't make sense, right?"

"They've been off since we got here?" Rogan asked.

"It would explain the lack of heat we noticed down there," Ravan said.

"Those tanks are *huge*," Holt continued, musing out loud. "They're the heart of the Refinery, shutting them down means weeks of work to get them back online. Why would they . . ."

Holt figured it out before he finished. The way Ravan stared back at him indicated she had too.

"Oh, Jesus . . ." West breathed, and then yells from below cut him off. So did the violent, percussive sounds of gunfire. A lot of it.

Holt watched the color drain from Ravan's face, understood why the city had seemed so quiet, why there was no counterattack coming from some other Pinnacle. The counterattack had been planned from the beginning. They'd never taken the Refinery. They'd simply walked into the exact place Tiberius wanted them.

"Move!" Ravan yelled, grabbing her rifle and heading for the door.

The floor under their feet shook from an explosion. No one spoke, just grabbed their gear and ran.

AVRIL WAS A POINT of stillness in the chaos around her. Pirate fought pirate, guns blazed, knives flashed, people fell and didn't move. They had been locked in those tanks underneath the Refinery for more than a day before the top hatch had finally opened. It had been an uncomfortable experience, a strange, cramped environment, where the sounds of their breathing echoed off the metal walls.

The three tanks were huge, big enough to hold fifty pirates each. Tiberius had ordered them drained and cleaned days ago. He seemed to firmly believe, now that Holt and Ravan were helping West, that the Refinery would be their next target. So they climbed inside and waited and it hadn't taken long for her father to be proven right. They'd worked their way up to the top, dispatching West's men as they went, until they got here, the main platform.

Avril saw Quade snap the neck of one rebel, knock another out with the barrel of his sidearm, and he held her look as he did. She was the only person who knew where his loyalties truly lay, and she wondered what he was feeling, ordered to participate in the slaughter of the rebels he'd secretly supported. She still hadn't told her father, and she wasn't sure why. She wasn't even sure why she was here now, except that Tiberius had asked her to come, and she'd agreed, probably because of how it felt to hurt those kids a few days ago. Avril had felt more herself in that moment than she had in weeks . . . and it was frightening.

She was teetering on the edge of a line she never would have believed she could walk.

Avril was unarmed; no one had offered her a rifle or knife, because none of them trusted her yet. A pirate charged her from out of nowhere. Her instincts took over, she sidestepped his blow.

She saw another aiming a gun at her, and she dropped and rolled out of the way as he fired. One of her father's men took the slug instead.

Avril moved toward cover behind a—

Something hard and metallic sent her reeling. A rebel hovered over her with a tire iron, about to strike again. A bullet dropped him, and Avril saw Quade a few yards away. They shared a look before he was swept up in the fighting again.

A boot slammed into Avril's side. Another kick found her stomach. She felt the anger rising again . . . and the excitement.

She spun, the rebel who'd struck her was raising a knife . . .

. . . and she kicked it out of his hands, sprung up, and one roundhouse kick put him down. There were knives on the ground, guns too, but she leapt into the fray bare-handed. It felt better that way.

For the moment, she had chosen her side.

Avril was a blur, the Spearflow was dangerous and adaptable, even without a Lancet. West's rebels raised guns, slashed with knives, came at her with clubs, and they all fell, one after the other. Two. Five. Ten. Her training made her more powerful than any of these fools, and she embraced the feelings that flowed through her.

Then she froze.

Ahead of her, through the dwindling crowd of rebels, were two other blurs, moving almost identically to her.

One had a Lancet, streaks of color ripping the air. The other had no weapons, but he was almost as quick, even though he fought with only one arm.

When Masyn and Castor saw her, they froze too. They stared at one another as the battle raged, confused, uncertain . . . and then Masyn saw the bodies of the rebels at Avril's feet. Her stare changed.

Masyn advanced toward Avril. Castor, more reluctantly, followed, watching Masyn sling her Lancet onto her back. It wouldn't be a fair fight otherwise.

Avril felt her first real sense of anxiety as the two took positions on either side of her. She had been Doyen to both of them once, even helped Masyn forge her Lancet after she completed her Spearquest, and now they were, somehow . . . enemies. What did that say about her?

Then again, what did it matter? Nothing was as it used to be. Those days were gone.

Avril squared her shoulders toward each opponent, her fists clenched, and she closed her eyes, waiting for the attack to come, already deciding how to strike and where, knowing Masyn and Castor were doing the same.

She felt them tense, felt them move toward her, felt her own body instinctively begin to—

"Enough!" an older voice yelled and a shotgun blast punctuated its demand.

What was left of the fighting stopped. Avril opened her eyes. Masyn
and Castor were flanked now by her father's men, rifles all pointing at them.
A hundred rebels either lay dead on the platform or were on their knees,
with their hands behind their backs. The former far outnumbered the latter. Among them, she saw Holt and Ravan and the leader, Rogan West,
each bloodied and injured, and every one of the survivors was staring at
the figure who had appeared on the platform, surveying the scene with his
usual unreadable calmness.

The man's eyes swept over the crowd until they found what he was looking for: Holt, Ravan, and West. He stared at them intensely.

"We're through here," Tiberius said. "Which, of course, means we can
start all over again."

THEY FORCED HOLT, RAVAN, West, and what remained of the rebels
onto their knees. There was no sign of Olive or her crew that Holt could
see. He held a dim hope that they'd somehow managed to undock the
Wind Rift and flee west, but he knew that wasn't likely. Tiberius was too
thorough in his planning.

Holt stared through the Menagerie that surrounded him to the one person he was actually surprised to see. Avril stared back unreadably, Castor
and Masyn on either side of her. Then again, she knew now about the role
he'd played in Archer's death, and she'd been in the corrupting presence
of Tiberius Marseilles for more than a week. Maybe he shouldn't be surprised at all. The unconscious bodies of the rebels at her feet showed she'd
made her choice. It was too late for him now, anyway.

Masyn, however, had a different view.

She dashed forward in a blur of purple light, aimed straight at Tiberius,
slamming into the large guards who circled him. Two of them fell instantly,
two more staggered back, and Masyn waded into the rest. They swung at
the Helix, but she dodged them nimbly, flipping onto the shoulders of one
and dragging him to the ground. In the end, she was too outnumbered,
and her Lancet was still on her back.

A fist caught her in the face, another found her stomach. A knee sent
her crashing down. Then the others moved in.

"Masyn!" Castor yelled, rushing forward, ignoring blows from the pi-rates, watching as kicks and punches drove Masyn into the floor as she struggled in fury to get up. He fought to her side—and he did it with both arms, ignoring the pain of the broken appendage—and leapt on top of Masyn while the blows and strikes from rifle butts continued.

Throughout it all, Holt stared at Avril. The pain was apparent on her face, the horror at the beating. She took a step forward once . . . then stopped, went still, torn.

"Let them be," Tiberius said. "I don't want them dead. Not yet."

The pirates pulled off Masyn and Castor, but Holt couldn't tell what shape they were in. He looked up to the man standing above them, and Tiberi-us's eyes were on Ravan. Holt felt her hand slip into his, and he held it firmly.

"I guess we know now the answer to the question of when you will dis-appoint me," Tiberius said.

"I guess so," Ravan said back.

"Such a waste, and all of it for *him*," he said. Holt felt Ravan's fingers tighten in his. "Did you learn nothing from me? About power? About weak-ness?"

"I learned a lot," Ravan admitted. "Guess I just valued other lessons more."

Tiberius shook his head, genuinely dismayed, then pulled his eyes off Ravan to Rogan West. West had been beaten badly, his left eye was swol-len shut, blood caked the right side of his shirt. He stared back at Tiberius savagely all the same.

"Rogan West," Tiberius said. His voice, surprisingly, held no menace at all. "There is no shame in this. You tried taking power, as is our way. I respect it, but you have lost, and I'm afraid, this kind of failure comes with harsh consequences."

Rogan just shrugged, he seemed resigned. "Do your worst. I won't be the last."

"Without question." Tiberius looked to Quade. "Make it quick. He's earned that."

Quade's eyes moved to Rogan, studying him in an odd way Holt wasn't expecting. Did they know each other? Had they been friends once? Holt wasn't sure, but there was . . . something. At the rear of the crowd, Avril watched the exchange intently.

In the end Quade moved forward and drew his gun, standing over Rogan.

"And *you*." It took a moment for Holt to realize Tiberius's voice was directed at him. He looked up and met the man's glare. There was hatred there, a radiating menace, but a smile formed on his lips all the same. "I see it in your eyes. You *care* again." He looked down at Holt's hand interlaced with Ravan's. "So much the better. Now we can have all the moments we were always supposed to."

The gunshot rang out jarringly loud. Next to him, Rogan West fell dead, and Quade lowered his weapon. The crowd of pirates cheered so loudly, Holt almost couldn't make out Tiberius's next words.

"Prepare a Nonagon match tomorrow, these four will be its competitors." He meant Holt, Ravan, Masyn, and Castor. "Don't hurt them anymore. The crowd will want a good show for Faust's reunification."

The violent, malevolent cheers intensified, and Holt looked at Ravan. She stared back, and he could sense the same calmness in her as in himself. The strange tranquility that came with knowing you no longer had anything left to lose.

MASYN SAT WITH HER BACK against the wall of the small wooden cell pod. She wasn't tall, but could still barely stretch her legs outright. A few hours ago she felt the cell shake as it was moved down the giant rack system, onto the floor, disconnected, then transported somewhere else. Most likely they were on some kind of lift that would take them up to the Nonagon. Judging by the muted roar she could just hear outside from some huge crowd, the time for that was drawing close.

Her rings and weapon were gone, she'd lost them and was now shamed. Perhaps up there, facing death, she could restore some of her honor, she could still die well. Let it come, Masyn thought. If they expected her to be frightened, they would be disappointed.

Castor was curled up next to her, still and unmoving. Masyn had taken her share of pain earlier, but his had been far worse. She still remembered the way he leapt on top of her, ignoring his wounded arm, absorbing blow after blow meant for her.

She stared down at him softly. Like her, he had lost his Lancet and rings. Like her, he had fallen in battle. She should find him repellent now, dishonored and insignificant . . . but she didn't. In fact, she was more drawn to him than ever and it made no sense. She embraced Gideon's teachings. They were harsh because they had to be, but she was finding them difficult to swallow when it came to Castor.

The boy moaned, shifted a little, and Masyn ran her fingers through his hair. He calmed at her touch.

Masyn had never been one for tenderness—it was detrimental to survival, but Castor, in the last few days, had somehow brought it out in her. He had the same walls, all from the same source, and yet always reached out to her. She had seen it as an annoyance before, a sign of weakness, but now she wasn't so sure. If she ever had the opportunity again, she wouldn't push him away so quickly.

The cell rattled as someone landed on top of it. The impact was soft and muted, not the clumsy footfalls of a Menagerie, and Masyn frowned. There was only one person it could be.

An observation slit at the top of the cell slid open. As it did, the sounds of the roaring crowd somewhere above grew louder. A figure peered down from above and Masyn looked back. Avril's look was a mixture of emotion. Masyn's, she knew, was pure hostility.

"Come to gloat?" Masyn asked. "You can save your breath."

Avril said nothing, just looked at Castor on the floor. "How is he?"

"You saw what they did. Twenty of them kicking and beating him while he was unarmed and already hurt. There's no honor in that, your people have no understanding of the word."

"They aren't my people." Avril's voice was heated, but Masyn scoffed.

"Really? Then why aren't you in this cell? You can't even see how much you've changed, Gideon wouldn't even recognize you."

"Gideon's gone, Masyn."

"So that's your reason to spit on everything he taught you? You must never really have believed it."

Avril's hand shook on the edge of the observation slit. "My father told me what Holt did."

"So what? Holt told me too, why does that justify abandoning everything you used to stand for?"

Avril's voice lost its edge. "If I had been here . . ."

"But you weren't," Masyn replied. "Your father told you what Holt did . . . but did he tell you *why?*"

Masyn educated Avril, telling her everything. What Archer had been about to do, what Holt had stopped from happening. As the words spilled out, Masyn could see the horror grow in Avril's eyes.

"Brother or no brother, that wasn't right," Masyn said. "Holt stopped it. He sacrificed basically the same things you did in order to do so, and I would have done the same. What about you, Avril? What would *you* have done in that room?"

Avril was silent a long time. "Maybe I could have stopped him from becoming what he became. Maybe it's my fault."

"Gideon told me once that holding on to the past is like grasping a hot coal with the intent of throwing it at someone else," Masyn said, her voice dropping. "In the end, *you're* the one who gets burned."

Avril studied Masyn quietly. "I can get you out of here, both of you. You can escape, before the match."

Whatever sympathy Masyn had for Avril fell away, and she stared back with disdain. "You really have changed, haven't you? I'm supposed to run away now, like some scared little Outlander? *No*. We'll face what comes, we'll show all of you what *real* strength is. Maybe then you'll remember who you are."

"You're going to die, Masyn," Avril simply said.

"When did *that* become more important than honor?" Masyn held Avril's gaze a second more, then looked down. "Go away, Menagerie. No one knows you here. No one wants to."

The observation panel slid closed and Avril was gone. Masyn sighed and looked back to Castor on the floor. He moaned again, and she took his hand in hers.

RAVAN SAT CROSS-LEGGED NEXT to Holt, her stare fixed on the cell floor. She'd worked loose a rusted screw, but not to use for escape. Instead, she was carving pictures into the old, faded walls and floor of the cell, drawing the same thing, over and over: two mountains, trees in front of them, a body of water in front of that. It was crude, but Holt could make out what it was. Soon the only place that wasn't full of the image would be the ceiling.

"Why are you drawing that?" Holt asked. He wasn't sure she'd even noticed the cell being lowered and moved to the main lift for the Nonagon, or heard the muted roar of the crowd above.

"Keeps my mind off being in here." Her voice was shaky. "I hate being locked up."

It was her worst fear, being restrained, Holt knew, held in some tight, confined place, and this cell certainly qualified. "I meant why are you drawing *that*?"

"It's the only thing I *can* draw," she replied. "You remember that guy when we were kids? Taught you how to paint in that super-simple-looking method on TV?"

"Bob Ross?" Holt asked, surprised he remembered the answer.

"Yeah. Him. I got it from his show, my mom watched it all the time, not that I know why. She never painted a damn thing. Anyway, it was either this or play tic-tac-toe with myself."

"You know, not long from now, you might actually miss being locked up."

Ravan shook her head. "No way. We aren't getting out of this, but at least I get to go down being free, not caged up like some animal. The Nonagon, far as I'm concerned, is a much better option."

Holt watched her carve the final squiggly lines on the water, then shuffle back and start again on one of the floor's remaining blank spots. He understood the desire to not die in here, rather outside where she had some measure of control over her fate. The problem was, Holt wasn't completely convinced they were done.

Now that he was coming back, now that he was feeling again, he wasn't so eager to just throw in the towel. As bad as the Nonagon was, he'd survived worse. The battle at the Severed Tower came to mind, the onslaught of the Mas'Erinhah, the huge Spider walker falling and crushing him. He'd died there, but he'd come back. If he could make it out of that, he wasn't going to just resign himself to death now. Of course, none of that was to say it would be easy.

"How many Nonagon matches have you seen?" he asked, starting to think of possibilities. Only one stood out, an impossibly insane one.

"Dozens, I guess," Ravan replied, concentrating on her mountains. "Why?"

"How many teams have you seen *beat* it?"

She stopped carving and brushed back the long lengths of black hair out of her face so she could stare at him dubiously. "No one's beaten the Nonagon in three years."

"That just means someone's due up," Holt replied. "Beating the Nonagon is the only way out of this."

"How do you figure?"

"Surviving it doesn't help us, Tiberius will just keep throwing us into it over and over until we're dead. He wants a show. But if we *beat* it . . . we get the Boon."

The Nonagon had two victory conditions: surviving it and *beating* it. The Boon was only given out to those teams who beat it, and it functioned a lot like a Menagerie Solid. If it was within the power of Tiberius to grant, he had to do so. Of course, no winner had ever used it for anything other than sparing their own lives and being let free, which was sort of the genius of the design. You only really had one option when it came to the Boon, but Holt could think of another. Maybe the one loophole that could get them out of this mess.

"You really think Tiberius is going to let that happen?" Ravan asked.

"He doesn't have a choice; they're his rules, and rules are everything here. Whoever beats the Nonagon gets the Boon, and the Boon trumps it all." The next part, Holt said pointedly. "Even the rule that says only Consuls can challenge him for leadership."

He could see Ravan understood what he was implying, and she seemed even more skeptical. "We get the Boon, I challenge Tiberius, kill him, and take his place? *That's* your plan?"

"Who's better set up to pull it off than us? We have our experience, we know the arena. Not to mention two White Helix. Even without their rings, they're unbelievably agile."

Ravan's hard look began to soften as she thought it through. "We give them the high parts," she mused, thinking, "the combination unlocks."

"Exactly. You said it yourself, you wanted to go out with your fate in your own hands."

The sounds of the crowd above them seemed to be growing louder, more violent. Ravan shook her head and looked back down to the floor. "Well, it's not like there's anything left for us to lose. Is there?"

Holt could see defeat in the way she held herself. She had no real hope of any of this working, no real faith. He didn't blame her, it seemed crazy even to him, but something about how distinctly she had gotten to this hopeless place bothered him. Ravan had always been, if nothing else, full of confidence. Even in the face of death, she laughed and shrugged and waded into the conflict. It was something he'd always found attractive about her: her vitality, how alive she was. Now it was gone, that vibrancy, and it was his fault. His actions had led to her losing everything she ever wanted or achieved, had led to her being in this cell with him right now. It was a tough pill to swallow.

"I'm sorry I got you into this, Rae," Holt said, his voice soft. "I really am."

Ravan didn't react the way he expected. She smiled, exhaled a short, sarcastic breath. "Been thinking about the past a lot," she said, without looking up. "I told you about my father."

"Yeah," he answered. She'd told him all the details, and Holt knew he was the only person she had ever shared that truth with. He hated that man almost as much as Ravan did, for what he'd done.

"I left home when I was twelve," she continued. "Stole some money, bought a bus ticket. Right clothes, right mind-set, it's amazing how much older you can seem. No one even questioned me. I don't know if I ever told you, but I had a little sister, about two years younger. I could see him looking at her the same way, you know? But while I was there, he never laid a hand on her. I knew when I left that would change, but I left anyway. Left her there, with him. Invasion happened pretty quick after that, don't know if she made it or not."

She looked up at him, and he could see in her eyes just how haunted she was.

"Out of all the things I've done, all the choices I've made, you know what's funny?" she asked in a hoarse voice. "I don't regret any of it. Even leaving her with him, I don't regret it at all. What does that say about me? About who I am?"

"You were twelve years old, Ravan."

"So the hell what? That doesn't matter."

"It *does*." He tried to be firm, to get through to her. "If you could go back, right now, as you are, what would you do?"

She didn't hesitate to answer. "Save her."

"*Exactly,*" Holt replied. "The reason you don't regret it is that you know there's no call for regretting things you had to do, and in all the time I've known you, I never once saw you do something you didn't have to. Except . . . when it came to me." The last bit stung more than he expected.

"No." Ravan shook her head, kept staring at him. "That I had to do too."

Holt held her gaze. He knew she meant it, wished he could repay her somehow, but really what else was there at this point, besides words?

"I'm sorry I never said thank you," he said.

Ravan studied him back evenly, though he was unsure what exactly she was thinking or what she felt. He'd hurt her a lot recently, but he was glad she was here.

"What about you?" she asked. "What do you regret?"

Holt felt uneasy. "I have to play too?"

"Isn't that what we're doing? Dining on ashes?"

Holt was unsure how to respond. Not because he didn't know the answer, but because he wasn't sure how it would be received. Ravan could see his conflict, and her stare turned curious about what he would say.

Then the cell shook as it began to slowly move. They could hear the hydraulics of the giant lift begin to slowly push them toward the Nonagon.

It was time, apparently. They were being moved into position.

"Great . . ." Ravan said as she stood up, staring at the small door to the cell. "Now that I think about it, maybe I do have a few regrets."

Holt turned to Ravan, and for the first time in a long while really saw her, this person who had sacrificed more for him than anyone he'd ever known. He thought of all he'd done to her, all the pain he'd caused, and for no other reason than that her feelings had always come second to his. She was beautiful, standing there, and he found it a tragedy it was only now, at the end, that he really saw it.

"Hurting you," Holt told her. She looked at him, confused at what he meant. "My biggest regret. I do it over and over, I know that, and it kills me every time. You said before, you didn't think that I see you, but I do, Ravan. No one has ever felt . . . more like home to me. No one's ever given up as much for me. I *see* you." She stared at him, almost stunned. Clearly these were words she never expected to hear. "I don't know what's going to happen now, or what's waiting for us outside, but I promise you this. We're going to beat this thing, we're going to get to the other side, and after we do . . . I will never, *ever* hurt you again."

Ravan's eyes glistened, she stared at him more intently than she ever had. "Never's a long time."

"Yes, it is."

She studied him a moment more, her eyes moving over every part of him . . . then she stepped forward, grabbed him by the shirt, and pulled him to her roughly. The kiss was deep and long, and the reality of what they were about to face faded out for a moment. It was unlike any other kiss he'd had with her. She had always been passionate, and there was an intensity to it, but there was something else too. Something deeper, as if she had finally surrendered the walls around herself that blocked such things, and the release that came from finally expressing it was powerful. He felt her emotions for him in that kiss, and it stirred things, warming him, bringing him back, and the same feelings flowed from him to her.

Ravan pulled away and stared into his eyes. "See you on the other side then."

HOLT WINCED AS HE STEPPED into the bright sun. The lift had brought them up in the back center of the arena, near where the dirt ground encroached onto the metallic floor that covered the place's giant collection of hydraulics and parts.

The whole thing was probably twice the size of a football field. The stands circled around the entire length and they were completely full. The platforms of the Pinnacles were just as crowded, pirates pushing to the edge to watch what was likely the most anticipated Nonagon match of all time. The roar from the spectators seemed to vibrate the ground and it felt like the sound was trying to crush them.

"Looks smaller from the stands," Ravan said, with no small amount of apprehension.

On the field, to the side, stood about a dozen other figures, protected by guards, their hands bound behind them. Out front was a small girl, the pink strips in her hair reflecting the desert sun above. Holt's heart sank. It was Olive and her crew. They hadn't escaped, and most likely, had been put on the field so that they could be quickly executed once the match was done.

The world felt heavy. It was his fault they were here too.

Masyn and Castor stepped out from a cell next to theirs. Neither of them looked great, but they were moving, though Castor was still holding his shoulder and leaning on Masyn. When he saw Holt, he smiled regardless.

Like Ravan, Holt had never seen the Nonagon from the inside, and she was right. It was imposing.

Nine sections of seats stretched around the perimeter, each with a huge red banner hanging above it bearing the shape of some menacing creature: a wolf, a dragon, a scorpion, and so on, around the entire stadium.

The arena floor was divided into a large circle of metal, surrounded by a ring of dirt. In the center rose the Turret, three hundred feet tall, a tower of latticework full of gears, pulleys, and chains. At the very top sat a giant box full of windows with turnable images that could be lined up to create giant mosaics, like some primitive version of a display screen. Right now it was blank.

Spreading out from the Turret was an obstacle course of old cars and trucks and buses and other obstructions. Some had always been there, others were brought in new for each match, seeing as the configurations had a habit of destroying everything inside.

Menagerie guards wheeled away their cells, while others prodded them backward toward the starting position. Waiting there was the Dais, a metallic pedestal with four closed doors that held the items they would have to use. Each Nonagon configuration came with four unique objects to help survive or disarm it, and somehow, whenever the Dais opened, only those items were present. They must be shuttled up from beneath.

Masyn and Castor stared at the huge crowd with curiosity.

"They want a show," Masyn said, smiling.

"Well, you're gonna give them one," Holt replied.

He told them the plan, and their reaction was different than Ravan's. What he was proposing, trying to win instead of just surviving, meant more danger. They were on board from the onset. Castor explained to Masyn about the Nonagon's three rounds, the nine-minute time limits, the different configurations.

"What about the items?" Masyn asked.

"Each configuration has four," Ravan told them. "You can use them to help you survive, or to disarm the configuration. There are four matching slots somewhere on the machine or out in the field."

"So they're like keys?" Masyn asked.

"Yeah, you'll see the lights. They're color-coded to match whatever your item is, and there'll be a receptacle of some kind. Once all the items are in . . . the configuration disarms. Then you get to do it all over again."

A loud blast of staticky sound echoed sharply throughout the arena. The crowd silenced. At the far end, near the top of the central section, rested Tiberius's private box.

Holt could see the tiny figures beginning to fill it. Tiberius's inner circle, those ranking Overseer and above led the way, followed by Tiberius himself, and a smaller figure. Clearly a girl, and even though she was demure, she carried herself with more presence than the others.

"Avril," Masyn said with disdain. "She's just going to sit and watch."

"We all make our choices," Castor replied.

"If you ask me," Ravan said, "she made the right one."

Holt couldn't disagree. Compared to the rest of them, Avril had certainly come out on top.

Looking at the box, it was pretty obvious which one was Tiberius, if only because of his guards and the unassuming way he held himself. He stepped toward a microphone, and seconds later, his voice echoed back and forth between the sides of the arena.

"These have been trying times," he said. "But it has brought us closer. United us. Faust, once more, is a *whole* city."

The crowd erupted back to life. It was exuberant and triumphant and, Holt thought, relieved. Those who had stood by Tiberius had backed the right horse, and this was their day.

Tiberius spoke again, silencing the crowd, and this time the reaction was less approving. "Amnesty will be granted to all those who participated in the rebellion."

The crowd roared its displeasure, feet stomped on the metal bleachers, creating a percussive sound that echoed in the air.

Ravan looked at Holt wryly. "Guess that doesn't include *us*."

Tiberius waited for the roar to die down. "Power must be taken. Challenging for it is our *way*. The ones who survived are few, yet they are the strongest, and we are made stronger by them. They will bring us all profit and power."

"Profit! Power!" the crowd chanted once in unison.

"The second half of our creed says that power lost must be retaken. That is why we are here today. The four in the arena have all played their roles in the taking of *your* power. Today . . . it will be returned. Let the Nonagon begin."

The crowd roared even more hungrily than before. Holt could almost feel the thousands of eyes glaring down menacingly. The windows of the giant "screen" at the top of the Turret suddenly began to spin. The crowd cheered louder. It was going to show the first configuration, which meant the bloodshed wasn't far off.

One by one, the spinning windows froze in place, each clicking to a stop and holding a fraction of a giant image that formed one piece at a time. When it was done, a distinct shape was emblazoned at the top of the Turret.

A spider, its legs tensed as if ready to pounce.

One particular section of the crowd cheered louder than the rest, and the banner above them matched the one on the screen. As Holt watched, the banner rose higher than the others. That section's totem had been called, which meant should it win, their profit would be increased, an exciting prospect. After all, most times, the Nonagon *did* win.

"Tarantula," Ravan observed. "Better than Scorpion, anyway. Tiberius must not want us dead as quickly as I thought."

"Two minutes." A new voice suddenly filled the air from the same speakers that had carried Tiberius's. It was the two-minute warning, the time until the first round would start. Below the screen, the single hand embedded in the giant timer began to spin, starting at 0, with 120 at the opposite end. The Dais hummed and opened, revealing four items, each painted a different color.

A red, wooden staff, about six feet long.

An orange set of bolt cutters.

A green hand axe.

A blue metallic spike with a handle.

"Look on the field," Holt told Masyn and Castor. "Find the matching light."

The Helix looked and now saw spinning lights on different parts of it, in colors that matched the items. Inside an old tow truck there was a blue light. On a rusted storage container, an orange one. At the top of a bus, set on end and stretching almost twenty feet high, sat a red light.

"One minute," the loud, jarring voice proclaimed, and the cheers intensified. The hand of the giant ticking clock was at the very bottom, pointing to 60.

"I don't see the green light," Castor observed, and he was right, it wasn't there, at least not yet.

"You will," Ravan answered dryly. "Just hasn't appeared yet." Quickly, she went over the details of the Tarantula: the pits, the chains, their general strategy. As she did so, the two Helix actually seemed to grow excited. Holt wondered how long that would last.

"We get nine minutes to disarm it, that's how long the round lasts," Ravan told them. "You don't disarm the configuration in that time, it counts as surviving, and we can't win after that."

"Funny how surviving's become second place," Holt observed.

"Remember," Ravan continued, "once you get rid of your key, you can't use it anymore."

"Who's taking what?" Masyn asked.

Holt and Ravan looked at each other, thinking it through, deciding what was best. The Helix's agility and reflexes gave them an advantage, there was no doubt, but it wouldn't count for anything if they didn't match them to the right items and keyholes.

In the end, Castor took the axe and Masyn the staff. They could work together on the green combination lock, and Masyn was the quickest of all of them right now. The red lock was the farthest in; she could use the staff to her advantage in the meantime.

Ravan gave Holt the bolt cutters and took the spike. Both items were meant to help deal with the configuration's second phase, and they were likely going to need them. Holt's body still ached, he wasn't as nimble as he used to be. He just hoped the inevitable surge of terror-induced adrenaline he was about to get would compensate.

Masyn and Castor moved off a few feet, talking in low tones.

"You think they're ready?" Ravan asked him.

Holt shrugged, watching the two talk, seemingly unintimidated. "They're White Helix."

The voice from the speaker filled the arena again. "Ten. Nine. Eight," it intoned, counting down the final seconds. The crowd chanted along with it, their voices punctuating each number.

"And us?"

Holt looked at her. She was beautiful even now, he thought. "We are definitely not ready."

The countdown kept going. Holt tensed, gripped the orange bolt cutters in his hand. It was unlikely they were coming out of this alive, but right then, they still had a chance, and that was what mattered.

"Three. Two. One."

A loud, blaring tone of sound filled the arena as the timer reached 0. The crowd roared. The windows of the giant screen spun crazily, wiping away the spider and replacing it with the numeral 9, the number of minutes they had left. The Turret began to spin. The ground under Holt's feet began to vibrate.

The Nonagon had begun.

32. TARANTULA

THE CROWD HOWLED MENACINGLY as the four dashed over the Nonagon floor. Holt and Ravan separated, headed toward their respective keyholes, while Masyn and Castor stuck together. It was part of the strategy, and necessary to get to the combination lock, which was a Nonagon term for a keyhole that required more than one item to reach, though still only one to disarm. Holt hoped they'd explained the round well enough.

He dodged around and through what was left of a series of buried motorcycles, their handles and front wheels sticking up out of the dirt. Ahead, lines of old cars and other obstructions impeded his progress toward his goal: a rusted storage container, about a hundred yards ahead, an orange light flashing on top.

Without warning, a strange thing happened. The dirt under his feet gyrated and spun, and his pulse quickened as it did. It was anticipated, the Tarantula's primary trap, and an unpleasant one at that.

Holt leapt into the air as the ground fell away under him into a circular pit with a diameter of about twenty feet, and he knew if he looked he would see the giant orifice of geared teeth at the bottom, ready to chew him to bits if he fell in.

He hit the ground on the other side and kept running, watching as the others did the same, leaping over new pits as they formed. The pits were everywhere and unpredictable.

He double-timed it for the container, dodging around another pit that swirled to life in front of him, saw Masyn and Castor do the same. The combination lock hadn't presented itself yet, but it would. The Helix would be fine until then.

Holt saw Ravan reach the tow truck with the flashing blue light . . . right as another pit materialized under her.

The truck was in the center of the pit, but it didn't move, it was held aloft by a metallic column. Anyone approaching that keyhole would have to somehow get over the pit to reach the vehicle. Ravan had seen enough Tarantula matches to know how the blue keyhole was trapped, and had run all-out for it.

It paid off.

She reached the edge of the pit right as it began to form, which gave her enough space to jump and slam onto the side of the truck before the hole yawned open. The spike she was carrying came to a razor-sharp point, and she punched it through the old wheel well of the truck, using it to hold on. Slowly, she pulled herself up until she was close enough to grab onto the side, barely scrambling up and over into the back, then pushed forward and climbed through the truck's rear window.

Seconds later, another intense, staticky burst of sound exploded into the air, and the blue flashing light on the tow truck went dead. Ravan had placed her item in the receptacle and unlocked her keyhole. Holt watched one corner of the huge screen spin and then make a square of blue, indicating what Ravan had done.

The crowd under the Tarantula banner booed loudly. The closer Holt's team got to disarming their configuration, the more profit they stood to lose.

The screen above them now showed 6. Only six minutes left, and they'd only disarmed one of—

From a pit, something exploded up into the air. A mass of thick cables, lined with sinisterly sharp hooks. They were bursting out of the pits all over the arena. Some landed in his path, and he almost tripped as they were reeled back in.

Holt leapt over one strand, landed . . . and felt searing pain as another clawed into his leg.

He was ripped off his feet and slammed onto his back as the cable drew back toward the pit. The cable dragged him roughly across the dirt, the hook digging into his leg. It would pull him inside the giant hole, and down to the grinding gears at the bottom, and that would be that. The crowd rose to a fever pitch, sensing blood.

Holt groaned and sat up, tried to get the jaws of the bolt cutters around the cable as it yanked him forward. He could see where the hook sat in his leg . . . a few inches lower and it would have torn his kneecap off.

The pit was coming, he could see it feet away. He got the cutters around the cable, they slipped loose, got them again . . . then slammed the jaws shut.

The cable snapped. Holt was free, the pain lessened, but the hook was still in. He grabbed the thing and yanked it out, yelled in pain, but was relieved to see the barb hadn't gone all that deep.

That didn't mean it didn't hurt. He had to get up and moving, or the same thing was just going to happen again. More cables and hooks were about to burst out of the pits.

Holt pushed up, started moving, and heard the crowd's fervor grow again. In the distance, he saw Masyn fall, grabbed by a cable, saw Castor leap to help, the axe in his hand chopping down, severing the line. The crowd died down in disappointment and Holt smirked. They'd have to wait a little longer.

"Just standing around isn't gonna help." Ravan ran by, yanking him along with her, ducking around the side of an old water tank.

"Maybe you didn't notice the hook in my leg," Holt replied sourly, the pain searing as he ran. Ahead of them was the storage container and its flashing light.

"And on the very first cable shot too," Ravan replied sarcastically.

"That's the hardest one!"

The cables blew into the air again, raining their hooks down all over the field. Holt and Ravan slammed against the side of an old taxi, barely avoiding the sharp barbs. In the distance, Masyn and Castor ran for a green flashing light above one of the pits.

The combination lock had finally revealed itself, and as he watched, Masyn used the red staff to pole-vault over the pit, arcing through the air and landing on the other side. As she did, she dropped the staff behind her, resting it across the length of the pit. Castor balanced and walked across the thin shaft, then used it to kneel down and shove the green axe into a receptacle somewhere inside.

Seconds later, another burst of sound filled the arena, and a corner of the huge screen colored green.

Castor and Maysn had done it. They both leapt clear of the pit and dodged around new ones, leaping over strands of cable, headed toward the bus in the distance with its flashing red light that held the keyhole for Masyn's staff.

For them the hard part was done. They would make it, which, of course, meant it was up to Holt and Ravan now. The screen above showed 3 . . . they were running out of time.

They dashed out from the taxi . . . and stumbled as a new pit spun to life in front of them. More cables exploded into the air, landing around them.

Holt leapt over them, trying to focus on everything going on around him at once, which wasn't easy. Ravan dashed in the opposite direction, doing the same. They met on the other side and ran for the old storage container just ahead.

"You ever seen anyone beat Tarantula?" Holt asked.

"Nope," Ravan replied, barely avoiding another hook as it slid past.

"So you have no idea what's up with this keyhole?"

"Nope."

Wonderful, Holt thought. The Nonagon was a bad place to be a trailblazer.

They slammed into the container, scanned it, looking for the receptacle for the bolt cutters, but there was nothing. Ravan jumped and grabbed the top edge, pulled herself up to see the top, then dropped back down.

"Nothing," she said, confused.

Then the answer occurred to Holt. He yanked open the thing's heavy steel doors. Inside, at the very back, sat the receptacle, a long orange metallic box, with wires running out the ends and disappearing in a hole in the floor.

Far away, Masyn used the staff to spring herself into the air and land on top of the upended bus with the red light. Seconds later, the blaring noise. A corner on the screen shifted to red. The number there was now 1.

"Move it!" Ravan shoved him forward, and they scrambled into the container. Holt would have smiled if his leg wasn't killing him. They were going to beat Tarantula, they were actually going to—

The metallic floor underneath them began to vibrate. A rumbling sound grew outside. Holt and Ravan looked at each other.

Gravity pulled them back as the entire container suddenly upended and a new pit formed *directly under* it. Unlike the tow truck earlier, the storage container wasn't attached to anything, which meant it was being sucked down inside.

Holt heard the roar of the crowd intensify. Through the container door, he saw the dirt draining into the grinding gears at the bottom of the pit. Sparks flew as the metal box hit those teeth. Scraps of metal shot everywhere as the container was ripped apart and sucked down.

Holt and Ravan grabbed opposite walls, trying to hold on as everything kept tilting. It was about to be too steep, they would slide down the slick floor toward the gears below.

"Toss it here!" Ravan shouted, barely holding on.

He saw what she intended, and threw her the bolt cutters. She fumbled them, but held on. With the last of his strength and with both hands free, Holt grabbed the side of the container and propelled himself toward the receptacle at the end.

He slammed into the back wall, grabbed onto the box and the wires, holding on as the container kept tilting and the teeth ripped everything to pieces below them.

"Ravan!" he yelled, and she threw him the cutters. He caught them, yanked open the box, slammed them inside, and shut it closed.

Ravan groaned and fell backward, barely catching herself. Holt felt himself going too. The gears continued to grind.

Outside the blaring tone of sound came again. The gears whined as they slowly died, shutting off. What was left of the fractured container shuddered as the pit closed and it was lifted back level with the arena floor.

Then everything was quiet, and Holt and Ravan planted themselves against the metal wall, exhausted. The crowd outside howled in fury, but right then, Holt didn't care.

Ravan looked at him, spent. "Well, that's one."

AVRIL WATCHED THE FOUR tiny figures in the arena slowly make their way back to the starting area as what remained of the Tarantula's pits flattened out and disappeared, resetting.

The crowd was electrified, on its feet, and no section was more rowdy than the one under the giant Tarantula banner. Not only had their configuration not managed to kill a single competitor, it had been *beaten*, which meant they had just *lost* profit instead of gaining it.

The windows of the giant screen on the Turret suddenly began to spin. The crowd went silent. Haphazardly, the images froze in place, making another giant mosaic.

It took a moment for Avril to recognize it. It looked almost like a snake, but wider and more oblong, with a strange, triangular face. Electric bolts shot out from its sides, the clues that finally let her decipher it.

It was an Eel.

A section on the far right side cheered as their banner, with its identical image, rose up above the others. Nonagon workers rushed toward the Turret to reconfigure it, switching and modifying its giant pieces.

"Two minutes," the staticky, amplified voice announced. The giant timer began to tick once more.

Avril was full of conflicted emotions. Two of the figures below she was supposed to hate. One for bringing her here, one for killing someone she loved, but the lines that defined those feelings were becoming blurred. The other two she'd fought beside and trained with, commanded even. Avril was bonded to Masyn and Castor, and yet she had betrayed them in her own ways. All of it made watching the Nonagon surreal. She could neither entirely cheer the arena, nor root for its competitors.

There was envy too. She couldn't deny the allure, how much honor there was to be earned fighting to survive. It was the kind of challenge Gideon had instilled a lust for in all his children, but this had been dreamed up and created by someone much different.

Tiberius's eyes were locked on the four figures below. His expression, as usual, betrayed no emotion, but the intensity of his stare was apparent. Next to him, his inner circle, the Consul and Overseer star ranks debated what they had just seen, and most seemed worried.

"My point is, no one's ever *beaten* Tarantula," a short, stocky kid with a stubbly goatee named Monroe stated. He was Tiberius's Economics minister, an Overseer, and one of the few with the guts to openly disagree with her father. It made him valuable to him, but it also, certainly, put him at risk. "Seems pretty damn clear it was a mistake letting in White Helix, or at least, with all their limbs still working."

"That's against the rules," a lanky girl named Petra replied. She was Tiberius's Spymaster, and unlike Monroe, Avril had never seen Petra disagree with anything her father said or did. It made her equally valuable . . . and equally at risk. "Tiberius wrote them himself, are you saying he made a mistake?"

Monroe gave Petra an annoyed look. Such obvious political maneuverings became more common the higher up the command structure you went. "I'm just saying I would have broken some fingers or punctured a lung, that's all. Handicapping them's fair, brings them down to the level of the usual contestants."

"One of them isn't using his left arm," an icy voice observed. It was Marek, the only current Consul in the Menagerie, and Tiberius's most trusted advisor. There were two Consul positions, and it was widely believed that the second would go to Avril. After all, Archer had held it before. Marek, unlike Archer, had risen to the rank all on his own, without any nepotism at all, and it was a testament to his shrewdness. He was as ruthless as Tiberius, and most likely very displeased at Avril's return.

If she hadn't come back, Marek would have been the clear heir apparent. Even now, he studied Avril as he spoke. "These Helix seem able to compensate for weakness with new strengths. I'm not surprised, given how formidable . . . our Avril is."

The conversation disintegrated into argument, but her father just stared down at the figures at the Dais, readying for the next round. Quade was at the opposite end of the box, studying Avril with his simple, curious look. Would she betray him or wouldn't she? The truth was, she still didn't know which way she would play that card.

"Stop the bickering." The arguments ceased at Tiberius's voice, quiet and calm, yet somehow able to overpower the others. "Even if they win . . . they lose. There's no reason for concern."

The comment was cryptic, but the inner circle seemed to accept it. Something about the statement bothered her. She looked at Quade questioningly, and he looked back, clearly deciding how much to trust her. In the end, he casually glanced up to the very top of the Nonagon, behind their box.

There, where the seats of the stands gave way to the support beams that held the structure together, she saw movement. Two figures among the shadows, and a flash, the bright, hot sun reflecting off glass.

Avril understood. The reflection came off a rifle scope. The figures were snipers.

Tiberius had no intention of letting Holt's team win. Even if they did manage to disarm all the configurations . . . they would still lose. Just as he'd said.

"One minute," the voice announced, echoing sharply back and forth amid the stands, and the crowd wailed its approval.

33. EEL

RAVAN LISTENED to the one-minute warning and the cheers of the crowd with slowly building anger. She turned in a circle, glaring at the individual stands, and wondered what the conversation was like in Tiberius's box right about now.

"I'm going to shut you up!" she yelled back at the crowd. "Every *one* of you!"

She felt full of strength now, confident. Before she had been pessimistic at best about their prospects, but the victory over Tarantula had changed that. Now she felt something very different, she felt hope. Dim, certainly, but it was there. She remembered Holt's words to her in the cell, knew, finally, that he meant them, remembered him pressed against her in that old, familiar way. She had things to live for now, she had reasons for seeing tomorrow.

"That oughta scare them," Holt said, and she gave him an amused smile. He'd bandaged his leg using the first-aid supplies in the Dais and was walking better. Masyn and Castor seemed no worse for wear after the first round, they weren't even breathing hard.

Everyone held a new item, pulled from the Dais, and it had been Ravan who picked them. The Eel had always been a passion of hers—she loved how the items worked with the configuration, how each had a specific place on the Turret. Of course, that affinity had come as a spectator, not a contestant, but the point was she had a good understanding of strategy.

Ravan took the red rubber insulated gloves for herself. She was in a better position than Holt to use them, she wasn't as hurt. She gave him the two yellow hand claws, which were just what they sounded like. They slipped over your wrist with a handle to grab onto, and jutting out from the other side were three sharp, metallic claws. They were for climbing a specific part of the Turret. It was tough work, but easier than going straight up the supports with the gloves.

Castor was slipping on a green leather harness, with a geared ratchet on the front that hooked into a pulley system on the Turret. It would get him to the top of the giant spinning tower quickly, which was an important part of the strategy. Getting back down, though, was going to be the challenge.

Masyn held an orange length of chain with a long, sharp grappling hook tied to one end. It was usually used for simple climbing through the Turret supports, but Ravan had other ideas how Masyn could use it.

The timer under the screen was at the ninety-second mark. It was almost time. There was a groaning as the Turret slowly began to spin again, and she could see the workers running to get clear as long arms of cylindrical metal rose into the air, spinning along with the tower.

They could all see the lights flashing up and down the Turret, each a different color that corresponded to their item. There was something else too. A dim, bluish, sparkling light that crackled up and down the thing: the arcing of powerful electricity.

"I see where it gets its name," Castor said, though his voice sounded fascinated, not frightened. He should be, Ravan thought. That was lethal current, one touch and it was good-bye.

"I just want you guys to know," Holt said, staring at the Turret uneasily. "I never wanted to find myself here, and I know you didn't either, but after the way we beat the last round, there's no other group I'd rather be in this with than you. Whatever happens . . . I'm glad you're here."

Ravan looked at him. Holt looked back. He held out his hand and she took it, running her thumb over the rough outline of the unfinished tattoo. "Guess you might as well finish this," she said.

He held her gaze . . . then smiled.

The blaring tone of sound filled the arena. The windows on the giant screen whirred and slammed into position, creating a huge 9 above them.

Ravan held Holt's gaze a moment more . . . then they all ran toward the Turret as the crowd cheered for them to fail. That wasn't going to happen, she vowed.

They ran through the dirt, dodging around cars and old water tanks. Ahead of them, the dirt was replaced by solid metal, the interior floor of the arena.

"Watch the ground!" Ravan yelled to Masyn and Castor, both several strides ahead in their eagerness. They slowed down as they saw what she meant.

Parts of the metallic ground flickered in bluish energy. Tiberius had designed the electricity to be visible, even in bright sunlight; it wouldn't be fair otherwise, he said, though what he really meant was the matches wouldn't last as long.

Ravan found a clear patch of ground that wasn't electrified and headed toward it, followed by Holt. Right now the parts of the Nonagon that were electrified were set, they didn't change, but that wouldn't last long.

She hit the metal, felt herself slide on its slick surface. The thing was like ice. Ravan slowed, felt Holt do the same, but watched Masyn and Castor actually pick up speed. She envied their agility.

Ahead sat the Turret, three hundred feet tall, spinning powerfully. The arms attached to it varied in length up the entire thing, whizzing through the air as the tower spun.

A dozen more strides and Ravan reached it, ducking as one of the arms whizzed past and almost took her head off. She risked a glance at the screen; it showed 8. Not bad, but all they'd done so far was the easy part.

Masyn swung the grappling hook and launched it upward where it clung onto one of the Turret's support rods, about fifteen feet above. Instantly, she started climbing, fist over fist, pulling herself up.

Castor reached the pulley system for the harness, a length of cable that went straight up to the top, where the green light that marked his keyhole flashed. When he was hooked in, he yanked the cable down with his good hand, and shot upward.

"At least they *look* like they know what they're doing," Ravan observed, slipping on the gloves and dodging another arm as it whizzed past.

"Wonder what that's like?" Holt asked back, the fasteners of the two climbing claws already around his wrists. One whole side of the Turret was covered in metallic plating, and Ravan could see the slits that were cut into it in a stair-stepping pattern running up the whole way, slits that would only work with the climbing claws. About halfway up was the flashing yellow light, Holt's goal.

"Geronimo," Holt said . . . then leapt up and plunged both his claws into matching pairs of slits in the paneling, holding on as the spinning column whipped him away and he began to climb.

Ravan didn't have time to wish him luck. Another arm sailed towards her, and she grabbed it. The impact was jarring, but she held on. After that, it was no longer the Turret that spun past her, it was the world outside, racing by in a dizzying blur.

The crowd cheered louder: the four were on the Turret now, where the Eel could do its worst.

As she spun, Ravan looked up. She could just make out the red light that marked her keyhole about three-quarters of the way up, mixed in with the central supports that kept the whole thing standing. She was going to have to climb those supports, and she could see the flickering, blue arcs of electricity covering most of them. Only the gloves would protect her, and if she touched it with any other part of her body . . .

Ravan slid over the arm toward the center of the column, where it was attached. She studied the interior column, could see the supports, found one that was below her and somewhat isolated from the rest. It wasn't electrified, it was her best shot.

Ravan fell . . . and grabbed onto the support, almost slipped, pulled herself back up. She made it, but she didn't congratulate herself. That red light was a long way up, through a maze of crisscrossing electrified strands of metal.

The nearest support was electrified, she could see the flickering energy. She felt a sense of doubt. Would the gloves really work? Could they insulate her from that kind of current?

Get on with it, she told herself. No hesitation.

Ravan grabbed the support above, let her fingers close around it.

She didn't fry on the spot; nothing happened other than she could feel the vibration from the current running through it.

Emboldened, she grabbed another rung, swung over, careful not to let her dangling feet touch anything. She did it again, climbing, pulling herself through the maze of electricity as the world raced by. She tried not to think about the spinning—it was disorienting, which was clearly the point.

The crowd wailed suddenly.

Ravan looked and saw Masyn, the chain and its hook attached to one of the spinning arms, flinging herself through the air, using the momentum to shoot straight up and through the spinning arms.

The crowd cheered louder. They liked it, and Ravan didn't blame them. That was definitely *not* how that item was meant to be used.

Castor reached the apex of the Turret in his harness, and shuddered to a stop where his receptacle and the green flashing light lay. He didn't waste time, started unbuckling. The strategy had been to get him to the top as quickly as possible, because once the second phase of the Eel started, the entire top part of the Turret became electrified, making it impossible even for a White Helix to reach it after that. It was important Castor be the first to get rid of his item, and it looked like he would.

Nearby, Holt kept climbing, slipping the claws into the slits, one hand at a time. He stuck the right claws into their grooves, shifted his weight . . . . . . and the entire panel came loose and he fell. The crowd whooped loudly.

Holt barely caught himself with his left hand, dangling, trying to find a new panel for his right. Eventually he did, cementing himself in place, holding on.

He stared up at Ravan warily. She shot him back a pointed look.

His path up had fake panels in it, and you had to test them carefully. Hopefully, Holt had learned his lesson.

Ravan grabbed a nonelectrified support, then pressed herself up, wrapped her legs around it, and held on, catching her breath. All around her the electrified poles sparked and fizzled, and her receptacle was still a good twenty feet above, through a tight maze of more supports.

The usual blare of sound filled the arena. A corner of the giant screen shifted to green. Castor had deposited his item. The screen showed 6, they were making good time.

But once the countdown hit 5, the configuration entered its second stage. Which meant . . .

"Castor!" Holt yelled up at the Helix, who, like Ravan, had found a perch to catch his breath. "Get off!"

Holt was right, he had to get out fast. Even climbing down, he wouldn't have enough time to get out of the zone that was about to be hot, and he didn't have the harness anymore.

"Jump!" It was Masyn's voice, farther up, using the chain and hook to swing through the Turret.

Castor stared down at Masyn, but not with a worried look, rather a mischievous one. He waited another second, watching her swing, timing it . . . then he dropped into the air and fell like a rock.

There was a gasp from the crowd.

Masyn slammed into him, using the chain to swing her like a pendulum. Castor grabbed on and they soared over to a lower rung like trapeze artists.

The crowd went crazy, and it wasn't with menace or disappointment. Odd as it was, it seemed like the Menagerie were actually cheering *them* now.

Ravan didn't have time to contemplate it. The bar she was wrapped around suddenly began to vibrate. She felt her hair stand up.

The support, and all kinds of other things on the Turret, were about to get hot.

Ravan used the adrenaline to swing herself onto the support, and with her legs, kicked up and off into the air. She grabbed another rung above her, just as the one below electrified.

The Eel's electricity was no longer static. All around her, she watched it move in patterns, switching from one piece of the Turret to the next, up and down its length. It was now much more dangerous.

Ravan grabbed another bar, pulled herself up. Another, climbing toward the red light. She was almost there. She grabbed another rung . . . and her leg, just barely, flicked across the top of an electrified support beam.

The pain was intense. Every muscle in her body cramped hard and then she was falling. She got control back in time to grab another bar with a gloved hand, and the impact almost ripped her shoulder out of its socket. She groaned, but held on.

"Rae!" Holt shouted from above.

It took everything she had to just keep her grip on the bar. She could hear the crowd cheer, eager for blood, to see her tumble to the ground, and the sound filled her with more rage. She would *not* give them the satisfaction.

The screen showed 4 now. They were running out of time.

Ravan gritted her teeth and started climbing, pulling herself up and through the deadly maze. She couldn't say how she managed it—maybe it was the crowd, or the memory of Holt and her in the cell, or the thought of strangling Tiberius with her bare hands—but she pulled herself through that maze, one bar at a time, keeping away from the supports as the electricity danced along their spines, until she finally reached her receptacle.

It was a faded red box, and there was a single rung that wasn't hot for her to sit on. She pulled herself up onto it, unstrapped the gloves, and shoved them into the box.

Another blast of sound. A corner turned red on the screen. The wail of the crowd overpowered everything again.

She'd done it, but now she was trapped, surrounded by electrified supports, her only option was to hold on while the Turret spun and hope Masyn and Holt could do their jobs.

One was having better luck than the other. After depositing Castor in a clear zone, Masyn swung back down and through the supports, then flipped upward, grabbed a rung, twirled around it and shot up again, dragging the chain and the grappling hook behind her.

It was a sight to see, especially when contrasted with Holt's decidedly slower progress.

He was below, the only good thing about his receptacle was that it was the lowest of the four, and she watched him gingerly test one panel, stick in the claw, shift his weight, and pull himself up while avoiding the electricity. It was a painstaking process, and to make it worse, the giant screen now showed 2.

"Maybe we should have given yours to Masyn too!" Ravan yelled at him.

Holt didn't retort, he was probably too tired. The receptacle was just above him, almost in reach . . .

Another blaring tone of sound, and a third corner of the screen rotated to orange. Above, Masyn had unlocked her keyhole, she was done.

But if Holt didn't get those claws to the yellow light, it was all over.

As Ravan watched, Holt froze, his eyes widening. Ravan could guess what was happening. One of the panels his claws were in had started to vibrate, it was powering up. Desperately he tried to remove his right hand, but the claw stuck in place. He tried harder, bracing his feet against the panel itself, pulled.

The whole thing snapped apart, though it didn't break completely loose. It hung in place by the bottom rungs, but the impact was enough to jar Holt's hand loose from the claw, still stuck inside the panel, right as it electrified. Sparks flew as the current arced through it.

Holt jerked, lost his grip on the left panel . . . and *fell*.

"Holt!" Ravan screamed, watching him plummet. He managed to jam the claw into the slits of a panel, jerking himself to a stop about twenty feet below. His feet dangled wildly as he tried for purchase, supports and panels electrified all around him.

The screen shifted to 1.

Ravan's gaze moved from Holt to the missing claw, stuck near the receptacle. There was no way he could get there now, even with both claws he couldn't climb it that fast. It meant they weren't going to be able to disarm the configuration, which meant they could no longer beat the Nonagon.

The smart thing to do would have been for everyone to just hold on where they were, and survive the round, but Ravan could see the desperation in Holt's eyes, could see what this meant to him. It wasn't just that he would fail, but that he would fail people he'd made promises to. It meant he would never make it to that little girl in San Francisco. Everything he'd struggled for and been through would be for nothing.

It was a fear she knew well. Maybe that was why she made the decision she did. Or because, like she'd told him not that long ago, he was the only person she had ever sacrificed for. What was one more time?

Ravan let go of the railing and fell through the air. She slammed into a support, and it spun her. Another hit sent her reeling the other way. She felt a rib snap, felt the pain, heard the crowd gasp.

She could just make out the big metal box and the flashing yellow light. She slammed into the paneling, slid, grabbed hold of the box with her hands, and barely held on.

The claw was just below her, still stuck where Holt had left it. She kicked it once. Twice. Knocked it loose, reached down, and grabbed it, barely holding on.

The crowd erupted, watching her, and once more it seemed like they were actually cheering *for* her. She liked it, wondered right then how Tiberius felt.

She shoved the claw into the box. The panels and supports around her arced as electricity flashed through them.

"Ravan!" Holt yelled up at her. There was desperation in his voice, but not for himself. It was for her. "What are you doing?"

"Throw me your claw!" she yelled back down at him.

"Rae—"

"There's no time, Holt! *Throw it!*"

Holt hesitated a moment more, then clung onto a support, unhooked the claw from his left wrist, and tossed it up to her. She yanked it from the air . . . right as her fingers slipped. She fell.

Ravan barely grabbed onto what was left of the panel Holt had pulled loose. It wasn't electrified right now, and it groaned under her weight, bending, tearing free . . .

"*Ravan!*" Holt's anguished voice yelled below.

"I know you meant what you said," she yelled down to him, oddly calm. "But this isn't where you're supposed to be."

With the last of her strength, Ravan shoved the second claw into the box . . . and then the panel burst loose from the supports and she was falling and the world spun and the ground rushed up at her, and strangely, surreally, she smiled, feeling a sense of triumph, not for having beaten the Eel, but for having embraced a part of herself she had always dismissed as weak and fallible. She knew who she was. Finally.

And then the ground was there.

THE TURRET STOPPED its spinning as the final blaring tone of sound filled the Nonagon, but Holt didn't notice. He wasn't even sure how he got to the ground, didn't remember climbing or jumping, just remembered the need to find her.

The crowd had gone silent. It was eerie, he'd never heard the place not filled with clamoring and furor, especially when someone died, but this wasn't just another Wind Trader prisoner, this was—

She is not *dead,* he scorned himself. *She can't be.*

He hit the ground running, eyes scanning, trying to find any sign of—

He saw her. Ten feet away.

The shape of her, bent like that, unmoving.

The world was a slow-motion haze now, nothing felt real. Holt's legs moved without his involvement, propelling him forward, sliding him down next to her.

She lay there, still. There was no real blood that he could see. Her body didn't move or shake, it looked like a stone. Only her eyes moved, back and forth, finding his.

"Listen to that," she said, her voice a fractured whisper. "Finally . . . shut them up."

"Ravan . . ."

"It . . . doesn't hurt, Holt. Want you to know . . . doesn't hurt."

Holt couldn't feel any one part of himself, could barely focus, could barely think. "That's because you're going to be okay," he said, his voice just as ragged as hers. He didn't even recognize it.

"You're an optimistic idiot. You . . . always were."

Holt felt the sting of forming tears, the burning. "You have to hold on, Ravan."

"Could have used that advice earlier." She smiled weakly, and it filled him with a desperate anger.

"*You hold on!*" Holt shouted, and the ferocity shocked him. His hands shook, he felt detached from his body. He couldn't lose *her*. He couldn't. Ravan was indestructible, she was . . . This was wrong.

Her eyes peered into his, she didn't like what she saw. "You've lost so many people, haven't you?"

Holt couldn't answer. He put his hands on her chest, felt her weak heartbeat.

"You don't have to go back to who you were, Holt." Her voice was fading, getting harder to hear, and it terrified him. "It's a choice."

"What's the alternative?" His voice was bitter.

"Inspire them," she said, barely audible. "Make them believe. It's . . . what you were meant to do. You just . . . never . . . believed it."

Her fingers lifted off the ground, just inches, it was all she could manage. They crawled to his hand, found the tattoo there. Holt was ashamed of it now. He hated it. Not because it was there, but because it was unfinished. It *deserved* to be finished.

"Tell me . . ." Ravan breathed.

"Tell you what?" He took her hand in his.

"Was there . . . a time . . . long ago . . ." Each word took effort, her gaze was becoming glassy. "When you . . . loved me . . . ?"

Holt's eyes shut tight. He felt himself collapse next to her. He almost lost it there, almost just lay down next to her and followed her to wherever she was going. Let the next round start, let it wipe him away. But he didn't. He made himself speak, if only so that she would hear the truth.

"Look at me," he told her, gently. "Ravan, look at me."

Her eyes refocused a little, found his.

"Yes," he told her. "I still do."

Her smile, from before, returned, but weaker now. She sighed, seemed to relax, as if the words filled her with some kind of peace that melted away the pain.

"See you . . . on the other side . . ." she whispered. Her eyes focused on his one last time. And then she was gone.

As he watched her form sink into the hard metal of the Nonagon floor, Holt felt a stirring of emotion more powerful than anything he'd ever felt. His fists clenched, his head throbbed, his eyes stung. He wanted to scream, but nothing would come. All he could do was look at her, lying there, someone more full of life than anyone he had ever known . . . and she was absolutely still.

Every memory Holt had ever made with Ravan flashed through his mind—good, bad, painful, tender—merging into one massive stream that flooded his consciousness. That last question had been damning, he still felt the pain of it. *Did you love me?* She deserved so much more. She deserved not to have had to wonder, she deserved to have *known*, and it was his fault she never did. Now she was gone, lost to him forever. The shame and the grief he felt grew and morphed, became hot, became a focused rage.

He stared a second more . . . then pushed to his feet and started moving toward the Dais. He had a dim impression of Castor and Masyn nearby, watching him silently, stunned, unsure, but he didn't say anything.

Behind and above, the screen began to whir again, and Holt heard it lock into place, showing the next configuration, but he didn't even look. Whatever the symbol was, the crowd didn't seem interested. It was still virtually silent, but Holt wouldn't have heard them even if they weren't. He just kept moving toward the Dais, each step filled with new purpose. The pain of his injuries was a memory now.

"What are we doing?" It was Castor. His voice had lost all its eagerness. He sounded stunned.

"Finishing it," Holt said back in a firm voice. "*That's* what we're doing."

"The . . . three of us?" Masyn asked back. Her voice was dulled as well. "Isn't that impossible?"

"*Two minutes,*" the booming, staticky voice announced. The crowd still had yet to respond.

Holt reached the Dais, saw it was open, saw the items inside.

A red tire iron.

A strange blue, electronic device, with two handles, a thick, circular piece of grayish metal, and wires running everywhere. It was a handheld electromagnet.

A series of yellow straps, clearly meant to go around a person's forearm, with a big, actuated, metallic clip at the end.

And a strange, green collection of pieces and parts—rubber, wood, metal—all welded and formed together into a rounded shape. There was a strap for someone to slip their arm through like a shield.

Holt knew the items, had no need to look to see the image of the bird of prey on the screen, streaking down, claws extended, beak parted.

"Harrier," Holt said, grabbing the shield and slipping his arm through the strap, tightening it in place. "There's not much to say. See the arms the crew is raising?"

If the two Helix had looked they would have seen shafts of metal lifting from openings in the metallic floor around the Turret, each probably thirty feet tall, the entire length of which were sharpened to a razor's edge. More arms, on the Turret itself, were being unstrapped too.

But they didn't look. Masyn and Castor just kept staring at Holt, shocked and unsure.

"Some strike downward, some are going to come at you from the sides," Holt kept going, his voice a monotone. He felt the same energy from before building, the rage, the focus. "They're bladed. Castor, take the electromagnet, Masyn, take the clip. Two of the keyholes are on the arms, those items help you get on top and hold on. I'll take care of the ones on the ground. Just be ready."

"Holt," Castor said intently. "This is *crazy*. We can't do this with three people."

Holt grabbed the tire iron and spun to face them. His eyes must have been wild, because the two Helix each took a step back.

"We *are* going to do this," he said. His voice wasn't loud, but it was full of energy and anger, and it shook dangerously. He pointed back toward Ravan, to where she lay, cold and still. "Every promise I ever made to her I *broke*. Well, not this time. I promised her we would beat this thing. I promised her we would get to the other side. *So be ready.*"

Holt pushed past them without another look, feeling the anger, letting it fuel him. Out the corner of his eye, he saw Masyn and Castor move for the Dais and the items there.

"*One minute,*" the voice announced.

Let it come, he thought. Let it *come.*

AVRIL FOUND HERSELF ON her feet with the rest of the crowd as the black-haired pirate tumbled down through the Turret, bouncing off the supports, twisting and turning until she crashed into the metal ground cover on the arena floor.

The impact was jarring, even from this far away.

It took Avril a moment to remember to breathe. The crowd went near silent. Even Tiberius seemed torn, staring down at Ravan's unmoving figure. They had been close. Maybe he had even seen her as a surrogate for Avril, which wasn't surprising. Ravan was much more like Tiberius than she was.

Or was she?

Avril had more reason to cheer Ravan's death than most. The pirate had been the one who ripped her from her home, taken away everything she held dear, but in the course of their time together, Ravan had proven difficult to unconditionally hate, had shown herself to be much more than Avril originally assumed.

Ravan's loss and sacrifice, combined with the performance of Castor and Masyn in the Eel, had done more to shake the foundations of the choices Avril was faced with than anything else. The more of this match she watched, the more she wished she was anywhere other than in this box.

In the distance, Avril could see Holt, Masyn, and Castor conferring around the Dais, watched as they took their items, and, specifically, she watched Holt take *two*. The action wasn't lost on the others, there was only one reason Holt would burden himself with two items.

"They're going to try to *win*," Markel observed, a note of amazement in his voice. And something else too, something that sounded like respect. Even Petra was silent.

The single hand of the huge timer had almost completed its circle. The blaring, staticky voice counted down.

"Ten . . . nine . . . eight . . ."

The crowd didn't chant along this time, they just watched the three figures moving toward the Turret, spreading out. For the first time since the event had begun, Avril felt nervous, watching the people below.

Gideon, she thought to herself. Watch over them.

"Three . . . two . . . one . . ."

The blaring tone of sound filled the arena. The Turret began to turn powerfully. And the crowd, silent until now, roared back to life, but this time they weren't taunting the spectators or rooting for them to fail. They were *cheering* them. Or, at least, cheering for one. The huge swath of pirates that filled the arena chanted one word, over and over.

"*Haw-kins! Haw-kins! Haw-kins!*"

Next to her, Tiberius, the only figure still seated in the entire arena, slowly stood. His glare was pure heat, staring downward at the figure of Holt below, moving toward the Turret. Avril couldn't be sure, but it seemed, even from this height . . . that Holt stared right back.

HOLT MOVED FOR THE Turret, gripping the strange shield and the tire iron tightly. He could hear the crowd chanting his name, the sounds echoing from one side of the Nonagon to the other. Part of him registered just how unheard of that was, but it was a dim realization.

He simply didn't care. It wasn't like before, though. He hadn't closed down again—in fact, it was the opposite. There was pain for Ravan, and he felt it passionately, but somehow, her loss had galvanized him, had fully brought him *back*. It was sad that it took losing so much to get him to feel, to get him to *fight*.

Inspire them, Ravan had told him. He would do much more than that.

Holt stared up at Tiberius's elegant box, glaring at the figures there. He saw one of them slowly rise, knew it was him, and Holt held his stare as he moved, the rest of the world bleeding away until there was nothing but the two of them. He had no idea how this would all resolve, but somehow, Tiberius would pay for the brilliant light he had snuffed out here today. Holt would see to it.

Then those thoughts were ripped away as Harrier's first blade appeared.

It whizzed through the air, propelled down right toward him, and Holt leaped out of the way and it crashed into the ground with a thunderous impact.

The other blades were falling too, striking downward all over the arena. Masyn and Castor rolled nimbly, dodging the sharpened arms. They reminded Holt of the giant bars of some twisted typewriter, trying to cleave everything below them in two.

One of the arms, near Masyn, had a flashing yellow light near the center, marking the keyhole. Castor's light hadn't appeared yet, but it would soon enough.

Another arm flew toward Holt, and he avoided it as it split the metal frame of an old Volkswagen in two, spraying metal everywhere.

Holt looked and found where he was going. A red light flashed over the remains of a rusted tractor. Unlike before, he had *two* keyholes to unlock this time. The second was marked by a green light, the color of his shield, and it flashed from the windows of an old Winnebago, much farther away. Getting there in time, through the air blades, was going to be nearly impossible.

The screen whirred and showed 8. Holt started running for the tractor.

Arms fell and he dodged every one, kept moving. He reached the tractor and scanned it, the red light flashing on its top, but he didn't see—

He heard the whir of the blade before he saw it. He barely had time to get the tire iron up, holding it with both hands while the blade slammed down.

The impact slammed him into the dirt. The crowd gasped, watching. He managed to block the thing with the iron, deflecting it up and off, and another one fell toward him. He rolled out of the way, right underneath the tractor.

There, nestled amid its rusted pieces and parts, was the receptacle for the iron.

Holt yanked it open, shoved it in, and shut the door.

The staticky, distorted tone filled the arena. It was quickly followed by a second blast.

Holt peeked out at the huge screen. Two of the corners were marked now, one green, one yellow. Masyn had gotten hers too. It helped, gave them some time back, but the screen still showed a 5.

Loud thunking sounds came from the near distance as new arms detached from the Turret. They were sharpened like the first set, but these whizzed through the air *horizontally*. The vertical arms were adjusted with clockwork precision to fall in between the spinning horizontal ones. Morbid as it was, it was an amazing mechanical design.

Masyn rode on top of one of the vertical arms, while Castor ran for a horizontal one, this one marked with a flashing blue light. It was the Helix's keyhole, and he would no doubt get it.

About a hundred yards away sat Holt's last goal: the Winnebago. The air between him and it was full of giant, whizzing razors. Conventionally there was no way he could reach it in time. But watching the horizontal arms spinning past, an idea occurred to him. An insane one, but the thought of it stirred no fear in him. He felt only resolution.

Inspire them . . .

Holt rolled out from under the tractor, while the screen above shuffled to 4.

He got to his feet . . . and just as quickly ducked as a blade soared right over his head. He could feel the wind, it was so close, and he stared after the thing as it whizzed away.

That was the one he needed, and he probably had ten seconds before it made its way back.

He scrambled out of the way of another arm, then blocked a second with the shield, felt the thing try and drive him into the ground like a tent stake, but he pushed it off and scrambled on top of the tractor and lay flat as another blade buzzed by.

Holt saw the arm he needed, coming for him at one hell of a velocity. He gripped the shield and shoved it in front of him, braced himself.

This was going to hurt.

It slammed into the shield at full force and sent Holt flying through the air like a cannonball. He heard the crowd roar its approval, felt the stands shake as they stomped in excitement.

Holt hit the ground hard, rolled violently through the dirt, and the shield came loose, skittered away.

The screen above showed 2.

Painfully, he reached for the shield . . . then flattened himself as a low blade arced past. He had to hurry, he was almost spent.

Holt dove toward the shield, grabbed it and limped for the Winnebago. He risked a glance behind him and saw Castor, riding his own arm, spinning around the Turret, crawling toward the blue light.

It was about to be up to Holt.

He burst through the door of the RV and crashed against what was left of the old kitchen as one of the giant blades crashed down outside, barely missing him.

A blaring tone of sound announced Castor's victory. Holt had about a minute, he guessed.

He scanned the interior of the old RV, and found it, sitting on top of the dashboard, a giant box big enough to hold the green shield. He pushed forward. He was going to make it, he was going—

A blade sliced right through the ceiling of the RV, splitting the whole thing in half in a shower of fiberglass and aluminum, and Holt barely jumped out of the way in time.

Splinters of wood cut into him, the ceiling buried him to the floor, pain laced through his body.

The hot sun filtered down now. The blade yanked back up, unblocked his path.

Holt crawled forward, holding the shield, moving for the dashboard and the receptacle there. Outside he heard the whizzing of blades, knew that same one was about to come back down and end him.

His vision blurred, his muscles screamed. With what strength he had left, Holt shoved the shield into the box and slammed the door shut . . .

. . . then collapsed, waiting for the arm to end it, to slice him in half like the RV.

But it didn't. The tone echoed outside, signaling it was done.

The grinding of gears from the Turret silenced. The sound of whizzing blades went away. All he could hear was the crowd now, roaring with the power of a tidal wave.

Holt just wanted to lie there forever, but he couldn't. He wasn't finished. Not yet.

He crawled out of the Winnebago, shaky on his feet, barely able to walk. He was bleeding, he saw, in numerous places. His depth perception was gone, and it took a moment for him to realize it was because his left eye was swollen shut.

He kept moving all the same.

He saw Masyn and Castor nearby, saw them hug, saw them stare at each other awkwardly, then kiss, pulling each other close.

The crowd cheered louder than any Nonagon crowd Holt had ever heard, chanting one thing, over and over.

"Haw-kins! Haw-kins! Haw-kins!"

But he just kept moving. Kept moving until he had reached her again, where she'd fallen, where she'd left him. She was still there, eyes closed. She looked beautiful, peaceful, like she deserved.

Holt bent down and picked up Ravan's body, held her close, started walking, carrying her to the other side of the arena, to where victors were always received. Everything was silent for him, all he heard was the sound of his own breathing. All he saw was the dark-haired girl in his arms.

Holt set Ravan gently down at the other end of the Nonagon, exactly where he promised her they would be. He smoothed the hair from her face. He waited for whatever was to come.

AVRIL WATCHED HOLT DELICATELY lay Ravan's body almost directly below her, where the dirt of the Nonagon floor's outer edge met the stands and the huge gate that allowed workers (and victors) to exit. Some of those workers approached him, and he glared up at them defiantly, daring them to even try and take Ravan away.

That gesture, combined with all the others, cemented her feelings for the Outlander, the one who had killed Archer. No one who was anything but decent could have done what Holt Hawkins had just done.

Next to her, Tiberius tore his hateful glare from Holt, and reached down for something. It was a radio, Avril saw, and her father was raising it up to speak. There was little doubt that he was about to order the snipers to fire. It meant everyone below would die, after all they'd been through, after all they'd achieved, and Avril felt her anger begin to build.

She looked at Quade. Quade looked back. "I'm ready to play that card now."

Quade smiled. Then he drew his knife from his belt and tossed it to her.

She caught it, gripped the handle, spun . . . and plunged it into Tiberius's heart.

The knife sunk deep, punching through the bone, finding its mark.

Tiberius gasped, staggered back. The radio fell from his hand. The inner circle stared in shock. Stunned cries echoed everywhere in the stands.

Guns, hundreds of them, all drew from their holsters . . . but a booming voice stopped them, echoing over the Nonagon's loudspeakers.

"*Stop!*" Tiberius shouted as he fell to his knees, holding the microphone. Slowly, the guns lowered, silence filled the arena. "Avril . . . is my heir. And she is *your* heir. This . . . is the *taking* of power."

Tiberius slowly collapsed to the floor. Weakly, he looked up at Avril. She stared back, in shock and horror. The action had been so quick, so instinctual, she hadn't even had time to think, but now the results were in front of her, and she wasn't sure she liked them.

"Wondered . . . what it would take . . ." Tiberius managed to say, his voice fading. He reached into a pocket, pulled out a small black cloth bag, and handed it to his adopted daughter. "I'm . . . proud of you, Avril."

Then Tiberius Marseilles, like Ravan below, faded and was gone.

Avril stared down at him. The man had been a father to her in some ways, and a nightmare in others, but just as much as Gideon, he had made her the person she was. Avril looked around the stands, at the pirates, at the people of Faust, and they all stared back. There was a kinship in their gazes now, which pointed to the truth. One she had long denied.

She was one of them. She wondered if this had been Tiberius's plan all along.

Avril opened the black bag, let the contents fall into her hands. Three rings, each made of glowing crystal, red, green, and blue, and they shone brightly, even in the sunlight.

Avril slipped them on, felt their slight, familiar vibrations. It felt normal, it felt like home.

She looked up at the inner circle and at Quade. They all stared back warily, some with hostility, but it was to be expected in this place, in this city, her second home. She would just have to get used to it.

"There will be changes," Avril told them, looking each in the eye, letting them see her strength. "Any who feel they can do better should challenge me for power. It is our way. But in the meantime, I will profit all of you, and drag the Menagerie to glory whether you like it or not."

And with that she ran forward and leapt straight off the side of the stands. The crowd gasped, watching her plummet. It felt fantastic, the free-fall, soaring through the air again. She touched her middle and ring fingers together, and sighed as the air crackled around her and her vision colored with bright cyan. Her descent slowed, she landed on the arena floor in a crouch, and her eyes found Masyn's and Castor's.

The three stared at one another, and then Avril nodded to them, with respect. They nodded back.

She moved toward Holt, who hovered defiantly over Ravan's body, putting himself between her and the Menagerie guards that circled him. When he saw her, some of the fierceness died. They stared at each other a long moment, unspoken words passing between the two.

Then Avril held out her hand.

Holt slowly took it. She held his gaze . . . then held his hand up into the air, letting the crowd see them together.

The stands erupted in cheers and stomping that must have filled the air for miles. They all chanted the same two words, over and over.

"Avril!"

"Hawkins!"

"Avril!"

"Hawkins!"

"Avril!"

"Hawkins!"

Avril felt the lustful sensation of power flow through her. The rings on her fingers sparkled. The reality she was faced with was one she never considered. She didn't need to choose between one world or the other. She could have them both.

35. DRAGONS

ZOEY WAS BACK IN THE LIVING ROOM, the one with the fireplace and the soft furry rug. Aunt Rose sat on the chair, with her golden hair and the book in her hands, but this time it felt different. The imagery was smoother, more vibrant, and when Rose spoke, Zoey could now hear her.

"How could we forget those ancient myths that are at the beginning of all peoples?" the woman read, while Zoey stared up at her. "The myths about dragons that at the last moment turn into princesses? Perhaps all the dragons in our lives are princesses, who are only waiting to see us, just once, as beautiful and brave. Perhaps everything that frightens us is, in its deepest being, something helpless . . . that wants help from *us*."

These were the words that had been blocked before, and Zoey knew why she could hear them now. The dream swirled, Zoey's head ached, and everything went white as she was pulled up and out.

ZOEY WOKE IN THE strange bed with the red canopy, staring once more at the black, geographic room, with its wavy walls and strange mix of furniture, but it held little fear for her anymore. She knew who she was now. There was no longer a reason to be afraid, there was nothing they could do to her.

Her fears were for others now. People she loved would soon be fighting for their lives in a desperate attempt to reach her. She could stop them, keep them safe, but she wouldn't. Zoey needed them here, needed their help and their sacrifice. She hated having to do it, but there was no other option. By choosing to spare the Nexus and not destroy the Assembly, she had started a new path. She just hoped they understood, hoped they didn't hate her for it.

There was movement nearby, a quick intake of breath. The woman who had been Rose lay on the black couch. She had curled up into a ball, and

Zoey could feel the emotions pouring off her. Revulsion, distress, fear, and . . . softer ones too. Longing, fondness, a melancholy sense of loss.

Two sets of emotions, from two very different personalities, both of which were trying to overpower the other. It was not going well.

Before, she had been connecting to the dreams of the personality of Aunt Rose, and the entity inside had managed to block Zoey from them. Now, however, Zoey remembered that moment *herself*, she didn't need to share in Rose's dream of it. It meant the tables had been turned. Where before the entity inside Rose had to keep Zoey from seeing its human memories, now it was struggling not to experience *Zoey's*.

"I do not want this . . ." the woman muttered.

"Why do they scare you so much?" Zoey asked.

"I don't like how they feel."

Zoey studied the woman across the room, and felt the doubt that poured out of her.

"No," Zoey said. "They scare you because you *do* like how they feel. It's not like anything you feel normally, is it?"

The woman said nothing. Zoey closed her eyes, recalling the memory she had been dreaming a moment more, no longer closed to her.

So you mustn't be frightened, if a sadness rises up before you, larger than any you have ever seen . . .

They were the next words from Rose's book. Zoey fanned the memory's flames, moved it from her consciousness to the woman's.

The reaction was immediate and violent. "Don't!"

If an anxiety, like light and cloud-shadows, moves over your hands and over everything you do.

The woman who had been Rose stood up, her eyes were on fire. She looked pained and enraptured at the same moment. "I will *kill* you."

Zoey just pushed the memories further, harder.

You must think that something is happening to you. That life has not forgotten you. That it holds you in its hand . . . and it will not let you fall.

"*Stop!*" Rose yelled, falling to her knees. Then, softer, she breathed, "Sunshine, please . . ."

Zoey cut the stream off, studying the woman now, watching her shudder on the floor, dealing with what was a normal amount of human emotion, but for the entity inside, it was a torrent. The more Zoey forced the feelings, the more the woman's personalities seem to waver, the more of her aunt emerged.

"What is . . . this called?" the woman asked. Zoey knew she meant the feeling Rose had been experiencing, reading to her, her niece. They had been very close once.

"Love," Zoey said. She got up and moved to Rose. Gently, she ran her fingers through the woman's hair. It was as soft as she remembered. "And you are burying it. If you do what you say you want to, it will be lost forever, no one will ever feel these things again."

Rose looked at her with red, swollen eyes. "There is nothing to be done. We must be Ascended, and you will do it."

"How?"

"They will take you to where the Tone for this part of the world is broadcast. You will tap into it, and then use the power of the Nexus to force each of us into each of them."

Zoey nodded. "Because the Tone is the Whole, and it touches your minds as much as it touches theirs."

"The Nexus will be consumed," Rose told her, "and only *we* will remain."

"You'd use up the Nexus?"

"So that we would always be free."

Zoey studied her. "There's another way." The woman who had been Rose looked at her curiously.

Zoey projected the details into her mind, sharing with her what the Nexus had told her. As she did, the Feelings swirled to life, and they were worried, they didn't like sharing the information, but Zoey pushed them back. There was nothing any of the Assembly could do now to stop her, and Rose, the *real* Rose, the one she had loved, was coming back. Zoey *knew* it . . .

The woman absorbed it all, and as she did, Zoey could feel her shock.

"But, that is . . . so unlike what we believe," the woman breathed.

"That doesn't make it wrong. You have to trust me, Rose, because I need your help." Zoey noticed that the woman no longer objected to being called her human name. "We can bring these feelings to them all. It's what you've denied yourselves all this time. Help me, and you'll never need to be scared again, I promise."

Rose stared back at her, on the verge of speaking, and Zoey could feel the doubt welling up inside the woman . . .

The back wall reformed itself into an opening. Through it entered three Centurions, their armor colored blue and white, their tentacled arms hanging at their sides. Then the opposite wall shifted, making an even larger opening. As it did, two of the pod containers rumbled to a stop outside, hanging from the giant rack system there, and Zoey could see again into the massive interior of the Citadel.

"It is time," Rose said.

Zoey looked back down at Rose. The emotions from before were gone. So was the torn expression on her face, the confusion in her eyes. She was stoic again, the mask had returned.

They entered their separate pods. The doors closed and Zoey felt hers shake and begin to rise, straight up, farther than she had ever been, then vibrate slightly as it came to a stop. Pieces in front of her morphed out of the way, making a door for her to step through, and when she did her eyes widened at an amazing sight.

She was on some kind of balcony, perched near the top of the Citadel. Rose was there too, so were several Centurions, and a group of Ephemera. They were each perfect mixtures of blue and white, and she could feel their satisfaction as she stepped onto the balcony.

The ruins of San Francisco stretched out before her, giant buildings connected through a grid work of old streets, and eerily, it was all perfectly devoid of debris and old cars, like the Assembly had just swept the city clean.

While it may have been empty, it was not dead. There was movement everywhere, far below. The walkers, from this height, were just tiny dots on the ground, but there were thousands upon thousands of them, massed everywhere. Swarms of gunships and other aircraft, their lights flashing, flew through the air.

It was an uncountable number of Assembly, and Zoey could feel the emotions blasting up at her. Victory, lust, but also adoration and pride, and all of it directed at her.

"You see?" Rose asked. "Nothing can stop it now."

"I never said I wanted to stop it," Zoey said back. "Just that it won't be like you think."

"Everything relies on your friends making it here, and there's little chance they will. Look at what waits for them." She motioned to the multitude, the insurmountable army.

Zoey shook her head. "They always make it."

"Even so," Rose said, "they will be changed. They will not be who they were."

Zoey looked past her, to the east, back into the interior of the land, to where Holt and Mira and the Max were fighting to get to her.

"I know," Zoey said, and her voice held great sadness.

AS SHE MOVED PAST the train cars one at a time, Mira smiled. They'd done it, and it had only taken a week. Sixteen cars had been scavenged from all over the yard and hooked together behind the locomotives she'd found. Technically, they could pull more than thirty cars, but Mira didn't want to risk it. Sparks sprayed up and down the line as Smitty's men put the final touches on welding in the armor plating, which meant each boxcar was probably twice as heavy now. Large slits had been cut out of the plates, and she could see the barrels from salvaged Antimatter cannons.

Mira noticed something else new: names were painted on the armor that now covered the cars. Mira knew them, many she'd committed to memory herself.

They were the names of fallen Wind Traders and White Helix and of lost Landships. They blanketed the sides of the train, up and down its entire length. Mira tried not to focus on them, the smile fading away at yet another sign of all that had been lost.

"Got him pretty fine-tuned at this point," Smitty said, following along behind her. He, along with Caspira, Dresden, Conner, and some of the Doyen were walking with her, studying the train. "Took awhile to figure out the engineering, just getting the damn thing started was like a calculus problem. Idles pretty smoothly, though, or at least as smooth as you'd expect from the biggest diesel engine ever made."

"What about fuel?" Mira asked.

"Tanks are full. Got my guys barreling up extra diesel, should have enough for the trip, if I'm right about MPG for this thing. Then again, who the hell knows? I never even drove a car before the Assembly showed up."

"What do you think the top speed is?" Conner asked. His demeanor had improved over the last few days. Mira guessed he'd come to accept that this was probably the last option open to them, and even though he likely didn't believe in the furor around Zoey, he was committed none-theless.

"I bet he could do one-twenty easy," Smitty replied, "the manuals said these engines are rated for up to two hundred, but with the weight we're carrying . . ."

"No way the ships can keep up with that," Dresden said, "even if we burn the Zephyrs."

"We'll take it slower then," Mira assured him. "All that matters is we get there in one piece. Which leads us to you, Caspira."

The White Helix Adzer, her brownish hair in its long, tight braid, nod-ded back. "We pulled cannons from the scrapped Landships, actuated them up and down, left and right. They're on both sides of the cars, the ones that are armed at least. We wanted to arm all the cars but there just weren't enough spare cannons. As it is, we've armed twelve out of sixteen, so more than half."

"Either way, makes the thing a rolling gun platform," Smitty said, star-ing at the giant machine with pride. "I'd hate to mess with him. Plus we welded on every last scrap piece of metal we could find in this dump. He'll take a pounding, that's for damn sure, and then there's your Barriers."

Mira and the Landship artifact handlers had spent the week assembling Barrier artifacts and other combinations, installing them up and down the train, all of it from components from the *Wind Shear,* Dresden and Con-ner's retirement haul that was depreciating by the day. Conner hadn't liked them using it, no matter how committed he might be. Every time she or one of the handlers went into the *Wind Shear*'s hold he grimaced.

The truth was, though, more than half those components were dead, their powers gone, and the rest would follow. As long as the Barriers held, the train was pretty well protected, but there were no guarantees anymore.

"What are you going to do with the Helix?" Conner asked, and the Doyen in the group stared at him heatedly. The question could have been phrased a little more delicately. The White Helix may have been taking their cues from Mira, but she was a long way from replacing Dane. No one *did* anything with the Helix.

Mira looked to a tall female Doyen amid the others. "Dasha, what did you decide?"

It was the same girl who had challenged the Assembly what seemed like ages ago, back in the Currency shipyards. She still had her almost-white, razored hair, and all of the fire she'd exhibited that day, but events had focused and tempered it. Mira noticed lately that Dasha was always the first Doyen to speak up among the others and with the strongest voice. There was strength in her, like in Dane, but if she felt any of his secret apprehension about leadership, she didn't show it.

"Your idea sounds good," Dasha said. "Divide the Arcs between the train cars. If we run into trouble, they can take position on the roof or deploy around the train. The remainder can go on the ships. There's something to be said for having the ability to drop troops away from the train."

Mira nodded in agreement. The White Helix had come to accept Mira, almost as one of their own now. Where before any non-Helix would have been excluded from their campfires, Mira was welcomed. They even let Max come, if he was with her, which he inevitably was these days. Nemo had been a constant annoyance the dog was happy to leave on the *Wind Shear*.

She wasn't sure if it was Dane's last words or simply a gesture of respect, but she was glad for their acceptance. Not just because her own actions had cost them so much, but because she truly felt they would be with her until the very end, and there was comfort in that. It was like Dane had said: Zoey belonged to them too.

In her mind, Mira ran through their assets. The train now, of course. There were almost a thousand Helix, and eleven Landships, a number that stung every time she heard it. She could still see the glorious image of the full Wind Trader fleet moving through the Barren before they'd gotten to the train yard and everything had gone the way it had.

The Assembly count stood at eighty-eight, not including dropships. They were going to be the weakest link until they got to San Francisco, if only because of their speed. Even if they slowed the train down for the Landships, it would still be too fast for the walkers to keep up.

Mira and Ambassador had worked out a plan to deal with it. They would just utilize the Ospreys more: the dropships could keep up with the train and the fleet, even carrying Spiders. If they ran into trouble, they could deploy as needed, and the Brutes, even though they would be lagging behind, could teleport in additional forces. Mira had sworn that they would *not* get caught like they had before, and she meant to keep her word.

Mira stopped as she reached the front of the train, where the two giant locomotives stood, the rest of the cars snaking out behind them. Along the side of the engines, something had been painted in huge, red letters.

A name. SORCERER.

Mira stared at the words in surprise.

"Just a little name the boys gave him, hope you don't mind," the engineer said, studying the engines. "Thought of calling him Rolling Thunder, but it sounded too much like a seventies movie."

"*Her*, you mean," Caspira injected patiently. "All ships are female."

"Well this is a train, isn't it?" Smitty replied gruffly. "Not a ship."

"It's bad luck to—"

"*Sorcerer*," Mira said, cutting them off before they got going. They'd managed to work well together the last few weeks, but they still had their moments. "I like it."

"Yes," Dasha said approvingly. "A strong name." The Helix all around her nodded.

Mira looked back down the train, mixing in and out of all the ruined boxcars and the charred remains of Landships. Even though it was all covered in rust, seeing it—this thing that everyone had come together to make, where they had collectively placed what was left of their hopes—it seemed to sparkle in the sun. Mira smiled again, then turned back to the business at hand.

"You have the map?" she asked.

Dresden rolled out the huge map from the office wall they'd studied previously, and everyone closed in to look at it.

"Where is it we're meeting them?"

Dresden pointed to a small town about fifty miles west. "Burleson," he said. "We can pick up the Western Terminus for San Francisco there too."

Mira studied the dot on the map. The Phantom Regiment, the famous resistance group which fought in the San Francisco ruins, were waiting for them there. If they could find them, they just might make up for all their losses so far.

"And we know how to switch tracks?" Mira looked at Smitty. It was maybe the biggest part of this whole plan. If they couldn't figure out how to switch tracks at the old junctions, the train, no matter how fancy and powerful it was, wasn't going anywhere near San Francisco.

Smitty nodded. "Think so, yeah. Deal is, we'll have to stop and do it manually. In the World Before it was automatic, trains never even slowed down, but no one's running those controls anymore. It'll cost us time."

"And we'll be vulnerable while we wait," Conner finished for him, pointing out the obvious.

"I'd think vulnerability, by this point, we should be used to," Mira remarked. She looked up from the map and studied them all in turn, the Wind Traders, the Helix, all people who she'd come to care about, and who, once more, she was about to put in harm's way.

"I'm proud of all of you," she said. "This is . . . really something. Now let's get this big bastard rolling."

No one hesitated, they all moved off, heading to finish whatever needed finishing, getting ready to move.

When they were gone, and it was just her, Mira peered into the distance, over the flatlands to where the hills of the coast began to form. She could see the giant, faded black form of the Citadel, a menacing shape covered in haze.

"We're coming, Zoey," she said. "Just hold on."

THE *WIND SHEAR* RUMBLED forward under the bright sun, bouncing on the rocky terrain near the train tracks, and as it did, Mira couldn't stop staring at the giant machine to their right. *Sorcerer* in motion was a sight to see.

It thundered westward, pulling its detachment of sixteen armored cars, each painted with angry, wicked-looking figures. Demons and snakes and crude pictures of Mantis walkers with *X*s marking them out. The names stood out prominently too. So did the gun ports in the armor which had replaced the cars' doors.

Eight Landships escorted *Sorcerer*, each with two full Arcs of Helix on board in case of trouble. The three remaining ships ran a few miles ahead, scouting for obstructions or signs of Assembly. At the rear followed a dozen Osprey dropships, each carrying either a collection of Mantises or a Spider walker. She could feel the sensations coming off them, the joy that came with movement, the anticipation of approaching conflict.

"Didn't wanna ride on your new toy?" Dresden asked behind her, near the wheel with Parker and Jennifer. They were on the helm deck, and everyone watched the giant train cutting a path through the landscape. Max and Nemo were both asleep nearby, the cat curled up against the dog. Max may not have transitioned to outright affection for the feline, but at least he was tolerating him.

"Kinda got used to this one," Mira answered.

"It suits you," he said back. "You're good on a ship."

"You tried to recruit me once."

"I did?" Dresden asked dubiously.

"Months ago, back at that trading post, during that Assembly assault." It had been a harrowing escape, and the first time she or Holt had witnessed Zoey's true powers. In a way, many things had begun that day.

"That's right," Dresden said with a smile. "Well, I have an eye for talent. Right, Parker?"

"If you say so," Parker answered. The first officer still hadn't warmed to her, but she didn't blame him. In fact, she didn't blame any of the Wind Traders for whatever feelings they harbored. The lives they'd come to love were fading, and it was her fault, directly or indirectly.

"Where'd you 'recruit' the fleabag?" Mira nodded toward Nemo.

Dresden looked down at the animal with affection. "He found me, came on board at dock in Midnight, just like that, never left, like he'd always lived here. I liked his presumptiveness. Always liked cats better than dogs, really. They're survivors, they don't trust easy. You earn a cat's trust, it means something. Your dog though, he doesn't trust easy either. I like him too. He can stay when you leave."

"He's not my dog," Mira reminded Dresden again. "But he goes where I go."

Max opened an eye and studied her briefly, before yawning and closing it. It was as much sentiment as she was going to get.

Radio chatter flared to life from the scout ships. Mira didn't have her earpiece in, she looked back at Dresden.

"Understood," he responded. "We're cresting the rise now, should see it in a few seconds."

"See what?" Mira asked darkly.

"Smoke," Dresden replied.

The Landships and *Sorcerer* all came to the top of a large, rolling hill and when they did, they could see trails of thick, gray smoke drifting into the air probably ten miles away. That was the estimated distance to Burleson, where they were supposed to meet the Phantom Regiment.

"Not a good sign," Dresden remarked.

Mira moved to the railing and stared at the smoke. The fire had been a big one. The smoke was turning white now, which meant most of the flames were out.

"What do you want to do?" Dresden asked.

"Get the scouts back here, signal defensive formation," Mira ordered. "*Sorcerer* goes in hot."

Parker motioned to the flaggers in the crow's nest, and they started signaling the ships around them. More radio chatter erupted. The engines of the locomotives rumbled powerfully as the train picked up speed and thundered ahead.

Mira could see the gun ports opening up and down the sides, the cannons being primed. White Helix scampered onto the roofs, masks lifting up, Lancets pulled from their backs. A thousand of them covered the train as it roared forward.

In cases like these, *Sorcerer* would barrel into whatever location was questionable, armed and ready. In the case of a town or a city, where the Landships couldn't enter, they would circle the perimeter. Assembly drop-ships would follow and deploy walkers, and if necessary, Mira could guide in Brutes with reinforcements.

She reached out toward the Ospreys, told them what was happening. *Guardian*, they projected back. *We follow*.

Feelings of eagerness washed over her as the Ospreys roared past, hoping battle would find them. It would eventually, she knew, and Mira wondered how they would feel then. They didn't seem to factor in that most of them could no longer survive outside their armor, that they were vulnerable, but she had no desire to remind them. The truth was, she needed them ready and aggressive.

The *Wind Shear* broke off with the other ships to circle the city: the ruins of a flat desert town, not unlike Rio Vista, in a small valley. Mira could make out more detail. A lot of the city had burned, but the fires were mostly out. There was no movement she could see, but the memory of the trap a week ago was still heavy in her mind, and she let *Sorcerer* move in, watched the Ospreys unload their walkers and the Helix deploy onto the roofs of the buildings that were still intact.

They waited for any sign of a threat. More radio chatter erupted, and Mira slipped on her headset.

"No hostiles." It was Dasha's voice, predictably disappointed. "No nothing. Whatever happened here, we missed it."

Mira turned to Dresden. What was *supposed* to have happened here was a meeting of great importance, and now it looked like they had just taken several steps backward.

IT WAS CLEAR THE ruins had been the site of an intense battle. Buildings still smoldered and the burn marks up and down the streets were the distinctive, sulfurous-colored scars of plasma bolts.

The destruction moved through downtown, intensifying at what remained of an old brick schoolhouse. Most of the building was gone now, burned and crumpled, but enough of it was still standing to explore. Mira stepped into the ruins, flanked by Dasha, two Arcs of Helix, and a few Wind Traders, including Conner and Dresden.

Max pushed ahead, nose to the ground, and they soon heard him barking on the other side of a wall of fallen brick and mortar. When they dug through it, they emerged in the school's old gymnasium, the basketball court splintered, the scoreboard rusted and fallen. Everything else was covered in plasma bolt burns, a sign that Assembly fire had been concentrated here, and all around was the gruesome evidence.

Bodies littered the gym, lining what remained of the stands, or fallen in the center of the floor. Some hung from the rafters, where they'd claimed elevated positions to shoot through the topmost windows. They were either bent at strange angles that seemed inhuman, or charred to varying degrees. None of them moved.

Mira wanted to shut her eyes, but forced them open. She needed to see this, to remember that there were Assembly out there very different from Ambassador.

Everyone moved forward, studying the death. The place still smoked, weapons were strewn everywhere. The bodies were all kids, their gear was chalky white—it was intentional, Mira guessed, for blending in amid the concrete jungle of the San Francisco ruins. Their chest plates were each painted with a single black skull.

"Definitely Regiment," Dresden observed. "But there's way more here than were supposed to meet us."

"Maybe they were planning a trap," Dasha mused.

Dresden shook his head. "They wanted this meeting, they wanted help. They must have come here for something else, but I can't think why."

"They pulled back," Mira said. "Retreated."

"Out of the ruins?" Conner asked in a skeptical voice. "Phantom Regiment are fanatics, tough as nails, all the resistance groups are."

"Didn't . . . retreat," a weak, raspy voice stated.

Everyone spun and saw a figure near the edge of the bleachers, covered by two other bodies. A survivor.

Max growled protectively, but Mira had a feeling there was no need.

She yelled for someone to get a first-aid kit, but when she reached him, she saw just how futile that was going to be. The lower half of his body was mostly black, and he was bloody. She could see where it had pooled under him, and she was surprised he hadn't passed out.

His eyes were almost fully black. He was close to twenty or maybe even older. Mira had always heard the rumor that the Tone spread slower the closer you were to the Assembly Presidiums, which meant resistance fighters got as much as an extra year before they Succumbed.

"Water would be nice . . ." he told them.

Dresden kneeled and unstrapped his canteen, let him drink. Mira kneeled down too.

"You said you didn't retreat?" she asked.

The survivor shook his head. "We . . . pulled the young ones out of the city. Those were the orders. The kids and the girls, the nonfighters . . ." He looked at Mira with intensity, she could see the decision to leave the ruins had been hard. "Brought them here, but . . . they followed . . ."

"Assembly?" Conner asked, and the kid nodded.

Mira looked around the gym again. All she saw were the bodies of soldiers. There were no "nonfighters" here. "Where are they?"

A smiled crept onto his face. "They made it. We . . . held them off . . ."

It all fit. They had some sense the Assembly were coming, got the nonfighters they'd been told to evacuate headed off, then this kid and his cohorts bought time for the others to escape with their lives.

"Where's the rest of you?" Mira asked, though she was hesitant to hear the answer. If the Regiment had evacuated people out of the ruins, it must be bad. "The main force, are they still in San Francisco?"

The smile vanished. "Dead . . ." Dread filled Mira to her core, and she forced herself not to react. "If not now . . . they will be . . ."

The answer only gave slight hope, but it was something. *"Where?"*

"HQ," the kid told her. His voice was weakening. He coughed raggedly. "They were . . . overrun. More Assembly than I've ever seen . . . different colors, different types." A fit of coughing consumed him and Dresden gave him more water.

Mira looked at Dresden while he did. "Do you know where they operate from?"

He shook his head. "We always traded here, in Burleson, that's how I knew the place. Landships don't go near the Citadel ruins, it's suicide."

Mira turned to Dasha. "Get me the map. Hurry."

A Helix runner leapt and disappeared through one of the gym's shattered windows in a flash of yellow, headed back for the train. Mira turned to the soldier. His eyes were becoming glassy. "What's your name?"

"Major," he said.

"Not your rank, your *name*."

He shook his head, smiled again. "It *is* my name. My rank's . . . sergeant . . ."

Mira smiled too. "Okay, Major. I want you to rest, but I need your help. We have an army outside. We can help your people, but I need you to show me where they are."

He studied her oddly. "An army?"

Mira nodded. "An army."

The smile faded again, the notion didn't seem to bring much hope. "You'll need one . . ."

The words sent a chill down her spine.

The same Helix from before leapt through the same window, landing on the old wooden court. A few steps later she reached them, handed over the giant railroad map, and Mira spread it open.

"Major," she said, holding it up for him to see. "Where?"

He studied it . . . then raised a hand, pointed to a spot.

Everyone bent and looked. It was some kind of old manufacturing facility on the outskirts of Oakland.

"Good news, bad news," Dresden stated. "Place has a train yard, so *Sorcerer* can get there, but the Landships are a no-go. It was always gonna be this way. Closer we get to the old city centers and out of the Barren, there's just no room. Debris, fences, downed power lines, not to mention buildings."

"Highways . . ." Major said, looking at them.

Dresden shook his head. "Highways are crammed with cars, there's no way—"

"Clear now . . . All the roads are. No cars, no obstructions. Assembly . . . got it all."

"The Collectors," Mira said. She'd only seen a Collector once. They were giant machines the Assembly deployed in ruins to collect all the scrap that was there for recycling. In a way, she supposed it made sense they would have cleaned the streets. They used the raw material to build the Citadel, and the Citadel was beyond massive.

Mira looked up at Dresden and Conner. "If that's the case, then the Landships can operate *inside* the city. We can use them in the fight."

"Maybe," Conner answered. "Even just one car in the middle of a road makes it unusable, but, yeah, I don't see why we can't try."

"You hear that, Major?" Mira said, looking back at the kid. "We're going to go get—"

Major hadn't heard. He'd gone limp, his eyes closed. He was with the rest of his men now. He'd come here to save one group of people. The information he'd provided might save more, but he would never know. Mira sighed. As much as he deserved to be mourned and honored, the realization of just what was happening in San Francisco didn't allow for it. If what remained of the Phantom Regiment were fighting for their lives, then that meant Mira might lose them and their knowledge of the ruins. It might mean the difference between reaching Zoey and not.

Mira turned and looked at Conner and Dresden. "I hate to ask this, but—"

"We have to save them, I get it," Conner stated without irony or hesitation. "Without them, it's going to be a hell of a lot tougher."

Mira was surprised by his acceptance. They had come a long way, Conner and his people. They had all cast their fate to the same wind.

Mira looked at Dasha. Dasha nodded back, and Mira could see the eagerness in her eyes.

"Let's move," Mira said, and then they were all up, Max tearing back the way they'd come, blazing a path through the rubble.

"When we get back to the train," she told Dresden, "find Smitty, tell him to bring a welding kit."

Dresden studied her curiously. "You have a plan."

Mira did, in fact. One as dangerous as it was improbable, but all her plans seemed to be of that kind lately. But if there were as many Assembly where they were heading as it seemed, it might be their only shot.

"Do I want to know?" Dresden asked further.

"Definitely not."

THE DARK RUMBLED around Mira as she finished the Mercurian artifact, watching as the Interfuse took hold and the combination hummed to life. Sparks lit up the darkness as Smitty finished welding the last of the column in place. It was made out of bits and pieces he'd taken off the remaining Landships. It wasn't pretty, but it should work just like any other Landship Grounder. Mira handed Smitty the Mercurian and he started attaching it under the top edge.

Her artifact, the horrible one that manipulated the Tone, was wired into the Grounder, ready to be activated, and the idea gave her pause. She just hoped the Grounder worked, redirecting the effect of the combination into the superstructure of the train, instead of just amplifying it even further. If it didn't work, when it was switched on . . . she might Succumb the entire army all at once.

Never again, you said, Ambassador projected, and it carried a tangible feeling of betrayal. She understood the alien's reservations, and it was right, she *had* promised, but, as usual, things had gotten complicated.

I know, she projected back, *but you see the advantage it gives us, right?*

It is abomination.

Mira sighed. *Yes, I agree, but you* see *the advantage?*

There was no response from the alien.

Ambassador, she projected again, *I* need *to know you understand.*

Yes, it finally answered. *We understand.*

Just factor it into your strategy. It should push them toward you. When it does . . .

Rock. Paper. Scissors.

Mira smiled as her radio headset crackled, Dresden's voice echoed in her ear. "Mira, you almost ready?"

Smitty looked up at her and nodded.

"I think we're done, yeah," she answered. "Why?"

"Take a look."

Mira moved for a ladder inside the compartment and scaled it, popping open a hatch in the ceiling. It was night now. Outside, the wind blew her hair wildly and she felt the rumbling of *Sorcerer*'s locomotives vibrating through her. All that power, from diesel and fire, made for a much different ride than the *Wind Shear*.

She could see the Helix deployed on top of the train, crouched and ready. Osprey dropships roared along above, carrying silver Spiders and Mantises. Landships, shadows on either side, their sails plumed outward, rolled over the smooth cement of a highway, wide enough for them to run in pairs. It was like Major had said, the roads *had* been cleared, there were no obstructions, which meant they could use ships in the city. If only they had the full fleet, she thought.

Mira pushed the thoughts away. They *didn't* have the full fleet, she reminded herself, and there was no point thinking about it.

She looked ahead, down the line of train cars to where the tracks were taking them.

There were lights in the distance, coming closer. Tracer fire flared into the sky. Plasma bolts and missiles streaked through the air. Explosions blossomed up and, for brief moments, illuminated the large buildings that surrounded the old manufacturing facility that was their goal.

The scale of the battle, even from this far away, was striking. She'd never seen anything like it, and they were heading right for it. Looking at it all, it was hard to imagine they weren't already too late.

"Valley of Fires, huh?" Mira said into the radio.

"Yeah," Dresden replied after a moment. "Good luck, friend."

"You too, Dresden."

The ruins of San Francisco grew on the horizon. She could see the flickering lights of the Citadel stretching into the sky. It was all just miles away. She shook her head as the first of the projections reached her. Thousands of them, all in the ruins. She would have to fight them, push them away, and she hoped she was up for it. Mira had never had this many in her head at once.

Dasha crouched next to her, and Mira looked up at her. It was time.

"Seek," Mira said.

Dasha smiled. "And find."

She moved off and Mira hit the button on her radio. "Do it."

She felt the train rumble harder as it picked up speed, thundering for-

ward and leaving the Landships behind. Above, Osprey engines roared
as they accelerated, and she could sense the feelings of anticipation from
the silvers. There was no doubt conflict would find them this time.

Mira slid back down the ladder and moved for the Grounder. Smitty
was holding a rifle now, ready to fight with everyone else. The sight made
her hesitate. He wasn't a fighter, none of the Wind Traders were, but here
he was.

He stared at her and shrugged. "You go where the winds take you, not
the other way around."

Mira nodded, gripped his shoulder.

The train shook hard, she heard the hum of a Barrier combination ac-
tivate as plasma bolts sparked into it. They were in range, both to fire and
be fired upon. It was now or never.

She moved for her artifact. Her hands shook. Other than the quick use
of it with Ambassador, the last time she'd used the thing was in Midnight
City, and she'd watched someone she'd once considered a close friend
twisted and destroyed by it. If the Grounder didn't work right . . .

More explosions flared outside. The train shook.

Mira flipped open the pocket watch and stepped back. So did Smitty.
"What exactly does this thing do?"

The black, squirming light, like a mass of worms, slowly fizzled into
the air.

"Never mind, don't tell me." He backed up farther.

Mira tensed, watching the black light grow, a sign the Grounder wasn't
working, and that—

The blackness was sucked back down into the combination, and she felt
the floor under her vibrate strangely.

A mass of projections assaulted her mind from outside like an explosion. Her knees buckled, she went limp, and if it hadn't been for Smitty
catching her, she would have hit the floor.

The sensations were all the same. Revulsion. Shock. Fear.

She could feel the Assembly recoil as one, pulling back in a wave as the
train and the effect from her artifact rumbled toward them.

The loud harmonic pings of Antimatter cannons filled the air. She heard
Ospreys move into a hover, heard the loud thuds as the silver walkers cut
loose and hit the ground.

Sorcerer shuddered violently as it slowed, and Mira and Smitty moved
for the side door. When they reached it, he stared at her with emotion.

"Crazy to say it, I know," Smitty said, "but this is the most meaningful thing I've ever done."

Mira felt emotion swell in her, and she looked back at him. "Thank you for coming, Smitty."

Then they yanked open the door and stumbled out into chaos, planting themselves against the back of a rusted water tower.

Explosions blossomed everywhere in the night, colored crystals shot through the air, plasma bolts singed past. Distorted bursts of sound punctuated flashes of light as Brutes teleported in with reinforcements. Spiders, Mantises, Hunters, all adding firepower to the rest.

In the distance, she saw blue and white walkers explode, saw a flight of Raptors crash into an old warehouse and, all the while, the Assembly were moving back and away, trying to get as far from *Sorcerer* and the horrible perverted signal it was broadcasting as they could. It was *working*.

Mira could feel the same revulsion from the silvers, the same anxiety, but they held their ground.

"Move as one!" Dasha yelled as she leapt into the air, followed by a thousand White Helix, their Lancets firing as they darted through the old train yard.

Mira looked around quickly, trying to find any sign of—

She saw it, about a hundred yards away. The distinctive, strobic flashing of gunfire. Someone had taken up a defensive position in front of the biggest building she could see, with three huge smokestacks stretching into the air. It had to be the Regiment.

Mira started to move . . . then saw a small, gray shape bound out of the train. Its eyes found her almost immediately. Its tail wagged in spite of the destruction going on around it.

"Coming, mutt?" she yelled as she ran. Max raced after her.

They both dodged through explosions and plasma bolts. Blue and white gunships streaked over the battle, strafing the factory and *Sorcerer* and everything in between.

She saw new crystals streak through the air and connect, big ones, blowing the Raptors to pieces. Mira looked behind her and saw what she'd hoped.

The Landships had caught up, they were adding their firepower to the rest.

Her radio crackled. "Mira, you out there?"

"Go, Dresden."

"Gonna try and pull the Raptors off you, circle them back into the landscape, catch 'em in a crossfire."

"Be careful," she said with hesitation.

The Landships banked hard, their Antimatter crystals streaking back to their cannons. The Raptors took the bait, engines roaring as they raced after the ships, freeing up the skies.

Mira and Max ran, made it to the building, and prayed whoever was outside didn't blow them away as they approached. They didn't. Instead, they motioned her closer, and she and Max leapt over a ring of old cars that had been piled together to make fortifications.

There were about forty fighters there, some shooting through gun ports, others reloading . . . and many more lying in the middle, wounded, moaning. It was a testament to what they'd been through. The fact they were still alive showed just how tough they were.

"It's my sincere hope," a tall, muscular kid behind a rusted van yelled, "you're gonna tell me how in hell you pushed 'em back like that. Not that I'm complaining."

"You in charge here?" Mira shot back, moving for him.

The kid studied her skeptically. He was past twenty, his eyes almost as black as Major's, and he would have been good-looking if not for the shrapnel scars on his face.

"If you wanna call it that, sure," he finally said. "I don't think anyone could be in charge of this mess. Call me Shue."

"You got radios, Shue?" Mira asked.

"No, we use smoke signals. Of course we got radios."

"Tell your men not to shoot the *silver* Assembly," Mira said pointedly. "They're on your side."

Shue seemed beyond skeptical. "On *our* side?"

"It's a long story."

All around them White Helix flipped into the air in bursts of yellow and purple, their Lancets spinning blurs of color. Bigger versions of the crystals shot out from the sides of the huge, armored train that had pulled into the yard, exploding through blue and white walkers.

"Who the hell are you people?" Shue asked, studying it all.

"We were supposed to meet in Burleson, your leader set it up. We're here to help. What's your status?"

"Holding on, but without Isaac, things are going bad. He always pulls us out of scraps like this."

Isaac must have been the leader. "Where is he?"

Shue nodded up and behind them, to where the factory yard ended in a street lined with old office buildings. One was burning, flames licking the side, and it looked like something had crashed into it.

"Bastards brought in Vultures right at the beginning, when we were still bunched up. One of the claws got him, but I took the thing down with a SAM. At close range, those things go down pretty easy. Crashed right there, had Isaac and a few other kids in its grip. I sent a small team . . . but I don't think they made it. I've never seen anything like this, this many Assembly all in one place. It's hell. Even for Sisco."

Mira stared at the smoking building and scowled. It seemed like every time she finally made it somewhere, the universe just moved the finish line farther back. She tore her gaze away and flagged down a Helix. Then she hit the button on her radio.

"Dasha, I need you. Look up."

Mira nodded to the Helix, and he understood, shot the red end of his crystal straight up into the air like a flare.

Mira looked at Shue again. "I need this Isaac alive. I have to get to the Citadel."

Shue didn't laugh out loud or even look particularly doubtful. He just nodded, thinking it through, like the request was a normal one. Maybe it was for guys like him. "You got a good-size force here. Isaac could do something with that. Probably get you there, but . . ."

"Where's the *rest* of the Regiment? Where's everyone else?"

Shue tensed at the question. "You're looking at it."

The words hit her like a punch, anguish washed over her. The Phantom Regiment, one of the toughest forces on the planet, and the group she'd been counting on, were all but wiped out. She buried the emotions before they could form. They still had their numbers, and the artifact was working. If they could find Isaac, they might be able to still make it.

A small force seemed the only way, leave the rest here to keep the foothold they'd gained, such as it was.

Dasha landed next to her in a flash of cyan, and the Regiment soldiers all flinched in amazement. She didn't notice, her eyes were full of battle lust.

"We got something we need to do," Mira told her. Dasha smiled.

THE SHAFT HAD BEEN SEWER and utility tunnels once, Mira figured, but judging by the rough marks on the walls, the Regiment had expanded them over the years. According to Shue, the Regiment had tunnels like these running all through the city, which allowed them to move out of sight of the Assembly. Above, she could hear the sounds of explosions. More than that, she could feel them, the vibrations rattling down through the earth. She hoped the tunnel was as stable as it looked.

Three Arcs of Helix flanked Mira on both sides but none of them seemed happy about it. Every time an explosion hit, they looked up eagerly. Their brothers and sisters were fighting up there, accruing honor, while they were stuck down here. Mira had a feeling that wouldn't be an issue very long. Max was there too, but he'd pushed ahead into the dark, sniffing and exploring, the environment very much his kind of place.

Shue and two of his men guided them through the tunnels, and she could see them stop at the front and stare upward. One of them scrambled up a ladder and pushed open a rusted manhole cover. The sounds of battle echoed down into the tunnels as the Helix followed up after them. When Mira reached the ladder, Max was still there, whining up at the exit.

Mira sighed. "You're a real pain, you know that?"

"Hand him up," Shue told her from above, leaning back down through the hole. "Hurry, though."

Max growled slightly as she picked him up, squirmed in her arms, then, infuriatingly, seemed to calm when she handed him to Shue. Mira shook her head and climbed up, exited, and immediately looked for cover.

There wasn't any.

The street they were on, a wide one moving between large, decrepit buildings, was a strange mix of destruction and desolation. The rubble was recent, it looked like it had rained down from the building just ahead. She could see the hole in its side where the Vulture had crashed into it.

Other than that, the streets were empty. The Assembly Collectors had picked them clean of anything that could be used for raw materials. It was eerie, in a way, looking at it.

Explosions spiraled back the way they'd come, and Mira saw Antimatter crystals streaking upward, could even hear the punctuated noise that marked Brutes teleporting in with reinforcements.

The Assembly were being pushed back . . . for now.

Raptors roared past overhead suddenly, and plasma bolts sparked all around them.

Two Helix and one of Shue's men fell. Dasha lunged in a flash of purple and drove Mira to the ground. The gunships banked sharply, coming back for another run. So much for being undetected.

"We need to get inside," Dasha stated.

"I concur," Mira shot back.

They ran toward the building as the sound of engines grew behind them. Shue kicked open the big glass doors and they dashed in as more plasma bolts shredded the streets.

No one stopped, just kept moving for the stairwell. The edifice was probably twenty feet high, and the Vulture had crashed about halfway up. Hopefully, they'd know the floor when they got there.

Mira wasn't wrong. The door to the eleventh floor had been blown apart, and smoke was still thick in the air. She could see flames as the group pushed through.

A collection of dusty, unused cubicles and desks was blown forward in front of the crashed alien craft that had burst through the windows.

The wedge-shaped machine was fairly intact, rolled over onto its side, and Mira could just make out the blue and white color pattern that covered its armor through the flames that burned around it.

"Spread out!" Shue yelled with a note of desperation. "Find him, search the rubble."

Mira moved as fast as anyone, Max next to her, searching with his nose. Vultures had powerful grappling claws they shot from altitude to grab unsuspecting survivors. This one had grabbed Isaac, which meant he was riding underneath the ship when it went down. He would have been exposed when—

"Here!" Dasha yelled. Mira rounded the side of the craft to see the Helix and Shue lifting off rubble and bent metal from a small figure.

Before they could finish, plasma bolts sparked all around them as two Raptors appeared in a hover outside.

Antimatter crystals streaked forward and punched through the ships in green and blue flame. They plummeted out of sight and crashed, but there were more outside, and probably walkers on the way now.

"Get out there and hold them off!" Dasha yelled, and six warriors leapt outside in flashes of yellow.

Shue finished uncovering the figure, and Mira breathed a sigh of relief when she saw he was alive. Scratched up and bleeding, but conscious.

"Hey boss," Shue said with a giant smile. "You look like crap."

Mira moved closer and stared down at a boy covered in concrete and glass, and he wasn't anything like she expected. He was short and skinny, pale even, and the broken frames of glasses barely clung to his face. He studied the White Helix outside, just visible as they flipped up and down the side of the building, avoiding a storm of plasma fire and dropping another Raptor.

"White Helix . . ." he observed in fascination. Mira was surprised. Few people had any idea what Helix actually looked like in action.

"She's got her own Assembly too," Shue told him, helping him sit up. "And Landships. And an armored train with crazy guns on it. They're cleaning house back at base."

Finally, Isaac looked up at Mira, and in his eyes she finally saw the trait which had probably earned him his position at the top of the Regiment. A flood of intellect, apparent by how he studied her up and down, and it way he did reminded her very much of Ben. They had a similar way, and the sight brought a dull ache as she remembered his sacrifice back at the Severed Tower.

"Mira Toombs, I'm guessing," Isaac stated.

"We had a meeting in Burleson."

"Yeah," he answered without much enthusiasm. "As you can see, we got a little sidetracked."

"We have to get you out of here. Can you walk?"

With the question, both Isaac and Shue looked at her with conflicting stares. Shue's was almost hostile, while Isaac just seemed embarrassed.

"No," he said.

"Are you—?" Dasha began, but he cut her off.

"I'm paraplegic," he said, looking down at his legs, and it was then that Mira noticed just how thin they were.

Mira tried to hide her frustration. There went that finish line again.

"We'll get him," Shue told her. "Don't worry, heaviest part of this guy's his brain, right boss?"

"I hate it when you say that," Isaac responded as Shue picked him up and tossed him over his shoulder.

More plasma bolts sparked around them, ripping into what was left of the support structure of the floor, spraying sparks and debris everywhere, and it was coming from below. Mira looked down and saw a dozen blue and white Mantis walkers converging on their building, their cannons spraying plasma up at them. She could feel their lust, their desire for carnage.

The floor under her shook. The remains of the Vulture groaned as it began to tip and bend, loosening from where it rested.

Dasha grabbed Mira and pulled her up. Shue lunged forward with Isaac. Two Helix were cut down by plasma before the rest of them leapt away.

Mira and Max ran as everything vibrated like an earthquake. There was a horrible rending sound as the supports of the building caved in and the Vulture fell, taking most of the floor with it, falling in a shower of debris to the ground below.

Mira slammed to the floor just past where the whole thing had come down, and grabbed Max and pulled him back from the breach. It was like being outside now. The wind blew through her hair, there was nothing on either side, the whole building swayed precariously, and still the Mantises fired up at them.

"Stairs!" Mira yelled, and Dasha kicked the door open, let Shue and Mira burst inside. More plasma burned the air as she lunged through after them, and before she did she heard the whining of Raptor engines. They were in a lot of trouble.

They reached the bottom and Mira burst through into the lobby, followed by Max . . . then she pulled him close and ducked behind the remains of an old reception desk as plasma bolts shredded everything.

Shue, Isaac, Dasha, and a few of her Arc slid into cover with them.

"Can't get out the front anymore," Shue stated, looking over his shoulder.

"The rear!" Isaac yelled. "The older sewer grates. They're not directly connected, but—"

"I get the gist!" Mira yelled as more glass shattered.

"We'll buy time for you," Dasha told Mira, holding her gaze pointedly. "Get him out of here!"

Before Mira could argue, she and four Helix leapt up and dashed in flashes of purple, exploding through the glass windows, and engaging the Mantises outside. It did what it was supposed to: distracted the walkers, got their fire on something else. For now.

Mira grimaced, but there wasn't time to lament it.

"Tell me which way, I'll lead!" she told Shue.

"That way!" He pointed behind them, toward the other end of the building.

Mira and Max ran from the old reception desk. She could see the glass doors out the back and raced for them.

Then the ground shook under her feet. Not from an explosion . . . but from a footfall.

A huge machine stepped into view outside, past the boundary of another building. Eight massive legs held the Spider walker thirty feet off the street. Mira saw its body twist, felt the sensations wash off it as it spotted them.

"Down!" Mira pushed Shue and Isaac to the floor as plasma bolts blew apart the wall in front of them. Two more Helix were incinerated as the others crawled behind the building's cement support columns.

More plasma came from where they'd just run from, the Mantises at the front, and it was ripping apart everything in that direction. At first it seemed like indiscriminate fire, but Mira could sense the Assembly around them, their intentions.

"They're going to bring down the building," Mira said in horror.

The plasma kept coming, decimating everything. She could hear the building groan, could see pieces of it beginning to fall. They would be crushed, and there was nowhere to go.

She thought of Ambassador, she could maybe guide him in, but there just wasn't—

Max howled as part of the building came crashing down in a blast of debris, the rest of it about to go. She grabbed the dog, pulled him close. She wasn't really scared, just disappointed more than anything. To have come all this way, and to die this close to the end. She could just barely make out the Citadel outside in the night, mocking her.

Explosions suddenly consumed the giant Spider in front of them, dozens of them that sent the thing reeling and stumbling back. The explosions were from *conventional* weapons, not Antimatter. What looked like missiles streaked through the air, slammed into the Spider all over again.

Mira could feel the anger erupt from it, then complete shock as it realized it was falling. Cheers erupted inside the building as the giant machine collapsed in flames, the Ephemera bleeding out of the wreck and lighting up the night in brilliant gold.

Something else flew by as it did. Four small, strange machines, with high-pitched mechanical engines. They were gone as fast as they came, buzzing into the dark. Two more vehicles streaked past in the streets, followed by four more, with the same high-pitched engines. Mira couldn't see them in detail.

Outside she heard the loud, punctuated firing of large-caliber machine guns, could hear the distinctive concussions of missiles, not crystals from Lancets . . . and then it all went quiet. Whatever sounds of battle were left were far-off now, and much more sporadic.

Mira risked a glance at Isaac. He stared back, just as confused.

Then Max tore out of her arms, barking excitedly, running back the way they'd come.

"Max!" she shouted but something had his attention. Everyone pulled themselves up and followed after the dog.

MIRA PUSHED THROUGH THE RUBBLE of the building and stepped out into the streets. The broken, burning husks of Mantis walkers lay crumpled there, and Mira could see the golden crystalline shapes lighting up the smoke as they drifted away. Dasha and two other Helix landed nearby and nodded at Mira. She smiled, relieved. Whatever had happened apparently had saved them too.

The sounds of battle were distant now, blocks away. The Assembly had been pushed back, but even with all their combined firepower and the effect from her artifact, it didn't seem possible. Something had happened out here, but what?

The smoke was thick, cutting the visibility up and down the avenue to almost nothing. The distinctive smell of gunpowder filled the air.

She spotted Max, for just a moment, racing forward, then he was lost in the smoke. More shapes buzzed by above, their gasoline engines whining, but she still couldn't see them.

"I don't like this," Shue said next to her, Isaac still on his back.

"Be ready," Dasha told her Arc. Their Lancets tensed in their hands.

New shapes appeared. People. Hundreds, maybe more, surrounding them. Bright lights lit up the smoke with the sounds of more engines. The figures, whoever they were, moved cautiously forward until they were finally revealed.

They wore black gear, toted rifles and shotguns and shoulder-mounted missiles. One thing about them stood out, even in the smoke. They all had small, colorful tattoos on their wrists. On the right was a unique symbol, all their own. On the left . . . was a red, eight-pointed star, the points of which were filled in to reflect their rank.

Mira stared at them in a dreamlike haze. It took Isaac's voice to connect the dots in her mind.

"Menagerie?" he asked out loud, even more stunned now.

More lights appeared in the haze, colorful flares of red, green, or blue, carried by three figures. Mira realized in shock that she knew them. Very well, in fact.

Masyn. Castor. And . . .

"*Avril*," Dasha breathed.

From there the rest of the pieces fell together. Dasha and the other Helix leapt forward instantly, landing next to Avril and the others. They all hesitated, staring at one another as if in a dream, a wonderful one, and when it turned out to be real, they moved close and embraced.

It broke the tension.

Other Helix landed near Avril, Castor, and Masyn, the main force from the factory, hugging and gathering close. The smoke was lifting and Mira could see the Landships had berthed now, and the crews had disembarked. Hesitantly, the Wind Traders approached the Menagerie, and the pirates stared back oddly. Two natural enemies, suddenly finding themselves allies.

Dresden was the first to offer his hand. One of the pirates took it, and then the process continued, everyone greeting and acknowledging the other. Menagerie, Wind Trader, Helix, Phantom Regiment.

Mira's heart began to beat. She could feel it in her chest now.

If they were here, if they were *actually* here, then . . . ?

She pushed through the crowd, shaking hands with Menagerie and Regiment, but distracted. Her eyes were looking for someone else. Her mouth felt dry. Her hands shook.

The sound of barking echoed from her right. She pushed in that direction with growing urgency.

She saw Max, jumping up and down over a person she couldn't quite make out. She froze, watching them. The figure pet the dog and he seemed stunned, as if Max were the very last thing he expected to see. She watched his expression change, as a thought occurred to him. She watched him stand up, watched him scan the crowd in disbelief.

And then his eyes found hers.

Mira stared across the celebrations at Holt.

The world faded away, the battle from before, the losses, everything she'd been through merged into the background. She felt tears well up in her eyes, felt the emotion building.

They stared a second more . . . then they were fighting through the crowd toward each other.

The tears flowed freely. Mira didn't care about seeming strong anymore, or that others might notice. She pushed past everyone in her way, every-thing else forgotten but being with him. Every step she took made time seem to flow slower.

His arms grabbed her and pulled her to him. He lifted her off the ground, spun her through the air, looking over every piece of her, as if trying to convince himself she was really there, that she was whole and real and not some ghost.

A smile formed on his lips as she cried, staring down at him.

"I knew it," he told her, nodding. "I *knew* it."

Max jumped up and down next to them in circles. Holt lowered her, his hands caressing her face, but there was a strange look in his eye, a distance she wasn't used to. She noticed his right wrist. It bore a full tattoo, not an unfinished one. A black bird, identical to another she had seen before. Mira stared at it, confused, back in the dreamlike state she had broken out of seconds ago.

"We should talk," Holt said, and she looked back up at him. Nothing seemed real anymore.

41. PATHS

THE INTERIOR OF THE POD reformed itself into a doorway that Zoey stepped through, and the room beyond was like being inside some huge, black, metallic dome. In the center, about a hundred feet away, rose the Nexus. She could see where it passed through the roof and drifted up into the sky.

The ceiling was lined with thick, fragile-looking plates made of some kind of clear, silvery material. Golden energy crackled through them, lighting everything in amber. It wasn't until Zoey saw one of the Ephemera slowly seep out from within one that she understood the source.

There must be hundreds of entities there, filling each of those panels, working together as a huge transmitter for broadcasting one thing: the Tone.

Throughout the room hovered more than a dozen Mas'Shinra royals, their incredibly complicated, crystalline shapes beaming with blue and white energy. Oddly, Zoey noticed, there were no Centurions in the room, nor any walkers of any kind. In fact, it was noticeably bereft of anything mechanical.

"Your place is here," a voice said next to her. The woman who had been Rose motioned to a machine near them, a column with armrests and stirrups for feet and a padded backrest. At the end of each armrest was a small rod of bright metal that reflected the light from the ceiling. She was meant to stand inside, and to hold the rods with her hands.

"What does it do?" Zoey asked.

"What you wish," Rose answered. "Allows you to control the Tone, to shape and direct it. A machine of this type has been built in every Citadel in every world we have ever conquered. Not until now has one ever been used."

Zoey looked up at the royals and their feelings washed over her. They were beyond elated, excited and eager for what was to come. Of course, what was to come wasn't anything like they expected, and they would be frightened before it was all over. She could already feel the fear from the woman next to her.

"Are you sure?" Rose asked, staring at her with worry. "That this is the path you must take?"

The question made Zoey hesitate. Not because it was difficult to answer, but because the answer was disturbing. "I can't remember *not* being on this path. Do some people really get to choose?"

Rose looked down at her, a strange emotion behind her eyes. It looked like guilt. "Some do. Just not us."

Rose offered her hand to the little girl. Together they stepped toward the machine, and the sensations from the royals intensified.

Scion, they projected. *You are honored.*

The machine looked like it had been formed out of the floor, the way it rose up. The metal was black, but entirely smooth. It didn't ripple the way the walls did, and there were no cables or wires of any kind that Zoey could see. For a moment, she felt a twinge of fear, staring at the thing, but it lasted only a moment. She was the Scion, and she had nothing to fear in this place.

Zoey put one foot in a stirrup, felt it hold her weight, then stepped all the way in, resting her back against the support and, all at once, she gripped the two rods with her small hands.

Light and sensation flooded her mind, flooded everything she was. Her eyes snapped shut.

She could feel the Tone, could feel it slip and slide over every mountain and prairie, felt it wind its way through the ruins of giant cities and small towns, felt it push through all the dark places that dotted the surface of the planet.

She could feel the Nexus, its warmth and serenity. She could feel where it rose through the ceiling and streamed upward, into orbit where it met with the other streams from the other Citadels.

It was all, at once, glorious.

Zoey reached out, using the Tone, streaking through the minds of the survivors, hundreds at once, looking for the two people who could help her do what she had to do, the two people she—

The emotions of the entities shifted. The Feelings rose to the surface, swirling in alarm.

Zoey snapped her eyes back open, but it was too late.

She felt the cold sting of metal snap around her wrists. Two more clasps closed around her ankles, locking her into the machine.

In a panic, Zoey reached out, concentrating on the clasps, trying to force them open, to power them, but there was nothing.

With dread, Zoey realized the truth. The clasps were not mechanical, which meant there was nothing for her to control. She realized why there were no Centurions or walkers in the room. This time, they'd made sure she had nothing to use against them.

Zoey saw the woman below her, locking the final clasp in place.

"Rose . . ."

She looked up at Zoey, and she could see the remorse there. "I'm sorry, Zoey. Your way is just . . . not something we have the courage for."

The entities, the royal ones made of blue and white, floated toward her. Zoey could sense their intentions. Icy fear spread through her. She was trapped, she had underestimated the Assembly completely.

They floated closer, she could feel their heat.

"Please, no, I only want to—"

Zoey screamed as the first entity burned into her body, and the world went white. A second pushed inside, and the pain tripled. A third moved for her.

The Feelings swelled up, trying to help, but they were outnumbered fighting its own kind inside the little girl's tiny form.

Zoey screamed again, but not with her voice. It was a primal scream that came from her mind and she was still gripping the rods of the Machine, which meant it burst into the Whole and overtook it completely.

When it did, she felt a mixture of emotions from the millions of Assembly entities connected through the Whole. Shock and horror from some, ferocious anger from others, and still, from more . . . approval. A terrifying complacency in what was occurring, and it was all spreading, not just to the Mas'Shinra inside the Citadel, but to the rest outside.

The searing pain expanded as the third entity pushed into her form.

"You will survive," Zoey heard Rose's voice from somewhere. "But only long enough. You will Ascend us, Zoey, whether you wish to or not."

Zoey screamed again as the entities merged into her, felt the Feelings struggle and fight, but it was in vain.

She was being torn apart. Her mind was being overridden.

She felt her grip on the rods tighten, felt herself reach out into the Tone, following its path, a stream through mind after human mind outside the black walls of this horrible place. She knew what they were about to make her do, exactly what she and the Nexus had committed themselves against.

Zoey was about to merge the Assembly entities into every human being on the planet.

HOLT STOOD INSIDE the old factory with the other leaders. The Phantom Regiment, what was left of them, stood apart. Isaac was in his "chair," a small-framed buggy with thick, treaded wheels. Railings wrapped and twisted all through the factory's interior, probably so Isaac could move through it. In fact, the entire place had been repurposed. Sleeping quarters, a cooking area, storage, a workshop near the old forge, and some kind of elevator lift attached to one of the unused smokestacks that stretched through the metal ceiling far above. It looked like it had once been a very livable, comfortable place.

Max lay next to Holt, feet wrapped around his boot. The dog hadn't left him since he'd gotten back, and Holt couldn't help smiling. He was one of two parts of his life he never thought he'd see again, yet had somehow gotten back.

Mira was within the Helix and Wind Trader camps. He could see the bonds that had formed between them, no different than the ones he'd made with Masyn and Castor and now Avril. Olive stood amid the Captains, back with her own people. Her task, taking a Landship to Faust, the lair of the Wind Trader's mortal enemies had pretty much been a suicide mission. Yet, there she was, back in the fold.

The walls rumbled from distant explosions. The Assembly had been pushed back, but it wasn't going to last long.

They had a foothold now, a small one, and as impressive a force as they had, the truth was they owed most of it to Mira's artifact. It was funny, in a way. That thing had caused so much misery, and yet had turned out to be critical for everything to come. Did that vindicate it? If it let them reach Zoey, as far as Holt was concerned, it did. He realized just how high a price he was willing to pay to have her back. Holt glanced at Mira . . . and saw she was studying him as well.

Holt had no clue what she was feeling or thinking. To be honest, he didn't even know what *he* was thinking. The shock of finding her hadn't worn off, even if a part of him had always believed it, throughout everything that had happened. But so much *had* happened, and that was the problem, wasn't it?

After all, it wasn't just him who had changed, it was her too. He could sense a new strength in Mira. The way she held herself and gave her opinions. The way the Landship crews and the Helix went quiet whenever she spoke. Whatever she'd been through to get here, it had been just as tough a path as his.

After another moment, Mira averted her eyes back to the conversation.

"How many fighters do you have left?" The question came from Avril, standing between the Helix Doyen and the Menagerie leaders. Both groups seemed to claim her now, and they looked at each other with distrust. It was an odd sight.

"Maybe a hundred," Isaac replied, his voice low.

Holt felt a jolt go through him. The Phantom Regiment had been more than two thousand strong, supposedly. They'd been counting on their help, but it looked like they were out of the game. One more problem that needed addressing.

Holt studied Isaac. At first glance, he certainly wasn't what you expected, but the others all looked at him with respect and crowded protectively around him.

In the World Before, Isaac had been something of a celebrity, Holt discovered. A child chess prodigy that had beaten grand masters and computer programs back-to-back, all at the age of nine. Apparently, it had been those skills that eventually endeared him to the Regiment. Their reaction to his arrival in the first days after the invasion had been predictable: skepticism and scorn. A boy that couldn't walk, much less lift a weapon—but then they had begun listening to his advice and his unorthodox ideas. The Regiment went from being a force that lost most encounters with the Assembly to one that increased its survivability and kill count significantly.

Isaac, right then, however, was trying to hold back a seething anger. He stared at the groups in front of him with hostility. The deaths of his men had left a deep scar.

"We can push forward," Mira said. "*Sorcerer* can repel the Assembly for now, but I don't know how much—"

"Push forward for *what*?" Isaac cut her off. "You got here too late."

"We got here as soon as we could," Mira told him.

"That's not what I mean, I mean you got here *ten years* too late. You show up with the Menagerie and your army with their glowing sticks and I'm supposed to be grateful? This fight's been going on since the *beginning*! We've been living it the entire time, dying for *you*! And for what? What have you been doing out there? Running around some theme park with colored lightning or trying to earn points on a stupid wall. *This* is where you should have been the entire time. This is where *everyone* should have been!"

Silence gripped the group, no one said anything, because there wasn't anything to say. He was right.

"And I'll tell you something else," Isaac continued, "and it goes for all the Regiment, I don't have to ask them. We won't fight with those Assembly you brought. We've lost too many people to their kind, and so have *you*. Frankly, I find it disgusting."

Mira looked back at Isaac, not with impatience or hostility, but with understanding. As much as his words might sting, she held the crippled boy's gaze.

"Since the invasion, we've done incredible things," she said. "The Landships outside. Midnight City. The rings on a White Helix's fingers. There's an artifact combination out there, maybe the most complicated I ever built, and I thought it was something horrible, but it's keeping us all alive right this second. All of them are amazing in their own ways, but . . . if we had put all that energy and creativity into *fighting* the way you have, maybe the world would be different right now. We're all guilty. You're right, we weren't here. But we're here *now*."

The words seemed to calm Isaac, allowed the rational side to reemerge. He sighed wearily. "Push forward for *what*?"

Mira looked at Holt. She shouldn't have to bear the brunt of what was coming, she'd done more than her share already. So Holt was the one who told Isaac the whole story. About finding Zoey, the way the Assembly hunted her, her powers, what she had done at the Severed Tower, what the Librarian and Gideon believed, that she was the key to both the Assembly's agenda on the planet and to stopping them.

With every word he spoke, the Phantom Regiment looked more and more skeptical. Isaac, however, just listened, thinking it through. When Holt was done, Isaac was silent a long time.

"Boss, you can't be buying this," Shue said. "A little girl?"

"Would a little girl be any less strange a savior than all the things the Freebooter just rattled off the top of her head? She's right, the world's a strange place now, and a lot of it fits, if you think about it. All the new Assembly that are here? If what they're saying is true, they showed up the same time this Zoey did. The blue and whites are consolidating power, they moved all their pieces to protect the Citadel. It means two things. One, they're worried. Two . . . we're in the endgame."

"What are we supposed to do, then? Make a suicide run for the Citadel?"

"In the end, what does it matter?" It was Dresden. He stood with the other Landship Captains, near Mira and Olive. He'd changed too, Holt could tell. The mischievous glint was still in his eye, but it was muted now. Whatever had happened along the way, he'd become a believer, and that was no small feat. "You're in the same boat we all are. The lives we used to know are gone, there's no going back. Most people here have been to hell and back for this, done the kinds of things you don't do if you're not sure about them. You don't strike me much different. Maybe it *is* a suicide run . . . but at least we get to stick it to those bastards for real. No guerrilla tactics, no hitting and running. We take it straight at them."

The words seemed to resonate with the Regiment, the idea of really *hurting* the Assembly for a change. Even Shue smiled slightly. Clearly, they had a lot of payback coming.

"There's moves we could make, with all the assets you've got," Isaac stated. "But all it's going to do is get you guys to the Citadel. After that . . . the clock starts ticking."

"To what?" Mira asked.

Isaac and Shue studied her intently. "You haven't seen, have you? I keep forgetting, it was dark when you got here. Come on."

The kid wheeled his buggy around and headed for the other end of the factory. Everyone followed, until he reached the homemade lift attached to the old smokestack. Holt, Mira, Dresden, Avril, and a few other Doyen climbed on board with him, and it rattled as it started to climb, shaking and moving upward, passing through the metal ceiling into the early morning air outside.

The sun was rising in the east, casting its rays over the giant ruins that stretched to the ocean. Urban streets sat eerily clean of debris, buildings stood empty, crumbling and falling apart. Holt could see the Assembly Presidium across the bay, near the warped remains of the Golden Gate Bridge, where it had landed years ago. And he could see something else too, something much more massive.

The giant, twisting, black monolith of the Citadel. It climbed so high into the sky, clouds circled around the top, and a giant beam of swirling energy shot from it into the air. Surrounding it, in the streets, was movement. Thousands upon thousands of Assembly walkers of all kinds, aircraft swirling through the air in groups so thick they darkened the sky. Holt understood now what Isaac had meant.

"*That*'s where you're headed," Isaac said once everyone had absorbed the sight. "Like I said, once you get there, the clock starts ticking. No one going there's coming back."

Everyone stared, stunned, at the opposition ahead of them.

"The truth is, we may not be going anywhere," a voice said from below. Smitty and Caspira stood on a walkway that wound up the smokestack, independent of the lift. They were both bloodied and exhausted, and they both looked very worried.

43. SACRIFICE

SOUNDS OF BATTLE echoed around them, just blocks away now. Most of the silver Assembly were fighting at the perimeter with the Helix and Menagerie. The Osprey dropships were nearby, next to the Landships, and there were a few Mantises there as well, standing guard.

Move back, Mira projected as they approached. Isaac and the other Regiment were following, there wasn't a need to antagonize them, or force the issue, at least not yet.

Guardian . . . The Mantises stepped toward the Ospreys, farther out of sight. As usual, Mira felt no hostility or insult from them, it didn't seem to bother them one way or another.

When Mira saw the train, however, all thoughts of Assembly and battles vanished. Everyone stared at *Sorcerer*'s locomotives. The lead one had a blackened hole bored completely through it, and debris littered the ground where the engine had exploded. The second had detached from the first, completely off the tracks, its engine just as blackened and charred.

Mira shut her eyes tight. It was clear, even to her, that *Sorcerer* would never move from this spot, and the entire endeavor had just died. Without the train, they couldn't move forward, because the effect from Mira's artifact couldn't be amplified. She remembered the sight of all those walkers and gunships, the impossible numbers of them. There was no way to reach the Citadel now.

"So much for the suicide run," Isaac stated.

"There has to be a way," Holt said behind her. Mira could hear the desperation in his voice. Like her, he'd come a long way. "We could use the tunnels."

Isaac shook his head. "That's for a small force, not something like what you have, thousands of pieces on the board."

"There's still the Landships," Dresden said. "We could load everyone on—"

"You'll be cut down in seconds," Shue replied, "then it's gonna be a slog through the streets with whoever survives, building to building. Be lucky if you made it there with a tenth of—"

"Well, we have to do something!" Holt yelled at him. "I'll head there myself if no one else has the guts for it."

The comment stirred indignation in everyone, and it all disintegrated into argument, people yelling, some for giving up, some for moving forward, no one agreeing on any one thing.

Mira pushed past the crowd, ignoring all of it, her eyes on the train, the names written up and down its length. Each was a reminder to her. Before, there was a chance their loss could mean something. Not anymore.

Tears formed and she made no attempt to stop them, just moved down the cars, reading each name.

Guardian . . . On the other side of the train came a blast of static as Ambassador teleported in. She could see it standing there, through the gap between two cars, and she stepped over the train connections toward it. Everyone behind her was still arguing.

Ambassador's armor was dented and burned, it had taken hits, and given many of its own. Still, the presence inside the machine seemed . . . dimmer. Its colors less vibrant. It didn't have much time left, but, then again, neither did any of them now.

The contrivance. Unusable? Ambassador asked. It meant *Sorcerer*.

Yes, she projected.

Mira looked back to the train, to the names. She could almost feel the eyes of their owners staring at her.

There was a piece of pipe on the ground. Mira grabbed it, feeling the emotions building. She swung it like a bat into the side of the train. It hit hard and bounced off. The Mantises stepped forward, next to Ambassador, curious. The anger that had been building, one defeat after another, finally boiled over. She swung again. Again. Trying to knock the names off the side, to make them disappear, but they stayed right where they were.

She thought of everything she'd lost. She saw Dane leaping up into the drone ship. Saw Landships disintegrating. Saw the pyres of fallen Helix burning in the night. Saw the tattoo on Holt's wrist, fully formed and completed now.

Mira looked through two of the cars, to where the crowd argued. Holt was there, yelling at Dasha, desperate, angry. God, she was weak. Right then, she just wanted him to hold her. Wanted it to be like it had been, all that time ago. With Holt, with Zoey, even with the stupid, smelly—

There was a whine next to her. Mira looked down. Max stared up at her, head cocked.

The sight disarmed everything. She almost laughed at the sight of him, then wiped the tears away and reached out to pet the dog's ears. He didn't stop her. "So what do *you* think, huh?"

Max had no comment, but if he did, Mira knew what it would be, and she agreed. She would go on alone, like Holt had said. She looked west, to where the Citadel towered over the ruins, could see the thousands of gunships swarming around it. It was so close.

They would never make it, of course, but they would have tried. They knew, back in Bismarck, after the Tower, that this was a one-way trip. Holt said as much, and she accepted it.

From behind her, the sensations from the Mantises and Ambassador washed over her. They felt her pain. Her desire to sacrifice everything for the Scion, and indirectly or not, for *them*. She felt stirrings of emotion she had never felt from Assembly before, and she turned to face them.

Guardian . . . the Mantises projected. *We believe.*

She studied them quizzically. "What is there to believe in now?"

All is not lost, Ambassador told her.

Mira jolted as three more Brutes teleported back into the factory ground, their armor just as dented. They came from the battle, summoned here. But why?

The Mantises moved toward her and the train, and as they did, images and thoughts filled her mind. She saw what they intended, felt what they felt, and she understood, grimly, what it meant.

Hope filled her . . . and so did guilt, for so quickly being relieved at their intentions.

"I can't ask you to . . ."

You say . . . sacrifice? Ambassador asked, and Mira nodded. *It was foreign. To us. Before you.*

Her stare moved from Ambassador to the two Mantises, staring into their colorful eyes. Tenderly, she reached out and touched each machine, felt their fading presences fill her with light.

We believe, they told her.

Mira felt more tears forming, but these she pushed back. "You need my help?"

As a conduit.

Mira understood. The entities were too far gone now, they couldn't exist outside their machines. If they were going to do what they meant to, the only choice was go through *her,* and it would be their very last gesture.

Mira studied the Mantises. They had no names to memorize, so she tried to remember their colors in her mind. She turned and moved to the gap between the two locomotives, placing one hand on each.

There will be pain, Ambassador told her.

Mira nodded. "So what's new?"

The Mantises moved close. Mira looked and saw Holt, amid the arguing crowd. His eyes were on hers now, and she could see the worry there. He knew her very well. Holt started to push through toward her.

"Do it," she said.

Her vision went pure white as the entities inside the Mantises passed out of their shells and into her body. The pain was searing, even worse than being ripped apart by the Vortex. It felt like every atom in her body was on fire.

Distantly, she heard herself scream. She wasn't sure if she was still standing; the pain had overpowered everything, and it felt like it lasted forever, the two entities flowing through her . . . and into the two ruined locomotives, filling them with their energy.

As they did, she could feel them spread into the train's hydraulics and mechanics, felt power restored to its systems. She could feel every inch of the locomotives, and in spite of the pain, it felt amazing.

Then it was over. The white became black. She fell.

When she opened her eyes, Holt was cradling her in his arms. His concern and fear were palpable. People surrounded her on all sides, staring down in shock.

"What did you do?" Holt asked, aghast.

"What I had to . . ." she answered.

"Holy God," Smitty exclaimed, stunned. "They're . . . *working* . . ."

Mira weakly looked up at the locomotives. The lights on them flickered. Their engines rumbled.

She saw the big Brute walkers move forward and ram into the second engine, using their powerful legs and frames to slowly push it back onto the tracks.

When it was over, the crowd stared, mesmerized, Isaac and the Regiment among them. The shells of the two Mantises lay dark behind Mira.

"The Assembly did this?" Isaac asked from his buggy. His voice was confused and . . . unsure now.

"They did," Mira said weakly, sinking into Holt's lap.

Isaac looked at her, and she could see it in his gaze. He was way too smart not to understand that a sacrifice had been made. He looked away from her, to Ambassador, and the big machine rumbled uncertainly.

"Then let's make it worth it," he announced. "Get your leaders, we need to talk." Isaac's buggy backed up clear of the crowd, and then spun away, his men following. As he did, he shouted over his shoulder, "One of the silver ones should be there too."

Mira looked back up at Holt, and he stared back as the train engines rumbled beside them. His look was a mixture of emotions: relief they could go forward, yet horror at the risk she'd taken. He'd lost so much, she knew. Lost *her* even, once, and she had almost added to that weight again.

She reached up and touched his face. "I'm sorry."

Holt said nothing, just held her tighter.

44. INFERNO

MIRA STOOD ON THE OBSERVATION DECK, staring out over the ruins. Clouds were moving in from the sea, grayish ones that blocked out the afternoon sun, but she could still see the battle to hold the perimeter around the factory. The White Helix leaping from building to building, the Menagerie firing from windows, and Ambassador's forces on the ground engaging the Assembly directly.

It was not going well.

Plumes of smoke rose into the air as buildings burned and fell, and while her artifact kept them at bay, the Assembly were pouring more assets into the fight. Those that had the unlucky task of engaging them were quickly being wiped out. The bulk of their forces had pulled back, in preparation for the final attack. The ones that remained, it was understood, would sacrifice their lives to buy the rest time.

It was horrible, knowing that, and it was why she made herself watch. She never wanted to forget.

Below, plans had been made and, Mira had to admit, it was a great strategy. Even with the Regiment crippled, Isaac's tactics were worth just as much. All the plan had to do was get them to the Citadel . . . but how many more would die for what *she* needed?

Zoey was their cause too, she reminded herself, but as always, the thought seemed hollow.

After the meeting, Mira spoke with Olive, and it had been good to see her. The Captain filled her in on the events at Faust, and the story was . . . stunning. As bad as it had been for Mira, Holt seemed to have gone through something just as bad, and it made her heart hurt. They still hadn't spoken, not in depth, but it was coming, and a part of her dreaded it.

"Grim view, isn't it?" It was Avril, staring over Mira's shoulder at the battle below. Mira hadn't heard her approach, but that was one trait of the Helix she'd gotten used to.

Looking at Avril, though, it was unclear if she still *was* White Helix. She didn't wear their black and gray colors. She was dressed in the strict black of Menagerie, and Mira noted there were tattoos on her wrists now. On the right, a red phoenix, streaking up toward her arm. On the left, the eight-pointed star, with all of its points colored in. Mira stared at that star and all it represented. It meant she had made a choice.

"You ever see the Heisenberg Fountain when you were in the Strange Lands?" Avril asked.

The Fountain was a stable anomaly in the third ring, a strange one that rested in the middle of a massive field of glass. The Fountain itself was invisible, radiating a constant tachyon stream that superheated everything under it, fusing it all into a glasslike material.

"Twice, I think," Mira replied, remembering the sight, the shiny, smooth ground that reflected the sky and the clouds. Pretty as it was, the "glass" was deadly. It smoldered at a constant one thousand degrees centigrade.

"This place reminds me of it," Avril said. "The orderly environment, clean and precise, contrasted with death. I always felt it was beautiful."

"And do you feel the same about this place?"

"Yes," Avril stated simply, her voice lowering. Mira could hear the eagerness in it. "Maybe that's wrong, but I do. This is what we were made for. This was Gideon's vision, and we're here now. Thanks to you."

Mira felt a chill at the words. "I'm not sure how comforting that is."

Avril stared out over the ruins a moment more, then looked at her. "I came to talk about Dane."

Mira nodded. It was what she'd been expecting, though not looking forward to. Dane had become a friend, and she never would have made it without him. Any words she spoke would fall short of describing how she really felt.

"The others won't speak of his death," Avril told her. "It's their way, death is a reality. It should be forgotten."

There was a hidden question there. Avril didn't want to ask directly, but she did want to *know*. Mira looked the girl in the eye and told her what she wanted to hear.

"He died well," Mira said. "Fighting a great foe, against insurmountable odds. He was victorious, and he died saving us all." The death she described was the greatest a Helix warrior could hope for. It was also the truth.

Avril nodded, absorbing the words. Judging by the emotion the girl struggled to keep down, it wasn't easy to hear.

"His last thoughts were of you," Mira said further. "He started to give me a message for you, but . . ."

"He said I would know," Avril answered for her, smiling slightly.

The girls stared at one another with mutual respect. Their lives had branched off months ago, and in some ways they had each taken the other's places. Mira assumed a role of prominence in the Helix, and Avril had helped keep Holt alive. It was an odd thing to reconcile.

"Will you be Shuhan again?" Mira asked. "Dasha leads them, but hasn't taken the title."

"No," Avril said almost instantly. Her eyes glanced at the star tattoo on her left hand. "My path is different now. It's not one I'd have chosen before, but . . . it's funny where life takes us. And the Helix may not have a Shuhan, but that's because they have you. They see your strength."

Mira sighed. "I wish I was half as strong as everyone seems to think."

Avril studied her back, understanding, perhaps. "We waste too much time wishing we were something we aren't. Everyone has their flaws. It's only when you accept everything you are—and aren't—that you finally succeed."

It was a nice sentiment. "Gideon?"

"Something my father taught me."

Mira stared back in surprise, but said nothing.

There was movement below, and both girls turned. Holt and Max were climbing the walkway, and the sight caused Mira's pulse to quicken.

Avril watched him come closer. "What he went through to get here would have broken most men. Instead, he . . . inspired everyone around him. He finished Ravan's tattoo, but he didn't take the star. That was his choice. Whatever occurred between Holt and Ravan, *you* were the reason for that choice. Even when he thought you were gone."

Mira stared at Avril, unsure how to feel, but she was grateful for the words.

When Holt reached the top he stopped in surprise. "Sorry," he said. "I can come back."

"No, we're done," Avril told him. "See you in an hour." As she passed by, she touched his arm fondly, and then began her descent back down.

Holt and Mira stared at one another, the first time they'd been alone since the Menagerie arrived. There was a strange mix of tension and sadness in the air. It was not the reunion either had imagined back at Currency.

"Hi," he said.

"Hi."

Max moved toward Mira, tail wagging, and she rubbed the spot between his ears. Holt smiled. "You took really good care of him. Thank you."

"He's not all bad."

"She was here about Dane?" Holt asked.

"There wasn't much to say, sadly."

Holt moved next to her, where he could see the ruins and the Citadel and the battle. "Dresden told me about the rail yard. It sounds . . . horrible. I'm sorry."

Mira stared down at Holt's hand. The tattoo stood out prominently, glistening in his skin. She wanted to look away, but she couldn't.

"We've both been through a lot," she finally said. "I heard how she died. Olive told me. She gave up everything for you."

Holt was quiet, staring into the ruins and the fires that were building there. "She deserved more."

Mira agreed. Ravan, for all her faults, had always been more than she seemed. She remembered their time in the missile silo: about to kill Mira one moment . . . then the next they were sharing their darkest secrets and helping each other survive. It didn't seem real, the idea that someone like Ravan was gone, that Mira would never see her again. It was one more item for the list of just how much this endeavor had cost, and Mira knew, however conflicted her feelings were, she would hold Ravan's name at the top of the list she'd already made herself memorize.

"When I saw that ship go down, your ship, I . . ." Holt started, then trailed off. Mira's eyes shut, realizing it was the beginning of the conversation she'd been dreading. "I went somewhere, and I didn't want to come back. Ravan . . . *made* me come back." He looked down at the tattoo with Mira. "I finished it because . . ."

"I know why you finished it," Mira said. "And you don't have to explain anything to me."

She reached out and touched the tattoo. For a moment, Holt's fingers touched hers back . . . and then they both drew away.

"I knew, after the Tower, when we committed to this," Mira continued, "that so much would change, that *we* would change, I just never thought . . ." Her voice dropped, she felt a sadness forming over her. "Did we lose each other, Holt? In all this?"

Mira looked up and saw the same sadness in his eyes.

"I don't know," he said. "I've had my feelings turned on and off and back on again so many times, Mira, I don't know what I feel anymore. Maybe . . . maybe that's *our* price to pay, for doing all this. For all the darkness we created to get here."

Mira felt tears again, her vision began to cloud. In the distance, two old buildings collapsed to the streets, and more flames took their place, rising into the air. The light from the fires reflected in what was left of millions of glass windows. The sight was overwhelming.

Instinctively, Mira leaned into Holt, and his arms circled her. They both stared to the west, through the destruction and the fires. The Citadel loomed, waiting for them . . .

"It's like the world's burning," Mira said. Holt held her tighter.

MAX LED THE WAY as Mira and Holt exited the factory, and they were the last ones out. The fires from before filled the skies with thick, swirling blackness. The majority of the forces were here, in the rail yard. *Sorcerer*'s locomotives rumbled, in spite of the gaping wounds, the dying entities inside giving them their last breaths. Hopefully it would be enough.

Ambassador and the silver Assembly stood near the train. Mira could feel their emotions, and they were each awed, in reverence of the sacrifice the others had made. As she walked, the silver rebels turned and studied her. Mira looked back—Mantises and Brutes, Hunters and Spiders, their silver armor no longer gleaming, the entities inside dying, and yet they were with her.

Guardian, they projected. *We believe* . . .

The projections overrode her thoughts, and it was funny now. She no longer saw them as some horrible collection of crosses to bear. Their presence in her mind was still draining, but it had become comforting. She could feel the underlying emotion. They had faith in her, believed in her, and the realization gave her strength. Right now, she couldn't imagine doing this without them.

And I in you, she projected back.

Everywhere people were getting ready. Smitty and Caspira talked near *Sorcerer*'s engines. A thousand Helix piled onto its roof with the Menagerie, all of them checking their gear. In the background, Landship crews were unberthing the ships, getting them ready to move. She saw Dresden, Conner, and Olive there, and their faces looked worried.

In fact, as she looked around, everyone's did. A silence hung over the yard. They were scared, she knew. They might be willing to push forward, to go to the end, but they had very little confidence they could win, it was in their eyes. Even the White Helix seemed uneasy.

"It should be you," Holt said. He was studying the crowd too, could see the same thing: like this, they'd never make it.

"No," she answered. "It should be both of us."

He looked at her and for a brief moment she saw the old Holt, the tenderness and the emotion, and it was heartening to feel again.

Together, they climbed up onto the train, leaving Max on the ground. As they did, all the movement in the rail yard stopped. The army they'd built, the one they'd sacrificed so much for, stared up at them, waiting.

Mira wasn't sure what to say. She was no speechmaker. In the end, she simply opted for how she felt.

"Each of us . . . is weak," she began. "Each of us has doubts. Each is afraid. Some admit to it, others don't. Either way, you have all taught me that strength is not an absence of fear. Strength . . . is going forward in spite of it."

The groups at the far end of the yard moved closer, listening: Assembly and White Helix, Menagerie and Wind Trader. She tried to look as many of them in the eye as she could, so they could see her sincerity. None of them looked away.

"The Wind Traders speak of the Valley of Fires," she said. "The point where we are all tested. There's no doubt, we are at that place now. A place where we either plunge ahead into the flames . . . or burn where we stand. I choose to go *forward*. To fight. Because I believe everything we've ever wanted is on the other side of those fires. I believe that when the sun comes up tomorrow, this planet will be *ours* again." The army before her listened, she could see the will beginning to burn within them. "We've been through so much together, changed in ways we never thought we could. Take this one last step with me, not because you have to, but because you believe. If I'm going to fall, then it will not be because I stopped and waited for the fires to claim me. It will be because I pushed on, into the inferno, in spite of fear. With *you*."

"Seek!" Dasha yelled from below.

"*And find!*" the White Helix chanted together.

"Power," Holt yelled. "And profit."

"*Power and profit!*" the Menagerie shouted back as one.

Mira turned and looked to the Wind Traders, near their ships, the crews watching from the top decks, the colorful sails billowing in the breeze. "Winds guide us," she said, and she never meant it more.

Dresden and Conner nodded to her.

A chant went up from the Helix, and it was picked up by Avril. When the Menagerie saw her join in, they followed, and the words overpowered even the sounds of the explosions nearby.

"*Strength! Strength! Strength! Strength!*" They chanted the words, over and over.

Mira felt Holt look at her, and turned to him. "Let's go get our girl," he said.

45. DISPERSION

PAIN SEARED THROUGH ZOEY'S BODY and the world threatened to fade out, but she held on. If she passed out, the end she had fought so hard to stop would come. There were four entities inside her now, and as unique as her biological structure was, she was literally being torn apart.

Her hands were still forced onto the rods at the end of the armrests. She could feel the Tone, could feel where it passed through the minds of every survivor on the planet.

She was dimly aware of other things too. The sadness of the Nexus at what its children were doing. The conflict growing in the Citadel and outside, the divisions forming between those who believed in her and those who did not. She felt the resistance of the Feelings, fighting against the other entities, but they were too strong.

The pain made concentrating on anything but staying conscious virtually impossible. All the while, she could feel her presence within the Tone speeding, mind to mind, person to person. In a moment, the entities would make her force their own kind into millions of human hosts.

She had to find a way to let go of the rods, but how? Rose had clamped her arms and legs to—

Rose!

Zoey forced her eyes open and found the woman staring at her in horror.

"I'm so sorry . . ." she said. Through her pain, Zoey could just make out the woman's sense of guilt.

Zoey fought through the pain with what life she had left. She tried to recall everything she could about her Aunt Rose, about the time they'd spent together and all the feelings that went with it.

Rose and Zoey's mother, holding her in between them on the beach. Eating ice cream while riding on Rose's shoulders. Drive-in movies outside of town, Rose teaching her how to paint, Zoey crawling into bed with her aunt to nap.

All of it, the images, the feelings, Zoey thrust at her, forcing them into her mind like coal into a furnace.

Shock exploded from the woman as the memories came to life, one after the other, overriding her other thoughts, filling her with their resonance. She was terrified.

"Zoey!" She staggered back, holding her head, but Zoey just kept pumping the memories in.

The pain in Zoey's body intensified, the entities burning her apart. The little girl fought through it, trying to hold on. If she didn't, it was all for nothing. Holt and Mira and the Max were counting on her.

Zoey pushed harder, concentrating on every detail of every moment she could remember, and the horror Zoey felt from the woman slowly morphed into something else. Anger at what was happening, intense shame that she had helped bring it about, and a maternal, protective instinct that overrode everything else. The woman, more Rose than she had ever been, dashed forward.

"No!" she yelled, grabbing one of Zoey's hands, prying the fingers loose from the rod. When it was off, Rose grabbed it herself . . . and then shrieked as she polarized with the machine and the Tone.

Like Zoey, Rose held on, adding her own strength to the fight against the entities burning out the little girl. It gave Zoey some relief, she felt the pain lessen, she could *think,* but the Ephemera inside her were strong, and she felt them double their efforts.

Dozens of transmitter panels in the ceiling exploded as the energy in the room intensified. The Citadel rumbled. Zoey saw more of the blue and white crystalline shapes push toward her, about to reinforce the ones already there.

She tried to pull her hand loose from the rod, to sever her connection from the Tone, but the entities kept her fingers clamped tight. All the while she could feel them using her innate power and the power of the Nexus to bind and merge with the Tone.

Zoey was running out of time.

Rose struggled to stay standing. The woman's efforts had given Zoey her mind back, for however long. She put it to use, reached out through the Tone, scanning for Holt and Mira . . . but there were just too many human minds now.

The only entities she could detect with any specificity . . . were Assembly.

Zoey's eyes widened. She reached out once more, searching for an old presence, one she felt fondly for. Zoey found its specific colors, called them forth, and, seconds later, she felt its response.

Scion . . . Ambassador projected with dismay.

Over the pain and her fading consciousness, Zoey felt a slight twinge of hope.

MIRA GRIPPED THE WALL of the cargo car as *Sorcerer* began to move. Holt and Max were next to her, and no one spoke. There wasn't much to say. It was all about to begin . . . and end. Her artifact sat in the makeshift Grounder, shut down for the moment. Mira had no idea how much power it had left, so it was being saved for the "Endgame."

Isaac said there were always three phases in anything strategic. Early Game, Mid-Game, and Endgame. Victory was achieved by the proper use of your pieces in each phase. In their case, victory was getting the train to the Citadel, though Mira still wasn't sure what they would do when they did.

Sorcerer would no doubt hit resistance right out of the gate. The Assembly would come down hard, but the arrangement of all their pieces was designed to counter it. The problem was balancing speed against force. Move the train too fast, and you'd leave behind defensive forces. Move it too slow, and you'd be overwhelmed by Assembly firepower. They had to get the pace just right.

Isaac was on the train, in a car near the middle, surrounded by what was left of the Regiment. He'd insisted on coming, even with his lack of mobility. Like everyone else, he knew this was it. Besides, too many of his men had died here. If he was going to follow them, it would be in the same light.

Sorcerer barreled out of the rail yard as the skies darkened with clouds and the sun was almost down. In a few hours, the ruins would be dark, but it didn't matter. This would all be over before then.

Almost immediately, a hailstorm of plasma bolts began flying. Walkers, mostly blue and white, were in the streets, and they erupted in explosions of their own as *Sorcerer*'s cannons returned fire.

White Helix and Menagerie were on the roof, and bullets, missiles, and Antimatter crystals launched outward. Flanking the tracks, Mira could see the Landships shadowing them, their colorful sails disappearing behind tall buildings as they raced along. Among them were the Menagerie vehicles, dune buggies and jeeps, and the gyrocopters buzzed by above, dropping bombs onto the Assembly.

At the front of everything were the silver rebels. A group of them broke off and barreled down a side street, their cannons engaging a group of Mantises directly—more of Isaac's strategy: dividing the Assembly into "battle groups," each consisting of a Spider, two Mantises, four Hunters, and two Brutes. When the front of the train encountered resistance, a battle group could break off and engage, stopping the Assembly from impeding the train. Even though the groups would be outnumbered, they would still make their impact. It was the ultimate utilization of Rock, Paper, Scissors, and Mira watched the groups wade into larger Assembly forces and shred them. Mira allowed herself to smile, for one brief moment.

Then the gunships appeared, swarms of them. They weren't blue and white, and they weren't Raptors. They were pure *brown*, shaped like crescents, with the pointed tips facing forward, and they soared up the streets, cannons blazing, strafing everything in sight.

Barrier artifacts flared to life around the train, absorbing the hits. The same thing happened on the Landships, but the Menagerie vehicles near them weren't as fortunate.

Half a dozen gyros went down in flames. Dune buggies skittered out of control, cartwheeling and disintegrating to pieces.

"Look at *that* thing!" Holt yelled, peering out the observation slit in the armor.

A few miles away, hovering in the air, was the source of the gunships. A massive brown craft and they could see the fighters launching off it. It was some kind of carrier, and far larger than the yellow and black drone mothership they'd faced before. It could launch enough fighters to decimate everything they had.

Mira tapped the radio button on her belt, spoke into her headset. "Olive, Dresden, you read?"

A burst of static, then Olive responded. "Go, Mira." There were explosions in her ear over the radio. She looked and found the *Wind Rift*, a block away, rocking as plasma bolts flared into her Barriers.

"These gunships are gonna rip us up," she said. "Hate to do this, but maybe you can pull them away. Isaac, you agree?"

"Agreed," Isaac's voice said. "Target that carrier if you can, you're bound to get their attention that way."

"That sounds like a great idea," Dresden replied testily.

Antimatter crystals streaked upward from the Landships, aimed at the carrier in the distance. They hit with colorful explosions, rocking the craft, but not dropping it. It was just too huge. Almost immediately, the gunships broke off and turned toward the Landships, chasing after them as the big vessels rumbled through the streets. Half of the Menagerie vehicles followed, the other half stayed to defend the train.

Sorcerer shook, Mira heard the crackling sound of activating Barriers. She and Holt both peered out and saw the source.

New walkers, but different from any they'd ever seen. Solid gray, smaller than even a Hunter, maybe five feet tall, but with four legs like a Brute, lined with strange, mechanical claws almost like octopus tentacles.

The walkers, a hundred or more, dashed toward the train . . . then leapt straight off the ground, propelled upward by jetpacks that flashed fire behind them. They landed on *Sorcerer,* the claws on their legs clamping down, holding them in place. Plasma bolts ripped into the train from the grays, they were inside the fields of the Barriers. There was nothing to stop them.

Max whined and Holt tapped his radio. "Avril!"

"We're on it!" the girl shouted back, and White Helix on the roof dashed toward the new threat, flipping and dodging through the plasma. Some didn't make it, they fell and disappeared as the train rumbled on.

Holt looked at Mira. "Are we having fun yet?"

TWO MAS'ERINHAH ALLIES FELL in flames. Their Ephemera did not rise, their colors would fade, as would many today.

The shield of the one the Scion named Ambassador flared around it as it charged, absorbing the ordnance as it drove the first Mas'Shinra through the wall of a building, crushing it into the ground in a shower of flame.

Another fell in a torrent of cannon fire from the huge Mas'Phara that reinforced their group. Seconds later, the rest of their enemies were obliterated, proving that more Electives trumped a single, even with greater numbers.

Rock. Paper. Scissors.

But there were many more to take their place, and the silvers turned and barreled back toward the long human construct the Guardian had named *Sorcerer.*

Ambassador could see the humans fighting valiantly, watched them flip through the air, firing their strange-colored crystals, or shooting their primitive weapons. If it was still connected to the Whole, it was sure it would feel a sense of apprehension. These humans were resisting, and they were strong, but that would not prove enough in the end.

The machine focused its optics upward, staring at the giant black monolith towering over the city ruins. It was the Collective, it was where the Scion was, and its electronic gaze zoomed in longingly on the beam that shot from the top.

Every exertion seemed to drain its life force, it could feel its thoughts slowing. Soon, its colors would fade, but before then it would defeat the shells of as many Mas'Shinra as it could. It would help the Guardian reach the Scion. And maybe, just maybe, it would feel the warmth of the Nexus once more.

Ambassador saw a new sight. Grayish shells, with four legs, leaping and attaching onto the speeding train.

Mas'Nashana. It doubled its momentum, rushing eagerly to aid against the new threat.

Then a voice ripped through its mind, distorted, weak . . . and in pain; amplified somehow, as if it were connected to the Whole, which should have been impossible. It recognized the voice, felt new energy as her unique colors blossomed in its consciousness.

Scion, it projected.

Ambassador. There was surprise and joy in the sensations. *I need you.*

Ambassador could feel the Scion's pain . . . and it understood. They were hurting her. They were *forcing* her. Anger swelled inside it, a thirst for vengeance. Mas'Shinra must *fall*.

It thundered forward, blowing through a pack of five Mas'Nashana, as it looked for the two it knew it would need.

ONE OF THE SMALL, gray walkers exploded as Avril's Lancet punctured it. She rolled along the top of the rumbling train as another landed behind her in a blast from its jetpack. She aimed and fired . . .

. . . then watched as the machine launched upward again, falling right at her. She rotated, readying herself to—

Two thunderous blasts blew the machine backward in a torrent of sparks.

Avril saw Quade above her, shotgun in his arms, among the other

Menagerie. He stared down at her, offered his hand. "You should really get a different weapon."

Another gray walker landed next to them . . . right as an Antimatter crystal cleaved it in half. Dasha gave Quade a contemptuous look as she moved past. "What for?"

Quade stared after her as she flipped back into the fight. "I like her."

Avril started moving again, headed for the front, trailing behind her two camps of fighters, Menagerie and White Helix; each seemed eager to outfight the other. She was caught between worlds, and when this was over, it would be her last day in one of them. Then again, who was she kidding? Most likely it was her last day in both.

She stared at the furious fighting. Bullets and grenades, explosions, Antimatter crystals, Helix and Menagerie and Regiment fighting the gray walkers, groups of silvers pushing outward, engaging the larger Assembly. Whenever they fell, no Ephemera appeared, they were truly gone, while hundreds of the glowing Assembly entities filled the air behind them, floating back to find a new machine and reenter the fight. The odds were stacked so completely against them the outcome was certain.

Two walkers landed in front of her, clamping onto the train, one more behind.

Avril fell flat, felt the heat of the plasma bolts sear past and spark into one of the machines, sending it flying off the train.

She launched a crystal. A second walker exploded, falling away.

The third she cut in half with her Lancet, then lunged to the side, spinning, looking for—

A plasma bolt caught her arm, sent her sliding dangerously close to the edge. She grabbed on just in time, rolled back up. There was blood, but she pushed the pain away. There wasn't time.

More walkers were appearing, the air burned with ordnance from both sides. She watched the last of the silver rebels engage two blue and white Spiders stuffed between buildings, saw Helix and Menagerie deploying off the train, engaging on their own, trying to buy the rest time. They were virtually defenseless now, they had used most of their pieces.

It was then she felt something unexpected. The train began to *accelerate*, leaving the deployed troops and the silvers behind. Avril looked ahead, and her eyes widened. The base of the Citadel was less than three blocks away, stretching out of sight and towering over them. The train tracks dead-ended right *into* it.

The Assembly had placed the structure on top of the tracks, not to mention a hundred or more streets' worth of city real estate. *Sorcerer* was going to ram into the thing.

More of the gray jump-pack Assembly landed, and Avril spun back into the fray. Bullets from the Menagerie sparked into the walkers, as more and more piled on. Without the silvers running interference, it was clear they were about to be overwhelmed.

A gray walker advanced on her, its three-optic eye locking on . . .

. . . then it shuddered as a spray of plasma bolts knocked it away.

All around her, the gray walkers were being blown to bits by plasma bolts, and it wasn't coming from Ambassador's forces. It was coming from *blue and white* Assembly. And reds. And brown gunships. And every other kind of walker she'd ever seen—and they weren't just firing at the grays, they were firing at *each other* now.

If the streets had been a war zone before, they were now complete chaos.

The sound of a massive explosion rattled down from above and Avril looked up to see a plume of fire blow out from the side of the Citadel. She saw gunships engaging one another high above, streaks of light in the sky.

The Assembly, it seemed, had turned on each other . . . but why?

"Everyone hold on," Mira's voice shouted over the radio. *"Tight!"*

Avril saw the base of the Citadel looming, felt the train accelerating. She grabbed the roof as *Sorcerer* rammed into the Citadel.

The impact jarred everything violently and Avril held on as best she could.

MIRA SLAMMED INTO THE wall of the train car at the impact. Max flew toward her, and she barely caught him. The added hit knocked the breath out of her, and she collapsed to the floor, the world a blurry, dizzy mess of strange, slow-motion sounds.

It was dark. She could hear screams and explosions, gunfire, the sizzling of plasma bolts.

The Assembly were closing in. Now that they weren't moving, everyone outside would be overrun in minutes. There was only one thing that could save them.

"Mira!" It was Holt's voice, nearby. "How do I turn this thing on?"

Holt groggily kneeled in front of her artifact. Apparently, he was thinking the same thing.

"Open . . ." she started, trying to form words. "Open the pocket watch. Then get *back*."

With distaste, Holt flipped the watch open. The black, squirming light bubbled into the air . . . then was sucked back down into the combination. Mira felt the floor vibrate.

A flood of disgusted projections came from the Assembly outside. She could feel them pulling away, back into the streets.

Mira sighed. The artifact still worked. For now. Whenever it finally faded, everyone down here was going to die, but that was a problem for later.

Max barked wildly, moving for the exit, and Holt helped Mira stand up. "You okay?"

She gave him a look. "I haven't been okay since I *met* you."

"Fair enough."

They jumped out of the train, Max leading the way, bounding off into the dark toward where the two giant locomotives had come off the rails and plowed into the ground. When Mira saw them, her heart ached. The engines were dark, she couldn't feel the entities inside anymore. Two more sacrifices in a long list she promised never to forget.

The only real source of light came from the hole where *Sorcerer* had punched through. Through it, she could see the rear half of the train, most of it still on the tracks, and the battle raging around it outside. Its cannons were firing and recalling their crystals nonstop. She could see gunfire coming from the cars too, and from the buildings all the way down the street where the Menagerie had deployed. White Helix flipped through the air, engaging the Assembly directly.

Walkers of all kinds moved outside, firing and blasting not just the silvers and the Helix, but each other, confirming the strange sight she'd seen before. Something had happened to turn them against each other. Whatever it was, there was no doubt it involved Zoey, and it only made Mira more desperate to reach her.

Mira studied the darkness, could see what was left of the old city ruins—streets, traffic lights, the entrance to a subway—stretching out of sight into the shadows, and there was something eerie about how the Assembly had just built over the remains instead of demolishing them, like they didn't even exist.

Giant support beams ran in a gridwork all through the dark, stretching up out of sight. It was clearly the foundational superstructure of the Citadel, and the horrible thought occurred to her that there was nothing to climb. No ladders, no foot rungs, nothing to grab at all. There was nothing here to use, because the Citadel was simply not built for humans. How were they going to get *up?*

"We can defend this," Isaac said, his buggy rumbling through the debris. "For a little while."

Around him were the remainders of the Regiment, White Helix and Menagerie, including Avril. Mira suddenly wondered what had become of the Landships, and felt guilty for only remembering them now. She knew the most likely answer, and tried not to think about it.

"I say we put our pieces in position outside, do as much damage as we can, and when your artifact wears off and they start pushing, we fall back here." Isaac studied the hole where *Sorcerer* had punched through, nodded in grim satisfaction. "They'll bunch up, we can drop a whole lot before they get in."

"And when they do . . ." Mira said.

"It doesn't matter," Avril told her. "We'll hold this ground as long as we can, buy you time to get Zoey."

"Getting to her's the problem," Holt said, staring into the dark interior above. "Can you spare some warriors? Masyn jumped me and Castor up about three stories' worth of height back at Faust, maybe they can do something similar here."

Explosions rocked the ground outside. They could see a group of silver Assembly pushing forward, clearing a path, and when it was empty, one barreled through the hole toward them.

Ambassador. Its armor was smoking and dented, she could see where one of its legs was crumpled. She sensed a desperation coming from the entity, and it worried her.

"What is it?" Mira stepped toward the machine.

The Scion, it projected. *She fades.*

The sensations brought to life a similar desperation inside her. "There's no way up to—"

We see her, it interrupted, and Mira understood. Ambassador was linked to Zoey somehow, he could *teleport* them right to her!

She looked at Holt. "Zoey's in trouble. Ambassador can take us."

Holt nodded and looked at the others, he couldn't help it. He and Mira were leaving . . . and everyone around them, new friends and old, were going to die so that they could.

"Go," Avril said, next to them, staring pointedly. "Finish it."

More explosions echoed in from outside, the Menagerie and Helix were moving to join the battle. Mira looked at Avril one last time . . . then pulled Max tight against her. She closed her eyes and reached out, touching her consciousness and Holt's, and merging them with Ambassador's.

Colors exploded in her mind with prismatic brilliance, and she felt energy wash through her. There was a sound. Like a powerful, punctuated blast of static noise, and a quick wave of heat. Max howled. Mira's stomach clenched . . . and then they were somewhere else.

THE ROOM WAS HUGE, with strange black walls, and a domed ceiling of hundreds of sparkling panels that glowed with golden light. In the very center, a giant column of flickering energy rose upward, each particle drifting slowly through the ceiling.

It all would have been amazing, beautiful even . . . if not for the massive burst of static that ripped through Holt's head. He had never felt anything like it, it was like razor blades rending his consciousness. He crashed to his knees, and it was all he could do to not fall all the way over.

Looking up at the glowing panels, he had an idea where he was. He knew transmitters when he saw them, and the ceiling was covered in them. This was where the Tone was broadcast from, and he had a feeling if he hadn't been Heedless, he would have Succumbed the second he stepped inside. Heedless or not, it didn't make the pain any less.

He made himself focus. As he studied the room through the haze, he saw something that made his heart stop, something a part of him thought he might never see again.

Zoey.

She was strapped into some kind of machine and her face was a mask of pain and exertion. Energy sparkled off her body like lightning. Crystalline entities were floating toward her, and there was a woman in front of her, one hand holding Zoey's, the other grasped onto the machine. Her body was covered in the same arcing energy, and her expression was just as pained.

Mira struggled next to him, trying to stand. The only one who seemed unaffected was Max, and the dog barked wildly as three strange Assembly machines entered the room. Four legs, with thin bodies that had tendril-like arms, each painted blue and white.

Ambassador rumbled and charged, smashing them to pieces, as the static grew in Holt's head. He wasn't going to last much longer.

A desperate idea occurred to him. What he needed was to short this place out, and if those things up there really were transmitters . . .

His hands shook as he unstrapped his Sig, aimed upwards . . . and made himself pull the trigger.

The weapon flashed to life, he felt it kick wildly in his grip.

The panels above exploded. As they did, the light around the machine Zoey was plugged into blossomed brightly. A violent chain reaction took place, and every panel in the ceiling ruptured apart in brilliant bursts of sparks that fell everywhere like a meteor shower.

The static in Holt's head died. The light from the panels was replaced with the golden wavering light from the entities that had been inside them. Hundreds floated toward the column of energy in the center of the room, absorbing into it. They were retreating. Holt thought about firing at them, not that it would do much good, but Zoey's pained scream grabbed his attention.

Zoey spasmed as something *pushed out of her body,* glowing with brilliant blue and white energy. An Assembly entity, and there was more than one. Two more pushed out, one after the other, and as they did, Zoey's face scrunched in pain.

The entities floated toward the Nexus, and the little girl fell limp in the machine's grasp. The woman next to her fell to the floor.

"Zoey!" Mira yelled, scrambling toward her. Max barked and ran too, recognizing the little girl. Holt pushed to his feet, his head still full of fog, but he didn't care.

They skidded to a stop in front of her, Holt's and Mira's hands moving to the clips that held her hands and feet, and she fell like a rag doll into their arms. They lowered her to the floor, and she lay there limply. Smoke rose from her body, and her skin had a sickly gray-blue tint to it. She was hurt. Badly. Looking at her, Holt's heart rose into his throat.

"She's not breathing!" Mira shouted in a cracked voice.

Holt pulled the little girl to him, parted her jaw, clamped her nose, and breathed into her mouth. He pressed on her heart, finding the notch where the rib cage met in the middle of the chest. Then repeated. Again. Again. Again.

Zoey shuddered as her chest rose, filling with air as she took giant breaths, her body filling again with life. Holt sat back with relief.

"Oh, thank God," Mira said, leaning in. "Zoey?"

The little girl said nothing. She just lay there, her body still smoking. She may have been alive, but she wasn't conscious.

The black, metal floor shook as Ambassador stepped closer. It rumbled and then a beam of green energy shot from one of its diodes. Instantly, Zoey's breathing calmed, but her eyes still didn't open.

"Why won't she wake up?" Mira asked to no one in particular. "Why won't she—"

"Because she's dying," a voice said next to them. The woman lay crumpled against the machine now. She looked almost as bad as Zoey, but Holt could tell she was beautiful. In fact, looking at her, it occurred to him she looked exactly like Zoey, though many years from now. "And it's my fault."

"How?" Holt asked. "You were trying to help her."

"Too late," she only said. For a split second, Holt thought her eyes sparkled with slight golden light, but he couldn't be sure.

"There has to be something we can do," Mira said, almost begging.

"There is one thing," the woman replied, looking toward the column of energy. "Get her there."

"The Nexus . . ." Mira said with a note of awe.

"Yes," the woman said. "But you have very little time."

"Who *are* you?" Holt asked.

The woman looked back down at Zoey's still form, as if the answer to the question was somehow connected to her. "My name . . . is Rose."

The walls around them suddenly began to shift; the best way Holt could describe it was that they reformed themselves, growing and stretching, making new walls that completely sealed off the Nexus from where they were.

Holt's eyes widened, realizing what was happening. So did Ambassador. The machine charged forward and slammed into the walls, but it didn't make a dent. They kept closing. In seconds, the Nexus was sealed away. They'd have to find another way there.

More walls shifted, new openings appeared, and Holt saw strange, twisting hallways of the same black metal. In the shadows there, things rushed toward them. Plasma bolts flared to life and Holt leapt and covered Mira and Zoey. More flew their way, but Ambassador landed on top of them, its shield blocking the ordnance.

Holt could hear more walkers coming . . . and the distinctive whine of Seekers. This room was about to be very hazardous.

"You have to hurry," Rose told them, her voice worried. "You have to get Zoey to the Nexus."

"How?" Mira asked. More plasma bolts sparked against Ambassador's shield.

Rose looked at the opposite wall. She closed her eyes and concentrated. The same thing happened as before. The walls shifted and morphed, made a new opening, with a twisted hallway beyond.

"Through there," she said, focusing. "Follow it to the main expanse, you'll know it when you see it. From there, the Nexus will be visible. Do whatever you must to reach it. I'll hold the opening as long as I can."

More plasma sparked against Ambassador's shield, and Holt could see it was weakening, beginning to flicker. In fact the machine in general seemed weaker somehow, its movements slower, its lights dinner.

Holt stared at Mira, and they silently reached an agreement.

"You're coming with us," Mira announced.

"No . . ."

Holt sprang to his feet, and pulled Rose up. "*Yes,*" he emphasized.

"You don't understand," she said almost pleadingly. The opening in the wall near them remained open. "I've made . . . mistakes."

"Join the club," he told her. "Think of it as an opportunity."

"For what?"

"To make it right," Holt said pointedly.

Rose stared at him a moment more . . . then made her choice. She bent down and picked Zoey up in her arms.

"I can—" Mira started, but Rose cut her off sternly.

"I *have* her. Follow me."

They moved for the opening in the wall. All . . . except for Ambassador. The machine stood where it was, its flickering shield absorbing the impacts from dozens of plasma bolts. Holt could hear the whining Seekers buzzing toward them.

"AMBASSADOR!" MIRA YELLED, BUT the machine stayed put, its eye just stared at her, bobbing up and down.

We will hinder them, it projected, and there was a feeling of finality to it. It would hold the Assembly off as long as it could, until its shield failed and its hydraulics died and when that happened, Mira knew, it would not rise. It would go dark. Forever.

The truth was, they couldn't outrun the walkers that were coming, much less the Seekers. As brutal as it was, they needed this sacrifice, and that only made the pain worse.

Her eyes welled, she stepped toward the machine. The emotion she felt surprised her, for this thing that was so inhuman, yet had been with her through everything, had supported her in more ways than she could name. She remembered that night under the aurora, the wavering bands of color. Ambassador . . . was a friend, and this was the last time she would ever feel its presence.

She lay her head on its armor, let everything she was feeling pass through to it.

Ambassador rumbled, low but soft, as it felt her emotions. *Never have we felt this. Except for you.*

"I will *never* forget you," Mira said, her voice breaking.

Good-bye, Guardian . . .

"Mira . . ." Holt's hand gently touched her shoulder.

Mira lifted up, stared into Ambassador's red, green, and blue eye one last time . . .

Then the machine turned and bounded toward the oncoming Mantises. She watched the plasma bolts spark into its shield, watched it flicker and die, but still the walker charged ahead.

It slammed into the first three, blowing them apart, and rushed into the rest of the attackers. More plasma fired, the Seekers swarmed it . . . then Holt was pulling her through the opening, and the walls morphed and sealed the room away, and Ambassador was gone.

Mira forced all the emotions away, made herself focus. She had to, for Zoey.

The five of them ran down the hall, Max leading the way, Zoey limp in Rose's arms. The route twisted and turned, a strange tunnel that eventually spat them out into the Citadel's main expanse . . . and it was breathtaking.

The scale of the interior was beyond massive. It was a world unto itself.

As she watched, strange black cases flew up and down a complicated rail system. Platforms too, bigger ones, loaded with walkers, moving them between one part of the Citadel and another.

She saw other things. Daises built along the walls and attached to various interior superstructures. Factories, warehouses, repair bays, landing platforms.

Thousands of gunships streaked through the air. An equal number of walkers marched like ants along every walkway and platform, and they were all firing their plasma cannons at one another. Explosions flared everywhere, and Mira could see pieces of the Citadel falling into the dark in burning scraps.

And in the middle of it all rose the Nexus. If what Ambassador had told her was true, that the Nexus was, in its own way, the creator of the Assembly, she wondered what it felt now, watching the violence all around it. Was it disappointed? Horrified? Did it even notice?

Rose kept moving, running onto a giant walkway that headed down to a factory platform. When they reached it, she could see hundreds of half-finished machines in various states of construction. They dashed through them, moving toward the edge of the dais where it ended close to the Nexus.

"That thing can save her?" Holt asked. Max was running next to Rose, whining and staring up at Zoey. "You're sure?"

Rose hesitated. "It is where she needs to be."

"What does *that* mean?" Mira asked now. "What is Zoey going to do?"

"Save all of us," Rose simply said. "But she needs your help."

Plasma fire sparked around them. Holt pushed Mira down against one of the incomplete walkers, and pulled Max close. Rose ducked down with Zoey behind a welding machine.

Holt rammed a new magazine into his Sig. "What do we got?"

Mira peered over the top and saw what she expected, stomping toward them on eight huge legs. "Spider."

"Grand," Holt intoned, then looked at her. "All I can do is distract it. Max and I will pull it away."

"Holt—" Mira began with dread.

"Just *listen*. Max and I will pull it away, then you and . . ." Holt turned to Rose . . . and saw she was *gone*. She stood at the edge of the dais now, staring downward, Zoey in her arms.

Mira started to rise, but Holt shoved her back down as plasma blew holes in the dais around them.

"Rose!" Holt shouted.

The woman turned for one brief moment . . . then simply stepped off the edge and fell out of sight.

Max barked wildly.

"*Zoey!*" Mira yelled in horror. She struggled, trying to break free from Holt, oblivious to the plasma searing the air, the explosions rocking the distant walls.

The dais shook as the Spider stomped toward them. Mira heard the distinctive hiss of missiles launching, and felt Holt pulling her up. They dove for cover behind another incomplete Mantis shell, pulling Max down, as the ground where they just were exploded as the missiles impacted.

Mira could feel the heat from the blast, and the combined firepower being leveled at them was massive. She shut her eyes and buried her head in Holt's arms. He held her tight as the world disintegrated.

Then there was a strange mechanical clicking. One of the huge platforms used to transport the walkers rose up from below, surrounded by a dozen blue and white Raptors.

Mira's eyes widened in shock. She heard Holt suck in his breath.

"Son of a b—"

The cannons on the Raptors screamed to life, spraying their own plasma forward. Mira flinched . . . but none of it hit her. That's because it wasn't aimed at them . . .

The giant Spider behind the walker stumbled back, covered in plasma bolts from the gunships. Missiles fired next and explosions flared all over the machine. In just a few seconds, it buckled and collapsed into a flaming heap, destroyed.

The gunfire ceased, but the whining of engines remained.

Mira opened her eyes and saw the Raptors hovering around the platform. On one of them, balanced on the fuselage, were two figures. Rose and Zoey. Zoey stood in the center, her eyes glowing with golden energy, holding hands with Rose. She looked at Mira. Mira looked back.

"Hi, Mira . . ." Zoey said. Mira felt her emotions begin to ignite and spread.

Then the golden light in Zoey's eyes faded and the little girl collapsed to the platform.

THROUGH THE PAIN, Zoey was aware of only two things. A thick, electriclike oscillation in her mind, that slowed her thoughts and kept control of her body at a distance. She could barely move, and her insides felt . . . wrong. Like tiny parts of her had been scrambled up and put in the wrong places. She was badly hurt, but it was always going to be this way. She had made her bargain, and the time to finish it was here.

The second thing she noticed was some kind of furry creature. She could hear it whining, could feel its warm, wet tongue on her cheeks.

A small smile formed on her face. Zoey opened her eyes and saw the dog that had become her friend hovering over her protectively, staring down into her eyes.

"The Max . . ." Zoey breathed weakly.

Her vision was blurred, images seemed to twist and distort. It wasn't something that would get better, she knew. The entities inside her were gone now, but they had done their damage. She could barely detect the Feelings, they were just a weak set of sensations now, and getting weaker by the moment, just like her. It made her sad, feeling them diminish and fade. They'd become a part of her, a friend in their own way, and through her experiences come to believe in her. They did what they could, and hopefully it would be enough.

The blurry sight of the two people who moved toward her gave her faith that it would.

Zoey couldn't see their features anymore, but she knew them both. She could sense the same mixture of emotions coming from them: relief at finding her, guilt at not doing it sooner, anger and anguish at how hurt she was, and of course . . . love. They loved her and she loved them. It was why she needed them.

Mira and Holt swept the girl into their arms. Max barked and jumped back and forth.

"You found me . . ." Zoey heard herself whisper.

Even after everything they'd been through, after how much they'd changed, this feeling, the feeling of being with the other, of holding on, felt . . . perfectly the same.

The explosions and the shaking of the platform reminded her how little time they had. The Raptors that had helped her roared away and back into the chaos.

Zoey let Holt and Mira go. She could feel all they had been through, all they had experienced, and she absorbed it, letting herself feel it too, and it was painful. Zoey's eyes began to well with tears, she couldn't help it. All they had gone through . . . and all of it had been for *her.*

"I'm . . . so sorry . . ." she managed to say.

Mira shook her head, wiped her own tears away. "We would do it all again and more. Do you understand?"

Zoey could feel something new forming in Holt, and it wasn't surprising. Denial. He was trying to find a way around defeat, just like he always did.

"Just have to figure out how to get her down to the bottom, now." His voice held dim hope.

"Holt," Zoey said weakly, but he wouldn't listen.

"She can control the platform. It looks like it goes down."

"Holt . . ."

"We can use the abandoned walkers for cover, if we need to I can pull away any—"

"Listen to her," a voice said sharply from behind. It was Rose, Zoey could tell, and the memory of how she'd rushed to help her in that room came back. "She won't survive a trip down to the bottom, much less outside. She's *dying.* The ones who were inside her . . . used her up." Rose's eyes teared along with Mira's, and Zoey could feel her tremendous guilt.

"That's . . . that's not true," stammered Mira. "You *said* the Nexus could save her!"

"I said she needed to get there. Not that it would save her."

Zoey looked at the Nexus behind them, the giant, beautiful fountain rising serenely upward. It bent toward her again, eagerly, and the sight gave her strength. She was so close . . .

"Zoey, you have to listen to us," Holt said, turning her to face him. "There has to be something we can do."

"You already have, Holt." Zoey's voice was hoarse. "You've made it all possible: saving you . . . and saving *them* from themselves." She watched the chaos around them, Mantis fighting Mantis, Spider fighting Spider, the Citadel burning, falling.

Holt shook his head in scorn. "They don't deserve to live. They don't deserve *you*."

"Mira knows that isn't true," Zoey answered. "She knows they're more than they seem. They're . . . beautiful in their own way. Just as you are."

Mira touched the little girl, and she felt new emotions from her now. Resolution. Dreadful resolution. "Zoey, what do you need us to do?"

"The hardest thing I can ask," Zoey said. "Let me go."

She felt Holt's own dread join Mira's, and he looked past them all to the Nexus. "You're going in there, aren't you? Inside it."

Mira was horrified. "That's pure energy! You'll die!"

"I told you I made a deal with the Tower," Zoey reminded her. "I only put it off a little while."

"Zoey . . ."

"If I fade away out here, it was all for nothing. In there . . . it means something. What's left of the Tower's energy will release. The Nexus will grow. Together, we can draw the others to us, and . . . *you* will make it permanent, make all the Assembly one, as the Nexus always wanted."

"How?" Holt asked in confusion.

Zoey touched their minds, and filled it with all the imagery she had absorbed and retained over the last several months, and the extent of it, the beauty of it, surprised even her. "By showing them *you*."

She heard Mira gasp, felt an ache in Holt's heart. The moments played for her just as they did for them. One after the other, each as vibrant as the original experience, each with the same emotion.

"When you found me, I was blank," Zoey spoke in their minds. "I could have been shaped in hundreds of different ways . . . but I was found by *you*."

Holt pulled Zoey free from a crashed podship in a forest, long ago, carrying her through the smoke and out into the night.

"I am who I am . . . *because* of you."

Mira made a magnet, a copper wire, and two pennies spin into the air while Zoey applauded in an old hotel room.

Holt carried Zoey on his shoulders, pushing desperately through a crowd of kids, protecting her while they tried to rip her loose, to make her help them like she had just helped someone else.

Zoey rode on top of Max, shrieking gleefully as he dashed down a hill toward a landscape full of darkness and colored lightning.

"The Assembly are . . . so frightened of being who they are. They were born in the Nexus, but it scares them, so they push everything it is away, which means they can't feel these things . . . because the Nexus is *love*."

Mira took a bite of a Hostess CupCake, smiling at Holt.

Holt kissed Mira for the first time, inside an old dam, her eyes perfectly clear, her mind her own again.

"I can share with them the one thing they've never let themselves feel . . . and I can do it because of you."

Holt shuddered and looked away as Ben lifted Mira up and kissed her.

Mira floated in Holt's arms in Bismarck, after the Tower, toward a bed where they touched and slid and were everything they were supposed to be.

Holt pulled Mira to him in Currency, at the end, as the Landships set sail around them, forcing them apart.

"Your love will tie them together. They will abandon their search. They will be one, as the Nexus always wanted. Don't you see? Without you, *none* of this could happen. I wouldn't be who I am."

Through it all, laced in between each individual moment and feeling, Holt danced with Mira around a campfire, long ago, as the stars filtered down through the trees.

Holt and Mira opened their eyes and slowly looked at one another. The past, everything they had been through, everything they had meant to each other, shown to them in the space of a few seconds. Zoey knew how much they'd changed, but she knew, more than anything, that they could find each other again.

"What do we do?" Mira asked, her voice barely audible. She believed now, understood. It made Zoey love her all the more.

"I have to . . . feel it," she told them. "What you feel for each other. So *they* can feel it. The rest . . . takes care of itself."

Explosions flared again, the platform shook. The three shared their looks. None of them could imagine how they got here, but knowing, somewhere deep down, it was the only true resolution there could be.

Holt was the first to move. Zoey couldn't see his eyes now, but knew, if she could, they would be red and sad. He pulled her close, hugged her tight, and whispered into her ear. "You're the bravest person I've ever known."

She touched his face and smiled. "Look inside yourself more often."

Mira was next, her arms wrapping around her, and she held on, as if committing the feel of Zoey in her arms to her memory, locking it in forever. "I just . . . want more time."

"We had our time," Zoey told her. "Now it's their turn."

Mira fought tears and nodded, pulled away, stepped back with Holt. Max whined, not understanding, but sensing something monumental was happening.

Zoey reached one last time for Max, grabbed one of his ears, ran it through her fingers, scratched him. "Do this, when you can. He loves it the best."

"We have to hurry," Rose urged Zoey.

She let Max go, and Holt called the dog to him, held him in place by the collar. Together, the three of them—Holt, Mira, and Max—stepped off the platform that held Zoey and Rose. They all watched one another a moment more . . . and then Zoey felt Rose reach out, find the platform with her mind, and power it.

It shook as the rail system lifted it back and away from the dais, leaving Holt and Mira there, staring up at her. Zoey stared back as long as she could, until they became distorted blurs in her fractured vision and she couldn't see them anymore.

Rose ran her fingers through Zoey's hair as the platform moved toward the Nexus. She could feel its energy and warmth, could feel it growing.

"You will live on for them," Rose stated, lying down next to Zoey, waiting for the inevitable. "Wherever they go, whoever they become."

"I know," Zoey replied, and the knowledge gave her comfort. The heat from the Nexus was growing. She could feel its eagerness. It had waited a long time after all. In spite of that, Zoey felt a tremor of unease. "I'm scared."

Rose nodded and pulled her close. "I am too."

"Will it hurt?"

"Only a little," Rose told her. "Only a little."

Zoey concentrated on the feelings of being in Rose's arms again, the memories the sensations brought. She would add it to the rest, she decided, share it as well. Maybe in that way, even more of both of them would live on.

The world began to lighten, growing brighter and brighter, until there was nothing left but warmth and feeling and memory.

Scion, the Nexus welcomed her. *You are home.*

The world burned away . . .

———

THE PLATFORM FLASHED AND buckled, seemed to warp somehow as it passed into the Nexus. When it did . . . it was gone. And so was Zoey.

Mira fell to the ground in grief as the world disintegrated. Explosions flared, the Citadel shook, Mantises and Spiders slammed into one another. All around them, the Citadel was falling apart. The giant structure was doomed, and they were at the very top, thousands of feet from the bottom. There was nowhere to go.

Mira felt Holt's hands on her. She fell into his arms, sobbing. Zoey was gone, truly, forever gone now, and the tension and anguish that had built to this moment over the last months was finally free. They'd run out of road, and if she were honest, she didn't really understand what the point had been.

"It's not doing anything," Holt said into her ear. He was staring at the Nexus in the distance, where Zoey's platform had been enveloped. "Why isn't it doing anything?"

"She said we had to feel it." Mira moaned into his chest. "So that *they* could feel it." Holt pulled her free, stared down into her eyes, and Mira voiced the unspoken fear they were both feeling. "What if we can't? What if we lost it?"

A violent explosion flared out from the wall across from them, spraying flaming debris through the air. Streams of new gunships poured in, thousands of them, all painted in shades of brown. The fighting intensified in the air.

"We didn't," Holt told her, trying to ignore the chaos.

"How do you know?"

Holt wiped the tears from her eyes, then his hands circled her face. "Because . . . I know."

He kissed her, gently at first, then with more passion as their stifled emotions, ones that had almost died, were reignited: by each other, by what Zoey had shown them, and by everything they had been through. Adversity and change didn't have to destroy feelings, Mira realized, sometimes it morphed them into something new, something more powerful . . . something better.

More explosions flared, gunships roared past, but none of it mattered now, except that they had made it, to this place, to each other, all over again.

Nearby, the Nexus flashed brilliantly . . . and began to *grow*, spreading outward, full of new light.

49. ASCENSION

"HOLD ON!" Casper shouted.

Olive did just that, as the Landship in front of them careened into a building and disintegrated. Casper pulled the *Wind Rift* hard right, and the wheels on the port side lifted off the ground, threatening to tip over.

"Jesus, Casper!" Olive shouted.

"Would you rather I hit it?"

The *Wind Rift* flew past the destroyed ship and the wheels slammed back down.

Two Menagerie dune buggies burst apart one street over. The radio chatter was frantic. They'd lost five Landships so far, which meant five batches of people Olive used to know. They were all gone.

The Barriers on the stern flared as the brown gunships rained down plasma. She felt slight satisfaction as her ship's cannons took one out, but there were far too many. The clock was ticking, and there wasn't much time. She hit the button on her radio. "Dresden?"

The ship shook, Casper barely managed to keep it on course. Any jarring impact at this speed threatened to knock the Landship off angle, and in tight streets like this, that meant you went bow-first into a concrete building.

"Yeah?" Dresden answered.

"Since this is pretty much it, there's something I've always wanted to tell you." She smiled as plasma flared by. "Your boots are stupid."

Olive heard him chuckle. "Says the girl with the pink hair."

She looked to starboard, past the buildings, and saw the *Wind Shear* dodging plasma bolts a block away, barely staying on course.

"You're a real pain in the ass," she told him, gripping the railing, "and the best Captain I ever saw."

"Don't get all mushy on me, Olive. This isn't the finale."

Olive frowned, looking at all the chaos. "Sure seems like one to me."

The air was rent with the sound of a massive thunderclap, and everything flashed bright. Olive flinched and peered behind them. It had come from the Citadel, a bright burst of light and energy directly above it, as something began to mass there. Golden, glowing energy swirled like some kind of mercurial pool of light.

Olive's eyes widened. "What. The. He—"

An explosion just above and to port rocked the ship. Two more behind them, another to starboard, fire and concrete sprayed everywhere. It seemed like an artillery barrage, but it wasn't.

The gunships themselves were *crashing,* falling out of the sky, exploding into the streets and buildings, and Olive could see why.

The Ephemera, the entities inside, were abandoning the ships, rising up and out of them. Hundreds of them filled the air, and they were all floating toward the energy field that was building above the Citadel.

Olive didn't have time to enjoy the view.

"Casper!" Olive yelled at him. He was staring behind them with everyone else. *"Eyes front!"*

Directly ahead, a dozen empty gunships slammed into buildings on either side of the street. Glass rained down like a hailstorm, the structures buckled and began to fall.

Casper shoved the Chinook to full. The wind roared louder and the ship jarred as it darted forward. Olive held on. There was no other option, they were going way too fast to stop.

Everyone held their breath as the buildings collapsed and tumbled into the street, ten stories each, showers of concrete and steel raining down.

Olive gripped the railing . . .

The *Wind Rift* roared underneath the cascade, racing through the last space of open air that was left. Then the structures careened into the ground behind, decimating everything under them.

The gunships rained down for another minute or so, and when it was over, everything was eerily quiet. Olive ordered full stop, could see the other ships doing the same.

The crew moved for the stern, staring back the way they'd come. Fires were everywhere, crumbled buildings, and the remains of Landships and Menagerie vehicles. And farther, at an unearthly height, the energy field continued to build over the Citadel. It was the Nexus, and the sky was full of Ephemera, thousands upon thousands, floating to it, sparkling like stars.

The Citadel itself glowed and shook. Explosions flared outward from it. Olive could see why. The Nexus was growing not just outside the huge building, but *inside* as well. It was going to burst the thing like a massive balloon. Watching it, all Olive could think about was that Mira and Holt were in there somewhere.

IT WASN'T THE EXPLOSIONS or Max's frantic barking that made Holt pull away from Mira. It was the heat. And when he opened his eyes, the sensations from their kiss fading away, he saw the source.

The Nexus was *expanding*. Filling the interior of the giant structure, and it was almost on them.

"Move!" he shouted, pushing Mira forward, and whistling for Max.

They dashed back toward the center of the dais. It shook badly, detaching from its wall supports. The air above them was full of Ephemera, all rising toward the Nexus.

Holt saw the walkway they'd use earlier rip loose and plummet down. Explosions flared everywhere. Behind them, the Nexus flashed as it touched the dais, beginning to dissolve it, and it shook violently under their feet.

There was nowhere else to go. Whatever they had started, it was going to be the end of them too.

Holt looked to Mira again, and she stared back. She seemed content, in spite of it all. Her hands took his, she moved close, and the feel of her calmed him.

"It was always going to be a one-way trip, wasn't it?" she asked.

Holt nodded. "It was."

There was so much he wanted to say. Like she'd told Zoey, Holt wished they'd had more time, but the little girl had been right, they had *had* their time.

A huge explosion blossomed above them. A massive shower of black metal rained downward through the air, plummeting toward them. There was no escape, it would take the dais with it, and that would be that.

"Come here." Holt pulled her against him, felt her shaking arms wrap around him. With his free hand, he pulled Max close. They shut their eyes, tightly, waiting.

The fire raced inevitably down . . .

. . . and there was a sound. Like a powerful, punctuated blast of static. In a flash of light, something big materialized almost on top of them. An Assembly walker, huge with five legs, its colors stripped away. It was dented and broken, two of its legs barely worked, the red diode on its eye was dark . . . but it was alive.

It had found them.

"*Ambassador!*" Mira yelled. Holt reacted, shoved her and Max farther under the walker, right as the flaming debris slammed into them.

Ambassador's shield was gone, and it rumbled as the debris slammed into it, puncturing and ripping it apart.

The dais shook one last time . . . then tore loose and they were all falling in a torrent of metal.

"Hold on!" Mira yelled over the chaos.

Holt grabbed Max as they plummeted, the bottom so far below it couldn't be seen. "Hold on to *what?*"

Then colors exploded in his mind, he felt heat wash over him. The sound again, the blast of static. Max howled in his arms . . . and then he was somewhere quiet.

THE LANDSHIPS APPEARED AT the last, miraculous moment, thundering through the debris near the battleground, as the giant building above Avril began to shift and groan. Avril couldn't see why from this vantage—they were still under it—but it was pretty clear what was about to happen.

The Citadel was coming down. Right on top of them.

Everywhere outside, gunships and walkers collapsed in the street or fell like meteors. They could take their chances out there, or be buried alive when the massive structure came down. It was an easy choice.

"Go for the ships!" she yelled. "Helix, grab someone and get them out of here!"

The Helix moved for what was left of the Menagerie and Regiment, then dashed them forward in blurs of purple toward the street.

Avril saw Isaac struggling with his buggy. She leapt for him, her vision covered in yellow, then started unstrapping him from the thing.

"Wait!" he yelled. "I love this thing."

"I'll get you a new one." She pulled him free, then dashed them both through the opening, out of there.

Outside, looking straight up, they could see the energy of the Nexus pooling above the Citadel and *bursting through* its walls. It must be *growing*. The air was full of Assembly entities, lighting up the streets as they rose.

Avril kept moving, carrying Isaac over her shoulder, running for the ships just ahead.

Explosions rocked the Citadel, the Nexus finally burst through the thing's exterior walls . . . and the inevitable began.

"FULL CHINOOK, HIT IT!" Olive yelled, watching the last of the Menagerie board the *Wind Rift*. Her sails plumed outward, the ship began to roll. The same thing was happening on the neighboring blocks, the other Landships loading up and engaging full sail.

The *Wind Rift* tore back through the streets, trying to get clear of what was about to happen. The Citadel shuddered . . . then began to *lean*.

A loud, awful groaning sound ripped the air as the whole thing started to come down, thousands of feet of black metal, caving in on itself.

Olive watched it fall right toward them. The lower parts hit and decimated the old skyscrapers there, flattening them like they were made of paper. The rest of the giant obelisk fell, its shadow looming over them, growing darker.

Behind them followed another Landship, and Olive recognized the color of its sails. It wasn't going to make it, it was too far away.

"Dresden!" Olive yelled into her radio. "You have to hurry!"

No response. The huge structure kept falling, crushing, swallowing up acres of ruins every second with a horrible rumbling.

"Dresden!" Her voice was harsh, she felt her heart pounding. "Please, you have to—"

From the front of the *Wind Shear*, rockets exploded into the air, trailing long lengths of cable that unfurled three additional sails and yanked the ship forward, almost bringing its wheels off the ground.

Olive watched the *Wind Shear* begin to *gain* on the *Wind Rift*.

The Citadel thundered down, decimating everything as the Landships raced forward, trying to get away.

The *Wind Rift* shuddered violently, every piece of it vibrating and tearing loose under the strain.

"She's going to break apart!" Casper yelled.

"Break her apart then!" Olive yelled back, keeping her eyes on the *Wind Shear*, still gaining. "Come on, you bastard," she said to herself, watching, gripping the railing. "Come on." The *Wind Shear* rumbled forward, the falling Citadel on its heels. She'd never seen speed like that, never seen a crew work so well together. It was beyond inspiring. *"Come on!"*

The remains of the Citadel slammed into the ground in a symphony of fractured sound unlike anything Olive had ever heard. The ruins vanished. The sky went dark. The shock wave from the impact hit, and the *Wind Rift* careened out of control.

"Brace for impa——!" Casper started, but it was too late.

The ship slammed into the side of a building, ripping the port side to shreds, flattening trees and old traffic meters before plowing into the corner of what had once been a bakery.

Olive flew forward, slammed into the helm. Casper slid by but Olive grabbed his hand, kept him from going over the side.

And then it was finished.

The horrible sound of the fall echoed in the ruins for what seemed like forever until it finally faded away. The air was full of dust and smoke, and she could hear people coughing nearby, could see shadows moving. Good. She wasn't dead.

She pushed up, helped Casper stand, and looked at him. "Hell of a piece of piloting."

He looked past Olive, to where the front of the ship had buried itself into the building. "I killed a bakery."

Olive smiled, rubbed the hair on his head.

She and Casper joined the rest, exiting the ship, filing into the streets, staring back the way they'd come. The dust began to clear, and they saw a giant swath of the city that was simply gone, a massive, burning debris field that stretched for miles, the final resting place of the Citadel.

In its place was an enormous, flickering field of brilliant, glowing energy, growing bigger by the second as the Ephemera of the Assembly, the radiant, crystalline entities, entered and absorbed into it, filling it with their luminance. Silence filled the crowd as they stared in awe at the sight.

The first cheer went up. Then a red Antimatter crystal launched into the air. Then dozens. Then gunfire. Everyone cheered and yelled and hugged, a mass of people, celebrating. Even though they scarcely understood what had happened, there was something monumental about it. It was, unquestionably, a victory.

Olive moved through the crowd, watching in a daze. She saw Avril congratulating her former Helix. Saw Wind Traders shaking hands with Menagerie. Saw Masyn pull Castor to her and kiss him. Saw Isaac, with what was left of his men, sit and lean against a telephone pole and close his eyes, as if waking up from some long nightmare.

And she saw something else. A very specific Landship, its crew disembarking, joining the celebrations.

Dresden led the way and stopped when he saw her. She shook her head and moved toward him.

"Sorry I didn't get back to you," he said, "it was kind of a hectic——"

Olive grabbed him and pulled him down to her height and kissed him. He didn't resist.

When she pulled away . . . she socked him hard in the stomach for the stress he'd just put her through. He groaned and took a wary step back. "What the——"

"You could have hit those sails anytime!"

"Flair . . . for the dramatic, I guess." He winced, holding his stomach. She moved for him again, and he took another step back.

Olive rolled her eyes. "Come here."

Dresden cautiously moved closer. "You send a lot of mixed signals, you know that?"

"Stop talking," she whispered, and planted another one on him.

Around them the cheering and celebration continued. In the distance, the Nexus continued to grow, lighting the city, taking the place of the sun which had just set in the ocean. The Ephemera kept filling it, becoming one giant mass of radiance in the sky.

MIRA OPENED HER EYES SLOWLY, unsure if she was even alive. Max hovered over her, staring down dubiously, answering the question for her. She smiled and pet the dog, then he trotted away, probably to check on Holt.

Wherever Ambassador had taken them, it was far from where they'd been. Everything was strangely quiet. Thick beams of reddish orange rose into the sky. Giant cables held lengths of asphalt above the ocean. It was a bridge. A famous one, the Golden Gate, spanning what had once been San Francisco Bay. It occurred to Mira, oddly . . . that it might one day be again.

Mira pushed herself slowly up and looked around. The sun had set, but the light in the distance was almost as bright. The Nexus filled the sky, and the golden light that drizzled down from it lit up the glass in the buildings there, making the whole thing look like some kind of giant altar of votive candles.

Thousands of Ephemera rose up, absorbing into the energy field, one after the other, making it brighter. The sight was impossibly beautiful, and it was only the movement of Holt nearby that dragged her attention away.

The bridge was as perfectly clean as the streets. Holt was nearby, trying to stand, banged and scratched up. Max nudged him to his feet and he and Mira stared at one another in a surreal haze.

There was a weak, distorted rumbling from nearby.

Ambassador's shell lay crumpled, smoking and sparking. They could see where the pieces of the sharpened black debris from the Citadel had punctured its armor, and they stuck out at every angle.

Mira and Holt moved it. The sparks meant the walker was still powered, but she couldn't sense Ambassador inside. Either it was too weak . . . or it was gone.

She put her hand on the armor, reached into the machine. There was a weak presence there, slight color that dimmed in the dark, but it was fading.

Mira shut her eyes sadly.

It didn't seem fair that this is how it would end. The rest of its kind were being absorbed into the Nexus and to whatever future awaited them. The thought that Ambassador, the best of them, the one who had fought from the very beginning for this moment would be left out infuriated her.

She punched the armor in frustration.

"What?" Holt asked.

"It's just . . ." she started, but couldn't finish, looking back at the ever-growing field of energy.

"Not fair," Holt finished for her. Mira nodded. "Is it gone?"

"Not yet."

"Then there's a chance."

She shook her head. "You don't understand. It can't leave its armor, it's going to fade inside."

"Why can't it leave?" Holt, she knew, was looking for a solution. It was maybe his most endearing trait, a refusal to blindly accept defeat.

"It can't push out," she told him. "It's too weak."

"What if it could?"

Mira sighed. "It couldn't live outside in the open, it would fade too quickly."

"But it's right there. *Look!*" He pointed at the Nexus, maybe five miles away, above all the buildings. "It doesn't have to survive that long, once it gets back there—"

"It will be recharged," Mira concluded, thinking now.

"There has to be a way to get it out, to give it a shot at least."

There was one way, she'd done it before, recently, allowed two of the entities to pass through her. She could probably do something similar now, draw Ambassador into the air, give it part of her strength. But . . .

"I'd need your help," she told Holt. "It's so weak I don't think I can find it on my own, but if we both try, together . . ."

Holt didn't hesitate. "What do you need me to do?"

Mira smiled. "Are you sure? It's going to hurt."

"It saved your life," he answered. "Mine too."

Mira touched him gently, thankful . . . then turned and placed both her hands on Ambassador's broken shell.

"What do I do?" Holt asked.

"Put your hands on me," she said. "I'm going to pull your mind inside the machine, then try and find Ambassador. If I do, and I can pull it out, it will pass through both of us. I can try and give it some of our strength. Are you ready?"

Holt wrapped his arms around her waist, pushed in close. "Ready."

Max whined under them, uncertain.

Mira closed her eyes, took a deep breath . . . and reached into Ambassador's shell with her mind. There was nothing but darkness, no color, no light. She felt her heart sink. Maybe it was already gone?

Mira reached back and touched Holt's mind, let its familiar confidence give her strength. Together they pushed inside further, exploring the dark, looking for any sign of consciousness.

Finally, she saw it.

A dim, flickering spark of color, twirling reds against purple. She felt her heart accelerate, pressed forward, pulling Holt with her.

Ambassador was weak, barely any sentience or energy left, but she reached out to it nonetheless. Mira felt a slight twinge from it, a hint of fondness, recognition. It was still there, Ambassador was alive.

She poured all her energy and intention into it, borrowing what she could from Holt, adding his focus to her own, suggesting to the dying entity what she intended, what she wanted it to do.

It flared slightly, grew brighter, as if committed not to give up.

Ambassador's presence moved toward her . . . and fire-like pain lanced through her body.

In the background, she felt Holt's arms flex around her, knew the sensations had seared over him as well.

Mira fought the dizziness and pain. It grew more intense, building and flaring as the faded colors of Ambassador tunneled through her and Holt, pushing on, burning bright, finally passing through the dark into the outside air.

As it did, Mira held on, pushing into it as much of her mental energy as she could, trying to fortify it, to give it enough life to finally get where it had longed to be for so long.

Then it was done. Mira collapsed to the ground, and Holt fell beside her. Max was on top of both of them, whining and barking.

Mira weakly opened her eyes.

In the air hovered Ambassador, its intricate crystalline form filled with purple, like an amethyst of pure energy, but nowhere near as vibrant as it had once been. The crystalline structure seemed to fluctuate, to break and remake itself. It had managed to escape its shell, but it wasn't going to last long.

Still, it hesitated, staring down at her, lighting the bridge in violet hues.

Mira could sense its feelings. Affection. Sadness, knowing it would never see her again . . . and deep gratitude.

Mira soaked them in, letting them fill her, but she knew it had little time. *Go,* she projected. *Hurry.*

Ambassador hovered a moment more, . . . then it flashed and floated away, over the edge of the bridge, over the bay, headed toward the others that were rising up into the sky toward the Nexus.

Holt sat up and leaned back against the smoking remains of Ambassador's armor. Mira did too. The pain was receding, the memory fading. Max squirmed his way in between them, and they both pet his head.

"Well," Holt finally said. "That hurt a lot."

"Perfect end to a perfect day," Mira agreed.

Both of them breathed in and out, exhausted and spent, too tired to move.

"Feels like forever since I just . . . sat down," Holt said.

They stayed that way a long time, watching Ambassador disappear within the mass of other entities, blending into them, watching the Nexus continue to grow.

"Look," Holt said, nodding to where the buildings met the ocean. There was something huge there, made of the same black metal as the Citadel, but nowhere near as big. It was also something Mira had seen before.

An Assembly Presidium, one of the giant baseships that had barreled out of the sky years ago. Looking closer, Mira saw why Holt had pointed it out.

Just visible in the light from the Nexus, she could see thousands of tiny dots exiting the structure, slowly walking out of its gateways and into the city ruins. They were people, she suddenly realized, and given where they were coming from, it became clear who they were.

"Oh my God . . ." Mira breathed, and she slipped her hand into Holt's.

It was the Succumbed. No longer affected by the Tone because the Tone was gone. Adults. Their parents and siblings and everyone they had lost. What they were watching here was probably repeating in every Presidium in the world.

Mira felt an odd emotion form as she watched the tiny figures. "I'm scared," she whispered, "and I don't know why."

Holt squeezed her hand. "Because it's all changed. Everything's new, all over again."

Mira looked back to the Nexus, watching it swirl and flash, colors of all kinds blending in and out of it.

She could feel the projections coming from the sky, and they were similar emotions to hers. Excitement. Apprehension. Elation. The Assembly were at a crossroads too. In spite of all they had done, she was happy for them. She hoped, with whatever new destiny awaited them, that they could begin to undo all the darkness they had caused. Maybe they could make it all mean something.

"Can you feel her?" Holt asked.

Mira smiled and nodded, closing her eyes, concentrating. "Zoey has her own colors within it all. She's . . . beautiful."

"What will they do now?"

"They don't know," Mira answered. "Leave. Travel. Explore. Everything the Nexus had always hoped they would. The same thing is happening all over the world, at all the Citadels. When they leave, it will be as one Whole. Zoey brought them together in a way they never dreamed they could be."

As Mira spoke, there was an ironic melancholy to knowing that when the Nexus was gone, the host of feelings and projections that crowded her mind would be gone as well. She'd grown used to the sensations, to the thoughts of the others. She'd come to see them as family.

"She loved you, you know," Holt said quietly.

Thoughts of Zoey swirled in her head, memories she would always have. She would always be with her. "I know."

There was a pause before Holt spoke next, feeling the words before expressing them. "*I* love you."

Mira sighed. Emotion and warmth spread through her. They were just words. Words that events had almost denied her of hearing, but the relief she felt at finally hearing them was intense. She had no idea just how much she had wanted those words until now. "I love you too."

She held Holt's hand tighter, never wanting to let go. "I know we said no more promises," Mira told him, echoing something he'd said to her once before, "but, whatever happens next . . . promise that you'll always be here. With me."

Holt slowly turned to her. She did the same, studying his brown eyes, his disheveled hair, the calmness he exuded. Everything about him made her feel safe, made her feel home.

"Where else would I be?" he asked. Then he leaned in, slowly, and his lips found hers. They kissed while Max rested between them, eyes closed serenely.

In the distance, beyond the bay, thousands of survivors walked slowly out of the Presidium. Landships gently rolled to a stop in front of the enormous structure, their colorful sails the first sight Earth's adults had seen in years. The crews watched, nervous, apprehensive . . . then slowly, the two groups moved toward one another.

Above, the Ephemera glided up, absorbing into the Nexus, thousands of them, bits of golden light that streaked across the sky. They would leave soon, as one Whole, and when they did, they would be like every other form of life in the universe.

Where they went didn't matter, what mattered was that they were free . . . and no longer alone.